Robin Gardner was born in Reading in M.   , ..., ... resides in
Flackwell Heath, Buckinghamshire. He lived in Reading, was educated at a
Secondary Modern school and enjoyed five years of woodwork, his main
hobby. Robin joined the RAF in 1951, becoming an electrician and later
commissioned in the Supply Branch. He served in Aden, Cyprus and Oman,
and after leaving the services in 1978, he was employed in the production of
security equipment. In 1955 Robin married Valerie Rowe from Reading and
they have three children, five grandchildren and three great-grandchildren.
On retiring in 1997, they purchased a motorhome, travelling in the UK and
Europe until 2013. Robin's other hobbies include stained glass and an 00
gauge model railway.

DEDICATION

I dedicate this book to:
My wife Valerie
Our children
David, Melanie & Cherie
Our grandchildren
Michelle, Charlene, Wayne, Katie & Kara
And our great-grandchildren
Tiffany, Angel & Jessica
and their partners.

Also
anyone I met while in the RAF, who became my friends, but unfortunately,
over a period of time, we have lost contact.
I would very much like to hear from any of them who remember me, and
hope if they do, I remember them also!

I donate any proceeds that I may make from selling all or part of these
writings to

THE ROYAL BRITISH LEGION

Robin Gardner

KETURAH

Beverly

a friend for many

years

Best Regards

Robin Gardner

AUSTIN MACAULEY PUBLISHERS™

LONDON · CAMBRIDGE · NEW YORK · SHARJAH

A CIP catalogue record for this title is available from the British Library.

ISBN 9781786931986 (Paperback)
ISBN 9781786931993 (E-Book)
www.austinmacauley.com

First Published (2017)
Austin Macauley Publishers Ltd.™
25 Canada Square
Canary Wharf
London
E14 5LQ

Having had my work rejected by other publishers, I was very grateful to Austin Macauley for seeing that my book was worth publishing, and to all the staff there with whom I have been in contact and were most helpful and guided me through to producing a finished work.

KETURAH

The tale is centred on events during the battles of the Great War, on the ground and in the air, about a couple, both originally living in different parts of England, unknown to each other. One from the nobility, the other from the country working class, that fate brings together by chance in the final years of the 19th century, telling of the highs and lows of their association.

In 1895 a young country girl, Keturah, arrives in London to ply her trade. She gives birth to two boys, two-and-a-half years separating them, each having a different father. As soon as they were born, she left them on the steps of an orphanage, never expecting to see them again. She soon falls in love, leaving her past behind her, marrying the son of an Earl, bearing him three children.

They were both deeply involved in the Great War, as were her two illegitimate sons. The first son joined up soon after the war had started and fought in the Ypres area. The second son, under age, uses an alias to get accepted into the army. He is wrongly condemned to death by a Court Martial, escapes the firing squad and finds the best way not to get recaptured is by taking the unique step of crossing no man's land to be taken as a POW by the Germans, escapes and returns to England to fight as pilot. Keturah becomes a member of the Women's Emergency Corps and later becomes a ferry pilot, interspaced with trying to find her two sons. Her husband starts as a fighter pilot on the Western Front, eventually becoming a senior officer.

All four were to receive decorations for their bravery during the four years of conflict. Three of them would take to the skies, but not all would survive the war, all having to endure the ups and downs of warfare in England, France and Belgium.

FOREWORD

Keturah lived in about the 17th Century BC and married Abraham, becoming his second wife, bearing him six sons. (The Holy Bible, Genesis. Chapter 25, paragraphs 1 to 4) Her name means fragrances or incenses and was of Hebrew origin. Later it was a name commonly used by Puritans after the Reformation in the 16th Century AD.

Keturah; you may ask, why call a book by that name? My brother Tony researched our family tree and discovered the name of Keturah Ball who was our Great, Great, Great, Great-Grandmother on my paternal side, born in 1757. I think this is a lovely name, and would have been happy if one of our daughters had been called this, but I found out the name too late. What either of our two daughters would have thought of it if they had been blessed with Keturah, I have not asked! Let's hope one of my descendants will take it up, I hope so. So, this story is in part to the memory of that lady. While I know nothing about my ancestor, I'm sure she was not like the one I have portrayed in my story!

Service numbers used in the story are part my brothers and mine, the remainder are made up and do not refer to anyone, and is a coincidence if they do. All departures from historical fact are my responsibility as are any mistakes in history I have made or perverted.

Finally, without the help of my wife Valerie, in proof-reading and correcting my hundreds of dyslexic mistakes, my efforts would have remained a disaster, bigger than they now are!

Table of Contents

THEY SHALL BE REMEMBERED

'Twas far from over by Christmas,
The 'boys' weren't coming home,
In Blighty they sat around their tables,
There was a chair that stood alone.

When the 'Star' above the stable stopped,
Both sides laid down their arms,
To climb out from their trenches,
To meet on land that had been farms.

All hopes and aspirations at the start,
Had began to fade from sight,
Where had everything gone wrong?
Did they really want to fight?

More came out to join the cause,
To bolster those who'd left afore,
The blood shed there was never ending,
And crosses stood as sentinels before.

The food was not like Mum had made,
'Twas under open skies they had to eat,
Nor was there beer as they had at home,
Just a tot of rum before the enemy to meet.

The trenches were deep and wide,
They zigzagged for miles on end,
Your bed a ledges cut in the side,
The view was yonder to the bend.

The weeks to months, the months to years,
The mud, the lice, the rats all there,
As were love letters from across the sea,
'Twas more than hearts and souls could bear.

Just over four years on, at 11 of the clock,
The guns went silent; the birds sprang into songs,
Nature reclaiming the ground and woods around,
And Flanders's Poppies now gather in their throngs.

They Shall Be Remembered

© Robin Gardner ~ 2015

This poem is dedicated to the memory of those who served their country in the Great War from 1914 to 1918, either in the Army, the Navy, or the RFC & later the RAF, or as civilian personnel, in all occupations in all theatres of the conflict throughout the World.

To those who never came home, to those who suffered injuries, in body or mind and never fully recovered, to those who did recover, and finally those who fought and were fortunate enough to eventually return home uninjured, all serving their own Country, which and where ever it was, with distinction.

CHAPTER 1

A Country Girl

William Perry was born on a cold snow-covered day on the 18th of January 1896 to a prostitute. His mother was a girl of just 18 years of age, called Jane Perry; a name she had chosen to hide her true identity and break all links with her past life. She plied her trade from a large house in a quiet secluded byroad in a better part of Marylebone.

The owner of the house was a widowed lady, who had had to let out all the other rooms in the building she did not use after her husband had died with his salary, the rent now her only source of income. On the death of her husband, all the servants and kitchen staff had to go and she now only occupied the ground floor room. She found this income from the rent paid by tenants more than adequate for her needs once all the rooms had been filled and continued to live in the style she and her husband had been accustomed, finding she could now afford a housemaid. As long as Jane paid her rent promptly, which she always did, and was a quiet tenant, which she was, there were no questions asked as to how she earned her living.

Jane's accommodation were two rooms in the basement of the house which was entered from the pavement, through the servant's gate, down the area steps into a small yard, which all her clients would descend for a night of pleasure with her. Across the yard was the front door where previously the house staff would enter and tradesmen ply their trade. Behind this door had been the kitchen and scullery, which had now been converted into a small self container basement living quarters and was well suited for Jane's purposes. The other side of her front door was the living room, with a small curtained-off cooking area to the right, while to the left was a doors leading to a flight of stairs to the ground floor, only ever used by Jane when she went up to pay her landlady the weekly rent. The other door, opposite her front door, was her bedroom, where Jane entertained her *"friends"*.

Jane, in her first bloom of adulthood, was young and extremely attractive, five foot and six inches tall, taller that the average girl, with long shapely legs, a slim waist and a firm well developed bust that caught the eye of every young hot-blooded male and the envy of not only all the young girls in the

Marylebone area, but where ever else she went. Behind her full red lips were dazzling even white teeth all set in a heart shaped face that always had a ready smile like Mona Lisa, and dimples in her rosy cheeks. Her eyes were green that augmented her long glossy chestnut-coloured hair, that when not put up, was half way down her back with gentle natural waves, there was a similarity between her and Nell Gwyn in figure and good looks, but no oranges! Wherever she went, she turned men's heads, much to her pleasure and the disgust of their wives or girlfriends. Men would smile at her when she passed, and would watch her retreating figure until out of sight. The more daring would sometimes follower her, but they did not get very far unless Jane was attracted to them or needed them to support her income.

Customers were of a better class and were willing to pay more in and around Paddington, had it not only been a village in 1835 when the railway arrived, than could be found in other parts of London or in the country, near Bedford where Jane hailed from. She had many patrons daily, so many she had to turn many away, only picking those who were the better well heeled. Paddington Station was a good place to find a lonely client who had missed the last train home! She could live for a whole week from one wealthy client for a night of her pleasures. She soon got to recognise those who were well off and those who were not, she always chose well.

***

That year, Swan invented electric filament lamps, and Cleopatra's Needle arrives in London. It was in 1890 that the Army took its first tentative step into to the world of flight with balloons. The same year, the first deep-level tube line opened in London, the City & South London Railway between King William Street and Stockwell.

***

In 1878, in a small village in Bedfordshire, Jane Perry was born and christened Sarah Smith, and was the third child of six, born to Eliza Smith and her husband, Thomas, the village blacksmith. Sarah had two older brothers, Mathew and Mark, two younger sisters, Mary and Maud and a younger brother, Luke, the last to be born to the Smiths. Like most working-class families of this period, the Smiths had had their fair share of sorrow, having lost three children in infancy. Thomas was strong, with muscular biceps from working all his life as a blacksmith, learning the trade from his father, who had learnt it from his father in turn, and him from previous generations of the Smith family. He had a florid complexion gained from working near the forge for more years that he could remember. Now over fifty, his hair had turned grey and was starting to thin, but all this was hidden by a cloth cap he always wore, and with much beer drinking at the local village inn over the years, he was becoming more rotund as the years passed. His wife Eliza, on the other hand, was as slim as a bean pole topped by wispy mousey hair, now starting to be streaked with grey, but bearing nine children hadn't put much extra weight on her. All the children were a mixture of their parents. The two older boys were like their father when he was in his prime, muscular and lean, but both taller than him. There was no other lad in the village who would take on the Smith brothers! The youngest boy was like a rake, but growing fast, he would eventually be like his father and older brothers. Sarah's two younger sisters would remain plain all their lives, not ever being at all pretty as their older sister, they were both as thin as their mother with the same mousey greasy hair that they hardly ever washed and a blotchy completion, unlike Sarah who had her head under the pump in the back yard at least twice a week. Her sisters were the true 'ugly sisters,' their hair reminded Sarah of two floor mops as they walked out together, they would never turn the heads of any of the village lads as Sarah could and did at any time!

Sarah had a good upbringing in the small country village of Hartingford situated on a minor road about half way between the market towns of Bedford and Luton. Hartingford was like hundreds of other small sleepy villages throughout England, where everybody knew everybody and their business as well! It was hard to hide a secret in a village so small. Harrington was a peaceable little place, crime was non-existent, and the local country policemen, who lived in the next village and patrolled a number of surrounding small villages, including Harrington, on horseback, had little or no work to do, bar to ride his beat one or twice a week and show a police presence. Crime just did not happen in the small village, the worst that ever happen were a few young lads who had drunk too much of the local cider on a Saturday night and could not hold their drink, but they caused little or no problems, fathers soon sorted sons out! They had to be up and bright for church on the following day!

There was no Roman Hartingford, they had not come anywhere near the half dozen mud huts that there were gathered around the stream at the time of their conquest in 54BC to their leaving in 407AD. The first anyone knew of the village was written in the Domesday Book, compiled between 1085/6, and there were now over two dozen dwellings and a place of worship. When King John put his seal on the Magna Carta in 1215, it did little difference to the village. Nor did the fighting between the Cavaliers and the Roundheads at various places throughout the land, but not in Hartingford. The King nor Oliver Cromwell ever bothered the village during the Commonwealth from 1649, deposing Charles I, for 11 years, after which a monarch was again enthroned, Charles II, the son of the previous King. In 1752, Great Britain adopted the *New Style Calendar*. In 1804, a Cornishman, Captain Richard Trevithick designed, built and drove the first steam railway engine with a pressure of 150psi, hauling 10 tons of trucks, nine and three-quarter miles at 5mph on cast-iron flange rails. It was not until 1869 that the railway came near Hartingford at Ampthill station. The women of the village were ruled with a rod of iron by the men, the Suffragette movement, founded late in the 19th century to the early part of the next century never had a chance, but by 1928, despite any help from the women folk of the village, they all got the vote if over 21 years, equality with the men.

The main part of the village was centred around the village green which was in the shape of a long thin inverted triangle. The short base was at the highest point of the green facing northwards towards Bedford, running straight on an east to west axis, known as Church Row, while the other two sides sloped gently downwards and were slightly curved inwards to its point at the southern end of the Green, where the village pond could be found. The main road through the villages, known as Bedford Road, entered at the north-east corner from Bedford, ran down the east side of the green leaving in a southerly direction towards Luton. The road on the west side of the Green was known as Brook Lane, which ran parallel to the large village stream that had been damned to provide water power for the village mill, that ground flour for the villagers and the bakery, it being only a little distance to the west of the lane, where all water for the villagers was obtained until a local benefactor had installed a pump on the apex of the Green near the pond.

It was the main job of all the young boys, and girls if the boys had disappeared, to keep their house supplied with fresh water from the stream, and later the pump, carrying it in locally made clay pitchers made in the pottery or metal buckets made by Sarah's father. As time went on, a number of the cottages had their own pump in the back yard, which Thomas had installed as soon as possible; he needed a lot of water for his trade, and did not want to waste the time of his two older lads in water carrying, when they could be helping him, which increased their income, which was very welcome.

The village of Hartingford was situated about five miles east of the nearest railway station at Ampthill, on the line that ran between Bedford and Luton, with only three other stations in between; Flitwick, Harlington and Leagrave. The station was only accessible by a narrow heavily rutted cross-country lane running in roughly a south westerly direction from the west end of Church Row, nearly impassable in bad weather. Thus, the stage coaches were still well-patronised, and therefore continued to ply between these two towns where the roads were better maintained, income for their up keep being obtained from the Toll Houses at frequent intervals along the road.

On the Bedford Road was the coaching inn, The Black Horse, also doubling as the village "local", where all the stage coaches that plied daily between Bedford to Luton stopped to take on extra horses to assist it up the steep hill out of the village southwards. The publican of the Inn had the smartest building in the village where at the back he brewed all his own beer and pressed locally grown apples to make his own rough scrumpy cider with the help of two of the local lads. It was a popular stop for coaches, offering rooms for anyone who wished to stay overnight, frequented by the majority of male villagers to quench their thirst after hard days toil.

With the advent of trains, the long-distance stage coaches between Bedford and London had ceased just after the railways had opened from the north, through Bedford, Luton and terminating at St Pancras on the Midland Railway or via Hitchin into Kings Cross on the Great Northern line, taking all their passengers. Local stage coaches that were still running would stop anywhere on their route to pick up local passengers, they needed the trade, calling at all the small villages *en route* which the railway did not serve, as one had to walk miles to get to the nearest railway station. But the writing was on the wall for the stage coaches, their days were numbered to the motor vehicles.

The coaches ran on a regular daily basis, between six and eight times a day and even more on market days, there was much horse drawn traffic continuing until a few years into the new century when motor vehicles were reliable enough to make this trip over the torturous road of the time; lorries for freight and converted lorries with seats for passengers, the first omnibuses of the day. With the increase of traffic, the roads were improved and more vehicles could be seen plying along the main road. Even the road to the station was improved by the railway when they realised they were losing trade to motor vehicles with the poor state of their thoroughfare serving the station.

Each coach carried a carriage clock which was checked once a day against the railway station clock before it departed on its first run of the day at either Bedford or Luton, supplying towns and villages *en route* with the correct *Railway Time*. The land lord of the *Black Horse* always checked these times with his clock in the only bar of the inn and those who had clocks or pocket watches would check the *Bar Time* and on most occasions, stay for a drink or two! It all helped trade.

19

Most of the village was grouped round the outer edge of the Green. The village had two places of worship, both being well attended every Sunday and on all other Holy Days. The Anglican church of St Mary's and vicarage were at the top of the village along Church Row, while the Hartingford Baptist Chapel and the Baptist Minister's house were at the lower end of Brook Lane.

At the top of Brook Lane were some Alms Houses, a small shop where one could buy, sell or barter goods for exchange; small cottages and dwellings that butted up to the Baptist Church. The village school was on the Bedford Road, near to its junction of Church Row. The School was also the home of the two spinster teachers who ran it, charging a penny per day per pupil.

Not too far away from the school was a small pottery, that obtained all its clay from a local clay pit, and its output provided the village with all the kitchen and tableware that was required and the surplus was taken by horse and cart to the markets at Bedford and Luton.

Situated at the top of Bedford Road, after the *Black Horse*, was the village bakery, large for the size of the village, where all the village bread, cakes, pies and biscuits were baked, was the second dwelling one passed on entering the village from Bedford. The baker, Abraham Ashworth, Doughy to his friends, who was rotund and looked like one of his cottages loaves, was a good business man and sold more of his output at the markets of Bedford and Luton than he sold in the village shop all week. By the 1890s, trains where taking the majority of passengers on long distances, but there was a minority who still could not stomach trains and remained loyal to the stage coach.

One of Doughy' s many products were sweet biscuits and he soon realised that when a stage coach stopped at the village coaching inn. Stage-coach passengers were often hungry when they arrived, and as the stop to change horses was not long enough for a meal at the inn they would pop into his shop to buy something to relieve their hunger. He found he had a ready market for his produce so he started to bake more biscuits. His trade was not as he hoped, but he realised a pretty face and a radiant smile sold more biscuits than he could, and as he had two sons and no daughters he employed young Sarah Smith, who had now left school, to take biscuits over to the coach to sell them to the passengers while horses were changed at the inn. With her good looks and charm, she did a roaring trade.

Doughy first sought permission from Sarah's father for his consent to employ her and as there was little or no work for a young girl in the village, except going into service at the manor, and those jobs were in short supply. Thomas soon gave his approval when Doughty told him she would be paid two-and-a-half percent of the profit of the biscuits she sold. He told Doughy that all the money Sarah earned for her labours were not to be given to Sarah but passed direct to Eliza, much to Sarah's disgust, which was given over under much sufferance! Thomas told Doughy that Sarah got all her meals free and her clothes made by Eliza, she did not need any money, and she had nothing to spend it on. Unlike her brothers who got paid, they needed beer money! Doughy had a soft spot for Sarah, she was like the daughter he never had, and if she did well he would tap his nose and gave her a wink and slip a few pennies in her pocket. Sarah started off carrying a tray slung round her neck, but as trade increased, Doughy got the local carpenter to make a small two-wheeled covered pushcart that Sarah loaded up early each morning with all the freshly baked biscuits and cakes. She would then wheel the cart out and set up her stand on the Green opposite the Inn as one of the many coaches plying back and forth between Bedford and Luton stopped.

She would only wheel her cart back into the bakery after the last coach had passed in the evening. As time passed, Doughy added other items of his daily output to the trolley, so Sarah was now selling, cakes, buns and loaves of bread and hot pies, kept warm on preheated bricks; his complete range was now on display for sale. Not only were passengers now buying for their current needs, but buying extra to consume later on their journey, if it was long one, or to take home. The word soon got around and trade was good. Doughy knew it was a lot to do with Sarah pretty smile and friendly chat that his sales were so good, so the few pennies she got when she started to sell were now a lot more. Doughy knew Sarah's parents were tight with their money, unlike Doughy, so he and Sarah had an arrangement. He gave Eliza Sarah's basic wages, while Doughy gave Sarah another 2½% of his profit as a bonus, and he was still well in pocket.

Many of the passengers were not bothered about receiving their change after they had purchased cake or biscuits; they were usually in a hurry as the stage did not stop long and also thought that the pretty girl deserved a tip, especially standing out in all weathers. She never told her parents about this income or Doughy's bonus, her father had only said she was to give to her mother the money the baker paid her for her services, nothing was ever mentioned about the extras! This she considered was fair game and rightly hers and was the start of her making money, and saving it. She was honest with Doughty and told him of the tips, but he said that was her perks, and gave her a daily peck on the cheek, that was his perk!

Sarah had a shrewd head on her pretty shoulders and was very astute where money matters were concerned. She only purchased her needs, not her wants! Her parents eventually gave her a meagre allowance, which did not go very far; but if they saw she was buying things over what they gave her, they would want to know where the extra money had come from. No one ever got the better of her where money matters were concerned. She realised from the start, she had to keep the tips and bonus separate from the money she handed over to Doughy, and she never ever cheated him out of any money she received. She made sure she wore a very thick full-length skirt, which she had sewn in a number of deep hidden pockets, where she could slip all her tips in and the bonus that Doughy gave her after she handed over all the takings for the day. This money was slipped into the various pockets, so the weight was spread around, and the coins did not chink together as she put small pieces of cloth in each to deaden the sound.

Sarah soon realised some of the stage coaches carried more wealthy clients than others and also private coaches came and stopped to buy from her with 'well-to-do' customers. She mentioned this to Doughy, and between them they had a two-price tier, for the upper class and the middle class. Not only did this make more money for Doughy, but it increased Sarah's bonus. Her coffers started to build up.

Sarah had once been told by a wise old man of the village that an income of £1, outgoings of 19s - 11¾d, you were solvent, but income of £1, outgoings of £1 - 0s - 0¼d, you were in poverty! *'So be penny wise and not pound foolish'*. She never, ever forgot this adage, and considered it to be a very astute statement; it was the basis of her accounting and spending for the rest of her life. She was never 'in the red' and was to become a very astute woman where money matters were involved. She never kept a written account of her money in her youth, in case it was ever found, but once she left home she did.

Next to the Bakery were the Smith's house and the Smithy, which was attached to one side of the house, having a back, another side and roof, partly open to the front in all weathers, where horses were hitched while they were shod. On looking in to the smithy, one could see the forge, with its large bellows, the anvil and all the tools of the trade of a village black smith and horse shoes hanging all along the house wall; cold to work in the winter, and very hot on a sunny summer's day.

Next to the Smithy was Chippy, the village carpenter, who made all the village and surrounding area needs in wood. Between his workshop and the Smithy was a pit where hoops made by Thomas could be heated up to be shrunk on to wooden wheels made by Chippy. The two workshops together were no coincidence; both their grandfathers had set them up over 100 years previous and had ever since been working well together. Chippy also had a son who was learning the trade. The last business was the butcher, and then the rest of this side of the Bedford Road were cottages and small houses.

If anyone had any animals they roamed and grazed freely on the Green, and one could always see horses, cows, sheep, chickens, and the odd goat for milking, peacefully grazing together. Not far from the Green was a farm that supplied the villagers with daily fresh milk and eggs.

The butcher had first call on any animals that the farmer was ready to sell at market, otherwise he went into the market at Bedford to purchase animals the farmer did not have and would bring them back to the village for slaughter, to sell in the village or make into local sausages to sell when he went on his visit to market next time. The village always had some fresh meat, be it beef, mutton or pork and birds from chicken, ducks and geese.

On Market Day in Bedford, the farmer, his wife and farm hands would be up early, driving the animals for sale to market, and return with cows, pigs or sheep, depending what he could get at a good price, to supplement his stock or increase his breeding animals.

Thomas and Chippy both got the majority of their work, not only from the villagers and farms nearby, but from the Lord of the Manor, who owned a big estate a mile towards Bedford and employed a number of local people, and had many horses to keep shod. Coaches and farm carts that always seemed to need repair and attention, the hooped wheels, damaged by the bad roads in the area, that required repair, brought them both a lot of hard work, but good business.

There were three ways to enter the Smith's house, through the front door that lead immediately off the main street, the side entrance from the forge, or a rear entrance into a garden where Eliza grew vegetables to help eke out their small income. Like the Inn and all the businesses, they had their own water pump at the bottom of the garden, their privy. Entering the front door was a living room which was the only place where they all gathered as a family, mainly for meals and bible readings by Eliza on a Sunday; Thomas could not read very well. Off to one side of the living room was a door that led into a passage where the three bedrooms were situated, while at the rear of the room there was a door that led into the kitchen. From there you could either turn right into the scullery and then into the Blacksmiths Shop, or straight on into the garden. When the cottage was built many years ago, for an earlier generation of the Smiths, it was small with only a living room and one bedroom. But the Smiths over the years had had big families and two extra rooms had been built on the side, one for the girls and one for the boys. Any new babies slept in the parent's room until old enough to move out, or another infant arrived to takes its place.

As Sarah was the eldest, her younger sisters did as she told them; they had been on the end of her wrath more times than they wished to know. Once they had told their mother of what Sarah had done to them and she was given a mild dressing down; it was like water off a duck's back to Sarah, and nothing compared to what her two young sisters received later, they had bruises for a week or more afterwards; they never snitched on their older sister again!

For privacy from her sisters, Sarah erected a partition with the help of her brothers, halving the room nearly down the centre so the door was in her sisters' half. There were two windows in the bedroom, each half having its own; an advantage that Sarah made good use of later. She had left an opening in the partition, from which to hang a piece of sacking that covered the aperture from top to bottom, which no one was allowed to enter - even her mother, who was a timid woman. So she had her own private room within a room, where she could keep all her secret purchases and her savings that she knew her father would not allow if he knew.

Not long after she had made her own *private suite* she discovered a loose floor board. On taking it up she found a small space underneath, and from thereon she kept her precious possessions that she did not want anyone to know about. After her days work selling Doughy's products, she would go to her room, making sure her sisters were not about, and hide her takings under the floorboards, in a purse she had made. Unfortunately, having removed the board a number of times, it became obvious of having been taken up, so to conceal her secret place she made a rag rug from an old sacking and off-cuts of material from clothes her mother had made. She was never without money of her own from then on and for the rest of her life her savings grew as the years went by.

Eliza bore all their children over a period of ten years, and because there was so much for Eliza to do in running their home and raising children, as soon as a child became old enough, they were not only expected to assist around the house but look after their younger siblings; it was considered their duty. Sarah's two older brothers first assisted Eliza, but when Sarah was old enough, she found she was now looking after the younger ones, while her brothers now had to help their father in the blacksmiths forge, not only to assist him there, but to learn a trade and take over from their father when he retired. They were only paid a few shillings a week, but never complained, as there was nowhere else to work.

Sarah soon found she was not cut out for looking after children, or helping her mother round their home, and was glad when she had to go to school. Her schooling was in the village school and being a quick learner, was an above average scholar, well versed in the 3Rs. In later life, this came to be a great asset. She also had another attribute; she was an excellent mimic, she had a good ear and memory which also served her well. As she started to move in better circles, she found this an asset and copied those around her, abandoning her local country accent and phrases, and was soon accepted in those new circles in which she mixed. This attribute was to come into use later in her life.

The main highlight of the year that Sarah and most of the villagers looked forward to was the May Fair, when suddenly the village green, that was normally empty all the year round except for grazing animals, was filled with gipsy caravans and the fun of the fair associated with such an occasion. What little the young lads and lassies had saved up over the previous year was blown in one glorious day on rides, side shows and food that they only saw but once a year at the fair. The main ceremony was the crowning of the May Queen which Sarah won when she was in her last year at school; many said she was the prettiest Queen they had had seen for many a yea. Her beauty and radiance attracted the attention of the majority of the village lads, and a number who and come from the surrounding villages. She had come into womanhood!

One thing Sarah was very good at when she came into her womanhood was the art of lovemaking, in which she did not require any tuition. Making love came quite naturally to her; she was an expert and did not require any schooling, but that came later, and not in the village of Hartingford. God had also been very generous when he created her, and she knew from an early age how to make the best of herself, much to the consternation of her strict Baptist parents. While in her early teens she was spreading her charms around the little village lads, but so far she had kept her virginity intact. She soon got herself a bad name in the village with the older generation, into trouble with her parents and worst of all, as far as her parents were concerned, with the fiery local Baptist minister who on many occasions had to remonstrate to her in strong language, quoting from the Bible on many occasions, pronouncing the errors of her ways. He also offered wise advice to her parents as what they should do with their wayward daughter. When her father and mother chastised her about her behaviour she would listen, agree with what they said, saying she would mend her ways, then carry on as before as if nothing had ever been said to her; all the advice wisely given to her went in one ear and out the other, as far as she was concerned, it was water off a duck's back!

When she was in her early teens her teacher took the six oldest girls from the school, which included Sarah, into Bedford to visit the weekly market. Sarah had never been there before and was amazed what was there and how much fun there was to be had. Besides the selling and buying of horses, cows, pigs, sheep and all types of birds, there were stalls selling goods from animal feed, ironware, tools, meat, and farm products brought in from surrounding farms. Stalls that for a small outlay you could gamble your money away with little chance of winning, and stalls of items that were of interest to ladies; jewellery, clothes, bonnets and scents, to Sarah like nothing she had smelt before.

But what interested her most were the stalls selling finery for young ladies to help them make themselves look more beautiful and glamorous. From her savings she made purchases, but looked around at all that was on offer, not buying the first she saw. She was not going to squander her hard-earned savings on any rubbish, she was not going to be duped by any fly-by-night stall-holder. With a few pence, she purchased a small bottle of cheap scent which she would put to good use the next time she was going to see the local boys!

The other thing she noticed was the number of young local town lads who were there, loitering around, about her own age. While she did not let on, many of these lads were giving her the eye and making cat calls after her, which she pretended not to notice, but a certain thrill passed through her body when they started to pay attention to her. Young men were certainly on her menu from then on!

Sarah soon got bored with the local village lads; they were not much fun and were lacking in any imagination or dress sense, unlike the lads at Bedford Market. Remembering her first recent visit to Bedford, just before she left school, she decided that there was more life there than in Hartingford. Sarah decided that she should seek fresh fields and pastures new and she considered that Bedford Market was her fresh fields and pastures new!

The day before Market Day she made her plans carefully. It was now June, the weather was hot and dry, just the time to pay a visit. It did not enter her head to consider the consequences on her return home in the evening - that was a bridge she would cross later! She would leave early, having to walk nearly 5 miles to the market, which would take her just over an hour. She told Doughy when she handed in the days takings she felt a bit off colour and would not be in the following day, and as it was Saturday, trade was always poor. He agreed, and even suggested that they cease trading on a Saturday as he was away most of the day at Bedford market with his wife while his son left in charge, considering it too much work for him to be responsible for on his own. This was music to Sarah's ears, she had the day off. When in Bedford she decided not to go anywhere near Doughy's stall; she knew she could trust them both, they were kindred spirits, but if they saw her they might let something slip when taking to the Smiths or any customer back in Hartingford. Word would soon get around the village when anything like that happened!

To make things easy for herself, as she was going to creep out before anyone else was up, she would hide her shoes, a purse of money and a bonnet in the outhouse behind the forge, seldom ever used; she knew a good hiding place in there which no one would ever find. While she slept in the same room with her other two sisters, she knew them to be both heavy sleepers, it would be best not to get dressed in her room, in case she made any noise, but sneak out without them knowing and change outside. She went to bed early that evening, before her sisters, saying she was tired and had a headache. Once in her room, she made her preparations by ensuring the sack cloth door was well sealed from her sisters' half and the window was open ready for her escape as dawn was rising. She undressed and slept only in a pair of very baggy and unbecoming knickerbockers with a tight fitting, revealing dress folded under her pillow. She had no intention of concealing the shape of her full ample bosom under a loose fitting high neck dress, what the boys would see is what she had, and she had no intention of hiding her contours for anyone, she was proud of what she had and no one could take that away from her. She knew she outshone any of the other village girls by miles, and hadn't she been the best *May Queen* for all the time she could remember; and what competition she had seen at Bedford Market, did not cause her any problems either!

The dress she was going to wear to the market had been made by her mother, like all their clothes, and being the oldest girl, she had to help, and as time went by, she was doing more of the work, until she could make dresses without her mother's assistance. But that did not mean that her mother did not keep a close eye on what her daughter was making, she knew the child had a wild streak. All the clothes produced were very plain and dowdy, which was to the liking of her Baptist parents. What her mother did not know, that while the dress she was going to wear to the market was plain, Sarah had done some alterations. The hem of the skirt was raised so her trim ankles could be seen, the waist was nipped in as tight as possible, and the neck line lowered as much as she dared to show her ample breasts and deep cleavage. Her aim was to be noticed by as many boys as possible.

Sarah woke up early, just as it was getting light; before she moved she checked that her sisters were fast asleep, which they were. She moved around making as least noise as possible and gathered the dress she was taking with her, plus a sum of money, hidden in a concealed pocket she had made in the waist band of the dress; she had heard all about *pick-pockets*. She then climbed out of the open window in her half of the room with her dress under her arm, wearing only her knickerbockers. Outside, she went round the back of the forge and washed under the pump in cold water, the water freshened her up and caused a tingle through her body. As she stood up the water running down her cascaded over her ample breasts and ran through the deep valley of her cleavage like a mountain stream. The day was already warming up, so she did not mind pulling her dress over her nearly naked wet body, and as she pulled her dress down, she also pulled her knickerbockers down as well. The long skirt of her dress was enough of a hindrance as it was, she did not want any other obstacles getting in the way to what she had planned. She retrieved her belongings from the outhouse, hiding her knickerbockers in the same place and she was on her way along the Bedford Road, in less than ten minutes of leaving her bed.

She was soon out of the village on the turnpike road, passing the Toll House situated on the northern edge of the village boundary, not having seen a single soul as she made her way towards her goal, the Bedford Market. She soon dried out, and started to plan her day. She would first stop at a tavern on the out skirts of Bedford for breakfast, and once eaten it would last her till evening, if she did not get someone to buy her anything, which she was sure she could.

The day, as far as Sarah was concerned, was a great success. Young lads her age, and a bit older, swarmed round her like bees round a honey pot, and with her chestnut coloured hair, half way down her back, the very tight-fitting dress and her pretty bonnet the crowning glory, how could they resist? It was far from surprising, that she got the result she wanted, to be admired and drooled over, and a number of hands she felt fondling her breasts, as she had hoped and thought would happen. She was plied with food and drink, but she kept off anything alcoholic. While there was a row when she got home, she considered it had been well worth it, and she now had plans for more visits, regardless to what her parents or the Baptist Minister had to say.

The only thing that was a drawback, as far as she was concerned, was her dress. She had done everything she could do to make it attractive, but the material, which she could do nothing about, was plain and boring. A lot of the other young girls at the market wore dresses with bright patterns, which showed a lot of ankle and a neck line that was low enough to guarantee getting noticed. She had to have one of these, come what may. The next time she went to the market, she went round all the dress stalls and she saw a number of market stalls selling dresses exactly to her requirements. She had the money from all her tips and bonuses and after a lot of looking, selected and purchased two dresses that showed a lot more ankle than the average, and a neck line that would raise the blood pressure of any hot blooded young lad who looked at her, and give her parents and the minister a heart attack! She had seen how buyer and seller bartered, so she joined in the game and got a few pence knocked off the price, giving the stall holder a charming smile and a good deal more boson and cleavage than was necessary and would have sent her parents into high dudgeon. The acquisition of the dresses gave her great pleasure; it was the start of her becoming a first-class business woman.

There was no way she could take the dress home, even in her private room, it would be impossible to smuggle it in and out unnoticed. She had to find a hiding place for it. Then she had an idea. When she was younger, she often played with other girls; a favourite game was *hide-and-seek* in the woods near the village, just off the Bedford road. She remembered the time while hiding behind a bush, the lower part of a big old oak was concealed by the bush. She turned round to find it was hollow, this seemed a better hiding place than the bush. She squeezed in through the gap and found there was a lot of room inside, dry and cosy. She stayed hidden but no one ever found her. When the other girls called for her to come out, she never revealed where she had been. This was her secret hiding place that she never told anyone else about it. This is where she decided would hide her dress. On the way home, she made for her hollow tree, and found the hollow part of the tree was even better concealed than before, the bush concealing the entrance had grown over the passing years. She could still squeeze in, but more effort was required; while she was still as slim as ever, she had developed since the *hide-and-seek* days! The hollow part was dry and inside she found a projection above her head that she could hang her dress from, all wrapped up as when she had bought it, in a cloth bag. Before she left the hollow tree she immediately stripped out of her old dress and tried on her recent acquisitions over her naked body, they were both a perfect fit, and showed off her figure in the way she had always dreamed. They were perfect and displayed all the assets she had to the best of her advantage. She had every intention of showing and exploiting them as much as possible. The lads in Bedford were in for a treat next time she went!

Her parents soon found out Sarah was going to Bedford Market every Saturday. They tried to stop her, but it was in vain, she was to wilful, and she was of marrying age, so they had to let her go, much to their annoyance. On market days, she would go into Bedford, by the hollow tree, and pick up one of her dresses and carry it to the market. She had no intention of wearing it along the dusty roads, and the word would soon get back to her parents if someone her parents knew saw her and told them. It was bad enough going to Bedford in an old dress as far as they were concerned. She would have breakfast in a tavern on the outskirts of Bedford and change there.

On her arrival at Bedford she found that the local lads there started hanging around waiting for her to arrive. As she got to know them, more liberties were taken, and eventually one had his wicked way with her, soon others followed, and she found that she enjoyed the experience! She was a popular and pretty girl and had now got into the wrong crowd, offering her services free of charge. She was soon advised by other girls who were plying their bodies for money, she was taking trade away from them, to stop being an amateur and become a professional! She was soon on the game, part time in Bedford on market days, and soon found that the better heeled the person, the more they would pay. It was not long that she had a client by the name of Jacob Parsons, a married gent who regularly came from London, travelling up by train on business at the Bedford market and always spending the night before market days at the large coaching inn in the centre of the town.

Jacob was a merchant venture, and visited two or three markets a week out of London, always Bedford on a Saturday. He was at the market as soon as it opened and being a shrewd business man, he would purchase anything that he knew he could sell in London at his shop near Baker Street station, always at a good profit to him, which was run, in his absence, by his two sons. After nearly twenty years in his profession he was extremely rich from buying cheap and selling dear. While he was now in his early fifties, he had lost his slim build of youth and was putting on weight, not only in the body, but around the face which was becoming flabby, not being much taller than Sarah; she made him look very stout. He also had gone prematurely bald, for a man of his age, and was self-conscious about the fact and always wore a wig, to the amusement of Sarah, but never to his face, she knew which side her bread was buttered!

Sarah met him one Saturday afternoon when he had completed all his business and he soon propositioned her, inviting her back to his hotel room that he still occupied until the evening. Sarah was soon spending the afternoons of her Saturdays each week with Jacob and he told her his wife was a cold fish, sex had only one purpose in life to her, or so Jacob thought, as Sarah found out later, to conceive a baby. They had enough children, so there was no more sex for him, so what else could Jacob do? She listened carefully to the way Jacob spoke and the idioms he used during the time they spent together, adopting his posh London accent. Being married Jacob did not want a permanent relationship, but wanted Sarah closer, so that he could have more nights with her, so suggested she should go to London where the money was better and he would help her find her a place to lodge.

After the afternoon together she would arrive back in the village very late in the evening. Her parents eventually got to know what was going on and they threatened to throw her out if she continued in her wicked ways. She continued in her wicked ways, so her parents showed her the door, telling her never cross the threshold again, which she never did, or wanted to! Before she left, she took up the floor board in her bedroom and removed her not too small cache of money, secreting in her pockets of her skirt.

Sarah was soon on the road to Bedford and visited her tree for the last time and removed all her clothes, she had bought a number of new dresses since her first purchase so could now ring the changes, putting them in a large soft carpet bag she had made from material she had got from Doughy's wife and had made in their kitchen, out of the way of prying Smith eyes. Doughy and his wife were both more broad-minded than the Baptist Smiths, their first son had been conceived out of wedlock. They were members of St Mary's, but were not strong believers. Sarah told them some of her secret trips to Bedford, but not all that happened!

With her schooling, she was prudent and wise with money, only spending on what she needed, never on what she wanted, never on anyone else, especially her parents. She did not let on to anyone the amount of money she was saving. She was earning much more than her blacksmith father in one good night stand than he could earn in week, not that anyone ever knew. She had now saved enough money by then when she was thrown out. Went she got to Bedford she took a room at the coaching inn that Jacob frequented when he came up from London, and stayed there until he arrived on the next Saturday Market.

To make a clean break from her past Sarah and decided to change her name to Jane Perry, her maternal grandmother's maiden name. It sounded posher and more up-market than plain old Sarah Smith, and no one could then trace her back to Hartingford. Her grandmother had lived all her life in a little village north of Huntingdon, never venturing any further than the adjacent town. The only time Sarah ever saw her grandmother was when her mother, on very rare occasions, took her visiting. No one, she felt, could ever make any connection with her or the family. When she eventually left home, she had no Birth Certificate to take with her, in fact she never knew if she had ever had one in the first place. If she ever thought about it, she considered she was better off without one if she wanted to retain her anonymity.

When Jacob turned up next, she offered him a free night with her if he took her back to London. He had told her a lot about London, where he lived and the surrounding area and she asked him if he could find her somewhere to live not far from his London home in Primrose Hill, where he could visit her more often than once a week and she could entertain most anyone, but only from the middle classes upwards. Jacob accepted her offer and suggested somewhere in the Marylebone area not far from his home, just over a mile across Regents Park. He wanted something on a more regular basis with this lovely girl and living nearby would suit his needs. She was sure trade would be better in London, surpass what Bedford could offer and charge rates more appropriate to the Capital, and he was sure with her beauty she could be kept very busy, saving money that she felt she would need when her days were over in the oldest trade on earth.

She soon found that the prices she could command when she eventually got to London were well above Bedford rates and above what Jacob paid her. While she continued to entertain him, mainly in return for what he had done for her, she was pleased he could only make it about two or three times a week, more time for the better-heeled clients!

CHAPTER 2

The Birth of Two Boys

It was in the summer of 1895 that Jacob agreed to take Jane to London. On the day agreed they left for the capital on an early evening train, after having completed all his trading at the market by mid-afternoon, seeing all his goods packed and dispatched to the station for collection at St Pancras the following Monday, travelling on the same train as his purchases. On arrival, he took her to a temperance hotel he knew not far from Baker Street station for a couple of nights until he found a permanent place for her to live. There was less temptation in that type of hotel; no young bucks to try their wicked way with her, he was getting jealous of other men have their way with her now. While she was there, Jacob came and visited her two or three times a day. He wanted reward for his outlay.

During the days at the hotel, after Jacob's visits, she wandered around the district. She liked to know where she was, the geography of the area, and all the shops that were of interest to her, but in the main, where she could pick up potential clients. By the time she booked out of the hotel, she was very familiar with the area, which stood her in good stead for the time of life she was going to live for the next few years. She had high hopes, as trade improve with more wealthy clients, she could move up the ladder of her chosen profession.

Jacob soon found her lodgings in the Marylebone area, close to the south west corner of Regents Park and she moved in without any delay. The Park was a good place to pick up clients when the weather was kind, otherwise the stations of Marylebone and Baker Street were her haunts, especially when the conditions were inclement. Jacob lived nearby with his family, but would often call on her to sample her delights. His wife had offered him nothing for a number of years, sleeping in separate room. She knew he had something on the side and was glad of it, as she also made use of a male prostitute that Jacob knew nothing about, or so she thought. Her companion performed better than her husband! She always paid him well as Jacob paid Jane. They were both happy and were satisfied, the arrangement suited them equally!

***

The years rolled by, and in 1895 a German physicist, Wilhelm Röntgen discovers X-rays. The following year Queen Victoria celebrated her Diamond Jubilee, 60 Glorious Years as our Queen.

***

But there are always setbacks, and it was not long before Jane found that she was pregnant. Because of her trade Jane did not know who the father of her child was, which did not bother her in the slightest, but she presumed it must have happened by one of her clients at Bedford Market in about March before she had met Jacob. She carried on business as usual, as long as possible, and towards the end of her pregnancy she lived off her savings, so that she did not have to give up her basement room, which Jacob still paid part, but he had to accept she had to earn more that he could pay her. She had now turned her back on Hartingford for ever, as far as she was concerned, good riddance. The Smiths also were pleased to see the back of her, good riddance!

Before the birth was due in early 1896, Jane started looking for a suitable orphanage. There was no way she could bring the child up and carry on working. Who wants sex with a crying baby nearby? While she did not want the child, she was very concerned about its welfare and that it should not be left in a rundown workhouse. On looking around, and making discreet enquires, she found that a certain Dr Barnardo had set a home for deprived boys and girls in the Shepherd's Bush area. He had set up his first home in 1873 for 12 young girls in a cottage in the grounds of his home at Barkingside, Essex, to save these poor unfortunate females from a life in the workhouse. From then on, he had set up homes throughout the country.

On one mild day early in December, a day when trade was poor, Jane decided to have a look at this home, and had already made discreet inquires to its whereabouts and was told to take the Underground train from Marylebone to Uxbridge Road station, the best and quickest way to get there.

***

In 1845 Charles Pearson, promoted an underground railway system to transport passengers and goods to the 'City' to ease the traffic congestion on the streets of London, the idea taking 18 years to come into fruition in 1863, the world's first subsurface train 'steamed' its way out of Paddington Bishop's Road to Fenchurch Street, a distance of just over 3½ miles on Brunel's broad-gauge track of 7 feet. In 1869, the line was extended south westward, Uxbridge Road station being one of seven stations opening that year.

***

On leaving the station, Jane followed the directions she had been given, turning west in the direction of the small town of Uxbridge, passing a big church on the left side of the road she had been told to lookout for, St Stephen and St Thomas, and soon found the lane she had been told on the right, not too far from the station she had arrived at minutes earlier. It was more of an alley than a lane, just wide enough for two carts to pass in some places, not much traffic on the lane, two ruts each side and hoof marks in the centre. The only place to go up the lane was to Dr Barnardo's orphanage.

It did not take her long to find *The Home* which stood right on the edge of the track, unlike when it was originally built, surrounded by acres of parkland. The home from the outside had plainly seen better days, having been built in the late 17th century, and was, when erected, a magnificent London home fit for a Duke and his Duchess of that time when the area was in the countryside, situated in grass and woodlands where deer roamed free and partridges and other game birds and animals were there in abundance to be shot at! As London grew outwards, the area became less suitable for people of this high standing and the house and the majority of the grounds were sold off to lesser mortals. Houses were built on what once had been open countryside and roads now crisscross what had been open land, where now there was hardly a blade of grass could be seen. Eventually there was no one who could afford to live in such a big house of this size, and it became derelict and run down as the last occupants left. Then Dr Barnardo arrived, looking for somewhere in the area suitable to open one of his homes, which he felt, was much needed in the district. He eventually discovered this edifice build in the reign of William and Mary, which was vacant and for sale at a price so low, proving that no one else seemed to want it. While the house was in need of minor repair on the outside, it was ideal for what Dr Barnardo required and internally there was little need for much alteration, the cost of any work would be minimal, and he could always rely on those well-heeled people in the area who would give generous donations of support to his *Homes*, it helped to keep poor unkempt youngsters off the streets. Within a few months the first orphans were arriving.

While Jane was pregnant, she was not showing beneath her loose clothes, and decided to look the house over on the pretext of seeing if they needed volunteers to help out. On her arrival, she pulled the knob set in the wall besides the front door which she thought would ring a bell in the depths of the house somewhere, but was audible from the front door step. On the left of the door was a bay window, while on the right there were two more bays, while above on the first and second floors there were bay windows above each of the ground floor windows. There were four blocked off windows between the bays that had been sealed up to reduce the bill for window tax that had only been rescinded 185,1 having lasted 155 years, dating the house before 1696. In the roof at the rear, unseen by Jane, were seven dormer windows, which had been the servants' quarters in better days.

In response to her ringing, the door was eventually answered by a stout, soberly dressed lady. "How can I help?" she asked Jane.

"I'm looking for a job," was Jane's response, "do you have and positions vacant, if so, could I be shown around?" The stout lady informed her she was the Senior Matron, Miss King, answerable only to the Governor, Mr Newbury, of the home, and they did have vacancies from time to time, but none at the moment, but she was willing to give her a quick look around and would add her name and address on the waiting list if she wanted.

She explained as she closed the front door behind them, "This is the main hall, the left half and second floor is for the boys, while the right half and the first floor is for girls. The girls only use the front stairs to get to their rooms, while the boys use the servants' stairs to get to their quarters. Only the staff and the girls are allowed in the hall and use of the front door. The boys always use the rear door when they go out. There is no fraternising allowed whatsoever between the girls and boys," she added, pausing for breath for only a moment before she continued. "On the top floor, which is in the roof, is the nursery, for those just born until the age of five years, after five, the boys and girls are separated and go to their respective wings. The girl's main jobs are the kitchen and laundry and looking after the under-fives on the top floor, while the boys look after the garden and farm at the rear of the premises, where all our vegetables are grown, and we have chickens that provide the eggs and a few cows that give us our milk. In addition, if there is any maintenance required on the house, a local man comes in, and boys suitable to that work help him."

Miss King then took her on a tour of the house, the girl's wing, up to the nursery, back through the boy's wing, into the garden and finally the kitchen. When the tour was completed, Matron said, "Well, if you are still interested, shall I put you name on the waiting list?"

Jane agreed to have her name put down, but was prepared for this and gave her name as Miss Sarah Smith and a fictitious address, making sure the road she gave was a genuine one a mile or two away. She thanked Miss King, and said she would consider helping them, but could not until the New Year when her Mistress was moving to Scotland, and she did not want to go, so would be out of a job.

She liked what she saw and decided that this was to be the place for her child to be left and raised. It was somewhere to take the baby, but she wanted what she considered the best she could do. Jane still had enough money to afford a Hansom Cab to take the child to the Dr Barnardo Home as soon as possible after the birth. The main problem was she needed to carry on with her profession, as she was now eating into her savings, so she had to get back on the game as soon as possible.

In the early hours of 18th January of 1896, Bill was born in Jane's basement rooms from which she plied her trade. Beth Long, a good friend and another lady of the same trade she had met - and like her, not a 'street-corner girl' - was there to assist her at the birth, which went off without any problems. The baby was certainly not Jacob's; he looked nothing like him which she expected.

During the day she recovered, and when it was dark Beth called a cab after Jane had given the baby a good feed of her breast milk. He was then well wrapped up against the cold, and she ensured he was sleeping deeply after the feed. All three of them set off in the cab together bound for the orphanage, the journey only taking about half an hour, they were soon at their destination. Beth stopped the cab just passed the entrance of side road. They both got out with the baby and paid off the cab, which immediately turned around to try for another fare in Shepherd's Bush.

Beth went first, to make sure the coast was clear and no one was about from the orphanage. Turning back, she beckoned to Jane, who was now standing on the corner with the new born baby in her arms, to come forward. She walked down alley carrying her bundle towards the orphanage, stopping at the large wooden front door. Before laying Bill on the front door step, she gave him a last hug and a kiss; while she did not like doing this, she it knew it was best for Bill and herself. She then laid the baby in front of the door on the single door step, still well wrapped up, fed and fast asleep. She pulled the door chain and on hearing the ring echo in the hall behind the door, she retreated to a safe distance and standing in the shadows from across the road with Beth, both watched. The door was soon opened by a bearded gentleman and a rotund lady, Governor Newbury and Senior Matron King. There was no one there, they looked up and down the road, not a soul in sight, then they heard a cry at their feet and discovered what looked like a baby wrapped up in a bundle of clothes. The lady picked up the bundle and the gentleman pushed back the blanket from the babies face and discovered the note Jane had tucked inside and read it aloud to the matron:

> *"I'm very sorry; I cannot afford to keep my baby boy.*
> *His name is William Perry, he was born today, please*
> *look after him for me.*
> *Thank You, Miss J Perry"*

He looked up and down the street again, but did not see Jane in her hiding place, and after a few brief words together, the baby was taken in through the doors, which closed behind them with a bang, the noise echoing down the empty street. Bill was now an inmate of the Shepherd's Bush Dr Barnardo Home. Jane breathed a sigh of relief, the baby was now safe. The two girls then walked to the underground station and caught a train back to Baker Street and their rooms. Jane never saw Bill again or even gave him another thought at the time, she had to earn money to keep up the rent and buy food to live on, and in the last few weeks her savings had taken a beating.

***

All Bill had, the poor child, was his name and date of birth, the clothes he was wearing and a blanket, he did not even have a birth certificate to prove who he was. The orphanage was required to obtain this document, and when completed by the local Registrar of Births, Marriages & Deaths in the area, the Registrar entered *Unknown* for the father, the mother's name, *J. Perry* and the boy's name, *William Perry*. As the orphanage realised the baby was new born the date of birth was stated as *18th January 1896* and the name of the baby and mother were the only entries that were defiantly correct.

***

After the birth of the child, Jacob started to get possessive; this Jane did not want or need. He said if she agreed to see him and no one else, he would pay her well, and suggested an amount, and little did he know this was far below her present income. Jacob was alright as a client and he paid an average amount to what other clients paid, but basically not her type and she was only entertaining him for all he had done for her, so he had to go, but how? She was earning enough now to do without Jacob, her new clients all paid more than he did, so she decided to find and move to a new home. While she had been in London, she had explored the district and got to know the various areas well. So, when Jacob was not around she started seriously looking for a more suitable location to live and continue her chosen profession. It did not take her long to find a much more up-market apartment in the Ladbroke Grove area of Notting Hill, and the increase in rent was well within her budget, as her earnings had risen ten-fold in about two years. The apartment, on the ground floor, was much larger, and consisted of two large rooms, a lounge that looked over the street and her bedroom that looked out over a small but well-kept garden. On the other side of the entrance hall was the kitchen and bathroom. Compared with the cottage at Hartingford and her present flat, this was like a palace. It was also far enough away to make it unlikely to be found by Jacob, and not far from Paddington railway station, the main place where she now obtained most of her clients. It was only a short journey by Underground from Ladbroke Grove to Paddington, and she was always taken back at the client's expense by a Hackney Cab!

When Jacob went back to Bedford for one of his weekly markets, she upped sticks and was away to the new home, not leaving any evidence to where she had gone or where she could be found, but hinting to her landlady she was returning home to Bedfordshire. Jane decided to change her name once again, just to ensure she had covered all her tracks completely. This time she chose the maiden names of her father's mother, Keturah Bray. Jane Perry and Jacob Parsons were now no more. Lastly, she changed her haunts, Marylebone and Baker Street were crossed off her list, Paddington had much better clients who were better heeled, and all the regulars were ditched.

For just over two years, Keturah kept at her chosen profession, but she eventually slipped up again and she found she was pregnant for the second time, this being early in 1898. The baby boy was born on the 30th September, the child, as William two and half years previous, was not wanted. As soon as the baby was born, the same thing happened as before, Keturah, with the assistance of her friend Beth, left the baby on the same front doorstep of Dr Barnardo's Orphanage in Shepherd's Bush, with a note saying:

> *"My son's name is Samuel Bray, he was born today, but I don't have the money to bring him up. Please take good care of him for me*
> *Thank You, Miss K Bray".*

Samuel was now out of her life and out of the way, and again a birth certificate that had to be provide by the orphanage, carried only three entries as had her previous son before, his names were *Samuel Bray*, his date of birth *30th September 1898*, and only his mother's name, *K Bray*, while the father was entered as *Unknown*. While Keturah had named him Samuel, he was always known as Sam to everyone.

Keturah, at the time, never saw or cared about her two boys; she had a job to do and had to earn as much money as possible. She was still not interested in being reunited with the boys she have given up, she was still young, only in her early twenties, and as far as she was concerned, earning a living was paramount; as soon as she had enough saved up, she wanted to get a proper job, she liked clothes and dressing up, a boutique in a fashionable part of the Notting Hill area maybe. The boys were far from her thoughts over the next few years, but that would come later, time would tell, but she made sure she would not make another mistake and have further children.

***

Before the boys had left the orphanage, they each wanted to know who their parents were, not knowing that they both had the same mother, asking the Governor and Matron if they could help, but they found that they could do nothing in this matter. The Matron explained to them both, they had been left on the doorstep, late into the night, with only a note saying who they were and would the home look after them. Once they had both left the home and had started working they were too busy to look into the matter anymore and it slipped to the back of their minds and was forgotten. Before they left they were given their Birth Certificates, but the notes their mother had left had been filed away, and lost in the fullness of time.

***

In London, there were hundreds of second-hand clothes shops, but there was only a small number that dealt in clothes from the nobility. Ladies who lived in high society hardly ever wore a dress twice, it was never done, a definite no-no! They would be gossiped about behind their backs by their circle of friends. When Keturah had set her sights on wealthier clientele, she had to dress the part, and with more money coming in, she was able to afford these clothes. A sprat to catch a mackerel, and her catch of mackerels were good! She turned the heads of most men as she past them, much to the disgust of a lady on their arm.

Now that she was a well-dressed lady of fashion, she frequented better places, no loitering about on street corners or station forecourts. She found she could now enter high class hotels that included the Great Western Hotel at Paddington and the 1st Class Restaurant situated on Platform 1 without any problems. If asked what she was doing there she would say she was waiting to meet a friend, and in a way this was correct! In fact, she looked so upper class, no one had ever had the courage to ask her! It was where she now picked up most of her clients. And this is how the Right Honourable Algernon Cavendish came into her life.

Late one Friday evening, Keturah was sipping tea in the restaurant, seated near the door which was the best position to see any likely customers enter. She had had a good week, and was not too concerned if she did not obtain another client or not, she was considering a quiet weekend, perhaps she could meet up with her friend Beth tomorrow morning and walk the Saturday market in Notting Hill looking at all the smart dresses, hats and shoes on display. She always enjoying sitting in these opulent surroundings, it was warm, comfortable, and the tea was excellent. Out of the corner of her eye, she suddenly saw a tall handsome gentleman enter, not looking very happy; Keturah played one of her many tricks to get noticed, and employing the *getting knocked down* ploy. As he approached her table, she got up into his path and to the entire world it looked as if he had bumped into her. She stumbled and it appeared she was caught from falling by this gentleman's quick action, and he was immediately full of apologies. Her line had been cast! He saw that she looked like a lady of beauty and real class and spoke well when she answered his apologies, saying she was unhurt!

The least he could do to make amends was to offer to purchase her substance in recompense for his clumsy action. Her line was reeled in! Little did she know at the time, he was the last fish she would ever catch, and he never got thrown back! She never cast her line again.

When refreshment had been brought to their table, he started the conversation, saying that he had come to catch the last train to Reading, but he had been delayed getting to the station by the hackney carriage he was taking being caught in heavy traffic, so by the time he eventually reached the platform, he saw the tail lights of his train disappearing into the night. This had set him in a bad mood and when he stormed into the restaurant to have a drink to soothe his nerves, realising he would have to return to his house in Notting Hill for the night and make his journey early on the following morning, he did not see her in his frustration and anger, which is exactly what Keturah had planned!

They stayed chatting for some time, Algernon having been smitten by her from the time he had saved her from falling, but realised that she was not the lady he first thought she was; but was a very upper class *Lady of the Night*. Algernon, still a bachelor, had sought the comfort of these ladies before, but this lady was different, very different. This one had not only her body to offer, which, from what he could see was something to behold, a real beauty. She was also intelligent, she spoke well and could converse intelligently on most topics that they discussed. This had never happened to Algernon before; previously he had only one night encounters.

Algernon was now pleased he had missed the train. "Please, what may I call you?" he asked her.

"My name is Keturah Bray, Sir, so please call me Keturah" she replied.

"As I have missed my train Keturah, I have now to return to my house in Notting Hill to spend the night there on my own, would you like to accompany home and have a drink with me, where I have some very good wines, much better than anything they serve here, and a cold collation to offer you as well."

"Yes, I would love to accompany you sir, I always appreciate a fine wine, and never refuse the offer of good food."

"Keturah, my name is Algernon Cavendish, I would very much like you to call me Algernon"

Always ready to please, she replied, "Algernon, I would be very happy to do so," but it was the way she said it that sent a thrill through Algernon's body, and an arrow into his heart!

Algernon and his father were frequent visitors to London, mainly on business to do with their estate in the country, and the visits seemed to get more and more frequent as time elapsed. Travelling up by train two or three times a week and returning in the evening they found the journeys very tiring, so they decided to purchase a second home, situated on the outskirts of London, where they could stay while they had business to conduct. Notting Hill Gate was becoming a desirable and smart place to live, and many new houses of different sizes and styles were built in the area. They started to look around for suitable sites and designs for a residence, and were not long in finding either. It was to be a modern house with all the latest fittings of the day. From the purchase of the land to moving in was less than a year. While at first Algernon's mother though it a waste of money, she was soon a visitor, and as a lot of her circle of friends were doing the same thing, it became a home from home for her also. It was not long before they were giving parties there, or being invited out to similar residences to parties given by their friends in the locality. While it was only originally intended to stay there during the week, they found that during the *Season* they were staying there for a month or more, letting Algernon to return home to the country to check on the estate with their manager. Luckily for them both, it was out of *Season* and his parents were at the family seat

One of the reasons the family town house in Notting Hill Gate was chosen was it location, near to the Great Western Railway station of Paddington and from there it was only a short journey by express train of less than an hour to Reading. This was the stopping off point to take a waiting family by horse and carriage, or soon to be changed to the family automobile, north out of Reading for a few miles drive of about nearly an hour by coach or later, 20 minutes by car!

When they were ready, Algernon called a cab and they were soon rattling over the cobbled streets to his Notting Hill residence and Keturah realised when they arrived she lived less than a mile away, very convenient if she became his regular. Soon afterward Algernon was plying Keturah with the best wine from his cellar and a selection of cold meats and other delicacies from the kitchen. While Algernon was out of the room, she had a quick look round the room and thought the house was lovely. After spending the night with Algernon in the master bedroom, she realised this was the life she would like to lead.

After breakfast, he said he had to go to visit his parents, which was where he was bound for the previous evening, so he would have to say good-bye, but he would be back after the weekend, and would like to see her again and it was arranged that she would call on him the following Monday evening. He then went to pay for her services and much to Algernon and Keturah's own surprise she refused any payment.

"Algernon, I have had a lovely time with you and look forward to seeing you Monday evening. I will go back to my apartment and not leave home, or see anyone else until I see you Monday evening, and that is a promise that will be easy to keep"

Algernon was taken back by this remark, his feelings for her were not as a 'lady of the night' anymore, but were closer, like a very dear friend of old standing.

Algernon offered to take her in a cab to her apartment, but she refused, as she would like to walk back on her own, thinking about the last twelve hours. At this early stage in their friendship, she wanted to keep her whereabouts from Algernon a secret, just in case he was frightened off or she changed her mind about him over the weekend, keeping her options open.

When she got home, she sat and thought about Algernon for the next two days, she never thought of contacting Beth. She suddenly realised this was the first time her heart had started to flutter! She listened well to how he spoke, and while the speech and accent was easy, it was the idioms she found most hard to take on board and drop the old Bedfordshire ones that were not suited to the station in life she would be situated in if she took up with Algernon.

After a number of visits Keturah made to Algernon's Notting Hill home, their relationship became serious. As she had told him when they first parted, all the past men in her life were business; she had never had another man as a friend, this included Jacob, it was only her body he really wanted. Algernon realised what she had sacrificed for him, she now had no income, and with his financial support, he took her off the streets for good, she was now taking the first steps on the upward ladder of respectability.

Before the relationship blossomed any further she took him to her apartment, sat him down with a glass of wine, not of the standard Algernon would serve, and told him about her past life, of her wicked ways as a child and having two sons by two unknown fathers, purposely omitting to divulge her son's names, confessing she had given them away the day they were born. It made no difference with him; he wanted her to share the rest of her life with him. Keturah felt the same, she never wanted another man from the day she had met the Honourable Algernon Daniel Ian Cavendish, who changed her life for ever, taking her off the streets. Until the day she died, there was no one else in her life, she was not interested. If Algernon had not been what he was, she would still have loved him, his position and wealth were only second to the deep affection she felt for him as a person.

Like Keturah, Algernon never wanted another woman from then on. While, as an unattached bachelor, he had associated with high class *Ladies of the Night*, now they were a thing of the past. He told her about his past life and she found out he was the first of two children, but sadly the second child was still born and his mother could not bear any more children. It was his family duty to take over the estate when his father became too old to run it or died. He expressed his hope to Keturah that she would be his partner for the rest of their lives, support him when he inherited the estate and hoped she would give him at least one son to continue the line of Cavendish.

As he was now supporting her, he decided she had to have better accommodation to suit her new way of life, to the Cavendish standard and ensure old clients didn't come a calling! Until they were married, it would not be good to be seen by his circle of friends that he was living in sin together in his London home. It was not long before Algernon soon found something suitable, not far from his Notting Hill Gate house, that Keturah thought was wonderful, and could not thank him enough. Her new luxurious apartment was the centre section on the first floor of a Regency style house, having its own balcony. It was self-contained and had a butler, a lady's maid and cook, all on loan from the Cavendish's London residence, and he purchased for her, her own coach, with two horses and a coachman, that was stabled at the rear of the building.

Being new to the district Keturah had no friends as yet, so her only visitor was Algernon, and that was how she now wanted it. Keturah then told him how much she loved him, partly for all he had done for her but mostly as a person, a friend and partner. She had, almost overnight, changed from a girl of ill repute to a lady, be it a mistress. It would have made her parents and the fiery Baptist minister happy once they were married, except she had now become an Anglican, which the Cavendish family all were.

The Algernon, who came from a rich and titled family, was heir to the estates of the 6th Earl of Caversham, Jonathan Cavendish by name and his wife the Countesses of Caversham, Isabel. Unlike Jonathan, who was Edward VII's double, Algernon was tall, slim, clean shaven with dark brown curly hair, and was extremely fit. He, like Keturah, had a ready smile, that looked if was about to laugh at any time. He was always smartly dressed, not necessarily in the latest fashion, but still well turned out. He belonged to a number of London clubs, like his father, who had recommended him to them; there was never any doubt that he would not be accepted. When staying in London on his own he invariably dined in one of these, but things were soon to change for both of them.

While Algernon had accepted Keturah's past, he did not know how his parents would feel. He felt he could not lie to them, and would go and visit them on his own to apprise them of the situation, however unpalatable it might be. He was adamant that whatever they said he would never desert her, but how he could achieve this if his parents were not agreeable, he did not yet know or comprehend.

The following weekend, Algernon went to see his parents while Keturah waited in her apartment on tenterhooks. On his return, instead of returning to his London home, he went straight away to see Keturah and related the outcome of his meeting with his parents. He told Keturah that he had explained to his parents, and before telling them about her, that whatever they thought from what he had to tell them was their business, but he would not waiver from his decision, whatever they may or may not say. If what he had to tell them was not to their liking, he would leave them and return to London to save them any embarrassment with their friends. He said they looked quite shocked and knew what he had to say was very serious. He then told them, in an abridged form, what Keturah had told him. They were stunned and shocked, as he knew they would be. He also told them he was far from white as the driven snow himself, while in London he had used *The Ladies of the Night* on many occasions, adding, only the better class of *Ladies!* But they never pleaded with him to give up this girl off the street, as they knew it would be of no use. They realised they had to consider his and their future, Algernon was their only heir. Over the weekend much was discussed, the pros and the cons. One of their biggest concerns was how she, Keturah, would fit into their circle, which their son told them she would fit in perfectly; they would have no worries on that score. It was agreed that he should bring Keturah up the following weekend, before a final decision was made.

Before the following weekend, Algernon asked Keturah to marry him and she consented. He immediately took her to Bond Street and purchased an engagement ring, a three-stone diamond cluster crossover, followed by dinner at the Savoy where they drank champagne to celebrate and seal their betrothal. During the meal Algernon told her about his parents and their lineage, their country mansion in a big estate Oxfordshire. Their home stood in extensive grounds, with a number of tenant farmers on this vast estate, with its open parkland, a large lake, woods, pastures and streams. In 1738, a certain Cavendish had served his monarch well and as a reward was given vast tracts of ground north of the Thames, not far from Reading, that had become Grafton Magna Manor, and he was bestowed the title of Earl of Caversham, the name of a small village on the north bank of the Thames that would change from being in the county of Oxfordshire to the county of Berkshire. Each successive Lord Cavendish of Caversham improved the house and grounds to what Keturah saw on the day of her first visit. Finally, he told Keturah, that when his father dies, he would be the 7th Earl of Caversham, and she would become a Countess. She was not very knowledgeable about the aristocracy, with all their titles and position on the ladder. She hoped, as she said to her future husband, that she would make him a good wife and Countess when the time came.

During the week before the visit, they both went to Harrods to choose and buy suitable clothing just for the weekend visit, nothing too dowdy or too gaudy, something in between. It was the style of clothes that Keturah came to like and would continue to buy thereafter. This was the start of her new wardrobe.

Just after lunch on the following Friday they left the Cavendish residence, taking a 1st class carriage on a fast train from Paddington to Reading, travelling in style, she had only travelled previously in 3rd class with Jacob, for Keturah's first visit to Grafton Magna Manor. She felt there was a little foreboding; would she fit in, would his parents accept her, and what would happen if they didn't? What ever happened, Algernon would come into the title, but being his wife may not ever happen. On the train journey, she told him of her worries, but he said whatever happened, she would remain his for the rest of his life. She crossed her fingers and said under her breath that she hoped so!

At Reading they were met by Algernon's father's head coachman who had a coach and four horses waiting outside the station on the forecourt for them. On leaving the station the coachman turned in a northerly direction, making to the only road crossing over the River Thames for a number of miles in either direction. On crossing the bridge, they entered into the county of Oxfordshire and the small Urban District village of Caversham, and at the first junction, turned left passing the ancient Griffin Pub, a tavern having been there since the early 17th century where all *"Parish Business"* at the time was conducted while nearly opposite was the village Police Station, handy if the *"Parish Business"* ever got out of hand!

They continued along the road, climbing up a steep hill, where the team of four horses was needed to accomplish the assent up the sharp incline, and after passing the parish church of St Peter's were well on the way to Grafton Magna Manor, which was soon reached. On passing through the main gates of the Cavendish estate, they swept up a long avenue of lime tree, in a gentle curve, passing by the lake until the mansion came in sight. On her first view of this magnificent building, Keturah felt butterflies in her stomach, could she manage to fit into this society?

The head coachman pulled up under a solid brick built canopy that was supported by round white pillars, this covering the driveway adjacent to the double front doors, and giving shelter to passengers alighting from their coach or soon to be motorcars. As soon as the carriage stopped, the second coachman had descended from his seat at the rear and opened the door and unfolding a set of steps for them to descend. Algernon was out first, and turned to assist Keturah to alight from the carriage.

They then both made their way up shallow steps of the entrance, where they were met by the head butler who detailed other members of the staff to unload and take Keturah and Algernon's luggage to their respective rooms. At the top of the stairs they entered the house through double front doors, into a short well-lit passage, to pass through another set of double doors into the large baronial hall. A number of doors led off both sides of the hall while in front was a wide staircase, which, half-way up, forked to the left and right on to a 'U' shaped gallery that ran behind the upper flight of stairs and down each side. From the gallery were the various bedchambers and dressing rooms, each room having its own bathroom.

Behind the far wall of the hall was a concealed stair case, running from the and kitchen, *'below stairs'*, up to the servants sleeping quarters on the top floor in the eves of the roof. The servants sleeping quarters, with a strict demarcation, females to the right wing, males to the left wing, was instantly dismissible if one was found in the wrong wing and the person that was being visited! On the ground floor, at the rear of the hall and the back of the gallery, were concealed doors, for the servants to enter to carry out their daily chores.

The head butler conducted them to the drawing room where they were greeted by Algernon's parents. Their greeting was cordial and polite; they were very unsure what Algernon's lady friend was like. Since Algernon's visit to his parents, he had written and told them he had asked for Keturah's hand in marriage, which she had accepted, and hoped for their approval.

Keturah was very astute and with the assistance of her intended became an acceptable member of his society, and soon adopted the same language, accents and idioms as the ladies of the Cavendish circle in Oxfordshire and the Notting Hill area and the hotel and clubs of London that they frequently regularly, either entertaining or being entertained. Algernon's parents were soon won over by Keturah and expressed their pleasure and agreed to a wedding as soon as could be arranged. The weekend passed, and while Keturah and Algernon got better acquainted, his parents would soon have a daughter-in-law to love. The 6th Earl had briefed the Head Butler that Mr Algernon was bring his future wife to meet the family, and that a marriage would soon be planned. All the staff knew about this within less than an hour and the room next to Algernon's were made up for his 'Lady'. There was an interconnecting door between the two rooms where Algernon could visit; the only problem was that he would have to return to his own room before the servants brought them their early morning tea!

Keturah's background was kept a close secret between the four of them, no one else in the family, friends or staff ever found out about her background. Her old manners were thrown out as was her second-hand wardrobe as Algernon was going to purchase her more new clothes before they were married; she then became and looked the 'Lady of Class' that she was to become in a very short space of time, and the wife to the Honourable Algernon Daniel Ian Cavendish.

Algernon's parents soon realised that Keturah would easily fit in and be an accepted by all they knew, so they decided to throw an impromptu party for Saturday evening, inviting a few of their local friends round for drinks and canapés. The evening went well; Keturah's prospective in-laws were delighted how well she fitted in, dressed in the best of clothes to suit the occasion. Their close friends were congratulating both parents on what a lovely and suitable daughter-in-law they would soon have, and their only son a wife. Algernon was the least surprised to how well his intended was accepted by everybody. She was chatting and making good conversation the whole evening to each and every one of the guests. The weekend went very well for all concerned. On further visits to the Manor, all four of them visited the Earl's many friends in the area; she was an accepted member of the Cavendish circle of friends.

On Sunday morning Algernon had a small trap harnessed up and he took her on a tour of the vast estate, arriving back only just in time for lunch. By now Algernon's parents felt at home with Keturah and asked her in future to call them Jonathan and Isabel, which gave her an extra boost of confidence. After an early tea, the couple made their way back to London, the same way as they had arrived. All Keturah's trepidation before the weekend had now vanished, she felt she had crossed a barrier and was now accepted by the family and their circle of friends.

Algernon realised that marriage to Keturah was not possible without a Birth Certificate for his wife-to-be, and felt she should be registered in retrospect, so she was duly registered as Keturah Sophia Bray, having been born on the 9th January in 1878 in Notting Hill Gate. No one questioned Algernon about the validity of this information, his parents did not know there was no birth certificate, and they were too important a family to be asked any questions about this matter by the registrar. This was the complete eradication of Keturah's past life for ever, Sarah Smith and Jane Perry never existed, and it was as if those two women had evaporated into thin air.

***

The century changed into the 20th. ■ In 1901 Queen Victoria died on the 22nd January at her home, Osborne House on the Isle of Wight; Edward VII was proclaimed King ■ Marconi made history by transmitting a radio message across the Atlantic by using a spark transmitter.

***

Keturah and Algernon were married in the early summer of 1901 with a big wedding in Oxfordshire, married by the resident vicar at the village church which was in the grounds of the estate, where all the Cavendish's eventually ended up. The reception, with hundreds of guests went long into the night, was held in two large marquees on the large lawn at the rear of the mansion. The honeymoon, which a lot of people were doing at the time, was a *Grand Tour.* On their return Keturah Cavendish, as she now was, vacated her apartment and moved in to the Cavendish Notting Hill Gate residence.

***

In early 1902 the second Boer War came to an end, Paul Kruger, their leader, signing the surrender document on 19th August. King Edward VII was duly crowned King in Westminster Abbey.

***

On Thursday, 17th December 1903 at Notting Hill, a son by the name of Rupert John was born to Keturah and Algernon. There followed another son two years later in 1905, Benjamin Charles, and in 1908, a daughter, Joanne

Ellen was born. Keturah and Algernon were both devoted to all their children, as the children were to their parents. While the children had a nanny and later a governess to teach them in their younger years, they were not banished to the nursery all day, Keturah and Algernon believed that children should not only be seen but also be heard! They considered that they were modern parents and did not believe in sending their boys to boarding school from an early age, as Algernon had been. When their children became of that age they found a suitable private school, not too far away, that they could all attend as day pupils.

Algernon, as heir to the very large estate in Oxfordshire, spent, with his family, a lot of time in the mansion there, slowly taking over the running of the activities, which included the various farms, which were leased to tenants, forest management of the large wooded areas, and the adjoining village, Grafton Magna which all belonged to the Cavendish family. Jonathan was not only Earl of the Manor but the local Squire, in control of a very large estate, the size of a small town, with over 1000 total population. With all this under his control, the title of Earl of Caversham made him the local magistrate, to be passed down to Algernon on his death.

While all this was going on, Isabel showed Keturah around the house, above and below stairs, explaining to her the duties she would have to undertake when she took over, including supervising the accounts below stairs and her personal bunch of keys to the various doors that valuables were stored and their cellar, of a vast and expensive list of wines from France, Italy and other countries.

While the Earl entertained in the country, Keturah and Algernon entertained in the town. Keturah soon settled down into this life, making friends easily, at both locations, becoming very popular, mixing with many titled and well-known figures of society. She was used to the country life from birth, but was now seeing it from the top of the pile, instead of the bottom. While she and Algernon entertained, or were entertained in the evenings at least three times a week, Keturah had coffee mornings and afternoon teas for the new lady friends she was making with husbands help. But she did not forget her friend Beth, but both felt it best if they met on neutral ground where neither would be seen by anyone they knew.

Keturah never gave any thought to her parents, brothers and sisters; they came from another world that now did not exist for her. But little nagging thoughts started to go round her head, what had happened to her two boys she given away? As time went by, these thoughts grew, and with it guilt.

CHAPTER 3

The Growing Years

The Dr Barnardo's orphanage at Shepherd's Bush was similar to all other of his orphanages throughout the country but a cut above the majority of others at the end of the 19th century. The regime was very strict but fair, far from the Dickenson era, even though the boys and girls were kept in separate wings of the building, and only saw each other at meal times, and then only from across a gangway between the tables, all watched over by Governor Newbury, Matron King and their staff. The meals, while basic, were wholesome and adequate for growing children, just enough to keep away the pangs of hunger, there were no obese children in the orphanage! Even though there were some felt like Oliver Twist and wanted more, but no one felt it in their best interests to ask such a question!

The only other occasion when the boys came anywhere near the girls was when they were being marched to church for Sunday Morning service at St Stephen and St Thomas, and afterwards marched back, in all weathers. During the service, the girls were seated on the left of the aisle while the boys were on the right. On the seat nearest to the aisle was always a member of the orphanage staff to thwart any form of contact between the sexes.

Those entering the orphanage under 5 years old, started life in the *Nursery Wing*, at the top of the house. When the youngsters reached 5 years of age, boys and girls were separated and went into their respective wings, being the *Girls Wing* or the *Boys Wing*. It was the orphanage policy for those children of 10 years and older to look after those leaving the *Nursery Wing*. It was found that this discouraged bullying, kept them occupied and was the basis of good relationships between the children of all ages. They were encouraged and expected to bond with one of the new youngsters and look after them until the youngster was old enough to look after themselves and in their turn to bond with new youngsters coming up from the *Nursery Wing*.

It was the older girl's duties to wash all personal washing; staff, girls, boys and the daily output from the nursery, it first being boiled in the big cauldrons in the basement. Each girl and boy had two sets of clothes, one on and one in the wash, each with a label bearing their name and when out grown and not worn out, was passed down the chain! On the plus side, there was basic schooling for part of the day, girls in the morning, and boys in the afternoon by four teachers, three of them being women, all of them teaching mornings and afternoons. All schooling was conducted in their separate wings where they learned their lessons, the main subjects taught were reading, writing and arithmetic, a little history and geography, while art was never on the curriculum but could be done when there was free time. Sex education was a thing no one ever spoke about, a taboo subject, or how to mix with the opposite sex. While there were four teachers it was expected that the older children would help out and teach the younger ones under the supervision of the tutors. The other part of the day was taken up in doing menial work that would earn money for the institution, boys in the morning, girls in the afternoon. On Sundays, they were all marched to St Stephen and St Thomas church, built in the mid-19th century, on the corner of Coverdale Road; following the morning service, all the orphans went back to their respective wings where they had an hour religious instruction before their midday meal, given by two local lay preachers. In the afternoon, the boys and girls were taken, separately, out to Wormwood Scrubs for exercise and fresh air; when the weather was inclement, they all stayed indoors.

Corporal punishment, while used in extreme circumstances, was hardly ever called for, the strict regime stopped most misbehaviour. Bullying was banned, and anyone showing any signs of this crime, boy or girl, was severely punished, and it seldom happened a second time. This schedule to Bill and Sam was what they liked, an orderly life, they knew where they were and how they stood within the hierarchy of the home.

One occupation for the older girls was helping out in the *Nursery Wing* where all babies of both sexes lived until they reached the age for splitting to go into their respective wings. This was the only time girls had contact with the boys. The *Nursery Wing* was a part of the *Girls Wing,* and while the supervision and the daily overall running of the nursery was managed by the senior matron; the hard work of feeding, caring, cleaning and washing clothes for the under-fives, was done by senior girls, taking it in turns to stay up during the night to feel the tiny babies. Those girls that showed aptitude in caring for the youngsters were encouraged and were seen as potential nannies. So, when these girls were nearing 14 years of age, the age children would leave the orphanage and expected to start their working life and earning their living, it was in this area that the orphanage staff looked to seek positions for them. Positions for Barnardo girls who had done baby care, and were potential Nannies, were quite easy to find places to work. The upper and middle class had many children in their family, and had the money to employ a large staff, and girls of 14 years olds were cheap to hire, a few shillings a month, a bed, basic clothing and three meals a day, the leftovers from the Master's table!

The *Nursery Wing* was divided into four parts, each part a separate room. Room 1 was for babies from new born up to one year, Room 2 from one to three years, and a Room 3 for three to five-year -olds. The rooms were divided into two parts, girls in one, boys in the other. The other room, Room 4, was where the helpers went, when not looking after their charges, to carry out their many and varied chores and sit for relaxation, if there was any time left to do so! Each room was kept separate, and only the matron and the girls looking after the young ones were allowed into all the rooms, the youngsters had to stay in their room and not stray anywhere else. The inmates of Room 2 and Room 3 were taken out for daily walks, but at different times. On Sundays, two members of staff and six girls remained behind in the wing, while everyone else attended church, as the *Nursery Wing* could not be left unattended. They were considered too young to attend church services until they were over 5 years old, but the 3 to 5 year olds attended *Sunday School* in their rooms, instruction given by the two staff members, one to each room, assisted by two girls while the other two girls looked after and remainder in Rooms 1 and 2. To make up for missing the morning service, the two members of staff and the six girls had to attend the evening church service, while the Matron and six girls, on the waiting list as potential nanny nurses helped out.

When William was found on the door step of the orphanage in the winter of 1896, he went directly into new born room of the *Nursery Wing*, progressing to Room 2 after his first birthday, and then moved into Room 3, earlier than was normal. For those five years in the *Nursery Wing*, William matured and for ever afterwards was known as Bill. He grew into a strong and good looking young lad, was well behaved, a good mixer, always getting on well with others, and as he got older, was always willing to help out where he could.

Sam, like his half-brother two-and-a-half years earlier, also found on the door step in late summer of 1898, was also placed in Room 1. As Room 2 was overcrowded in the early part of 1899 when Sam was due to move up, he had to stay there until there was room enough for him. To help ease the situation, Bill, who they felt was mature for his age, went to Room 3 before he was 3 years. If it had not been for this overcrowding problem, Bill and Sam would have met in the early part of 1899, but fate was against it. Thus, Bill did not meet Sam until he was 5 years old and transferred from the *Nursery Room* to the *Boys Wing*. When Bill was transferred to the *Boys Wing* in 1901, an 11 year lad became his mentor and he soon settled in with all the other boys there, growing up as the years went by, to become a tall handsome young lad.

***

In 1901 an underwater vessel known as a 'submarine' was undergoing sea trials. The world's first air flying machine, piloted by Orville Wright, took off from Kill Devil Hill, at the sands of Kitty Hawk in North Carolina, USA at 10.35am on 17th December 1903. It flew for 12 seconds to a height of 10 feet and a distance of 120 feet.

***

When Sam arrived in the Boys Wing in August 1903, he was with three or four other lads who had all been born 5 years earlier in August 1898. While it was usual and expected for older boy to come forward to bond, Bill, on seeing Sam for the very first time, immediately felt a tie between him and Sam, which he could never account for and would never know why. It was also a surprise to the staff that Bill, only two-and-a-half years older than Sam, then aged seven-and-a-half, immediately took him under his protection. While the staff was surprised about this relationship, they did not discourage it, in fact it was most welcome, a natural bond was better than a forced one.

On Sam's side, he was drawn to Bill and was happy to be taken under his wing. From then on until Bill left the orphanage they were hardly every separated, the staff ensured that they had adjacent beds in the dormitory. Not only was there a physical bond, but they looked alike. As the Governor of the orphanage remarked, when it was brought to his attention, "They always say everyone has a double somewhere in the world, this time they have come together. If it was not for the age difference and having different parents, they could almost be mistaken for twins!" What little did the Governor know! If the orphanage had kept the notes that had been left with Bill and Sam when they had been left on the door step, they would have seen that the handwriting was the same. But as there were many babies left on their door step and many notes, they had better things to do than keep and file them away.

The staff soon realised there was a strong tie between the two boys, and while the regime was strict, they did nothing to keep them apart, but encouraged it. If it was possible, Bill improved in all ways and was a model inmate. On bonding with Sam, Bill spent most of his time looking after him, and made sure he was never bullied. Bill became one of the best-behaved children in the orphanage. His good behaviour was passed on to Sam, the bonding got stronger as time went on. If they were ever apart, and something

54

happened to one of them, the other sensed this and would immediately try seeking out his half-brother to ensure there was nothing amiss, and if there was, both would try and rectify any problem that might occur. The two brothers grew up together; the bond between them grew stronger, never faltering. Outside their world of the orphanage they knew little, or at that young age, cared even less, they were kept busy within.

Dr Barnardo would often visit his homes and on a numerous occasions he visited Shepherd's Bush where Bill and Sam met him on several visits. Dr Barnardo's aim was to get employment for all his orphans when they left the home and was pleased on one of his visits to see Bill and Sam helping a carpenter who was carrying out some repairs in the home, and remarked to the Governor that they were learning a good trade that could be useful when it was their time to leave and seek their living.

***

In 1903 London had its first electric tram and it was driven by King Edward VII. Motor vehicles were seen more frequently on the streets, and traffic jams and gridlock were an everyday occurrence in the streets of the City of London and the West End. ■ The Hon. Charles Rolls and Mr Henry Royce started a factory to manufacture cars in 1904, and the first **Rolls Royce** appeared on the streets the same year. The distinctive **RR** appeared in red on the radiator of the cars from then on. ■ When Dr Barnardo died 1905 he had set up 112 homes for deprived children, but his orphanages continue to live on and flourished after his death.

***

In 1905 Algernon purchased his first car, a Rolls Royce, and over the years, when he wanted a new vehicle, it was never anything else than an **RR**. He garaged it in the stables at his Notting Hill home, one horse drawn carriage plus two horses were soon put up for sale. The coachman, who was interested in cars and their workings, learnt to drive and become their chauffeur. Algernon was always interested in anything mechanical and hearing that a club had been formed for motorists in1897 had joined the Automobile Club, later to be patronised by the King and having Royal added as a prefix. It was through this club that he had heard about Charles Rolls & Henry Royce going into partnership to manufacture cars. Not many years later, after Keturah had learnt to drive, Algernon bought a second car as a town run-a-round for both of them to use, the remaining carriage and horses were sold off and the groom, who had no interest in anything mechanical, moved to Grafton Magna Manor with his family. From then on, when the weather was clement, they would drive down to his father's estate, instead of travelling by train. It took longer, but that was a small price for the joy of driving oneself, and soon afterwards the chauffeur found other employment with a large household who had a number of cars and the master of the house considered it beneath his dignity to drive himself. When Algernon's father saw the car for the first time, he said it was not for them, and he never owned for a long time, though he and the Countess did go for the occasional ride in Algernon's! Later his father gave in, and purchased a car, with the help of his son, but never drove himself, employing a chauffeur.

***

On 10th February, 1906 King Edward VII launched the most powerful warship the world has ever seen, HMS Dreadnought. The Government dropped plans to build a fast motor highway between London and Brighton. Robert Baden-Powell held the first scout camp in 1907 on Brownsea Island. Women's Social and Political Union, more commonly known as Suffragettes, were very active, being formed about 1886 by Emmeline Pankhurst.

***

Ever since the Wright brothers had first flown in 1903, Algernon had shown a great interest in flying and closely followed the progress of flight and vowed to himself, that if he ever got the opportunity, he would fly. He soon found out in 1907, that there was a club for those interested in flying, the Aero Club of Great Britain and it was not long afterwards that The Honourable Algernon Cavendish became a member. Algernon felt that while he could not design a flying machine, he could at least learn to fly one, if others could, why not him? He immediately started to look to where he could learn to fly; he had on good authority that the Wright brothers had started a flying school in Alabama earlier in the year, so surely there must be a flying school somewhere in England.

***

In 1908 the Franco-British Exhibition was held at White City west of London. In July 1909 Louis Blériot was the first person to fly across the English Channel, and in the same month Mr A V Roe became the first Britain to design and fly his own aeroplane. Pigs might fly! - Claude Moore-

Brabazon proved they could, he took one aloft in November! In 1910 the King granted 'Royal' to the Aero Club of Great Britain; Moore-Brabazon received the Royal Aero Club's first 'Aviator's Certificate', Charles Rolls the second: In May, King Edward Vll died and was succeeded by his son, King George V. In July, Charles Rolls became the first Britain to be killed in an aircraft crash at Bournemouth. Mr Henry Royce changed the **RR** logo on *Rolls Royce* cars from red to black in respect of his late colleague and friend. In July the War Office authorizes the establishment of a flying corps. Hendon became the first official civil airfield for London, and not long afterwards Brooklands became the second. The Royal Flying Corps was created in April 1912 into two wings, the Military and the Naval and, to the Navy's disgust, both as a part of the Army. In 1914 the Royal Naval Air Service broke away, forming its own flying branch.

***

Through Algernon's membership with the Aero Club, he got to know many of the pioneer flyers and it was suggested to him that the best place to learn to fly was at the Sopwith School of Flying, situated on the edge of Brooklands motor racing track.

***

The sport of motor racing was growing fast, but the majority of meetings were on the continent. The only recognised race track of any sort in England before 1907 and was a short straight, with a downhill start on the sea front at Bexhill on Sea, no wonder the cream of foreign motor racing drivers never came to this country to race their cars. But Hugh and Ethel Locke-King, both motor racing enthusiasts were far from satisfied with the state of British car racing in this country. They designed their own purpose-built motorcar racing circuit constructed on their estate. The course, when built, had two straights joined by banked curves at each end and a finishing straight in the centre. To one side of the finishing straight was the club house with a parade ring in front. In close proximity were refuelling points, garages and workshops, in fact all the paraphernalia of a racing track. This was Brooklands. It was opened in 1907. When opened it was run on the line of horserace meetings, not surprising as many members were from that field of sport. There was still plenty of spare in the centre of the course, and an airfield was opened there the following year, initially for people flying to the race meetings. It soon came into commercial use as well, where Tommy Sopwith set up his flying school, followed by his aircraft factory. It was soon to be followed by another aircraft manufacturer, Vickers Aviation. Brooklands was now a motor racing course, an official aerodrome and a base for aircraft manufacture. The Locke-Kings had now realised their dream, it became a centre for motor racing in the British Isles, attracting drivers from all over the world.

***

Algernon immediately applied for a place on a flying course at the Sopwith School of Flying which would set him back £75. He was accepted, but there was a long waiting list, behind Hugh Trenchard, who was at the time commanding the Military Wing at Farnborough and later became Marshal of the Royal Air Force, colloquially known as the *Father or the Royal Air Force.* He was advised that flying was only a part of the test required by the Aviator's Certificate. He had to have a good knowledge of navigation using map and compass, sketching skills, an aptitude for mechanics including the maintenance of the aircraft that included the engine and airframe and finally, be a good sailor. While Algernon could do nothing about being a good sailor, which he was, having only recently sold a sea faring 30-foot yacht he had owned for many years, but he could work on the first three; he had plenty of time to practice these skills. He purchased a number of books to help in his quest to be a pilot and navigator.

It was not until the following year that Algernon was offered a place on the course. Keturah was very interested in flying and they studied and helped each other together. She told Algernon, that if he could be a pilot, why could not she. Algernon had a lot of sympathy with the Suffragettes, and believed where possible women should have equal rights in voting and pay. Once he had gained his certificate he promised she could learn to fly also and secured her a place at Tommy's school.

***

The orphanage was always in need of some sort of maintenance work, be it large or small jobs, and there were no members of staff capable of carrying anything but of a minor nature, the larger tasks were beyond their capability and the tools they possessed. All this work was contracted out to a local firm who had been doing the tasks there for over ten years. When any job was required, a note was written of the problem, and a senior boy who could be trusted was sent with it, walking to Bert Frost and his son Fred's workshop in Shepherd's Bush. Both were skilled joiners and carpenters, and also proficient in other building trades. Bert was in his early fifties, of medium height, clean shaven with a middle-aged spread just starting to show. Fred, on the other hand, took after his mother, just a litter shorter than Bert, but already a bit on the plump side in his mid-twenties, and walked with a permanent slight limp since being hit by a wheel of horse and trap when he was young.

When Bert came to the orphanage, he often left Fred back at his workshop because of their work load or if he was having a bad day with his limp and walking long distances, especially carrying tools, did not help. Many jobs required assistance and he would ask for volunteers from the senior lads. A number of the lads volunteered, including Bill. They all helped out the best they could, but Bert soon saw that Bill had a natural ability, soon picking up the craft of a carpenter, perhaps working with his hands he had inherited from his grandfather! It was not very long after Bill had started helping out whenever Bert came to carry out any jobs at the orphanage, he was soon asking for Bill. In fact, whenever they required Bert's services, the Governor would send Bill with the note, and if Bert did not return with Bill after he had left the note, Bill would be waiting at the front door for him when he arrived.

Bert soon noticed that where ever Bill went, a young lad was always with him, and on enquiring, was told that he was Bill's bonding partner, Sam. When Bert first saw the two boys together he was struck by the strong likeness between the two of them. Bert also noticed that at first Sam only watched, encouraged by Bill, then he was passing tools, getting to know their names and uses, holding the wood that Bill was working on. It was not long before Sam was starting to do small tasks, just as Bill had done when taught by Bert. When Bill was coming up to 14, towards the end of his stay at the orphanage home, Bert got permission from the Governor, to take Bill to his workshop, less than a mile away. Bert knew Bill was very close to Sam, and sought permission to take Sam as well. They walked down to his premises together, and as they approached saw a crudely hand painted sign board displayed at the front, stating:

Bert Frost & Son, General Carpenters

The two boys on first entering Bert's workshop saw it was not a cramped sweat shop that they had heard was the norm that small work places were at the time, but was light and airy, windows on three sides and windows in the sloping roof. There were outward opening double doors where raw material entered and finished products departed. At the rear was a door leading to Bert's private living quarters. There were five work benches, but now only two were being used, Bert's and Fred's; work over the last few years had dropped off, from having a staff of five now down to two. But things were just picking up, and Bert had ideas about employing an apprentice, who could learn a trade, and would be at the bottom end of the pay scale, not that Bert minded paying good wages for good employees, but as they were pulling out of recession he had to be careful, he felt an apprentice would be an answer to his problems.

Bert soon realised that Sam was just as good as Bill, and with their visits, which became more frequent, their ability soon progressed, and soon started to make items that Bert required, first from copying items that Bert or Fred had made, then from drawings. Four benches were now in use, and the home was only to pleased to let the boys work there, it looked as they both had a job in the near future.

***

The brothers Oswald and Eustace Short had started in the flying business in 1902, making balloons in a workshop under two railway arches in Battersea, convenient to the local gas works where there was a ready supply of coal gas. They then decided that making aeroplanes was the way to go forward and opened a factory on the Aero Club's flying ground at Shellbeach, near Eastchurch, on the Isle of Sheppey in Kent, in 1908. They were now joined by their third brother, Horace, who was the older of the three. In 1909 they established the world's first airplane production line. They had recently negotiated with Orville and Wilbur Wright to make six replicas Wright Type 'A' biplane, for members of the Aero Club, and were visited by the two American brothers at Shellbeach the same year to see how they were progressing. Not long after that they were designing and making their own flying machines. With the use of the new medium of radio telegraph, the arrest on 31st July 1910 of the murderer Dr Crippen was made as he was escaping to Canada on board a liner with his mistress Ethel Le Neve. He stood trial for murdering his wife, found guilty, and was hung.

***

Early in 1910, Bill Perry reached 14 years of age, and had to leave the orphanage and seek employment in the outside world. But that was not a problem, he had already been offered a job by Bert, working in his carpentry workshop, but as they got bigger, the workshop was usually referred to as the *Factory*. With the job came lodgings and keep, which he accepted without hesitation. While the two boys were separated, they saw each other most days as Sam continued to come to the workshop and help. The orphanage was only too glad to let Sam work at Bert's as the orphanage were always on the lookout for jobs for those who were coming up to the leaving age, it was an up-hill struggle, so if there was a place on offer they gave all the encouragement they could to find someone to suit the position.

Bert had set up his workshop about the time Bill was born with the assistance of his 14-year-old son who was already a competent young carpenter, but who had never been in the best of health because of his leg injury. Bar for his son, they had no other family members they could employ, and after they had laid off the three workers they had employed soon after they opened because of dwindling orders they had to work on their own, the way they liked it, a small family business again, just making ends meet! He soon built up a reputation when the locals realised how good he was; his work was of a high quality and much in demand in times when people had money to invest. But this came with a price, he could not take up all the work offered and did not feel like taking on another skilled carpenter. He did not have much confidence in his ability to govern other staff about his own age and felt others may not have the same high standards as he had. He knew of other carpenters in the local area and none were as good as he was, he always got the cream of the jobs in the area, and could demand a higher price without having to quibble much. But he saw the opportunity to overcome his problem by taking on Bill, also realising, after two-and-a-half years, while Bill would be getting competent, Sam would be ready to leave the orphanage, making a team of four. Once Bill had started, Bert was able to take on more work, and when Sam came, even more work and the business was expanding.

***

When Algernon went down to Brooklands to learn to fly he was surprised that Tommy Sopwith, with all his expertise, had only recently decided to learn to fly himself, being self-taught. On arrival, he was greeted by Tommy, the first time the two men had met. They got on very well together, after all, they spoke the same language! It was a friendship that would last a life time. Sopwith had four machines attached to the school, his new Model F and two of Howard Wright's; all three were biplanes and fitted dual controls and his Blériot monoplane was an advanced trainer.

With Sopwith's chief course instructor, Algernon took to the skies in one of the dual seaters, alternating between one of the three planes, to gain more experience, as each aeroplane was different, each having its own characteristics, some good, and some, unfortunately, bad! The experience of flying he had never had before, he now knew what it was to be like a bird!

He was not long to master the art of flying; his instructor remarked to one of his colleagues that, "Cavendish is a natural, born to fly, he must have been a bird in a previous life!" It was not long before he flew solo in the advanced trainer and was passed as a qualified pilot and in late August he was awarded the *Royal Aero Club Certificate.*

He now wanted his own aeroplane, but first he had to find some where to store one. That was no problem in Oxfordshire, he could soon get a carpenter to design and erect a hangar in one of their meadows, as near as possible to the mansion. He had to find something near their Notting Hill home, but where? While he was training to fly at Brooklands, he remembered someone else who was leaning to fly mentioned that there were a few spare sheds which were situated on the perimeter of the Brooklands flying area that were available to rent for a nominal sum, big enough for a small light aircraft. That was the solution, and in a short space of time he had a shed to store his aircraft. When he next went to see his family, he had a good look round the estate close to the house and soon realised that one of the pastures, near the mansion, was an ideal place for planes to land and take-off, and there was adequate space to build a hangar to house a flying machine when purchased. On his next visit, he took the opportunity to seek out a local carpenter who was capable of designing and erecting a hangar similar to the ones at Brooklands. There were a number of trees on the perimeter of the pasture and the carpenter, under the supervision of the Estate Manager, cut them down, which he took in part payment. He also got the Estate Manager to let sheep graze on the pasture to keep the grass down! Not long afterwards he purchased a wind sock and got the manufactures to erect it in a suitable prominent position at one corner of the paddock.

The beauty of this was the family would still go by train to Reading while he could then drive the 16 miles to Brooklands, garage his car in his shed, and then fly Oxfordshire. The journey by car to Brooklands took about the same time to fly from there to Grafton, but it was faster than by train, and much more exhilarating. The only down side was the weather, if on their return journey it was too bad to fly, then it was the train again, having to return when there was a break in the weather to return his plane back to its home!

He now had a hangar at Brooklands and would soon have one on the estate. More importantly, however, a flying machine had to be purchased. He decided before he bought one that he would look around, ask the members at the Aero Club, and try to have a trial flight if possible of any aircraft on offer. After over a year of looking around at what was available he made his choice. His enquires had led him hear about the Short Brothers, Oswald, Horace and Eustace, and he had heard very good reports about their flying machines. He decided when he was ready to purchase an aeroplane to make them the top of his list and the first ones to contact.

***

June saw the Coronation of King George V which the 6th Earl and Countesses of Caversham attended. The first British Air Mail service was inaugurated on 9th September, flying between Hendon to a meadow on the Royal Farm at Windsor, with mail for the King, a distance being 19 miles. Hilda B Howlett was the first woman in Britain to be awarded the Aviator's Certificate.

***

The creation of the Air Battalion of the Royal Engineers was an event not missed by Algernon who knew that Britain was lagging far behind other countries in establishing a military flying service, which grieved him. While Algernon wanted a flying machine of his own as soon as possible, he was not going to be rushed into buying the first thing that became available. Aeroplanes in these early days ranged from the very good to death traps, he did not want to end up with the latter. It was just over a year after he had received his *Aviator's Certificate* that he first made acquaintance with the Short brothers at the Royal Aero Club in London towards the end of 1911. They told him of their background, explaining how they started their association with the Wright Brothers and that they were just about to launch a two-seat biplane of their own design which they had called S.36. If he was interested, he would be welcome to visit them and see their new plane in flight. Algernon had only thought of buying a single seat aircraft, but a two seater aircraft was ideal. Keturah, from the time he started to fly, wanted to go aloft as well! So, in the future when they had their own aircraft, going to visit Algernon's parents in the country would be done by flight. Their nanny and other members of staff that always travelled with them would take the children on their own by train and car would be arranged to meet them at Reading station when they got there. Algernon had now purchased a third vehicle which was kept at *Grafton*. In the meantime, he and Keturah would motor to Brooklands, swap the car for the aircraft, and fly to Oxfordshire, getting there quicker than by train. It was an ideal situation, which he knew Keturah would be thrilled by.

In mid-December, on a cold, clear sunny day, Algernon took a train down in to Eastchurch where he was met by one of the brothers at the station and driven to the airfield in Shellbeach, the first aircraft company in the world.

Two of the S.36 aeroplanes were parked outside one of the hangars, either ready to be flown.

One of the brothers took the S.36 to show it off to Algernon, they hoped, a potential customer. On landing, Algernon was invited aboard for a test flight and was soon out across the Kent countryside. Once they were airborne, Algernon took over the controls and found it was a joy to fly, going at a cruising speed of 60mph. After half an hour, they landed and they were confident enough to let Algernon take off on his own, fly the aircraft again and land himself, which he did like an expert. After the flight, they all went back to the factory office and discussed with Algernon his opinion of the S.36, his answer was how soon could he have one. They had a number of orders on their books for their new aircraft, but promised he could take delivery in early March 1912. The deal was sealed; he would return to them to collect his purchase when they advised him, the following year. It was agreed that they would only call him when they had clear, calm weather as he had to fly the aeroplane some 60 miles to his hangar at Brooklands.

In mid-March, Algernon received a letter from the Short Brothers informing him that his aircraft was ready for collection at his convenience, stating the agreed price of the machine. On arrival, he would be asked to test fly the aircraft, accompanied by one of their pilots, and on acceptance of the aircraft, after any problems that may have risen from the flight had been resolved, and payment made, the aircraft was his. Algernon on receipt of Shorts letter phoned the *Company* arranging a date acceptable by them both for the collection, writing a letter confirming these arrangements. The same evening, with the assistance of Keturah, they planned his route. After taking off west over the Medway, then keeping the Thames in his sight on his starboard quarter until he got to Weybridge and turning south, with the Brooklands only a mile further on. It did not seem to be a problem, but only if the weather was clear. They also noted any green open spaces in case of a forced or emergency landing, one could not be too complacent.

As Algernon wanted an early start on the day he flew from Eastchurch to Brooklands. He travelled down on the previous morning by train and would put up in a local hotel for the night, but not before he had test flown his aircraft. On arrival at the factory he was soon airborne, taking it up for the acceptance test flight, accompanied by their test pilot. He flew the S.36 for an hour, going through all the manoeuvres he knew to ensure that everything was in good order. As there were no problems they returned to the airfield, Algernon being well satisfied; he could not wait to own it. After all the paperwork was completed and the payment made, he was taken back to the hotel and was given dinner, courtesy of the Short Brothers.

He was up early on the following morning, it was another clear sunny day with light easterly winds that would help to blow him to his destination. After breakfast, he made his way to the airfield to find his aircraft standing out on the apron, fuelled and ready for him to take away. He had his route as he and Keturah had planned, all he had to do was to work out his ETA and wait for the wind. Once done he rang Keturah to advise her when he would get to Brooklands so she could drive down by car and meet him. Algernon donned his flying clothing, thick jacket and trousers, boots, helmet and goggles, and once ready was soon airborne in his own aircraft and on his way to Brooklands.

The flight went off very well, over the Medway and follow the Thames as planned, it was clear so he could fly more south making more or less a straight line to Weybridge. When Weybridge came in sight he turned south; he had already seen the landing strip at Brooklands. As he circled to land, waiting for the all clear to do so, he could see Keturah standing by their car, waving a bright red scarf for all she was worth. He was there before lunch and on landing he taxied in to the hangars to be met by two of the airfield ground crew, who chocked the aircraft. As he got out of the aircraft he turned round and was pleased to see a grinning Keturah waiting for him. Unbeknown to Algernon, Keturah had purchased a full set of flying clothing which she was wearing, and insisted that Algernon took her up for a short flight before the aircraft was put into the hanger. They were soon airborne and flew to Notting Hill Gate looking down on their home; she loved the aircraft and the sensation of flying from the moment they took off to the time they landed. On return to Brooklands he checked everything was OK for putting the aircraft in the hangar and was helped by the ground crew and Keturah to push his new acquisition into its new home. On the drive back to Notting Hill the talk was nothing but flying and when she, Keturah, could start to learn.

***

Just over two months after Algernon's flight from Eastchurch, the Royal Flying Corps was formed on the 13 April 1912 from the Air Battalion of the Royal Engineers into a Naval & Military Wing, but was still a part of the Army. The Navy were far from impressed with this situation. If the Army could have a flying service so could they, and not long after the RFC was founded the Royal Naval Air Service had their own air branch. The first military flying school was opened at Upavon on the 19th June, becoming the Central Flying School for the RFC. On Sunday 14th April 1912, the White Star liner SS Titanic struck an iceberg off Cape Race on her maiden voyage to America, and sank in a little over two hours at about 2.15am the following morning. The liner was carrying 2,340 passengers and crew, of these 1,513 were drowned in the icy waters of the North Atlantic. There were not enough lifeboats for all passengers and crew on board. The SS Carpathia, being the only ship near enough to respond to the emergency SOS call, saved 827 people on lifeboats in the area of the tragedy.

***

Very soon Algernon started the journey to Grafton in the S.36 with Keturah by his side after she bullied him to take her flying as much as possible while the rest of the household went down by train. The night before they had planned their route with care, but after a number of trips they knew the route like the back of their hands, both ways. In a straight line, it was just less than 30 miles. From Brooklands, taking turns to pilot and navigate, they passed over Sunninghill and Bracknell, going to the north side of Wokingham, Woodley and Caversham, landing between Whitchurch and Cane End on the Grafton estate. It was not long before he let Keturah take the controls and he soon found she had a natural aptitude for flying just as he had, they made a good pair.

***

For Sam, the next two-and-a-half years could not come soon enough. He missed his friend Bill, unbeknown to him, his half brother, even though he was allowed to visit him on a regular basis. On Sundays, Bill would always visit him in the orphanage, often both going out walking on the common at the nearby Wormwood Scrubs on warm days or to go back to the Frost's for a meal. To be able to live and work alongside Bill was the main thing that kept him going. On the last day of September 1912, a Monday, when there was a decided chill in the air first thing in the morning, the leaves on trees had started to turn from green to shades of yellow, orange and brown and only just starting to fall, and the nights were now longer and the days shorter, Sam was 14 years old. He had reached the age when he had to leave the orphanage. It had been a good home for him all those years, the best he could have had or wanted without parents, and he was very grateful for everything they had done for him and Bill, but now was the time to go, he had out grown the home he was now about to leave and ready to start earning his living in the outside world of commerce. Rising early on the day he was leaving, he packed his few belongings in a canvas bag, ready to depart as soon as breakfast was finished. He said his goodbyes and thanks to the Governor,

Matron, and all the staff; and as he was a popular boy, too many lads also awaiting their time to leave. As he left, the sun was shining in a cloudless sky, and while it was nippy, it had no effect on him, nothing was going to dampen Sam's spirits in his first day in the adult world.

Soon both the boys were installed in Bert's workshop, living on the job and getting three good meals a day as part of their wages, supplied by Agnes, Bert's wife, a woman of plump build accentuated by her short height with a jolly disposition who was helped by their young daughter, Alice, who had been born early in 1898, the same year as Sam. She was more like her father in build, but like her mother with a ready smile, with looks that made men turn their heads, all hoping to get acquainted, but so far no one had yet caught her attention. While Fred, their son, had been born two years after Bert and Agnes got married, they had not been blessed with another child until quite unexpectedly Alice arrived, and was very welcome. They now had a pigeon pair.

With the two boys now a part of the work force Agnes did not have to assist her husband in the workshop anymore, keeping the place clean and tidy, so she could devote her time to looking after her family, the house and the supply of three meals a day to four hungry men. Agnes now did not require Alice's help in the house, and as she was good with figures, she was the *'Company Secretary'*, looking after all correspondence and the accounts. Woe betide any customer who did not pay up on time, or any supplier who failed to meet his delivery target, they soon got the sharp end of Alice's tongue! With the extra income that was now coming in to the business Bert purchased a typewriter that Alice soon mastered through evening classes, even taking short hand writing lessons. Bert mentioned to Agnes one day, as there was more money coming in and more could be spent on food and she was in the kitchen longer, that the meals had improved, which earned him a clip round the ear from her for his troubles! With three lads to help Bert, it took a great weight off Agnes's shoulders, no longer having to worry about him working too hard. He was over 60 years old now and was starting to slow down.

At the orphanage, there had been no fraternising with the opposite sex, and Bill therefore had no experience with girls, unlike Alice, who had her brother, and mixed with his friends when they came calling. While they were strict with Alice they gave her a certain amount of latitude. She did not have any serious boyfriends, but it did not stop her teasing and mildly flirting with the boys that came calling to see Fred, to the amusement of her parents, even though they were a good bunch of lads and a great deal older then her. They would often tease Alice but she could stand up for herself, she gave as good as she got! When Bill arrived to take up residence he was 14 while Alice was only 12 years of age, but this did not stop Alice flirting with Bill and she treated him the same way as Fred's friends. Bill, with a lack of experience with girls, was highly embarrassed and would often blush, much to the delight of Alice, which made it more fun, and egged her on to do more teasing of Bill. But as time went on, and they both got older, Alice suddenly realised that the flirting that had once been fun was now developing into something of a more serious nature. She kept this to herself, Bill did not notice anything, but her parents did, and they felt she could not do much better than Bill for a partner. They trusted both Alice and Bill not to do anything stupid, which she did not want to, she was sensible enough to realise that they were both far too young, while Bill, himself, was not yet a man of the world and was not sure about girls or what to do with them! But life progressed, and while Alice matured and her feelings for Bill became more serious he was very busy in the workshop, between 10 and 12 hours a day, but during this time, he started having thoughts about Alice, but did nothing to display his feelings towards her. If there was a war, he felt it would not be fair to be serious with a girl, so he did nothing about Alice's minor advances towards him. She was disappointed about Bill's lack of response, but she kept on trying and was determined to wear him down, somehow!

***

At Epsom Racecourse, on 4th June 1913, Emily Davison, a Suffragette aged 38, was knocked to the ground when she ran out onto the racecourse and tried to seize the reins of the King's horse Anmer at Tattenham Corner as it was running in the Derby, dying of her injuries 7 days later. On the 14th of June she was given a Suffragette State Funeral, thousands of her fellow Suffragette attending, the coffin, draped with a purple cloth, inscribed 'Welcome the Northumbrian hunger striker', and drawn on an open carriage, pulled by four black horses, being taken through the streets of London, followed by four coaches carrying hundreds of wreaths, followed by ten bands and watched by tens of thousands of spectators.

***

In April 1913, the son of a wealthy French arms dealer, Jacques Schneider, set up a flying competition for float planes, to taxi on water half a lap, then completing the 173 miles course over 28 laps in the Roquebrune Bay in Monaco. The second Schneider Trophy race was held in Monaco in April 1914. On one of his many visits to Brooklands, early in 1914, Tommy Sopwith approached Algernon and asked him if he had heard of the Schneider Trophy, which, not to the surprise of Tommy, he had. Tommy continued, "You might be interested to know I am entering a plane for the contest this year, it's something new I have designed especially for the race, I'm calling this aircraft the *Tabloid*. It has just been completed at my Southampton works and will undergo flying trials next week from the RNAS base at Calshot, where I have a hangar." Algernon congratulated him on his achievement, and hoped he would do well, saying he would like to go and see the race. "That can be easily arranged, you get yourself there, and I will get tickets in the viewing stand if you let me know. I could offer you a cabin on the boat taking the plane, there and back, but that would take too long for you I expect, a sleeping train is your best bet."

On his return to Notting Hill he discussed it with Keturah, who could not wait to go. They arranged to take the children down to Grafton and as Tommy Sopwith had suggested they took a sleeping train from Victoria to Folkestone, crossing the English Channel to Calais, thence a train to Paris, across the city to take another train to Monaco in the south of France. Tommy and his aircraft were evident when they got there and they paid him a visit to his moorings and meeting his pilot Howard Pixton. The visit, which was a two-week holiday for them both, was a great success, the climax being that Tommy, Howard, and his *Tabloid* won the race for Great Britain. The Tabloid completed the course at an average speed of 86.8 mph, which was just over 40mph faster than last year's race winner, to the great pride of the Sopwith team and the excitement of Keturah and Algernon. This was the last race until 1919.

***

As dawn rose on 1914, storm clouds were starting to rise over Europe. In Sarajevo, on the 29th May, Archduke Francis Ferdinand and his consort were assassinated. The first seeds of The Great War had been sown!

CHAPTER 4

The War To End All Wars

War was on the lips of everyone after the assassination of Archduke Francis Ferdinand and his consort on the 29th June in the capital Sarajevo in Bosnia and Herzegovina. The assassin Gavrilo Princip, a Serbian nationalist and a member of the Black Hand secret society, was arrested within minutes of the crime. This set up a chain reaction that could not be stopped. Serbia was blamed for the felony and Germany, under Kaiser Wilhelm II, guaranteed Austro-Hungary its support if it went to war because of the incident. Russia immediately sided with Serbia. The international situation now spiralled out of control.

On the 29th June, Austria declares war against Serbia, and a month to the day, Germany declared war on Russia. On the 1st August, Great Britain declared war on Germany who was led by their bombastic and impetuous leader, Kaiser Wilhelm II. Three days later Britain was in conflict with Austria and on the 12th August the British Expeditionary Force lands in France. The conflict began.

When war is declared, Truth is the first casualty
Hiram Johnson *(speaking to the US Senate in 1918)*

The Government was closely monitoring the situation in Europe, seeking advice from their senior Army and Naval staff and their various Embassies on the Continent. The war machine was gearing up. Both services were now placing orders for new equipment; production was on all fronts for military hardware, guns for the Army, ships for the Navy and aircraft for the Royal Flying Corps and Royal Naval Air Service. While in June at Netheravon, on Salisbury Plain, the RFC gathered its six squadrons for a month of training.

***

When the RFC was formed they had very few aeroplanes. Many new contracts were put out to tender by the Ministry, to all the five major plane builders, one of them being The Sopwith Aviation Company, headed by its

70

founder Tommy Sopwith, who had started his company a few years earlier, based originally near Southampton for seaplanes and now near Weybridge for landplanes.

***

With the sudden expansion of work, Tommy was well pleased, but this brought its own problems. He did not have the facilities or space at the Brooklands hangars to make all the parts he required in-house, as he had been doing since he originally started his company two years previously. The only way out, as he saw it, was that the factory would now only be for the assembly shop of parts that had been outsourced. These parts would have to be made by local firms in and around London.

This would allow Tommy quick access to parts he required as there were always delivery problems with suppliers who were far afield. Deliveries by train or lorry over long distance were always notorious for delays and loss of product, he would stick to suppliers in the Home Counties that he knew and that he or his staff could visit without an overnight stop. He now had to sublet this type of work to suitable companies and word soon got to Sopwith of the reputation of Bert Frost & Son, Bespoke Carpenters of Shepherd's Bush, and he was only about 15 miles away, out of London on the west side, that suited his purpose admirably. If he was employed, they had to find a suitable method of delivery.

It was not long into the war that both the Navy and War Office soon realised the importance of aircraft in the war, initially as reconnaissance, scouts and trainers, not until much later as fighters and bombers. The RFC and RNAS were both in urgent need for aircraft and pressed their respective Ministries to place order at the up most urgency. Orders were soon let out to tender to the aircraft industry, once the suitable tenders had been accepted and orders placed with aircraft manufactures, including Sopwith, mass production began all over the country. The flood of orders soon outstripped Tommy's capacity and he had to sub-contract other companies to make his aircraft under licence, firms such as Vickers, Boulton & Paul, Failey Aviation, Nieuport, to name but a few; some were even made in France!

It was not long before Bert received tenders from Sopwith's for the manufacture of aircraft parts. The amount of work they required was more than Bert could undertake with only him and the three lads, he would need more staff, space and up-to-date machinery. He returned the accepted tenders and with the rest of the family, and Bill and Sam, all got round the table in the Frost's living room one evening after work for a meeting to discuss and plan for the expansion that was badly needed, with Alice taking shorthand note of the meeting, which she would type up the following day, all in the hope of getting Sopwith to accept his tenders and offer him contracts, a gamble they all thought worth taking.

Within a week Sopwith contacted Bert and asked to inspect his premises and they arranged a visit the following week with his production manager. After the inspection, they realised that the capacity was small, but Bert explained his plans which they considered would be satisfactory once they had been implemented. They were duly impressed by the workshop and Bert's plans and invited Bert to Brooklands to view the assembly of the aircraft and the finished product. This, Bert felt, was a good sign; it was now up to them to prove their worth.

Bert and Fred visited the Sopwith factory and after being shown around they soon realised there was nothing that they could not produce, provided they got the staff. A single contract was given, on the provision that if the goods and delivery targets were not met, and they were not up to the Sopwith standard, they would be out. Bert and the three lads were soon making parts for their first contract, well into the night, which was completed and delivered before the dead line, and, after inspection, they were told they were accepted contractors and would, in the not too distance future, be getting more contracts, provided they increased their staff to meet the output that was expected of them.

The rewards for Bert's Company were better than his wildest dreams, and to keep up the output his contractor required they would have to modernise their production methods. With the money they would soon be getting for all this work, Bert had to purchase an up-to-date plant he could now afford for the modern machinery he required, that would save them time. What one man could now do with a modern machine had previously taken 3 or 4 men to accomplish. This was one of the solutions solved if he was to fulfil all the work that had been ordered. Bert knew that other firms would be having the same idea as he had, so he got in on the ground floor, ordering all the new machinery that he required, before most others had started making a list, and received all he had ordered long before anyone else in the surrounding area had placed their orders. Bert's firm was up and running before most others had left the starting gate!

The other problem was he now needed more staff to operate all the new machinery. Once he had confirmation of the work from Sopwith, he saw his local bank manager and got a short-term loan to buy the necessary equipment he required. With the amount of work coming in, increasing all the time, he was soon able to repay back the loan, which pleased his bank manager no end! Once the loan had been repaid Bert was never in the red again!

The delivery of product on time was soon solved. A local delivery firm had a fleet of Lorries, which had lost a lot of contract work, mainly delivering leisure products; that manufacturer having now ceased for the duration of the war, there was now not enough other work to keep his fleet employed. As he had lost most of his staff to fight in the war and the Military had requisitioned most of his lorries, he was up a creek without a paddle on two fronts. But Bert Frost came to the rescue, and contracted him to make at least one daily run to Brooklands. The haulage owner was not a forward-looking person, and said no drivers, no deliveries. Tactfully Bert suggested employing women, which initially he was against, being very against the suffragettes; *a woman's place was in the home, not the work place.* But he soon realised this was the only solution, and his wife, all for the suffragettes, told him there were many women looking for work now there was a war on, their husband and boyfriends away and time on their hands, and she was happy to drive for him, which she soon did, and was often seen at the Frost's Dispatch Bay!

Bert also decided to smarten up the place inside and out, and over one weekend, Bert and the three lads repainted the place in a pale cream, to give the workshop a fresh and airy finish. He got a local contractor to paint the outside and replaced the firm's logo sign, the original had been done by an amateur and was a bit crude to say the least; the result of the new sign was very pleasing:

> **Bert Frost & Son, General Carpenters**
> *Contractors to the Sopwith Aviation Company*

Bert knew once he got the staff he wanted this would increase his profits still further, so he could consider offering higher wages. As such and because all the hard work his son and the two lads were putting in, he increased their wages as starters, to a level which they thought they would only achieve after many years of experience and toil.

Now came the recruitment of staff. Up to about a year ago the joinery trade had little work, there had been a slump, times had been hard, but now business was now on the up, they had jobs to offer and were looking for skilled carpenters and there were many around and many currently unemployed. Things had now turned around by 180 degrees, jobs now out stretched available workshop space and there were vacancies for good experienced tradesmen everywhere you looked.

To get contracts you had to get a bid that was acceptable to the contractor, the lowest bid was not always the best, cost and quality was what Sopwith was looking for, only high standard products were good enough for fitting into flying machines. He knew he could get this from the firm of Frost. From a year back, when there was little work and many people were unemployed, it was now the other way round, loads of work and not enough good carpenters around, nearly all the young men had joined up. Bert knew he would have to pay higher wages if they wanted a suitable workforce of the calibre he required to meet the high standards of the Sopwith organisation.

Bert decided that men in their 20s and 30s, if still around, would soon be wanting to volunteer to join the Army or Navy or be conscripted. The younger ones would have less experience in joinery, while older men, with more expertise behind them, would probably be less keen on joining up. He had heard they would not be calling up people over mid-thirties of age initially. So, Bert started looking in the 40-plus bracket for staff, and had little trouble finding suitable men in that age range, in fact he was spoilt for choice with the wages he knew he could now offer, and he was able to pick the cream that came through his door for interviews. A lot of the men he employed and been made redundant in the slump, or sacked to make way for younger blood, but now the younger blood were the ones volunteering to join up, the older ones were now needed again to support the war effort.

Bert was well satisfied with those he recruited, they worked hard and stayed with him for the duration of the war, they would never be called up as they were making equipment for the war effort and that would mean that their job would be classed as a reserved occupation. He divided the workshop into three teams, his son Fred was in charge of one team, while two of the more senior men, who both had been foremen before they had been made redundant, took charge of the other two teams. Bert explained to Bill and Sam that at present, while they were good at their trade, they were not as accomplished as the older staff, and they did not have the managerial skills to be the boss of a team. They both agreed with Bert's decision, they were not disappointed and had not 'The Governor' increased their wages. But they both had other ideas as to what they wanted to do to help their country win the war, which they kept to themselves. If they were team bosses, it would be harder for them to leave. Bert split up Bill and Sam, putting each one into a team supervised by the new team leaders. He made Fred the overall foreman of the workshop, and when Bert was away, he was the 'Boss'.

Another problem arose, it was space. Bert needed every square foot of space that was available, and decided that the two rooms at the rear of the workshop that the boys used as their free accommodation was what he now required and would be converted into one small parts workshop where one of his three teams would operate. He told the boys they would not be turned out until he got Agnes to find them suitable accommodation in walking distance of the factory. It did not take Agnes long to find lodgings for her two boys, as she now considered they were, as there were many room available to rent; lads who had vacated their lodgings and joined up and gone away to fight, wives who moved out of the *'front room'* and into the *'back room'* to allow for a lodger that brought in a bit of extra cash, service allowances were low for the women left behind. It hurt Bert to do this, but the lads understood, and between themselves it helped with the plans that were germinating in their heads, so they were soon living a short distance away from the workshop. Agnes said they would still have all their meals with them as before, and Bert said he would pay their rent, so Bill and Sam were no worse off. In fact, they now had more freedom after work. The only person who did not like this arrangement was Alice, who now had a large crush on Bill. While Bill was quite flattered, he had never taken her out on his own, he didn't want a deep relationship if he was going off to join the army, and he was no fool, people did get killed, and he could be one of them. He felt that he should keep his distance.

Once Agnes had found them a decent place to stay, a room each in the same house, both on the first floor, and in walking distance, they soon moved in. The four men worked together over a weekend converting a two-bedroom ground floor flat in to a workshop, housing four benches and a clerk's desk for the foreman to keep a tally on jobs and their progress through the system.

While the services desperately needed hardware, they also desperately needed personnel. Bill was now of an age to join up, but Bert had applied to the Government department dealing with war workers as soon as he got his confirmation from Sopwith Aviation of major contracts for his firm having dispensation as a reserved occupation, which was granted for up to 12 employees, none of his staff were now liable for call up from now on, their work was far too important to let them go.

While Bill knew he did not have to join up and fight, like all the young men around him were doing, he felt that his country would be better served if he eventually joined up. With the new staff Bert had recently employed, it would not be detrimental to the firm or affect their output for long if he left. He knew Bert had retained all the personal documentation of men he had turn down, telling them if he required more staff, he would contact them. Bill realised if he did join up, it would make a vacancy for someone else who may be unemployed, so he would be doing that someone a favour, and most likely a wife and children too.

Bert had often said to the boys they were lucky that they had a reserved occupation and would not have to join up and fight. While he realised most young lads without a reserved occupation were eager to join up and were required to do their bit, Bill and Sam did not have to. The lads knew Bert did not want to lose them, not only because they were good, conscientious workers but were considered a part of the Frost family.

With all the new machinery now installed, Bill considered the firm could still fulfil all its contracts without him. He did not talk about his feeling to Bert or Fred, but he did with Sam, the bond was as strong as ever. Bill did not have to tell Sam of his disquiet about the situation, somehow Sam knew. They did not discuss this in the factory or in the hearing of any of the Frosts, but away from the workshop they talked about it a lot, it was easier now they did not live on the premises. Sam was of the same opinion as Bill, he also wanted to join up as soon as he was old enough, so they both agreed if there was a war Bill should apply, and Sam would also, when he became of age. They knew Bert would stop them, but if they left and joined up, without telling Bert, it would be too late to do anything. Bill said to Sam, when he did join up he would not let on to where he had gone, including to Sam, so it would not be possible for anyone to track him down. He knew that the Army would not give such information away, it was confidential, besides, if they had got someone to enlist and had taken the Kings shilling, there was no way they were going to let him go back from whence he came!

Bill decided that he wanted to join The Berks & Hants Light Infantry, and considered that the best place to join up would be at their base in the home of the British Army, Aldershot. It was not too far to travel, but far enough away from Shepherd's Bush for anyone to trace him. If he applied at a recruiting office, he could be sent anywhere; he decided he wanted to make the choice.

Now they were living in lodgings on their own, there was no problem in receiving any mail with any military connections. When it was time to leave and join up, he and Sam agreed that Sam would plead ignorance of Bill's disappearance to the Frost's to where he had gone. Bill also planned, but did not tell Sam, that he would leave four notes. One for Bert and Agnes, one for Alice, and one for Sam, to make it look as if Sam knew nothing of the reason why he was leaving, ensuring they were found together in Bert's office. The last one would be for his landlady. Bill was a sensible and practical person in the affairs of his and Sam's life, and before he left he would leave with Sam all his personal effects and his Birth Certificate, in case anything happened to him. When Sam joined up, Sam would pass these on to Bert, with his own effects, again leaving it impossible for Bert to find where he had gone.

The boys carried on working as if nothing had happened, but were keeping a close eye on what was unfolding, especially after the assassination of Archduke Francis Ferdinand and his consort. They could see the writing was on the wall, and war was not far off. With Britain declaring war against

Germany on the 1st August and a few days later the British Expeditionary Force leaving these shores for France, Bill knew it was time to act. It was the poster of Earl Kitchener that made it for Bill, it was pointing to him, and he had to join up! Bill and Sam discussed their next move.

Within a few days of the declaration of war, Sam, on arriving at work, told Bert that he and Bill had gone out for a beer and a fish and chips supper the previous night and this morning Bill was not feeling very well, probably due to a bit of iffy fish. He was sick during the night, and still feeling a bit queasy when he woke up, but he was sure he would be back the following day, and, emphasizing that he was getting loving tender care from their landlady, making sure Agnes did not go down to see him! Sam could tell white lies if the need arose!

In fact, Bill had left early that day, taking a train from Waterloo down to Aldershot. On arrival there, he asked directions to The Berks & Hants Light Infantry Barracks, but was directed to a central recruiting office and was pointed in the right path and it was not long before he saw the main gates of an army camp. Guarding the gates were a pair of smart armed sentry each side and a Colour Sergeant, complete with a highly polished pace stick under his arm and a broad red sash diagonally across his chest denoting his importance, directing the steady stream of recruits to the reception office that was easy to spot by the size of the crowd of young men queuing outside. He immediately tacked on the end and it was not long before a Sergeant Major, in full dress uniform that befitted his rank, walked down the queue, checking Birth Certificates. If the Sergeant Major came across any young man without a Birth certificate or under age, he was turned away and told to come back with it to prove his age, or wait till he had reached the age of enlistment.

When Bill's turn came to start the joining process, he had to show his Birth Certificate again to an officer, and once he was satisfied was told to join the queue for a medical inspection. On entering a medium size room, he saw at the top end a number of officers in white coats, each checking naked man. An orderly was by the door and told Bill to remove all his clothes and place them in a large basket, then join yet another queue, carrying his clothes in the basket with him. This led him to the officers in white coats at the far end of the room, doctors he suspected. Part way up the room, they were stopped by another orderly who entered his name, address and other personal particulars on an official Army Record Form, with a second form attached that was for entering his medical records, again with his name. He noticed in the top right corner of each form a block that stated 'Service Number' and six blank joined squares in a row; he would keep an eye on that one. He was then weighed, had his height measured, and his blood pressure and pulse rate taken, all which were recorded on the medical form. He was given the form and told to hand it to the doctor who examined him. When it was his turn, he handed the form to the doctor, who put a stethoscope over his back and chest and told to breathe deeply. He looked into his ears as well as his mouth. Told to bend down, he felt the doctor hold his testicles before being told to cough. What this was for, Bill did not know, and never found out! Lastly, he was given an eye sight check by reading letters on a far wall, which was no problem, but it made him wonder what happened to anyone who could not read. He was told he had passed fit to fight for King and Country and all his medical details entered. He was then instructed to get dressed and report to the orderly at the door while the doctor completed the forms and put it in a box with a lot of others medical forms. He also saw another box, with only a few forms in, this was, and he found out later, the reject box, there would be no fighting for them unless their health improved, if that was possible. The doctors completed his other card and gave it him and told him to hand it in when ordered. *Ordered!* He was not in the army yet!

The next queue was outside another room for those who had been passed fit. They were told to wait their turn until called forward and would be interviewed one at a time. When Bill was called to enter, he saw the room was small with only two chairs, a desk and an officer and in front of the office on the desk, and asked for the form he had been given. It was the officer's job to assess the recruit's capabilities and what they would be best suited, whether they were to be rank and file, or be considered for a commission. It only took a few minutes, there was a long queue waiting, and as he knew, he was not officer material. He asked if he could join The Berks & Hants Light Infantry, and he got what he wanted, and told he would be attached to them for initial training as a soldier to make sure he was round peg in a round hole. It was just what he had come for and was very pleased he had made it.

Once all this had been completed, he was told by a Staff Sergeant go to another large room and to wait to be called for, it was all 'waiting' and being 'called for'!

Eventually, with nine others, he was called forward by name to the final room by a junior office holding what looked like the form that had been following him around. On entering the room there were two officers behind a table at the top of the room, joined by the third who had called their names. In front of them were two rows of five small tables, but no chairs. They were all told to stand behind a table on which there was a Holy Bible, a blank piece of paper, and a pen. The junior officer told them to raise their hand when their name was called; Bill's was the fifth name and he was handed the forms that were following him around. The first thing he saw was the block in the top right-hand corner was now filled in with a five-figure number in bold print.

They were instructed to complete the empty space in the forms in front of them with their religion, home address and next of kin, but not to sign it. The two junior offices then went round the room to check all the forms had been correctly filled in helped one of the lads who had difficulty in reading and writing. When this was completed to the senior officer's satisfaction they were told to take the Bible in their right hand and hold it at shoulder height and repeat what the officer would now say, as they were going to swear allegiance to King and Country. When the 'swearing in' was completed, they were told to sign the form on the dotted line, Bill did so, signing himself as before:

William Perry

When everyone had signed the form, the two junior officers came round and both signed on each of the ten forms as witness. They were told to remember the number printed on the form, write it down on the blank paper provided if necessary as this was their personal *Army Service Number*, never to be forgotten and must be given to any Officer, NCO or a person in authority who asked them for it. The final act of joining up was when he handed in the form and was to be given the *Kings Shilling*; he was now in the Army.

Bill looked at the form that he had filled in and where he had first seen the number in the corner, but had not thought anything about it at the time, and this was his own personal number:

-	7	5	2	8	1

He had heard somewhere that when you joined up, you were not a name any more, but a number! They were told to hand the signed form to one of the officers in the entrance hall and report to the Sergeant Major who was seated in a large room off the main entrance, behind a table on a platform to await further instructions.

As they were now in the Army, the were ordered by a Corporal to stand in three lines and wait to be called by the Sergeant Major, who had now been given a list of all the accepter recruits. The Corporal briefed them, when called; they were to march smartly up to the table, stand to attention and say their last three numbers, their name and their initials.

The list was long, there were many who wanted to join up, Bill had to wait ages it seemed as other were called and given their instructions, until suddenly his name was summoned. He marched up in a manner what he considered smart, halted, and stood to attention and said in a loud voice, "281 Private Perry W, Sir." On completing all the formalities, he was told to return home and wait for his call-up papers which would be accompanied by a railway travel warrant, this should be with him in about two weeks' time. And as a bonus, he was reimbursed with his train fare today, the Army was not too bad after all! His train fare and a shilling!

All this had taken all day, except for a brake half way through about midday when they were taken to the soldiers' mess hall for a lunch. It was now mid-afternoon, but no more food was offered, he was getting hungry again.

Lastly, they were all given a printed letter which had their service details written in at the top, to be handed to their employer, if they had one, telling them that they had joined the Army and would soon be called away for active duty; it was an official notice terminating their employment. Bill would destroy this; he could never give it to Bert. He then made his way back to Shepherd's Bush, exhausted but pleased with what he had achieved. Sam was back at the lodgings before Bill, and as Bill had not eaten, they went out and got a beer and some fish and chips, which they had not had on the previous evening! Sitting in the centre of Shepherd's Bush Green, Bill told Sam all about his day, and on hearing all this, Sam could not wait to join up himself!

The boys often went back to the orphanage, sometimes working, at other times just friendly visits, helping out with the boys there. It was not long after the landing of the BEF and Bill had been to Aldershot that he made his last visit to the orphanage, not that he let on to anyone there that he had joined the Army.

***

In Notting Hill, Algernon was getting very concerned about the war and he and Keturah decided to go to Oxfordshire and discuss it with his parents. The children and staff went by train and Algernon and Keturah flew in the S.36, as they had done many times before. Keturah loved it, wearing her warm fur lined flying suit, helmet, goggles, boots and leather gauntlet gloves. She had initially had to badger Algernon a bit, but he was now teaching her to fly, and she proved to be competent pilot. With the help of Algernon, she was studying map reading, the mechanics of the aeroplane and why they flew, doing a lot of sketching which, while she had never draw before, had taken to it and quite liked it. The next thing was to pass her flying test and then apply for an *Aviator's Certificate*. Neither took long to arrange and she was one of the early female aviators in the country to gain this coveted certificate.

Algernon had started to put out feelers in the right places in early June, after the assassination of Archduke Francis Ferdinand and his consort in late May, as how best to become a pilot in the RFC. His father, now 64, was in very good health and was quite capable, as he was always telling his son, of running the estate for a few more years with the help of his long serving estate manager and their staff and Algernon must not worry about him, he must join up and go and serve the country, giving much needed support, which he considered was more important than worrying about his father and the estate. His father's words were to him, "It's your duty Algernon, to join up as soon as you possibly can, in the Army, perhaps in my old regiment. Just say the word and I will get you a commission." But Algernon had different ideas!

Algernon's father Jonathan had been a career soldier, and before his father had died, had served in the Army for over 30 years retiring as a Brigadier General. He was serving in India at the time Queen Victoria had been declared Empress of India in 1876, but was back in England when news came through that his father, after years of very good health, was suddenly taken ill. Jonathan was advised by the doctors attending his father that he did not have very long to live. He therefore felt that he had to retire from the Army and take over the running of the estate. He had not long left the Army and returned home and was now running the estate when his father had died just before the turn of the century. Jonathan became the 6th Earl of Caversham.

Jonathan should not have been surprised when Algernon told him that while he was going to join the Army, it would not be in his old regiment, not even in any other regiment, but in the Royal Flying Corp. Jonathan felt he should have realised this as he knew his son had got bitten by the flying bug and was flying home nearly every weekend.

And so, when the Cavendish's returned to their town house at the end of the weekend, Algernon joined the Royal Flying Corps. To become a pilot in the RFC around this time, you had to hold an Aviator's Certificate, so Algernon had a head start. As he was just over 40 years old, he was given a thorough medical examination; eyes and fitness were a main consideration. On the plus side, he was now a very experienced pilot; they were in short supply in the Corps and was accepted and given an immediate commission as 2nd Lieutenant Cavendish and was posted to Larkhill in Wiltshire, on probation to see how he shaped up, joining 3 Squadron there.

There were an assortment of aircrafts at the station, and every pilot was expected to fly each type to become familiar with all the current service aircrafts. At this time aeroplanes were only used for reconnaissance, and armament was not even considered to be fitted at the outbreak of war in August. The top Army brass were very sceptical in the early days of the war in the use of aeroplanes, and a lot of them felt they should not be there, which included the whole of the RFC.

The initial job for aircraft in the war was to fly over enemy lines and report back what they observed with sketches or, later, take photos of troops and gun positions and any movement of these since they had last flown across that area. They were considered only to be scouts or reconnaissance, the name by which they were known, even though by the end of 1914 machine guns were starting to be fitted. The planes that were in service throughout the war were, save for only two, all biplanes. Algernon's first flight was in an Avro 504, a single seater, then unarmed, but later some were fitted with a Lewis machine gun, but only for home defence.

He then flew a two seater aircraft, a BE2C, and carried an observer thus leaving the pilot free to fly the plane and navigate, while the observer did the sketches or take photos, later to man the gun fitted in the rear cockpit. The last plane he flew while at Larkhill was a Vickers 'Gunbus' FB5, an early aircraft designed to have a mounted gun fitted. The propeller was a pusher, at the back of the fuselage, while the pilot sat in the rear of two cockpits and the observer, gunner, had a front cockpit with a very good field of vision forward to observe and fire his Vickers gun; but the danger spot was behind and below, no rear facing guns.

Farnborough in Hampshire was the hub of anything to do with aircraft in the RFC and was titled *The Royal Aircraft Factory*. As well as designing and building their own aircraft, they were responsible for vetting all aircraft designs that manufactures sent for their approval, before a prototype was ordered. When the prototype was built, it was sent to Farnborough to be tested, and was either approved or rejected as deemed fit. If approved, then the Ministry would order. With so many aircrafts to be test flown, they needed pilots with high flying skills. Algernon's squadron and flight commander soon realised that he was a gifted pilot; the probation period was soon over. After only about six weeks at Larkhill, Algernon was selected to be a test pilot, and a post to Farnborough soon followed, with promotion to full Lieutenant.

***

Young men all over the country were now joining up, gaps were appearing in the work places and to fill the gaps women were now being employed. The suffragettes curtailed their campaign of civil disobedience for the duration of the war; ladies could now be seen working in all walks of life, from tram drivers to working on the land.

***

At Grafton Magna Manor, all the young men working in the house or gardens left, and the 6th Earl had to start looking around for female staff or older men to fill the gaps by those who had left to join up. He was lucky that the head butler, head gardener and senior game keeper were all well over calling up age, so he had a continuity of staff at the top to train the new comers. They found that there were many girls looking for places in service, and local farmers were only too happy to have a daughter working at the Manor, if they could be spared, be it serving in the house or the tending of the land. It was not long before all places were filled and things got back to normal with a majority of female employees, even though it was hard to accept that young girls were serving at the table! The duties of the game keeper were curtailed while hostility raged across the channel.

***

Bill continued to work as if nothing had happened, though he was on edge and he and Sam only talked about Bill's secret away from the factory and never on the premises; walls have ears! He was now a bit tense, which he hoped no one had realised at work, waiting for a buff envelope to arrive with his call-up papers.

Before the war had started, there were 5 deliveries of post a day, but now, as the majority of postmen had gone to war, their jobs had also been taken over by women, and to ease their task, deliveries were cutback to only 3 a day, early morning, midday, and late afternoon, all while the two boys were at work. The boys had never received any mail, but Bill asked his landlady if any post came for him to hold it back, and he would collect it from her on their return from work, without Sam knowing.

While Sam knew Bill would be leaving soon, he did not know when, and Bill was not sure either. While he had been working for Bert, now for over two years, he had saved money, as all he earned was pocket money, as he and Sam had all their meals free with the Frost family, and Bert was paying their rent and clothes, which was little. He had found a local savings bank and regularly put money away, all gaining a small interest. While he had been at Aldershot, they were told to make a Will if they had anything worth leaving; as such they were all given an Army Will Form. Bill did this and got his landlady and another lodger to stand as witnesses, unbeknownst to Sam.

Before Bill left he wrote four letters, the first to Sam

Dear Sam, my best friend,

When you get this I will have gone to do my bit for King and Country.

I have given you as my Next-of-Kin on the forms I had to fill in when I signed on. I have put my Birth Certificate in as well and one or two bits of paper that are official, including my Savings Book and my Will in a sealed envelope, which they suggest you do when you first joined up. I have sent a letter to our landlady, explaining I will not be back and she can re-let my room. As you will now know, I sent this letter with one to Bert and Agnes and one to Alice

In my bedroom, in the bottom drawer of the chest of drawers, there under some old clothes you can chuck out, my pocket watch and chain, please look after it until I return, but if I don't come back, it is yours to keep and look after. If all goes well, it should be all over by Christmas, well that is what everyone is saying. Lastly, please keep an eye out for Alice for me, not too closely, but look after her while I am away. On my return, I hope she and I can make a go of it together.

Your best friend

Bill

The next letter was to Bert and Agnes

Dear Bert and Agnes,

I hope you both don't think too badly of me and feel I have left you in the lurch. With all your new

staff I don't think you will miss me, I know you have a waiting list of chaps who would like to work for you and have more experience than me, you will soon fill my place, I'm sure. I feel that being young and fit I should offer my services to the country, and have joined an infantry regiment. If what

they say is true, it should be all over by Christmas, if so I may have to apply to you for a job! Don't have a go at Sam, he did not know anything about this. Lastly,

thank you for everything you have done for me over the years, and for Sam of course.
All the best
Bill

The hardest letter he had to write was to Alice.

Dearest Alice,
Please don't think too unkindly of me in going away without saying Goodbye, but I felt it was better this way. The country needs as many men of my age as there is an important job to be done and I have joined an infantry regiment. We all hope, as everyone is saying, it will be all over by Christmas and I can then come back and take up my old job where I left off and I hope, with your father's permission, we can start walking out together, if you will consent. Sam knew nothing of what I have done. The day
I went to Aldershot, I said I was not well, that Sam told you. After he had gone, I went out and joined up, and was back before Sam returned from work. Lastly, I have the picture you gave me recently which I will keep with me always. Take good care of yourself until my return, I've told Sam in my letter to him to look after you if you have any problems.
With my greatest affection, yours,
Bill

The last letter he wrote was a brief note to his landlady telling her that he had joined the Army to fight for King & Country. He would not be needing his room anymore and she should let it as soon as possible, as Bert would stop paying her any rent.

He put all four letters in separate envelopes, and addressed them by name, except the landlady's, on which he put her full address. The other three envelopes were put into one large envelope, sealed and addressed to Bert at the workshop. He then stuck a postage stamp on the two envelopes, with stern King George V looking to his left. As he would be leaving very early, before dawn had broken, he would not post the envelopes until he got to Aldershot, that way they would not be delivered until the next day. While

Sam knew Bill was off to Aldershot at some time in the near future, but did not know the day, Bill never let on to him.

The boys had separate rooms in their lodgings, so Bill had no worries about creeping out before the sun came up, without waking Sam, on the day he was leaving. When he received his papers he would depart without telling Sam that he was going, so it not only would be a surprise for him, but the Frost family and his landlady as well. At the end of each working day, on their return to the lodgings, Bill, without Sam's knowledge, would slip back down to see if their landlady had any mail for him, as he had asked her to take it in for him. She was a very goofy landlady, and did not ask any questions.

About ten days later, his landlady passed him his 'signing on' letter from the Army complete with his joining up instructions and rail warrant, he was ordered to report to the Victoria Barracks, the home of The Berks & Hants Light Infantry in Aldershot by 1200 hours in two days' time. Unbeknownst to Sam, Bill had purchased a small cloth bag especially for the journey, and had already packed it, bar for his everyday essentials. On the eve of his departure Bill did not want to give the game away that he was leaving in the morning, so he made sure they did nothing special, just sat and chatted after they had returned from work after their evening meal, about the war, joining up, and how would the Frosts feel when Bill eventually left without telling them before he went.

Bill got up when it was still dark, dressed and put the last things in has bag. The last thing he did before he left his room, was to put his watch under some old clothes in his drawer, with a note on his bed to say where his watch was, as he knew that Sam would come looking for him in the morning if he did not shout to him as he did every morning to let him know he was awake. He had made sure his bedroom door would not squeak as he had oiled it well on his return from Aldershot. In stocking feet, he opened his door and crept down the stairs in the dark, letting himself out of the front door. He put his shoes on and was on his way to the station without a backward glance. If he had, and it had been light enough, he would have seen Sam looking out of the window, watching him go, and silently wishing Bill all the best of luck in the world.

CHAPTER 5

Two Men Go to War

Bill made his way by the underground from Shepherd's Bush to Waterloo. As he ascended the steps into the main station from the bowels of the subterranean world of the tube to the light but smoke-filled, circulating area from which all the platforms radiated, he was greeted with the sound of music, even at this early hour of the morning. He checked the main train indicator board for the platform that the next Aldershot train was departing from and asked smartly dressed railway official directions. As he made his way there he saw who was providing this jolly music to help travellers on their way, a Salvation Army Band. He felt it was a nice send-off, he did not hear many bands in the Shepherd's Bush area, and he did not expect to hear any when he was on the front!

When Bill arrived at the platform that he had been directed, there were many lads of his age, all laughing and joking together, some he recognised from their *intake day*, and all it seemed making their way to the home of the Army at Aldershot, all joining one of the many regiments based there. There were also a number of women there, wives, fiancées and girlfriends, teenagers and early twenty-somethings and older folk, mothers, fathers, and wives and younger children, all seeing their son, brother or husband off, they looked less happy than the young lads who were soon boarding the train, they were in a more sombre mood, most could remember the losses from the two Boer Wars, the last having only ended in 1902.

The train was crowded and it was impossible not to talk and make friends, they all had one common purpose, to save Great Britain from the Kaiser and his followers and it was all going to be over by Christmas, so everyone said. On the journey Bill soon found a number of lads also joining The Berks & Hants Light Infantry, they could all make their way to the barracks together.

As they got off the train at Aldershot station, they were met by a number of smartly turned out SNCOs and a lot of Corporals. They were told to assemble into groups of the regiment or corps they were now joining, as they had been directed to go by their joining instructions. A number of corporals were shouting like there was no tomorrow, calling out the regiment or corps they represented, similar to market traders calling out their wares. Bill, with his other comrades soon made their way to the JNCO, assigned to take the in charge, calling out, "B and H, B and H, B and H, over 'ere," for all his worth. He soon had his flock gather around him, and once the train had left, he knew there would be no more until the next train arrived and making sure there were no stragglers left on the platform he made a short curt comment, "Right you lot, follow me, keep up and don't lag behind. Got It? And try and look smart, you're in the Army now!" He did not wait for a reply, he was off out of the station as he made his way down the road to the Victoria Barracks, marching smartly, swinging his arms shoulder high at 120 paces per minutes, followed by a motley shower of men, shuffling along and trying to march, having a job to keep up as he was setting a good rate and was not hampered by carrying a suitcase or holdall of their personal belongings.

By the time they arrived at Victoria Barracks, the group of lads were a shambles, they were all puffing and blowing, like the steam engine that had hauled them from London, way behind the corporal and straggled out in a long sausage-shaped group. After handing over his party inside the main gates to the Company Sergeant Major, the corporal returned to the station for the next batch of recruits.

They were met by the six foot six Company Sergeant Major standing out side the Main Guard Room. He was dressed in an immaculate khaki uniform, well pressed with creases that would cut paper, all topped by a peaked cap with shiny peak pulled down so he had to lift his head to see anyone. Across his chest was a diagonal red sash, to denote his standing in the barracks and a row of decorations he had been awarded from both Boer Wars. On the opposite side of the road there were six corporals, all well turned out and smartly standing at ease, spaced out in intervals of about four yards in a straight line.

They had hardly crossed through the gates when a voice, which Bill reckoned could be heard miles away bawled, "Right you lot, you are in the Army now. The Berks & Hants Light Infantry, and don't forget it. You don't stroll around *MY BARRACKS*, you *MARCH*. Now get fell in in three ranks in front of me you 'orrible little men, and *AT THE DOUBLE*, if not sooner, *GOT IT*? They *'GOT IT'* with a lot of pushing and shoving by the motley crew of exhausted lads in front of him, getting themselves sorted out into some sort of three ranks for the first time which was not a thing they were yet accustomed to. They weren't laughing and joking as they had been at Waterloo!

The voice continued, "I am the Company Sergeant Major and you will remember that from now on. I'm God here. You will always stand up straight and stand to attention whenever I address you, and call me Sergeant Major."

When he paused, Bill then saw that a sergeant was standing just behind the Company Sergeant Major. Without looking over his shoulder he announced, still in a loud voice, "When the Colour Sergeant behind me calls your name answer *"Present Sergeant"* so it can be heard over a mile away, *'GOT IT?'"* There was a mumble of agreement. This did not impress the Company Sergeant Major a bit. "I want to hear *'Yes Sergeant Major'* echo off the building, *'GOT IT?'"* he shouted. They got the message and, *"Yes Sergeant Major,"* echoed off the buildings. The Sergeant Major continued, "The Colour Sergeant behind me will tell you which Corporal on the other side of the road to stand behind, and when I say stand, that means standing to attention. And you do all your movements at the double, *'GOT IT?'"* for which he received a good and loud *"Yes Sergeant Major."* They found out later that his name was Eveleigh, but his nickname, behind his back was *'Old Got It'*.

The Colour Sergeant stepped forward and started calling names from a list attached to a clip board. Bill's name was just over half way down and he was detailed to stand behind a Corporal Davis of 'D Squad'. He found out a little later that Corporal Davis had seen many years of service in the Army, another Boer War veteran, the last time he had been in any conflict, and carried a leg wound to show for it, this making him medically unfit for action again. On his left chest, he carried two rows of decorations for his bravery. He had made it no further than his current rank, and while a good solider, three stripes would never be his because of his injuries. The last few years of his service life would be at Aldershot, his job to change civilians, now raw recruits, to become fighting men. The Army was his life, he was happy in his rank and did not wish for anything more. While he appeared to be a hard man and a disciplinarian, and would run them into the ground with their short training, they were all *his lads* and would defend them to the end against all other who interfered with him. He had served with *'Old Got It'* for many years, fighting in both Boer War under his command; he a private, *'Old Got It'* his half section corporal at the start, they had great respect for each other.

No sooner had Bill and all the other lads arrived, they the hit the ground running, there was no rest from *Reveille* to *Lights Out* for the next six weeks they were under training. When about half the compliment of 50 recruits had arrived to join 'D Squad' they were all marched from the Guard Room carrying their personal belongings, a ragged bunch of men as one could ever imagine, to the Bedding Store to collect their bedding, a Dixie, and a knife, a fork & a spoon (known colloquially as irons). If they were bad at marching to the stores, coming back was even worse, carrying their first issue of army equipment and their luggage. Corporal Davis was not slow in telling them what he thought of them, which happened many times a day for the next six weeks, when he hoped at the end they would be useful fighting men.

Corporal Davis was in charge of 5 sections of 10 men each that made up his Squad, billeted in two adjacent unheated wooden huts. Bill was glad the weather was mild, and he hoped he would never have to be there in the winter. In charge of each section was a Lance-Corporal who had been selected from recruits that had only been in the army for about two weeks but showed potential in commanding men, some were later commissioned. They all reported directly to Corporal Davis and had the privilege of sleeping in small room at the end of the hut, known as bunks.

They had their first meal, lunch, which was basic army grub, not like mother made, and on the stodgy side, but it was food, it filled the many holes they had in their stomachs during the next six weeks, and it was piping hot, just what an active young lad required. To some who had joined up, who had no job, were in poverty and always hungry, it was manna from heaven to them. To those who had dined out in the country's top eating places, a minimum of five course and unlimited wine, it was hardly palatable, but after a week, with all the energy they expended, they soon ate it, even if they and their stomachs still complained!

In the afternoon, they were kitted out with uniforms and told to get changed into them, then parcel up their civilian clothes and post them home. While the well-heeled complied with this order had to send their expensive apparel home, those at the other end of the scale arrived in the only clothes they had which were near to rags, dumped them in the nearest bin, as Bill did. Once in uniform, they were all now on a level playing field. They were recruits, known as sprogs, there was only one class for them in army terms, and they were the lowest of the low. The last thing the new recruits had to do that evening was to fill in a form with details of who their *Next-of-Kin* was. Had Bill not done this when he had enrolled about weeks ago? That was the Army, make doubly sure! Bill entered Sam's name and but gave Bert's address, just in case Sam moved.

Before they were dismissed for the day, they were all issued with their *'Dog Tags'* the common name used for the two identification discs they had all to wear round their necks for now on. When Bill received his, it was brief:

> **B&HLI**
> **75281**
> **PERRY W**

If they were killed, one would be left with the body, while the other was removed and handed in to those in charge to commence the train of events to inform the nearest and dearest back home.

When the working day was over, and after an evening meal, a different stodgy foodstuff from lunch, they all went to the Army Canteen on the base. There were all told they had to be in bed by 2100hrs, and if they were not up and dressed, and had made their bedding made into a bed packs by 0630hrs, they would all be in deep trouble; extra duties in the Cook House, peeling spuds, washing tins in the tin room or some other unpleasant task would befall anyone who strayed off the straight and narrow.

After breakfast, on their first full day in the army, the training started in earnest. They were told that while they were under training they would train in sections, Bill being put in 'Section 5'. They would be known as 'D Squad ~ Section 5' and the Lance-Corporal in charge of them said woe betide anyone who did not pull his weight, as slackers would be severely dealt with. No Section had ever let Corporal Davis down, so they had not better be the first. The Lance-Corporal who was in charge of them was Lance-Corporal Richardson, from a middle-class background and was in his mid-twenties. Bill felt that before he had joined up he had held a position of responsibility, as he had a natural ability of commanding men. Bill decided this was a man to look up to and take tips from his actions. He could learn a lot from him, which could prove useful later on. By his attitude and demeanour Richardson would easily earn respect form those under his command, and they would follow his orders without question as any trained soldier was expected, another attribute Bill felt was worth watching. Bill found out that Richardson had been in the Officer Cadet Force at the public school he had attended, and had a head start above most of the rest when he joined up. When he had completed his basic training, he was accepted for training for a King's Commission, which he gained and was a 2nd Lieutenant Richardson serving on the front in less than three months.

The first day was a mixture of foot drills, PT, road runs, assault courses, and the skills of combat; the following day the same, but in a different order. At the start of the second week they were issued with the current service rifle, the Lee-Enfield. With this additional piece of equipment their foot drill now incorporated the rifle. They were told how to clean the gun with a 'pull-through' with a two-by-four-inch linen cloth, known as a '2-by-4', which was soaked in oil and put in the middle loop at the end of the 'pull-through', dropping the weighted end into the breech until in emerged at the muzzle. They pulled the cord and 2-by-4 through the barrel, finishing with one cleaned and oiled rifle barrel. Finally, they were taught how to fire and kill with them; either with 0.303 bullets, a maximum of 10 rounds in the magazine, or with the 18-inch sword bayonet fixed to the end of the rifle, stabbing sacks filled with straw and making blood curdling noises, to frighten the enemy!

Bill got stuck in to all this with gusto, he considered himself fit when he arrived at Aldershot, but soon realised fit to him was not fit to the army. After the first day Bill did not know he could ache in all the places he did. Each day of the first week it got no better, but after about 7 days in, he started to feel the aches less, he felt stronger, and could do more without wanting to rest or getting puffed out, not sounding like a steam engine they could hear in the distance; he was improving every day. Some still found it hard, others were pulling through, but Bill seemed to cope better than most of the others, he had been doing a certain amount of heavy work at Bert's.

Before he had left Shepherd's Bush, Bill had said he would write to Sam once a week if possible, even if it was a short note to say he was still alive. Sam was relieved to get the first letter just over a week after Bill had left, and having read it a least twice, he could hardly wait to join up, but he would just have to. He always replied to Bill's letters promptly telling him all the news from Shepherd's Bush.

Towards the end of the second week, they were given tasks in the army exercise ground in the plains outside Aldershot. They were divided into teams of about ten men, two from each section, each man being a team leader for at least one task. These tasks were varied, all using a map and compass; getting from A to B, finding a "wounded" solider, crossing streams by homemade rope bridge, navigating "minefields" and many more similar exercises. This went on for a week, Bill taking his turn as leader, and felt he had done himself credit when he had completed his task. Offices and Instructors, who had watched all these tasks being performed, were on the lookout for potential Officers and Junior Non-Commissioned Officers, JNCOs.

At the start of the third week, the results came through, and Bill was made an Acting Paid Lance-Corporal and now in charge of 'Section 3', a section of new recruits who had arrived two weeks after Bill. During the day, he was still training with 'Section 5', while the rest of the time he was billeted with his 'Section 3', helping to turn them into soldiers. Bill now reported directly to Corporal Davis and he found he was human after all. There were perks that went with the rank, more pay, status, and he could now use the Corporals Club, a better place than the Army Canteen, even having the occasional drink with his Corporal and a bunk at the end of the billet, a room for only one with bed, locker, table and chair.

Training continued, with no abate, but the whole squad was improving, they were working as a team, each week they were assessed on their ability, only one failed during the whole 6 weeks, and he was put back to retake the week he had failed, as another solider who had been put back to their squad. At the end of six weeks they had their final assessment and all passed, completed with a Passing Out Parade, marching past their Section Commander, a Captain, taking the salute. After the parade, they were taken into one of the lecture huts and told that they had the weekend off, a 48-hour pass, and on their return, would be making their way by train to Dover, then boat to Calais. When they arrived there, they would be informed as to which area of the fighting they would be going. The entirety of 'Section 5', except Bill, and three other like him who had been made Lance-Corporals, would be staying with the section they were in charge of, and when they passed out they would travel to France with them. Because of his position, he had no 48-hour pass; he had to stay and look after his Section and would get his leave when his section passed out.

***

Sam watched Bill walk down the road hoping he would look back and give him a wave, but he never did, and soon disappeared around the corner. Sam went into Bill's bedroom hoping to find a letter from him, but he found nothing. He left for work with a heavy heart having little appetite for food, arriving purposely late, after breakfast was over and would not have to face the Frosts, going straight to his bench and got on with his work. The foreman of Bill's team came over to where he was working and asked him where Bill was, to which Sam had to lie and say that when he got up Bill was nowhere to be seen, omitting to say he had seen him leave before dawn, and that his room was empty and he was not at breakfast. The foreman reported this to Bert who was soon asking Sam the same questions, for which he got the same answers. Bert said he would like to know as soon as possible if Sam heard anything from Bill.

When Sam stopped for lunch, Alice also wanted to know all the details. Again, he explained as best he could, but felt awkward and embarrassed whenever he was in her company. He always knew Alice was very fond of Bill, and while Bill never said anything to Sam, he was sure Bill had some strong feelings towards her; he knew they had never been out together. Bill had once said to him, that it was not fair to have a steady girlfriend when you were going to war, no one knew if you would ever come back. But Alice was never mentioned in connection with this. Sam's embarrassment was mainly due to the fact he fancied her also, but as she only had eyes for Bill, and he was sure Bill had some feelings for Alice, he would never make any advances towards her while there was a bond between both of them. He would have to look elsewhere.

On the way home after work he had a feeling that most people had a good idea that Bill had joined up. But what was he going to do, if only Bill had left some sort of note, it would take the pressure off him, he was asked questions by most of the staff on and off during the day. On return to his lodgings he asked the landlady if there was any post for him, but she had none. He did not mention to her that Bill had gone and joined the army, he was sure she would find out in good time.

On arrival at the workshop the following morning, Bert asked him about Bill again, but still he had no answer to give them. Part way through the morning, there was a scream from the office where Alice worked. Everyone stopped working and looked up while Bert dashed to the office. A short time later, Bert came out and walked over to Sam and handed him an envelope.

"We've just had a letter from Bill, in the envelope were three letters, one for Agnes and me, one for Alice and one for you," which Bert passed over to him. "The silly lad has joined up, its broken Alice's heart, did you know anything about it?"

Sam had to admit to Bert, Bill had mentioned it. "I did not take it seriously," he lied, "he must have done all this in secret. It must have been the day a couple of weeks ago, when he was sick, that he enlisted, but that is only a guess"

Bert had to accept what Sam had said, but he had a funny feeling that Sam knew more than he was letting on, but there was no way he could prove it. He was not going to badger the boy, he could tell he was also upset, but not like Alice.

While Sam wanted to read the letter from Bill, he wanted to do this when he was on his own. After work when he had got back to his lodgings, in the privacy of his room, he opened the envelope and read its contents. Having finished the letter, he went into Bill's old room and found Bill's pocket watch, the only time Sam felt like crying. When he had sorted his feelings out, he went down stairs and spoke to the landlady. She told him she had had a letter from Bill also, saying he had joined the Army and was not coming back. She asked Sam to check Bill's room and take anything out that he may have left behind as she had a girl from the other side of London who had got a job locally and urgently needed a room.

For the next few days there was a cloud hanging over the factory, Bill had been a very popular member of staff. By the end of the week things seemed to be getting back to normal, except for Alice who looked red eyed and hardly spoke to anyone. She spoke to Sam on his arrival at work to ask if he had heard from Bill since he left, but he told her he had not. As time wore on, she asked him less, even though he had now started to receive letters from Bill, but he never told anyone as he had asked him not to. The Frosts assumed that Bill had decided to break off all contact with everyone and the Landlady never asked any questions, she now had a new occupant in Bill's room.

***

In the early morning sunshine stood a number of aircrafts on the apron outside the Royal Aircraft Factory at Farnborough. They were all awaiting evaluation for consideration as potential RFC aircraft. Algernon had been detailed to test one of these aircraft and he was well aware of the dangers of these machines. The RFC were desperate for new fast aircraft and would test anything that could be flown into Farnborough. The aircraft Algernon had to test was made by a company he had ever heard of; Lloyd Scout Mk Inc. He had a good look round the aircraft, got in and tested all the simple controls got out and had another look round, then got back in again getting the ground crew to start her. She started after the third go, and seemed to run all right. He had certain misgivings about this aircraft, he could not put his finger on what it was, but the misgivings would not go away.

He waved the chocks away and taxied out to the threshold of the airfield, lining himself up into the wind for take-off. When he was given the, *"All Clear,"* he opened the throttle and started to move forward, bumping over the grass runway. He gave himself a good long run before pulling gently on the control column and the aircraft left the ground, in a gentle climb. It was when he passed over the airfield boundary at about 50 feet he realised things were far from right. There was very poor control and the engine started to run rough. This was a plane that should have never left the drawing board, let alone the ground. As soon as the engine started to smoke he switched it off, luckily the smoking stopped. The aircraft was now a glider, and a poor glider at that. Algernon was now heading for the ground at a descent too fast for his liking.

In front of him was a small field that looked fairly flat but a railway line was ominously near, he felt he could just about avoid that, he did not have any choice of going anywhere else. At the far end of the field was a hedge and what Algernon did not see on the other side of it was a twenty-foot drop into a narrow country lane. He tried to level out to make a forced landing in the field, but with lack of height he was in trouble. He slowed the descent by a small margin, which helped, and just keeping the nose up at the last minute and instead of doing a nose dive into the ground, pancaked onto the flat field with considerable force, the undercarriage too weak to take the impact, collapsed. If the field had been longer he would have been OK, but it wasn't, the slithering aircraft ploughed through the hedge at the end and as it descended the embankment, flipped over landing across the lane, the plane upside down making a form of bridge, the engine and tail supported by the two banks of the lane, a very sad and sorry state it looked, never to fly again.

With the sudden de-acceleration and impact of the aircraft, Algernon's straps broke and he was thrown to the ground, landing heavily in a heap in the middle of the lane, luckily not hitting any part of the aircraft as he made his unscheduled rapid exit. As he landed, his head hit the ground, and even with his leather flying helmet on, which offered little or no protection to him, he was knocked unconscious. What Algernon obviously did not know was that the leaking petrol from the punctured fuel tank did not go anywhere near the hot engine, and luckily there was no fire as so often happened. Had the plane turned over on flat ground, the pilot would have most possibility crushed and killed under the body of the fuselage. He was lucky for the path he landed in.

When Algernon opened his eyes, and regained conscious he looked up, he saw through the mist what looked like white clouds, was he still flying, he thought! As things came into focus, he heard voices, smelt disinfectant, eau-de-nil coloured walls were on all sides, sunshine streaming through an open window, and it was then he realised he was lying in a bed, aching all over with a thumping headache. The white clouds turned out to be a staff nurses in her stiff white starched uniform, blazoned with a small red cross placed centrally on her chest, who was bending over him and holding his hand. He realised he was in hospital.

"Hello, good to see you back in the land of the living, Sir," said the pretty young nurse, sitting down beside him. "I'm afraid you have had a crash in your aircraft, but nothing is broken which is the good news!"

Looking at the nurse and getting his eyes into focus he felt he had to say something, "Thanks," he murmured.

"How do you feel, Sir?" she asked. "I ache all over, like being put through a mangle, and my head feels as if doesn't belong to me!" he replied. The nurse continued and told him his wife would be visiting him later that day. When he was up and about, and that should not be too long, he would be getting a few days sick leave, before going back to flying again.

He felt he had lost time somewhere and asked his nurse how long he had been unconscious and where he was. "Not long, I was told you crashed just after 8 o'clock this morning, and lunch is about to be served, and you are in the Royal Military Hospital in Aldershot. Now would you like something light to eat, how about a little soup?"

Keturah arrived soon after lunch had been cleared away and was very concerned about her beloved husband, telling him all the children sent their love and looked forwarded to seeing him when he came home.

Algernon was very fit and soon recovered from his injuries, being discharged two days after the accident. A RFC car arrived to take him to their London home. He was given a week of sick leave, and told to report back to Farnborough after his local doctor had given him the all clear. When he returned to Farnborough, he was seen by a service doctor there, who considered that he was fit again to fly, far from the aircraft he had crashed in! While he was on leave he made a report about the aircraft he crashed in, saying basically it was a death trap and should be rejected. On his return, his report had been implemented and the firm of Lloyd Aircrafts was struck off the list of potential suppliers and were told it was their responsibility to remove the wreckage from the crash site. It was a great relief to Algernon and all the other test pilots that a Lloyd aircraft would not appear on their test list again.

But his accident had given him food for thought. While no parachute would have saved him in this incident, he had been far too low for one to be any use, but if he had been high enough, he could have jumped and floated down safely to earth, otherwise he most probably would have been killed without the aid of such a device.

The current War Department policy was that pilots of the RFC and the RNAS were not allowed this life saving piece of equipment, they had to stay with the plane under all cost; keep a British stiffer upper lip and all that! But it was different for the spotters in observation balloons, they were issued with a chute and wore them all the time while they were aloft, and on many occasions saved lives when the enemy had shot their balloon down from above them. The thinking behind this was that balloon observers had no other option while pilots may take the easy way out and jump when they were in any danger of being attacked. It did not bother the high command, sitting in their comfortable arm chairs behind their desks in Whitehall, safely away from the action, hundreds of miles behind the front lines and 21 miles of the English Channel between them, not even considering that pilots and aircrafts were both very fragile and could easily be destroyed under enemy fire. There were plenty more pilots and planes where they came from, they only appeared as statistics on the overall casualty board. The writing was on the wall for pilots under these conditions, he could stay in his aircraft and crash and burn to death on the ground, or jump out to a quick death, or, as some did, carry a revolver and shoot himself. New pilots were often known as '20-miniters' as this was the average time a new trained pilot lasted on their first patrol after on a few hours' training before joining a front-line squadron.

Pilots often teased their girlfriends about jumping out of aircraft, saying they slip down the beams of the search lights to safety!

Algernon could not wait to get back into the air and was soon testing aircrafts again, but he was making a much closer inspection before flying, doing taxiing trials and mini hops before he felt safe to take to the air, he had learnt his lesson the hard way! He did not have any further mishaps while at Farnborough, but he did reject a number of aircrafts before he took them into the air, once bitten, twice shy! Also, he now had a parachute that was a part of the seat of the aircraft, which those at Farnborough, while they could not officially say anything, were in agreement with him. He had approached the company he purchased the chutes from and got them to teach him and Keturah to pack them; Keturah seemed to be a better packer then him, a lady's touch! Both did a drop each from a tethered balloon at 1,000 feet, which while Algernon was a bit apprehensive, Keturah seemed to have no fear and relished the experience and badgered them to let her have a second drop while Algernon watched safely from the ground. Flying was one thing, dropping by parachute was another! They both flew with parachutes while they owned the light biplanes that were common at the time, neither would ever fly without one.

He had not returned to Farnborough very long when he was given two pieces of news. First, he was to go to France and join No: 5 Squadron flying B.E.2C, a two-seater reconnaissance aircraft which he had flown many times at Farnborough and was a product of the Royal Aircraft Factory, and the Avro 504, an unarmed single seat plane, unlike the B.E.2C which now carried a Lewis machine gun. The other news was he was promoted to the rank of Captain and would command C Flight, reporting directly to the Squadron Commander, a Major Brown. He was replacing the previous Flight Commander who had been lost over enemy lines recently.

The Germans hardly ever flew across the British line while the British were always fighting on the German side, this was the pattern for the duration of the war. Any shot down German aircrafts, if they landed safely, were safe amongst their own people, while the British aircrew who were downed and landed safely either made it back across the German and English front to return to their unit or were taken prisoner for the duration of the war. The latter was the most likely scenario.

It would be a wrench for Algernon to leave his family, but it was to be expected. He had 7 days leave to get all his affairs in order and then he would travel by train to Folkestone and be taken by boat to Boulogne. On arrival, there he would take a train to Ypres, the nearest railhead to where his squadron was stationed. The squadron was based in a tented makeshift airfield, 10 miles behind the front line in the vicinity of the town Ypres, a few miles north west of the town. The NCOs and other ranks slept in tents on the airfield, near the canvas hangars, with their own messing facilities, while the officers had taken over a deserted château situated in the local area that had became their mess, being about 2 miles west of the airfield, the original occupants having long fled because of the German shelling.

The evening before Algernon left, his father had a family gathering and they all dined together in the great hall in the mansion, a final gesture to send Algernon on his way. The following morning there were tears from Keturah and the children. With a final wave, he was driven away down the drive to catch a train from Reading, making eventually for Folkestone Harbour.

***

Bill's section passed out, and because fighting men that were now urgently needed at the front, there was no leave allowed before they departed. Within a few days they marched out of Victoria Barracks through the streets of the town to Aldershot station, where a special troop train, made up of old 3rd Class carriages, was awaiting in a bay platform to take them to the same station that Algernon was traveling to. There were crowds of well-wishers there to see them off, like it had been just over six weeks earlier at Waterloo, but more so, euphoria for the troops leaving, with heavy hearts and some tears for those left behind at home to worry. How many troops on board the train had only booked one way tickets?

***

In another train, Algernon was travelling 1st Class to the same destination. Both trains arrived within an hour of each other, in the pouring rain. The soldiers were marched from the train wearing their waterproof capes that gave them some protection in the pouring rain, down to where the boat to take them across the channel was due to dock, but the quay from which they would embark was empty, so they had to stay there until the boat arrived. When the boat eventually docked two and a half hours later, they were cold and wet from the rain, eating the damp packed rations they had been given before they left Aldershot. Algernon meanwhile, on arrival, was taken to a waiting room and restaurant that had been converted into an Officers Mess for the duration of the war, which was heated and where he was served with a hot meal and alcohol beverages if needed!

The soldiers were boarded first, in the 3rd class deck, first on got to get under cover, while the remainder were out in the open, to all the English Channel elements. Not so good if it was a rough crossing, on a boat built in

99

1885, old, rusty and creaking, which had been requisitioned for trooping for the duration of the war, only if it did not sink from enemy action or old age, which ever came first, and by the look of it the latter! All NCOs were under cover in one of the 2nd class saloon, while the JNCOs were in the other. Half an hour before the boat was due to leave all officers embarked, being taken to the 1st Class Saloon and dining area, where on the crossing they were served another meal of their choice and more strong liquor if required.

The channel was not without its dangers and perils, as the Germans also had their shipping patrolling up and down, mainly in the form of their "U" boats and submarines, inflicting damage on slow and unescorted boats. The ferries that did not have mounted guns were chaperoned by Royal Navy destroyers or frigates, whatever was available at the time.

***

After Algernon had left, Keturah had to return to their London home with the children; there was still school for them to attend. Her own staff would take the children back by train while she would fly back to Brooklands and then drive to Notting Hill. On the flight back to London, she began to think of the future without Algernon. She had no intention of sitting around until the war was over and Algernon returned to her, she never contemplated him being killed. But there was war work to be done, and with the shortage of men, there were a lot of vacancies, and it was obvious as there were not enough men around to fill them, women would now have to take their places. She started to look to what she could do, it had to be practical, no sitting at home knitting or making clothing, she still considered herself young, only 36, fit, well and strong, so no soft job for her. It suddenly came to her, her first born, William, was now old enough to fight, she wondered where he was and what he was doing, she would love to know. She started to wonder how she could find out, and what about Sam, he must be working, but too young to join-up.

On her arrival back at Notting Hill, she found that the children had not yet arrived so she decided to take their car to Paddington to see why they had not returned and if there was any problem, only to find the train was running late, because of war traffic, but would be there in about half an hour. She looked around the station, which was thronged with men in army khaki or naval blue in the large public circulating area at the head of all the platforms, to accommodate arriving and departing passengers, constructed in the early 1880's, known as the *Lawn*. When the land was purchased for the site of the station in the middle of the 18th century, the area where the *Lawn* now is, formally included six cottages with their gardens and lawns, where the name originated.

Keturah saw two large canteens parked more or less in the middle of the *Lawn*, each thronged by service personnel taking refreshment. The two canteens, different from the each other in design, one being static, the other semi-mobile. The latter was mounted on road wheels and in its previous life had been use at fair grounds and country fairs as a mobile snack bar with a towing bar and hook at one end (that had replaced two horse shafts in the recent past,) allowing it to be towed to other location as required by a lorry, while the other would require to be mounted on a trailer to be moved. Keturah, when she first saw them, wondered where they had come from; requisitioned or commandeered she surmised. The one on wheels was a bright shade of green, with a different colour of green used to paint out the original owner's sign, while the other was in a drab shade of khaki, similar in colour to the uniforms worn by the ladies manning the canteens. Some of the uniforms were made of coarse serge, ill-fitting and baggy on the staff who wore them, whiles others who could afford it were wearing tailor made barathea uniforms and were of a better quality; them and us! Three things brighten up the surroundings, the bright aprons that the ladies were wearing to protect their uniforms, their cheerful disposition, a smile a chat for every one of their customers, and the Salvation Band playing bright and cheerful tunes on the *Lawn*.

There were two 'A' boards beside each canteen, stating what they were, that read:

> **Refreshments for The Troops**
> **Women's Emergency Corps**

Keturah watched as these ladies handed out tea and sandwiches to the servicemen passing through the station. On enquiring she found out the canteen was open throughout the day and night, operated on a three-shift rota basis by many of these ladies.

While she was waiting for the Oxford train to arrive, she walked around, watching the women go about their work. When a large lorry arrived, painted bright green and with the inscription in bold yellow letters, stating:

> Harry Smith
> High-class baker

The sign had obviously been commandeered by the WEC for the duration of the war. She wondered what had happened to Harry Smith and would he ever get his lorry back after the war, if it, the vehicle, lasted that long? Also in the drab khaki uniform were the crew of two young girls, hardly old enough to drive, both in a buoyant mood. When it pulled up between the two canteens, the rear doors were opened and new supplies were unloaded. When this task had been completed, between a lot of chat, laughing and joking among the other young girls there, the van drove off to go back to their supply depot for more supplies for other stations. When the lorry had left, Keturah went over to speak to one of the ladies from the larger of the two canteens, who was obviously in overall charge, she wore a smart fitting barathea uniforms!

"Can you tell me about your organisation, and do you need any more volunteers?" she asked.

"Well it depends on where your sympathies lie," was her reply. "I'm Lady Patricia Cornish, and may I enquire who you are please?

"I'm Keturah Cavendish, my husband is the Honourable Algernon Cavendish who is serving in the RFC across the channel," she replied.

"If you father-in-Law is Jonathan Cavendish, I know him, our family seat is about an hour's drive away, and now I recall my husband came to your wedding, must have been ten or more years ago".

"It was in 1901, but I'm sorry, I can't remember you, I was new into the family and there were so many guests there."

"Not to worry my dear, nearly 14 years on, time flies, I don't either. Now to get down to business. A lot of us were members of the Women's Social & Political Union, better known as Suffragettes. Within a couple of days of the war starting in August we suspended all our protesting until the hostility is over, we must support our country in its hour of need. The Governments response was to release all our loyal women who had been incarcerated in prison for no good reason, it was the least they could do. All our girls are from all walks of life, we don't hold with positions in society. You would be surprised how a situation brings the best out in people, and potential leaders, class does not come into it. As soon as the war is over, the Suffragettes will be back protesting, with more vigour than before. But for the time being, this is one of the ways we can help, the war effort and our cause. We are now the *Women's Emergency Corps,* known as the WEC, started by Evelina Haverfield and Decima Moore. Are you interested in helping the cause?"

It did not take a few moments for Keturah to decide. "Yes, I would like to help, please tell me how I can join the Corps?" Keturah knew all about the Suffragette movement, and both Algernon and she had great sympathy with them, and on many occasions she was tempted to join, but with young children she had felt that they came first. Now they were getting older, she had more spare time. She would give up visiting and visits for afternoon tea with friends and other social outings she often made, and as the lady said, "We must support our country in its hour of need."

After discussion, it was suggested that she go to the Suffragette HQ, which was now the WEC HQ, in the West End of London, being in the Kensington area, near Hyde Park Corner, just west of Buckingham Palace. She thanked Patricia Cornish and made her way to meet her children, whose train had just arrived.

It was the following day when she got the WEC HQ, finding it to be a large four-storey house with a servant's basement and kitchen, set round the edge of a large square with many similar houses with a garden in the centre for the occupants of the houses to use. There, all the WEC war work was coordinated. At the time they were very busy, and the lady in charge of recruitment was currently indoctrinating six new members. She was asked to report there in a couple of day's time when they would be expecting her, being asked to fill in a form with her address and details of any qualifications she had, so they could find her suitable employment with in the organisation. And that was how Keturah joined the WEC.

At the start, she helped in various ways, using her car to ferry people around London, driving any of their delivery lorries, visiting the all the various terminal stations in the capital, and, when needed, even ambulances in time off air raids which she was told they must expect if the war lasts for years. Being a competent pilot and owning one's own aeroplane, she was often in demand to fly people around in about 100 miles of Brooklands. She had no worries about the children, they were all at school during the day, and had staff to look after them when they came home. She now wore the smart barathea uniforms of the *Women's Emergency Corps*, sometimes covering with her flying clothing.

***

The boat eventually left and headed out into a channel storm. The crossing took over an hour; the enemy was not the Germans, not to be seen on this occasion, but the gale force wind and the strong tide flowing up to the North Sea. While Algernon was comfortable and dry, the soldiers were now cold, wet, tired, hungry and fed up! From leaving Aldershot, Bill kept his section close to him, like a shepherd looking after his flock. On the quay he found them shelter, on the boat he did not go to the 2nd class saloon with the other JNCOs, but stayed with his men and found cover for them near the boiler room, where they were warm and dry. In addition, he had wangled some extra rations for all his section before they left Aldershot so they did not go hungry either like most of the rest. When the boat eventually docked in Calais, Bill's squad were in the best condition of all the soldiers who landed.

Waiting on the quay side in the French port was another troop train, but this one had all classes. It was to take them as near to Ypres, as fast as possible, depending if the Germans hadn't shelled the lines en route. The train, once loaded with men and mail for the front, left the port, soon crossing the border from France to Belgium, arriving at Ypres, still in the rain. At their destination, Algernon was taken by an RFC vehicle, whatever was available, while the Troops were marched to a holding camp, a few miles behind the British lines. There they would stay for a few days for briefing and local training. For the troops it was tented accommodation, which was luxury compared with what they would be living in in just over a week, a waterlogged, muddy trench within yards of the German trenches.

Algernon had to accept that his transport was a lorry, the cab and back were both open to the elements, the best that was available apparently, or so his driver told him. He also said that the only car had taken a direct hit by a shell a couple of days ago, killing the driver and two pilots who were traveling from the airfield back to the mess. As the driver informed him, one of the pilots who had been killed was a member of C Flight. So, it seemed he was already short of one pilot before he started and made a mental note to speak to the CO at the earliest opportunity, to ascertain what the situation was on a replacement pilot.

The lorry soon arrived at the château and his only bag was unloaded, the lorry departed for the airfield to pick up the pilots after a day's flying. He was taken in to the main hall by a mess steward, Private Bayliss, who he soon found out, was his personal batman. Also in the hall was a young 2nd Lieutenant, who had been detailed to meet the new member of the squadron. As Algernon entered the young office approached him, limping and using a stick in his left hand, offering his fight to his new Flight Commander.

"Welcome to 5 Squadron Mess Sir, I'm James Oliver," he announced, shaking hands. "I am a member of your flight. At present, I'm afraid I'm grounded with a minor leg wound I got last week, rifle fire from the ground, but the doc said I will be OK to fly in another week. The rest of the squadron are still at the airfield. While it's a bit wet, they have been flying, doing some spotting over enemy lines, getting info for the top brass at HQ. They won't be long now, light is fading, and dinner is sharp at 1900 hours."

Algernon groaned inwardly, another pilot lost, even though he would be back, he hoped, in a week. "Tell me Mr Oliver, how many serviceable planes does C Flight have, and how many operationally fit pilots?"

"Well Sir, I haven't been to the airfield today, but when the lads came in last night, our flight consisted of 4 pilots, including me, and six planes, two B.E.2Cs and four 504s, all serviceable, what the score will be tonight, we will have to wait and see Sir".

Algernon was taken to his quarters by Private Bayliss, up two flights of stairs to a small and sparse room in the eaves of the roof with a dormer window. The floor was bare boards with a small rug by the bed; the furniture was very basic, a bed, a small wardrobe with shelves and a wash basin on a tripod stand. The window looked out on the front of the house, over the extensive ground, once as good as the gardens back home in Oxfordshire, but these had been left for over a year and now nature had taken over, wilderness was the order of the day. While the rain had stopped, the drive was a sea of mud. He then saw a car and a lorry coming up the drive, fully loaded with young officers, the pilots and returned form a day's flying.

Algernon made his way back down stairs to arrive in the main hall at the same time as the occupants of the car and lorry, led by Major Brown. The Major seeing Algernon immediately came up to him and introduced himself. "I'm James Brown, you must be Algernon Cavendish, pleased to meet you, welcome to 5 Squadron, I expect you are tired from your journey, when did you leave Blighty and what was your journey like?"

"I left yesterday morning sir, staying in London last night, and travelled most of today. It was a bit tiring, the crossing, while wet it was not too lumpy, just the drive from the train was about the worst part, but flying in our planes one gets just as wet, even more so, as I have experienced."

"Did you get any leave before you came over?"

"Yes, my parents live just outside Reading, I spent a few days there, as I said I stayed in London at our town house for my last night."

While the Major was at least 15 years his junior, there was an immediate rapport between the two men. "Come and have a chat in my room," was the invitation to him. The Major's had two adjoining rooms; one was his office in the Mess while the other was his personal quarters. The first thing he did on entering his office was to take from his desk a half full bottle of whisky and two glasses and offer Algernon a drink. "To 5 Squadron, and may you have many safe flying hours and landings with us," was the Major's toast.

The Major continued, "Now, to get down to business, and I won't beat about the bush. Your predecessor, I'm afraid was not a good pilot, he should have never flown, but we are short of pilots, as you may realise, and because of some string pulling he was made a Captain and assigned to me as a Flight Commander, he lasted less than two weeks. Whoever did that signed his death warrant. Any rate, that is by the by. You are now here and from what I hear you are a capable pilot. Tomorrow, if it's quiet on the front I will take you up and we will have a stooge around together. If you feel happy, then you can take over the C Flight and you will then be operational. Sorry, but that is all the time I can give you. We will go up at first light as we don't do much an hour after sun up normally, nor do the Hun!"

After their chat, they joined the rest of the squadron in the anteroom for drinks before going into dinner. He found out from Major Brown that his flight still had four pilots and six planes, all serviceable. Besides Oliver, he had three other Second Lieutenants: Adams, Halsey and Warren. After dinner, he took all his pilots to one side in the anteroom to get to know them and find out what they were all like. Oliver was the most senior, he had been with the squadron three months, the others between two to six weeks. It was obvious that there was a fairly high turnover of pilots. He wondered to himself, *was the enemy better than us*, aircraft or pilot wise, and *how did our aircraft and pilots compare with the Germans?* He would soon find out when they flew tomorrow for the first time.

***

At the holding camp, Bill and his squad were billeted in two bell tents, and as accommodation went, it was not bad. There was a washing area and a mess, where the grub was not too bad either, good army stodge! They found out later that this camp is where they would come for short rests away from the ravages of battle from time to time and when enemy action allowed. To have a good wash, clean up, and repair or exchange items of clothing, if any were available. The Officers and SNCOs came round, keeping an eye on everyone, but they were not to be seen after the evening meal. The SNCOs had their own tented area about mile away, while the Offices were billeted on the outskirts of Ypres, where the town offered some sort of night life!

***

After Bill had left, Sam was at a bit at a loose end, without Bill's company in the evening he had to look for something to do. While he got on well with the Frosts, and they considered him one of the family, he was not all that close, Alice was only interested in Bill, and Bert and Agnes were not his generation, and Fred was 14 years older than he was, so he felt a bit on the lonely side. But it was by accident that he did make a new friend. Now Sam was earning good money and he decided he should improve his wardrobe, and purchase some new clothes, a suit would be a good starting point, a good one, but not too expensive. He would have to look round for a tailor to make one, but it would have to be in the local area. In the next few evenings, after work, he looked around and eventually found a small shop in a side street off Shepherd's Bush, going under the name of:

Eighteen's, Bespoke Tailors

In the single fronted shop window were bolts of cloth, and a couple of suits displayed on stands, with a notice that all suits were made to measure, and their prices were the best value for money in the area. The following day he told Bert that wanted to buy a suit and as he had been working a lot of over time, could he have a couple of hours off when the shops was open, promising to make up the time in the evening if required. Bert was only too pleased to help Sam out, he had never asked time off before, and he thought Sam deserved some new clothes if he could afford them.

One lunch time Sam cut short his lunch break and told Bert he was off to the tailors and hoped to be back in about an hour's time. Bert had complete trust in Sam and was happy for him to be back a little late.

He made his way straight to the shop, pushing the door open, which was accompanied by the ringing of a bell attached to the top of the door. There was no counter, but a large flat cutting table centrally on the shop floor, covered in green baize. There were shelves on the two side walls that contained bolts of cloth while in the rear wall there was a door that lead to a room behind the back of the shop, and, he found out later, stairs to the living accommodation. The rest of this wall was taken up with shelves that carried work in hand and the tools of a tailor. On entering, two men were bending over the cutting table, cutting out cloth against a pinned-on pattern.

They looked up as Sam entered; the older man was wearing a pair of pince-nez glasses and had a short goatee beard, while the younger man was clean shaven but wore more modern glasses, both wearing traditional Yarmulkes. The older man smiled and introduced himself, "Hello, I'm Isaac Eighteen and this is my son Joseph, how can we help you sir?" This was the start of a new friendship between the three of them.

The older man Sam reckoned was about sixty, the father, while the other, the son, must have been in his late twenties. It made Sam wondered why he had not been called up, as he looked as if he should have been, but he soon realised when they both came round the table to greet him, Joseph, walked with a limp, and out of the corner of his eye, Sam could see, one leg was shorter that the other, the younger man was wearing a built-up boot on his left foot.

"I would like a suit made, can you tell me how long it will take and how much will it cost?" was Sam's reply.

"My boy, you have come to the right place, let us measure you up, tell us what type of suit you require and what you want it for? We will show you various cloths and various prices, and then you can choose what you would like, but please, may I have your name".

"It's Samuel Bray, Mr Eighteen," he told them.

"Thank you, Mr Bray, now let us get to work." While Isaac did the measuring, Joseph took down all the details. Sam was surprised that he had to be so many measurements and was all these measurements necessary to make a suit, some measurements he did not know ever existed, but everyone to his trade. When the measuring was completed, they started to display their cloths. Again, Sam did not realise that there were so many patterns and styles of suits, morning, afternoon, evening, and holy days, summer, spring and autumn and finally winter, to name a few. He told them he wanted a suit that would serve most occasions and let the Eighteens advise him of the style and material. He was advised wool was the best material and hard wearing, so Sam agreed, and after about 10 minutes a pattern and material was selected.

After they had come to an agreement they arranged a first fitting at the same time the following week. Sam's idea of buying a made to measure suit was nothing like what he envisaged, only having ever purchased second hand clothes after he had left the orphanage, and later when he had a bit more money, new *off the peg*.

As they chatted about the suit, Sam leant on the cutting table, which wobbled alarmingly, and both the Eighteens, asked him not to lean on it, as it needed repair, but they just never got round to it, and they did not know any good carpenter who would do that type of work, there were too many cheats around, all trying to make a fast pound, with shoddy work in return.

Sam then told Isaac and Joseph that his profession was a carpenter, and would be glad to look at the table and give his assessment of what was needed. They were well pleased and Sam suggested that he came to see them after work the following day if that was convenient, which was agreed by both the Eighteens. They told him if the shop was closed, to come round to the back door.

When Sam packed up work the next day, after making up the time lost from the previous day, he decided to have a chat to Bert about doing work in his own time. Bert was happy about this, and he could have any scrap wood free, but if he wanted anything new, he could have it at cost, which was much cheaper than going to a timber yard. As Bert purchased so much wood in bulk and paid on time, he could get the best prices, which no one else could, so Sam had a good deal.

On arrival at the shop, as expected, he found it was *Closed*. He went round to the back door and his knocking was soon answered by Joseph, who said his father was just coming, as he was upstairs. When Isaac arrived, Sam gave the cutting table a professional examination. It was bad news for the Eighteens, the table was old, it had been neglected over the years, it could have been saved it had been attended to earlier, but all the joints were worn and loose, and the more the table moved, the worse it was on the joints, there was nothing to save the joints or the table, in Sam's opinion, it did not have much life left! They told Sam they had got an estimate for the repair, but it was far more that they could afford, so they soldiered on with what they had. Sam did not tell the Eighteens, but was sure that who had ever given them this was either a shark or was a bad carpenter.

Sam examined the table thoroughly; it was clapped out, only worth fire wood. He explained the situation that it was not worth repairing, but was willing to make a new one, which they could design together, and the wood would be at cost, plus his time. The old table was just a basic frame, four legs, a top, and bracing strips. Sam suggested that the new table should incorporate shelves and drawers, where they could store the tools of their trade underneath, which would then free up much needed space on the shelves at the rear of the shop where the tools were currently stored. They were pleased with this suggestion and agreed to the new design as suggested by Sam. He gave them a price which was far less than the repair price they had been quoted, so a deal was struck. It would take about two weeks to make the table, which included doing drawings, which he would like them to approve before he started any construction. They were only too happy with this and even said they would pay up front, which Sam declined, pay only on delivery and only if they were happy with the result. What Sam did not say was that Bert had said that he could pay him for the wood, once he had been paid by his client. Bert never asked him what he was making or who it was for, which was a good thing, as he was to find out later.

After all the discussion was over they invited him into to come up stairs to meet Marie, Isaac's wife, who like her husband and son, was a rotund, cheerful soul. He spent a pleasant evening with them, telling them about his background and of his friend Bill who had recently joined the army and was now in France fighting somewhere.

He made all the drawings in the evenings in his flat, he wanted to keep as much of this work to himself. When the drawings were completed, he was down to see the Eighteens for their approval, which was soon given, the table being slightly larger than the present one and they would have no problem fitting in. They did not tell Sam, while they understood tailoring, construction drawing was beyond them. They did understand the three-dimensional drawing of the table, which satisfied them.

They had become good friends, and they told Sam to come down whenever he wanted, not to stay in his flat on his own. When asked he had explained that he had no friends of his own age, so would be happy to visit them, but to himself, he thought he must not outstay his welcome.

As soon as he got approval, he started work on the table after everyone had ceased work. After his evening meal with the Frosts, he went back down to the workshop and worked on the table. Alice, while still missing Bill, would often pop down to the workshop and see Sam at work and would bring a mug of tea and have a chat. Even giving Sam a helping hand if needed.

Sam had decided to make everything in kit form, and as each piece was completed, he would take it back to his flat and store it there as long as there was room for him to sleep. He agreed with the Eighteens, when he had a number of parts, and his flat was getting overcrowded, he could bring them down for storage in the yard behind the shop. In all the table took ten days to make, and when finished, the final parts were taken to the shop ready for assembly.

As the Eighteens had a business to run, they required a table all the time they were open, and if busy, which they were, in the evenings also. It was agreed that the following Sunday would be the changeover day. Sam asked if it was all right to arrive at 8am, and assembly would be completed by about 4pm, which was his estimate on doing all the work himself. He was told not to bring his lunch, as Marie would be only too happy to feed him.

Prompt at 8am, Sam was there with the final parts. It only took a few blows to demolish the old table, and dump the remains in the yard for firewood. Sam had numbered each part, and with the help of Isaac and Joseph, even Marie was there, she was not going to miss anything, they brought the parts through as Sam called out the numbers he required. They were also a great help in holding parts together before they were permanently fixed. They were so helpful that the table was completed before lunch, and stood firm where the previous one had stood for over 25 years. The final part of the table was done by Marie herself, and with the *men* out of the way, she was to cover the smooth bare wooden surface with a new piece of green baize cloth she had purchased as soon as the drawings had been agreed. When Marie had finished, they had a rearrangement in the shop, their tailoring tools from the shelves were put into the new drawers under the table that then released space for more cloth to be put on display on the empty shelves where the tools had been kept. The table was ready for use, and they were all sure it would last much longer than the last one!

Isaac, Marie and Joseph were very happy with the result, and Sam was very embarrassed when Isaac added a five percent bonus on the original price, and try as he might, Sam could not get them to change their minds. With this extra, it was still much cheaper than they could have got anywhere else, and they considered it a first-class job. Sam's pleading made no difference, he was paid, and the Eighteens were very happy. Bert would be happy on Monday, when Sam paid him, and he would pass on half of his bonus to him, for all the help he that had given and for not asking questions!

While Sam now had his suit, which was less than the original price they had quoted, they told him the material they used was cheap as it was the end of the line. This happened to be untrue, which Sam never found out, what they did was to let him have the cloth at cost, and did not add the total labour costs to the final bill. To them having a table that was rock solid and was not likely to collapse was worth not making any profit on Sam's suit! In fact, with a larger table, Isaac and Joseph now could both work on the table on different orders, without getting in each other's way, and their output increased.

From the ordering of a suit, to Sam leaning on a wobbly tailor's table and making a replacement, a new friendship had been struck up between Sam and the Eighteens. Joseph was nearer Sam's age than Fred Frost and the two of them found they had a lot in common. Sam and Joseph soon became close friends, and in their spare time would often go out together. As Joseph found walking tiring, they would take rides on the electric trams to different parts of London, or a bus to the West End, and take leisurely walks at Joseph's speed in the various London parks.

CHAPTER 6

The Front at Ypres

On the first day in Belgium, as dawn was breaking, Bill and his Squad were up, had a hasty breakfast and paraded ready for inspection and to start learning about fighting on the front, and what was expected of them. They never stopped all day until their evening meal, except for half an hour break for lunch. It was like that for the rest of the week. They repeated everything they had done at Recruit Training, but crammed into a few days, and much more intense. Digging trenches, simulating *going over the top*, cooking meals in the open, at times in the pouring rain, and getting used to being wet 24 hours a day and up to one's knees in cold mud and water. The worst part, as most agreed with Bill, when he expressed his opinion, was sleeping on a ledge, dug out of the side of the trench, fully clothed, including a heavy coat, and covered only by a ground sheet. After two or three nights like that, most of them got used to it and could sleep on and off, even during the day, when they were given an hour or two stand-down. The final detail they were given was a night exercise. They were split up into pairs and were given a map, with five points marked on it, a compass and a torch; they had to navigate from point to point in order, as quickly as possible, each point manned by an NCO, noting the time of their arrival. Bill had a good sense of direction and completed the course in under average time, but no thanks to his partner, who could get himself lost in an orange box, blundering and crashing around in the undergrowth! His result was duly noted by those in authority, as was his partner, and was told that he could be in line for his second stripe if continued to perform as he had done on the exercise. Bill wondered what they said about his mate, but he never heard, he was thankful he wasn't one of his squad at training, and was pleased he did not see him again. He was pleased with himself that he had completed all the tasks with little or no discomfort; Aldershot had prepared him well!

***

On Algernon's first day, he and the Major were up before dawn, but no breakfast for them. Transport took them to the airfield where the Major's

Avro 504 was ready for take-off, the engine running and getting warmed up, having been started when the ground crew saw their car headlights approaching in the distance. The engine would be nice and warm by the time they arrived, allowing for immediate take-off. The Major had chosen the 504 as its maximum speed was 95 mph, against the BE2C's of 72 mph, He suggested to Algernon that he make the 504 his personal aircraft, while if he had the BE, he may not always keep up with the 504s, plus the fact, as an experienced pilot, he could act as a *Shepherd* for the rest of the *Flock* with his superior speed and flying skills.

The Major sat in the front cockpit, Algernon in the back, only a bench type seat and with no safety straps, an anchoring wire from a shackle on the floor to a hook on a belt round his waist. His contact with the pilot was via a Gosport speaking tube, through which the CO gave Algernon a running commentary of everything they saw and what the Major considered were important landmarks and danger areas to be watched carefully. A weak sun started appearing over the German lines when they took off, Brown climbing over home territory as quickly as he could. The 504 could climb to 6,500 feet in 25 minutes, so that they would have height in their favour and to their advantage. If they saw trouble approaching, they could dive for home, nothing would catch them then. After half an hour over German lines things started to move on a Hun airfields that they passed over; they both saw aircrafts taking off. Brown put the nose of the aircraft down and made a hasty retreat for base, heading west, and going down to tree top level. As the Major had said before they left, employing this tactic, no one would catch them, including the flak guns, they could fight another day! By the time the Germans in the trenches had woken up, they would be long gone.

They were back at the airfield without any problems. Once on the ground, they handed over the aircraft to the ground crew for checking for the next flight, then they breakfasted in the small Officers Mess tent on the airfield, awaiting the rest of the aircrew to arrive.

When they had finished eating the Major spoke about the forthcoming flight. "Now, whenever I fly, depending on the circumstances, I usually fly with one of the flights, not leading the squadron. So today I will fly with you as one of your flight, but you will be leader, if you get into any trouble I will be there to help you out, is that OK with you Algernon?" He agreed, he was happy with that. The Major continued, "The Army want us to have a look at a railway junction and sidings, and drop a few bombs on it and take a few photographs if there is anything worth taking. The BEs, we have six in total, there are two in your flight and they will carry a full complement of bombs, including three in the other two flights. The remaining BE will only have a camera, and be faster, and bringing up in the rear. The 504's are there for protection and while initially flying in formation, once battle commences they will go where they are needed. When the BEs have dropped their bombs, they will be a bit quicker, but we will have to stay with them. I have planned the route that will keep us away from all the Hun's airfields and as much flak as possible, we will fly low there and back except when we carry out the bombing raid. We are not penetrating deep into enemy territory so we will be in and back in no time at all. The target is about 25 miles over their lines. The BE with the camera onboard will be taking photos of the damage we hope to have cause, and on landing the exposed plates will be removed from the cameras and immediately taken away for processing in the mobile darkroom on camp, once processed, they will be taken by despatch rider back to the Brigade HQ. As soon as the photos have been analysed the *power to be* will decide what to do next, more bombing by us or if we have done a good job I expect the big guns to start shelling the place, just when the enemy start to clear up after what we have inflicted on the railway with our bombing, serves them right."

By the time he had finished the aircrew had arrived, having had their breakfast in the comfort at the château. After the Major had briefed all his pilots, they made their way to their respective aircraft. The air was soon filled with the noise of twelve planes preparing for take-off for the first day's sortie. The BEs took off first and got into formation, soon to be followed by the faster 504's who gather round them like a chicken with her chicks!

***

Bill's squad completed their weeks training, and were told to prepare themselves to go up to the front to relieve one of the squads due for a rest after breakfast the following day. Having eaten their final meal in the camp, they were marched with two other squads, who had been on rest, by a sergeant who had come from another part of the front line. The weather, while not raining, was cold and windy, which was a plus as it helped to dry out the mud that was everywhere. Bill had never seen anything so desolate in all his life as the shattered town of Ypres. The town had taken a battering, there was only a few inhabitable buildings left, the star shaped citadel was the only landmark recognisable. All the ditches and dykes had been long clogged by the shelling, and with all the rain that seemed to come down every day, everywhere was flooded, and all traffic was sinking into filthy slimy muddy water that oozed everywhere.

As they got nearer to the front, things did not get any better. There was nothing green to be seen anywhere, all the ground was either mud, water filled shell holes or scorched earth. What buildings that had been were shells of their former existence. The only vegetation to be seen was blackened tree stumps, looking like a mouth with a few rotten teeth. Scatted everywhere were the remains of shells and other missiles that the Germans had fired onto and behind the British lines, the shattered remains of large cannons could be seen abandoned where they met their demise.

It took about two hours for them to march to the front-line trenches passing causalities being stretchered back to a field hospital; dead horses were left to rot beside the roads.

When they arrived, it was quiet, there was a lull in the war. Bill viewed the landscape, or what there was of it; it was devoid of life, and the training area they had been in for the last week was paradise compared with what he could now see. What he saw was bare earth everywhere, tree stumps, potholes made from shells filled with water and trenches that disappeared in both directions along the front, farther than the eye could see. The trenches, their total length Bill had been told was in the region of 460 miles, starting in France at the Swiss French border going north into the high grounds of the Vosges on through the wide expanses of Champagne and the Somme areas passing Ypres, where The Berks & Hants Light Infantry were encamped, and finally ending up in the industrial heartland of the Artois on the coast of the English Channel. Bill had seen better trenches and ditches in a farmer's field and at road works; a building site had more character than this barren landscape. This was the battlefield of Ypres. The only recent construction were narrow gauge railways that supplied the front and returned with the wounded. This form of transport, provided it was maintained and laid on what firm ground could be found, did not sink or get stuck in the quagmire of mud to be found everywhere when the skies rained forth. It was also easy to repair or move the track to other locations as needed.

During the day, the German guns opened up to pound the trenches, it was either in preparation for an attack or a variation of their strategy, a bit of a bluff just to keep the British guessing. On the other hand, they could either have been given the wrong coordinates as their target or their aim was just inaccurate, which was often the case! At night the tactics were different, the heavies opened up, and, with their 6-mile range, they could reach well to the rear of the front line, and if their aim was good they would hope to obliterate the British big guns, ammunition dumps or other vital storage areas. The British operated the same tactics, no wonder it was stalemate!

Bill was one of three squads that made up a half section in charge of a corporal, while a sergeant was in control of two half sections. At the top of the pyramid of the two sections was a junior office in charge of the platoon, usually a Lieutenant or 2nd Lieutenant. In turn, he was answerable to the Captain who had command of a number of platoons.

The length of trench that the two sections covered was no more than two hundred yards, midway between each end was the Control Centre which had been dug into the trench wall, the entrance faced away from the enemy being over six feet below ground level, for protection from what the Germans were sending across. This is where the Platoon Commander, 2nd Lieutenant Hughes, slept with his two SNCOs, Sergeants, Butler and Molineux. The Control Centre was primitive compared with the Command Centre at Staff Headquarters, over ten miles behind the front line, three camp beds, a table, three chairs and a field telephone connected by wire to the Control Centre. Any break in the 'line' caused by shell damage or, as most often happened, by a truck cutting the cable was an urgent repair job for the Royal Engineers Signal Service linesmen. The Control Centre was also used to store ammunition, the only dry place in the trench, but a direct hit from a German shell would be curtains for those in Centre and anyone in close proximity.

Then there were the communication trenches, these had a twofold purpose, to connect each trench system to the ones either side and also lead away from the front line in a zigzag pattern to give protection to personnel entering or leaving the area. Lastly, there was the Improvised Stations, that could be there one day and could be gone the next, depending on the action and damage done to the trenches by enemy fire. The main purpose of the Distribution Area was for the distribution of hot food and drinks when brought in during the lull in the battles, if possible. If the battles were particularly ferocious and lasted all day, or even days, no hot food would get through. If they could light a primitive fire making sure the enemy could not see the glow from the embers, they could cook bully beef from tins and water could be heated for tea, if not, it was cold and only water to drink, and hard tack biscuits. The only other drink they got was a tot of rum if they were going *Over the Top*. Lastly there were the Listen Posts, designated points in the trench system, which would call for silence in the nearby trenches when all was quiet and there was no action on either side, to try and detect what the enemy were about, perhaps digging tunnels underneath them to plant explosives to blow those above to kingdom come! From the trenches, the enemy had to be viewed by looking over the top with a box periscope, a safer way than poking one's head up to only get it shot at.

The corporals and men slept in horizontal ledges dug in the side of the trench wall, the side nearest the German's trenches, covered with their water proof ground sheets, well off the trench floor which was covered in duck boards, and if it did not rain too much, the water level was below the boards, so they were not treading in the oozing sea of mud!

The squad, on their arrival, made their way down to the part of the trench which they had been assigned and would live, sleep, fight and defend and may die, until it was their turn for a rest. The outgoing squad were waiting to go, and within minutes of Bill and his men arriving, they were off. Bill organised a 24-hour shift system of *'Lookouts'*, but once action started, they all came to readiness. It was not long before firing started from the other side, shelling passing overhead, exploding behind them. This was a usual occurrence, two or three times a day, the British doing the same at other times, but no one made any charges, they all stayed well protected in their trench. They did no *"Over the top"* unless they were ordered by the Staff Officers from the Command Centre; it was all holding your own position. It was 10% action, 90% boredom!

When evening came, the German's opened up with shell from the big guns in the rear and small arms fire from the trenches. Behind Bill, the British guns responded, and the platoon was ordered to return fire. After about half an hour of this action tragedy struck, a shell landed at the other end of their trench, exploding killing three and wounding another five solders. The incident was too far away for Bill to know anything about this until later; they continued firing until after about an hour of this action, when the order for cease fire came through. They all stood down, cleaned their rifles through ready for the next onslaught. Word was passed down that a brew would soon be coming along the line with tinned rations and biscuits, many made by Huntley & Palmers of Reading, usually called dog biscuits as they were so hard, it was best to have a drink before trying to eat one! When the rations came along they heard of the tragic incident that happened earlier, they found out this had killed a lance-corporal and two soldiers. The office had sent for replacements immediately, which they hoped would arrive early the next morning. The dead and wounded had been removed as soon as ceasefire had been given. Bill and his squad being new in the trench did not know any who were involved in the incident.

After the meal, they went on *'Stand Down'*, and *'Lookouts'* were posted for the night. They had a quiet night, getting used to sleeping in these primitive conditions. In less than a week they were all sleeping as well as could be expected under these circumstances.

***

The Frosts were coming to terms with Bill joining the Army, but in different ways. Upon reading Bill's letter, Alice was distraught, and no amount of comfort from her mother was of much help. She went to her room and shut herself in, lying on the bed, crying into her pillow. For Bert and Agnes, they initially found it hard to take in, mainly because there had been no indication that Bill was going to do anything like this. They both assumed, incorrectly, that Bill and Sam, having reserved occupations, would be there for the duration of the war.

Bert's first task was to find a replacement for Bill, which was not a problem, as he still had all the names and addresses of the applicants he had to turn down. He contacted the most suitable carpenter on the list, and by the following day he had taken up his new appointment. Work had to go on.

Agnes made frequent visits to her daughter's bedroom, and by late the following day she eventually got Alice to return down stairs, pale, puffy faced and red eyed with all the crying she had done, not wanting to eat for a couple of days until her Mum had done a lot of coaxing. Just over a week after Bill's departure, Alice got a letter from him, it had two effects on her, another bout of tears, but also relief that she was in contact with him. Bill told Alice the training was so hard and intense, it was not possible for him to leave camp and meet her, even if she came down to Aldershot, but if they were granted leave before they left for the front, he would see what he could manage. She wrote back immediately catching the late evening collection with her letter. After that they exchanged letters about once a week. These Alice would take upstairs, unopened, to read in the privacy of her bedroom, so no one could see her emotions. Having read them at least three times, she would then settle down and reply, sending all her love, and hoping for his safe return. Did not everyone say it would be all over by Christmas?

Sam had also received letters from Bill, these had a different effect on him than the Frosts, he now wanted to join up, but he was only 16 years old, and looking younger than his years, so there was little chance of him being accepted. One afternoon he went down to the local recruiting office to try his luck, but was turned away before he had hardly set foot inside, he was not surprised. The Staff Sergeant took pity on him and gave him a couple of coppers for a cup of tea and a bun at a nearby *greasy spoon!* Sam was determined that as soon as he could, he would join up, officially, but it would not be until September 1916, just over two years, to him, a long time to wait. But nothing of this he would tell the Frosts. Not long after Bill's departure, Bert reminded Sam that his job was a reserved occupation, and it was expected by the Government he should stay and work with them while there was still at conflict with the Hun; they were making items essential to the war effort. Sam felt the best answer to these comments was to agree and carry on working with that intention. In his replies to Bill, he was guarded in what he said, as he knew Bill felt he was too young to join up, and preferred him to say working for Bert throughout the conflict. One of them fighting was enough. Both the Frosts and Bill were against him jointing up, he had no support anywhere, what could he do?

***

Algernon, after his first flight with Major Brown in charge, was soon taking his flight over German lines on his own. They soon saw action, but at first neither side had mounted guns, they only fired at each other with hand guns, pilots with revolvers and observer with rifles. The biggest problem came from ground fire. Low down it was small arms fire, while at altitude it was the flak, losing one of his aircrafts to the latter on his second patrol. The pilot was hit, badly injured as his aircraft flipped over and dived towards the ground, being killed instantly. It was a sad loss, the pilot, like Algernon, had only just arrived but he had little experience as he had only recently left training. On return, the loss was reported, which set in motion the procedure to inform the next-of-kin and requesting another pilot and plane.

The squadron had a daily rota; a task aptly named 'Dawn Patrol', or to the ground crew, 'The Milk Run'. One crew each morning, at first light, would send up one of the 504's reconnaissance aircraft to spy out over enemy territory as ordered by Command HQ, making sketches, taking notes or aerial photos as appropriate, on any changes they saw from the last patrol. Only the experienced pilots and observers were allotted to this task. On landing the sketches, notes and prints from plates taken by the camera were quickly looked over by the squadron commander, then passed to a waiting despatch rider and taken back to the HQ, the same from the other squadrons, for analysis of all this information. It usually took less than an hour from landing by the time it arrived on the Staff Officer's desks, looking at the results.

Then, for the rest of the day, either the whole squadron or one of the three flights would venture over enemy lines as directed by orders from those higher up the chain of command to selected areas to spy, or harry German ground troops, mainly from the information they had collected on their first patrol. There was a least one loss a week, if not more, depending on what action they had to take on the other side. The Huns soon realised what these patrols were all about, and in retaliation now had their own 'Dawn Patrol' to thwart the enemy form the west.

***

Keturah was now fully occupied with her war work with the Suffragettes. At first, she was reporting daily to their HQ in Kensington, which, for like a lot of other volunteers was a long trek from the western suburbs and she felt much time was wasted which could be better used. As the WEC got busier, the system at their HQ was getting swamped, it took longer to sort out the tasks for the day, and much valuable time was being squandered.

Keturah regularly wrote to Algernon and told him all about her war work with the WEC as soon as she had volunteered and was accepted, in his reply he was one hundred percent behind her. As she became more frustrated with the problems at the WEC HQ, he suggested to her in one of his letters home that she offer the use of their home as a Sub Office. Her answer was in agreement with his suggestions, anything to help the forces and the war effort, how big or small it may be. Also he knew, which he did not mention to Keturah, it would keep her fully occupied most of the day, away from central London, as he had heard talk that the Germans were planning raids with Zeppelins on the Capital, and stop her worrying about him so much!

Towards the end of 1914, Keturah put her idea to the WEC Committee, suggesting that a branch office be opened further west to help ease the situation at the HQ, and she offered to set it up at her home. After discussion at the next committee meeting, they soon saw the wisdom of this suggestion, and the WEC London Sub Office (West), as it became known, was opened in less than a week after the approval of the committee. Later other sub offices were set up round the outer suburbs, covering the four points of the compass, modelled on Keturah's idea. Keturah cleared the large front lounge of their house, putting all the furniture into storage, converting it into an office, with desks, chairs, a typewriter and other office material, all second hand, new items were unobtainable. She selected five of her best ladies, first-class at organisation and with leadership qualities, as Team Leaders, taking on tasks allocated by Keturah, most originating from the London HQ. In addition to their personal house telephone, another telephone line was installed as special dispensation by the Government as they considered it was supporting for the war effort, but only for the use by the WEC Sub Office. They would then be in contact with their HQ and get their daily updates and orders, and they in turn would give the HQ feedback on their work on a daily basis and ideas of other projects, especially in the local area. It was because of her position as head of the Sub Office that she was elected as a full member of the WEC Committee. She was now totally occupied working for the Corps, there was little room in her life now for other activities, her diary had little or no spaces for socialising with friends, her visits to Oxfordshire were few and far between, her days were full, and, on the plus side, it took her mind off worrying about Algernon, as he had predicted it would.

***

In August 1914, Major Hugh Trenchard was appointed Commander of the RFC Military Wing. On 19th August, No.3 Squadron of the RFC carried out their first mission of the war, a reconnaissance flight into Belgium, 16 miles south of Brussels. In September, the RNAS were made responsible for

British air defence. Later in the month, wireless was first used in aircraft, to direct the fire of the howitzers. On the 21st November, the RNAS flew the first strategic bombing raid on Zeppelin sheds on Lake Constance. On 9th December, the first British aircraft carrier was commissioned, the Ark Royal. At Christmas, Princess Mary presented all troops on the front with a Christmas Box containing a photo of herself, a Christmas Card, cigarettes, sweets, and other items that a soldier could not get at the front.

***

Both sides now had aircrafts with guns as standard fit, both reconnaissance and fighter crafts, the start of aircraft fighting with each other in the air, the age of the 'dog fight' had begun! It was not long before Algernon's squadron started to receive the French built Nieuport Scout, having a much higher speed, the first aircraft to fly at over 100mph, 107mph at 6,500 feet and 140mph at sea level. Designated as a scout aircraft, it carried a forward firing gun making it into a fighter aircraft. Major Brown and each Flight Commander received the aircraft early in 1915.

***

For Bill, the fighting on the ground was fast and furious, he and his squad had been back for a few days' rest on two occasions, but his squad had suffered losses, half of the men he left England with were dead, another two were so badly wounded that they had to be taken back to a military hospital in England, leaving Bill and only two others from the original squad; faces changed all the time. He soon became the most senior lance-corporal in the platoon and unfortunately early in the new year one of their corporals was killed, and Bill was immediately made up to full corporal, now in charge of both the half sections. Bar for the two lads in his original squad, all he now knew were the officer commanding his platoon, now a full Lieutenant, and the two sergeants.

As time went on as each day passed, it seemed to Bill the same as the day before, and the next day would be no different; all they could do was to look forward to a few days of rest. It was hard to know what day of the week or date of the month it was, so tedious, but did it really matter to soldiers in the trenches? Soldiers came and went, either killed, injured or did not return from a patrol or charge and were they either lying dead or dying in a water-logged shell hole somewhere in no-mans-land or now captives of the Germans. Some of the injured were so badly wounded, they never saw them again either dying of their wounds in the field hospitals or returning to

England, they were no further use to British Army. Those with minor wounds were soon returned to the battle, men were always in short supply and urgently needed back on the front line. It was not long before Bill was the senior corporal, and, if he survived, he was in line for promotion if a sergeant was killed, dead man's shoes syndrome.

During one day of heavy fighting a charge was ordered just as it was getting dark in a period that was normally quiet, hoping to catch the Germans unawares and in an endeavour to destroy a machine gun post that not only had been inflicting heavy damage on the platoon, but also pinning them down in their trench. The Lieutenant briefed his NCO to their duties, Bill was to follow the officer and one of the sergeants to destroy the gun post while the other half section was to give covering fire with the heavy Lewis machine guns with their rapid rate of fire.

The platoon crept out under cover of the setting sun, which was shining directly into the faces of the Germans, which they hoped would blind their movements as they advanced through no-mans-land to the German's gun post and the trenches on either side, keeping well down so not to cast silhouettes against the sky line of the afterglow of the sun.

At the start all went well, they reached their objective, throwing grenades in and destroying the machine gun, the whole gun post and killing all its crew who were taken unawares. As they left a large amount of explosives was thrown in with a short fuse, time enough for everyone to clear the area. When it went off the post was blown to smithereens, the post was no more and not a threat to the British trenches until it was, if possible because of the damage, rebuilt. The noise had woken up the Hun who was resting in their trenches. The covering section were ready for this and started firing into the German lines as the whole platoon started to retreat, firing as they went. In the failing light, Bill could see soldiers dropping around him as he weaved from side to side in an endeavour to put those firing at him off their aim. Even running in a crouch position, they were sitting targets. He knew it would be unsafe to stop and help the fallen as they now showed up against the reddening sky. What was happening around him was carnage, soldiers were annihilated, limbs torn from bodies, bone protruding from arms and legs, heads torn off torsos and split open. The dead did not suffer, but those with terrible wounds did, death was the best way out as no doctor could put them back together again. To stop and help a comrade was signing one's own death warrant with the amount of fire power that was being thrown in their direction from the rear by the enemy, the only thing that was open to them was to get back to the safety of their home trench and consolidate.

Those who made it back in the trench immediately turned round and started firing back over the top, continuing to use their two Lewis guns to help quell the enemy fire. At least there was one machine gun post less from across the divide, which helped. The senior person who made it back was one of the sergeants, Bill now being the senior corporal was the next. With a quick check down the line of their troops, Sergeant Molineux, Bill's section NCO, soon established that they had lost at least 15 men, including Sergeant Butler, to him it had seemed more. One of Bill's men, who had been in the party to destroy the gun post, had seen the Lieutenant shot down, but was not sure what his condition was.

When the firing ceased they had a quiet period and called out to ascertain if any one of the platoon in no man's land was still alive. After a few minutes, they heard Lieutenant Hughes calling out, he was wounded and could not move, not being strong enough to drag himself back to the trench. A listening post was set up and silence was ordered along the trenches for about 100 yards both directions. They listened from different angles and worked out that his position was about 50 yards away from the nearest trench. The sergeant and Bill discussed the matter, and contact was made with Command Centre, but they had more serious problems and could not help, they had to work things out for themselves. After further discussion, the sergeant accepted Bill's suggestion that he would crawl out under cover of darkness and try and drag the Lieutenant back. The rest of the platoon would be in readiness but not fire unless the enemy started, then they would give covering fire to divert the attention away from Bill. Sergeant Molineux decided they would not make a move until it was completely dark, no silhouettes to show to the enemy.

Bill went out unarmed but with a small electric lantern and taking a hank of rope with him, which he would put under the arms of his officer and then under his arms and behind the back of his neck, and drag him back home that way. That was the plan. As soon as everyone was ready, Sergeant Molineux gave the word to everyone to take up their positions and not break silence until ordered, which they were told would probably be to return fire. When all was ready, the Sergeant gave Bill a morphine injection kit, and then ordered the start of the rescue. Bill was off, crawling flat on his belly all the way through the mud, littered with dead bodies, limbs and unrecognisable parts from this and other missions, mercifully the dark hid this terrible carnage from Bill's vision but there was the stench of rotting flesh from the dead who had been there days. It was too dangerous to recover their dead comrades, its seemed callous but their recovery would gain nothing, while on the other hand someone could get killed or injured in going out to retrieve them. All in all, while heart breaking, this was the best option. It did not take long to locate the Lieutenant as he kept calling out for help, still semi-conscious and in pain, suffering from bad arm and leg wounds. On reaching his officers side, Bill gave him an injection of morphine to reduce any pain as he dragged him back to the trench, but the drug did not knock him out as Bill had hoped, he was still semi-conscious. Bill got the rope round the officer and around himself, the rope being long enough to allow a gap of about two feet between the two of them. Everything so far had been done in complete silence, and no one in the enemy trenches had been alerted. But as soon as the officer was moved, he felt agonising pain and cried out. The enemy trench was immediately alerted. As the night was now ink dark, white flares were sent up by the enemy.

Bill stopped and lay flat as if dead. The Germans started firing, they knew something was happening, but they did not know what it was. The did not waste their ammo firing at the ground in no man's land at the dead, but fired at about two feet up in any direction hoping to hit something they thought was out there, mainly at the lip of the British trench line, hoping to shoot anyone who raised their head over the parapet edge. All hell broke loose as fire was returned from the British line, which was a good thing for Bill, as he could now continue his task, and the cries of pain from his officer were drowned out by the cacophony of the firing. Keeping very low, Bill crawled from one shallow shell hole to another making his way in a zigzag fashion back to the line of trenches, with bullets from both sides whistling only a foot or two above his head. The Germans sent up more white flares, which had the reverse effect of what they expected as the wind, blowing from the west, blew the flares back across their own lines and lit them up like day, they could not see anything to fire at which the British did, now having the advantage. The British fire was now more accurate and concentrated on the heads of Germans they could see in their trenches. The Lewis guns opened up, doing immense damage to the enemy soldiers, the Germans soon saw the error of their ways and kept their heads down thus the firing was greatly reduced and no further flares were sent up. The white flares had not picked up Bill and under all this noise, lying prone on the ground slowing dragging his officer back to the nearest trench.

The fifty yards that Bill had to go was now nearly 100 yards as he had to keep changing direction, it seemed like fifty miles, but he eventually made it back without injury to himself or further injury to the officer. Sergeant Molineux had the foresight to have a medic and stretcher party standing by and as soon as the Lieutenant was gently lowered into the trench he was taken up the communication trench and on to the reserve trench where a waiting ambulance took him off to the Forward Dressing Station. The Medical Officer in charge took one look at him in the ambulance and told the driver to make haste and take him to the Clearing Station where he would most likely be sent to the Field hospital. On arrival at the Field Hospital he was operated on to remove any bullets, and when he had sufficiently recovered and strong enough to travel he was returned to England, to fight no more. The following day Sergeant Molineux reported the whole incident up the chain of command to the Captain in charge of the platoons, who in return reported the occurrence to Command HQ and eventually to Brigade HQ.

Things moved swiftly, as they often do in war time. Sergeant Molineux was given an immediate field commission as 2nd Lieutenant and Bill was promoted to Sergeant, in charge of one of the sections. Replacements were soon sent in and the platoon was back up to full strength. A further report was sent up the same chain, detailing Bill's action in rescuing the badly wounded Lieutenant Hughes under heavy enemy fire, all unbeknown to Bill. It was not long afterwards that Bill was awarded the Distinguished Conduct Medal for his bravery which he was told as soon as it had been promulgated in the London Gazette on the 12th February 1915:

Awards and Decorations
Distinguished Conduct Medal
75281 Sergeant Perry, William
Sergeant Perry of The Berks & Hants Light Infantry has been awarded the Distinguished Conduct Medal for bravery in the field of action on the 2nd February 1915.

At night and while under heavy enemy fire, he crawled into no man's lands without any weapons to rescue his Commanding Office Lieutenant Hughes who lay seriously wounded. With the aid of only a rope he pulled his

Commanding Officer back to the safety of the British front line without suffering any wounds to himself and his CO not sustaining any further wounds.

But for Sergeant Perry's prompt and brave action the Officer would not have survived, and was immediately taken to a field hospital and eventually made a full recovery

***

5 Squadron had also taken heavy losses; Algernon soon became the senior Flight Commander after the squadron lost the two other Flight Commanders in the space of a month. Then came the worst blow for the squadron, Major Brown, who had been the Officer Commanding of the

squadron since its inception in 1914 in England and had brought the squadron over to France just after the war had started, did not return from a particularly heavy raid over a strategic railway junction ten miles behind enemy lines. The good news was that he landed safely and was seen to walk away from his aircraft after setting it on fire, the bad news was he became a prisoner of war. Algernon, as senior Flight Commander, reported the loss of Major Brown to RFC HQ as soon as he landed back from the mission.

Before the day was out he received a telephone call and was told to report to the RFC HQ as a matter of great urgency. He flew his Nieuport Scout to the nearest airfield, close by the HQ, where a car was waiting to take him the rest of the way to the Château which had been commandeered by the RFC. When he reported, he was shown in and told to wait in an ante-room until called. He was eventually escorted to the office of Brigadier-General Hugh Trenchard. He entered the Brigadier-General's office as Captain Cavendish, OC 'C' Flight, and in less than fifteen minutes exited as Major Cavendish, Commanding Officer of No 5 Squadron.

***

Keturah was thrilled to hear his news, but apprehensive about his new role, hoping it would not put him into more danger. But with all her war work, it took her mind off the dangers that her husband might be in and of finding her two sons. She was so busy now and often away from the office, visiting HQ on committee matters, driving the WEC's various vehicles and even flying members around southern England in her aircraft, for all of which they were allowed a precious fuel allowance which she did not have to pay for!

With all these activities, the office was left without anyone in overall charge, and she soon realised that this state of affairs could not continue. It did not take her long to appoint her best lady as her Second-in-Command or Adjutant to take her place when she was away, and she also selected another lady who showed potential and had been a secretary before joining the WEC as deputy, permanently staying in the office to answer the telephone, look after all the incoming and outgoing mail, type letters and agendas.

Most important, while Katurah was still in overall charge, she did not have to be there every day and was free to carry out other duties that were more important. After a weekly meeting, early on a Monday, all jobs and tasks were allocated for the week, and Katurah would either visit two or three times a week, or phone in from where ever her commitments had taken her, but still attended her committee meetings at London HQ. She and her Adjutant then co-ordinated and organised the daily and weekly programs for all the Team Leaders at the Notting Hill house, who were now a part of her empire.

***

In Shepherd's Bush things were getting back to normal, the only two who were still affected by Bill's departure were Sam and Alice, in different ways. Sam the loss of a friend of over 10 years, while Alice the loss of someone she was deeply in love with, not realising how deeply until Bill had gone. Agnes and Bert had come to terms with the situation, Agnes in comforting her daughter and Bert replacing Bill.

CHAPTER 7

Tragedy on The Front

As the winter ended and the spring of 1915 began, the weather improved which signalled the start of the run up to the approaching summer campaigns. One particular position was considered by the Staff Officers at the Command Control Centre as a very important position to capture, was a hill that had been held by the Germans since the war started, known to the British as *Hell's Hill*, a strategic location that overlooked a large area of the front, where a control centre could be established if captured to spy on the enemy positions and direct fire as necessary and be more accurate. Currently the enemy had this advantage.

***

Early in May, 5 Squadron went out on a dusk patrol, the last patrol of the day, being led by their recently appointed commander. This was a normal patrol, one of which they had done many times. They were soon over the German lines and making their way to a point that they had been asked to review, *Hell's Hill*, where there appeared to be a large build-up of troops and supplies in the surrounding area. The squadron had been given orders to keep observation on the area, daily, and report any changes that they may see back to Command. A photographer had been sent down especially to take photos as that were deemed necessary. The Germans, firstly, did not want the British snooping around this sensitive area, and as the Brits were looking at them on a regular basis, the Hun was ready with guns any time the RFC flew over them. Algernon soon realised that the enemy fire was getting stronger after every visit, so they never arrived on the scene at the same time, approaching from a different direction on each occasion, in the afternoon, out of the sun, was the best time.

On one particular afternoon patrol, Algernon took his squadron in, swooping down with the setting sun behind them and had over flown the area before the Germans realised what had happened. As they turned for home, the guns opened up, but they were soon out of range, diving fast to cross their own lines for home before the German fighters could be scrambled to

128

intercept them. As they passed over the German front line trenches, they opened up with rifle fire, and a chance bullet hit Algernon in his left side.

Algernon's wound was burning with pain and he signalled to his senior Flight Commander that he was wounded and to take over the patrol. He immediately turned west, descending to gathering speed and headed for the nearest British airfield which was not far away, and though in pain landed his aircraft safely, which had suffered only a few minor bullet holes in the fabric, without any detriment to the aircrafts flying ability. The ground crew rushed over waving to the medics that their help was urgently needed. Algernon was soon put into an ambulance that had arrived close to the aircraft and was taken to the nearby field hospital where he was immediately looked at, given a morphine injection and given a temporary dressing before being sent to a major military hospital about 25 miles distance, well away from the direct fighting. He arrived there late in the evening, and was taken to the operating theatre where he was x-rayed, which showed the bullet has passed through leaving little or no major damage. This wound was cleaned up and dressed, but with a considerable loss of blood, he was very weak, and was still semi-conscious the following day. Later that day, Keturah was informed of Algernon's wound, but was told he was progressing well, and as soon as he was fit would be returned to Blighty for recuperation.

On the day Algernon arrived back in England he was taken to the King Edward VII hospital in London, final plans were being finalised to storm the strongly held German position of *Hell's Hill*. He was visited in hospital by a Staff Officer from the RFC HQ who told him a replacement had taken over his position as CO of No 5 Squadron, and when he had made a full recovery, he would be given a new appointment before he returned to France, and while he could not tell him, it would be an improvement on the position he had just relinquished. Algernon made good progress and after a week was up and walking about the ward with the aid of a stick, and after another week had passed he was discharged to recuperate at home, minus his stick, where Keturah was able to give him large amounts of tender loving care.

***

In 1915 there were two firsts in war air combats; an aircraft torpedoed and sunk a warship while another sunk a German submarine in a similar manner. ■ The War Office planned to increase flying squadrons from 108 to 200.In July '14, Lieutenant-General Sir Douglas Haig had dismissed air reconnaissance, saying, "There is only one way for a commander to get information by reconnaissance and that is by use of cavalry." In November 1916, he wanted 20 more squadrons for reconnaissance duties! An RFC reconnaissance plane had spotted a gas cloud moving towards French infantry lines. They communicated with the French commanders who ordered a retreat, saving the day and many deaths and causalities. Field Marshal Sir John French praised the RFC's performance saying, "Almost everyday new methods for employing aircraft both strategically and tactically are discovered and put into practice."

***

Bill's platoon Commander was informed that they would be one of a number of platoons who would be engaged in storming Hell's Hill in a few days' time, this information was passed on to his two sergeants but would not be passed on to the rest of the troops until a few hours before the charge.

On the 19th April, as dawn started to break, action started on taking the hill, firstly by the heavy guns and, after a softening up, followed by an assault by ground troops to assess the enemy's defences first-hand. The following day the main charge was made on the hill, spearheaded by Bill's platoon. Covering fire was given to all those assaulting the Germany position and the platoon, led by their officer, made good progress, Bill covering his CO. As they reached the top, the German resistance became fierce, they were fighting for their lives, even covering fire from those left in the trenches did not initially stop the enemy fire, the barrage was nothing as Bill had seen before. The Germans were not going to give any ground if they could help it, but things were turning in the favour of the attacking forces, not without terrible losses. Before Bill's eyes, his CO was killed, he could do nothing for him, the assault was the main thing. Bill took over leading the action of his depleted platoon and carried on the charge up the hill. Soldiers on both sides were still being killed or wounded, while the fighting was on, nothing could be done to help them. Eventually the enemy capitulated, the British forces took over all the hill positions and put all enemy guns out of action, taking those Germans still alive, who had not escaped, as prisoners. *Hell's Hill* was now in British control. Bill, as platoon commander, took over and held the position until fresh troops arrived to consolidate the position. The remains of the enemy had retreated, but they were not far off, and were firing at anything that moved. Bill made his way down the hill to where the remains of his troops had gathered, but tragedy struck at the last minute as a machine gun opened up from the retreating German troops on Bill's platoon, everyone running for what little cover there was on the bare hillside. Fire was immediately returned and the machine gun position was soon wiped out, but not without the loss of more soldiers. After the platoon had made their way back to the reserve trench, a Major carried out a head count. There were 23 wounded, 11 killed, one being the Platoon CO, the Platoon SNCO, Sergeant William Perry, DCM, aged 19 years and 4 months.

***

With Algernon at home in Notting Hill convalescing, in upstairs rooms not taken over by the WEC, Keturah took time off to stay with him. About half way through the 19th of April Keturah suddenly felt faint, and had to sit down; she became short of breath, and had to lie down on a sofa, where Algernon found her in a faint. A doctor was immediately summoned, and checked her over, but nothing could be found. All she could say was that she had a vision that someone close to her had died. They checked the schools in London and were told that their three children were alright, so who could it be. She suddenly thought of the two boys she had given away, and told Algernon that the eldest was older enough to fight, they both wondered it this could be it, and would she ever find out?

***

The following day, when Sam returned home after work, on opening the front door he found his landlady, looking anguished, waiting for him with a buff envelope in her hand. As soon as Sam saw it, he had a good idea what it was, bad news. Sam felt shattered. He thanked his landlady and took the envelope and with a heavy heart he went upstairs to his bedroom, sat on his bed, staring at the envelope. Eventually he plucked up courage and opened it, pulling out a telegram form, reading its contents with a sinking feeling in his stomach.

From:- The War Office, Whitehall, London

Dated:- 21 April 1915

To:- Mr S Bray, Flat 2, 24 Wood Lane, Shepherd's Bush, London

Subject:- 75281 Sergeant William Perry, DCM, with deep regret we have to inform you as next of kin of the above soldier that on 19 April that he was killed by enemy action stop his personal effects will be forwarded to you in the near future stop letter from his commanding officer to follow stop Major J M James, Room 406, The War Office, Whitehall

---

Sam turned around and lay on his bed and cried. He dreaded tomorrow as he would have to take the bad news to work and break it to the Frosts; Alice, he knew, would take it very badly.

When Sam had recovered sufficiently, he went down and told his landlady, who was much saddened by the news. He felt that he had to tell the Frost's immediately, and leaving his landlady with tears in her eyes, he made his way there. On arrival at the Frost's house, the workshop was closed after all the carpenters had left just after 6pm. After tapping on the front door, as he and Bill always did, he went in. Bert and Agnes were there, but Alice was out with a friend. When Sam told Bert and Agnes the terrible news and showed them the telegram there was a shocked silence until Agnes burst into tears. When Bert had calmed her down they discussed how to tell Alice. The did not have much time to discuss their problem, as suddenly the outside door was opened, Alice had arrived. As she entered the room with a smile on her face, she sensed that something had happened and the smile was gone in an instant and by the look on her parents and Sam's face, she knew it was bad news. She screamed and said, "It's Bill, he's dead," and collapsed on the floor in a dead faint. Bert took charge, he suggested that Sam return home and he and Agnes would cope the best they could with Alice. Bert suggested that he took a day off from work, assuring him he would not lose any wages. Sam returned back to his flat, dazed. Then and over the next few days Sam did a lot of thinking. Somehow he had to get revenge for the killing of his best friend, but how could he get into the Army? He was still under age.

Sam did not take the next day off as Bert had suggested and went back to work. Everyone knew of Bill's death and showed sympathy towards him. He worked in a dream, all his actions were automated and his mind was not on the job. Bert kept a close eye on Sam, but as the week drew to a close Bert noticed he was bucking up and started to return to his normal self, from the outside, no one knew the turmoil raging inside his head.

If Bert and Agnes thought Alice was bad when Bill left, it was nothing compared to hearing Bill had been killed. She was so bad that a doctor had to be called and she was given sedatives to calm her down and make her sleep. When she eventually made an appearance, she looked ten years older. But as the weeks wore on, she slowly came to terms with her loss and bravely realised she had a life to lead, and Bill would not have wanted her to shut herself away for the rest of her life and the world. She knew that Bill and Sam had been very close, almost like brothers, so at lunch breaks, she would seek Sam out and they would sit together. At first, talking about Bill and the war, but when those subjects got exhausted, they started to talk about other things closer to home.

Alice had never been close to Sam when Bill was around; she only had eyes for him. She now realised how very much like Bill was to Sam. Sam had always fancied Alice, but never tried to woo her in any way, as far as he was concerned, she was Bill's girl. After a few weeks, a friendship started to blossom, as far as Sam was concerned he was happy with the events but he did not rush anything, he let Alice come to him, but he showed her in a negative way that he was receptive to her advances.

***

Major Lanoe Hawker was awarded the Victoria Cross for his gallantry when he shot down three German Albatros biplanes. Major James McCudden was awarded the Croix de Guerre (War Cross), one of France's highest decorations. Captain Albert Ball was awarded the Military Cross, second to the Victoria Cross.

***

A day after Bill was killed he was buried in a large mass grave well behind the British front line. The only person Bill really knew was Lieutenant Molineux, who attended the mass funeral of all who had been killed in the same action, Hell's Hill. After the grave-side service, the grave was covered and wooden crosses were placed in the soft earth, one for each person buried underneath, each cross bearing the name of one of the dead. The Lieutenant took Bill's cross from his tunic pocket, on it was a metal plaque marked with his details:

75281
SERGEANT
W. PERRY
DCM
19 APRIL 1915
19

He pushed the cross firmly in the soft soil, "Thank you Bill," he said. "You were an excellent soldier, brave, courageous and a very good friend, I will miss you. Take care, if I have to die, be there to meet me." If anyone saw the Lieutenant walking away, they may have noticed a tear or two on his face, but no one noticed, everyone else there was also grieving.

When the Lieutenant returned to the control post, he gathered all Bill's few belongings together to forward to his next of kin, and finding letters from Sam, decided he would like to write to him, it was the least he could do.

22 April 1915
Dear Mr Bray,

You of course will have heard the terrible new of Bill's death as his next of kin, and as his Commanding Officer, I was deeply shocked, as not only was he the best soldier I ever had, he was a close friend. When on stand-down, or on rest, we would often chat, have a smoke, eat and drink together. He was, as you would know, very brave, having been awarded the Distinguished Conduct Medal, showing what he was made of, not many of these are awarded. The only shame is, he never received the medal he won so bravely, with little or no regard to his own safety. The safety of his own men was always paramount in his every action.

I have spoken to Staff HQ and I understand you will accept the medal on his behalf later and you will be informed no doubt by the War Office of how this will be presented.

Today we laid Bill to rest, I watched his coffin lowered into the grave and when it was covered I placed a wooden cross with his number, rank, name and decoration over the spot. I don't mind admitting it, I left the cemetery with tears in my eyes, which I have never done before. I have been asked to collect the few things Bill left, which will be sent on to you through official channels.

Words cannot express the loss Bill has meant to me, but I am sure you will feel the same. One thing I did find in his tunic pocket was a photo of a pretty young lady. Bill never mentioned that he had a girlfriend, but keeping it with him, she must have been someone special to him. I did not hand it in with his other effects, I felt it was too personal to let other people see it, and I did not want it to get lost, so I am enclosing it in this letter.

With kind regards
Jack Molineux (Lieutenant)

When Sam received Jack's letter, it helped the grieving process, but there were again tears, the thought that Bill had now been laid to rest in a known marked grave helped as he now could, after the war was over, visit the place he had been buried, not like some who had no known resting place or there was nothing left to bury. One thing that cheered him up was that he now had a photo of Alice, he would not say anything to her at the moment, and he had a good idea what reaction it would bring from her. Because of the reference to the photograph in the letter, he felt it best not to show this to anyone and not to mention he had received a personal letter from Bill's CO either. As time heals, he might leave it for another time, if he felt it would help, especially Alice. He wrote back to Jack, thanking him for the letter, everything he had done for Bill, and being a friend to him, to the end.

After having read the letter again, he then looked at the photo of Alice, which was a formal portrait taken by a professional photographer in Shepherd's Bush. The photo was just like Alice was now, it could not have been taken very long ago, had she had it taken especially for Bill, Sam had not seen it anywhere in the Frost home. He knew Bill did not want to have a close relationship with Alice as he was going to join-up, but Alice did not know this. He eventually came to the conclusion that Alice had the photo taken, unbeknown to anyone, and somehow gave it to Bill, how he would never know. It also made him wonder what Bill must have though when he received it. As he was carrying it when he was killed, he must have thought a lot about the photo, and, more importantly, about Alice.

About two weeks later he received a buff envelope through the post, emblazoned across the top were the words **ON HIS MAJESTY'S SERVICE**, the official letter from the War Office had arrived. Sam sat on the bed where two weeks earlier he had cried his eyes out reading and re-reading the telegram that had announced Bill's death to Sam. There were no tears this time, but his heart was still heavy as he opened the letter and took out the official letter. While he appreciated the letter, he knew it was written by a person who had never met Bill, and who was writing letters every day like this to the bereaved.

> **The War Office**
> **Whitehall**
> **London**
> **29 April 1915**
> **Mr S Bray**
> **Flat 2**
> **24 Wood Lane,**
> **Shepherds Bush,**
> **LONDON**
> **SUBJECT:-   75281   SERGEANT   WILLIAM PERRY, DCM**
> **Dear Mr Bray**

As the next of kin of Sergeant W Perry, please accept our deepest sympathy in the loss of this very brave solder. His section was detailed to attack Hell's Hill. Soon after attacking, his

Commanding Officer was killed; Sergeant Perry took over command, eventually taking the position from the enemy. When relieved and returning to the rest area with the remainder of the section, they were fired upon by the enemy, killing a number of soldiers including Sergeant Perry.

Before the attack the hill was held strongly by the Germans, and through Sergeant Perry's selfless and brave action we took the hill from the enemy, which we are still holding it today, a fitting final tribute to an excellent soldier.

Sergeant Perry was laid to rest in a grave not far from where he fell on 22 April last. The grave is marked with a Wooden Cross, bearing his personal details. Lieutenant J Molineux, his

Commanding Officer was in attendance at the service of burial as the Official Army representative. The position of the grave has been notified to the Graves Registration Committee, and after the war, if you wish to visit, they will be able to advice as to its location.

I have been informed by the Brigade HQ in his area of all these actions and his personal effects will be forwarded on to you in the near future.

He was awarded the Distinguished Conduct Medal last February which unfortunately he died before the award could be made. I understand because of his bravery in his last battle he is being recommended for a Bar to his DCM. I am led to understand, that as Sgt Perry's Next of Kin, you will be asked to receive the decoration on his behalf.

Again, please accept the Army's deepest sympathy in the loss of Sergeant Perry, who was a very brave soldier and you can be justly proud of him as he has served his country well.

Sir, I remain your

This time he took the letter into work, which was passed around the Frost family. Bert suggested some of the lads Bill had worked with would like to see the letter. Those who read it and knew Bill were moved, but some of them were secretly glad they had a reserved occupation and would not be called up. Not a good idea to tell anyone, except the wife perhaps.

***

Algernon soon recovered from his injury and when he was passed medically fit, he was told to report to Colonel Gordon at the RFC Wing of the War Office. "Now look here Algy," said Gordon as soon as Algernon was seated in his office, "we feel you have done very well since you joined up, but we are very concerned about all the flying you are doing, you are over 40 now. As you know when we started in autumn '14, it was only reconnaissance flying, but now we are fighting in the air, gun to gun action, dog fights, we think this job is for the younger men."

Algernon was just about to raise an objection when Gordon cut in, "Hang on Algy, just hear me out first. You have a lot of experience, you are exceptional pilot and have skills in leadership that we feel you will be better placed in a more responsible role where you can pass your expertise on to others. We don't want to you lose you in a dog fight, so we are therefore giving you command of a Wing in the rank of Lieutenant Colonel, what do you think of that?"

Algernon was initially speechless, he had only been in the RFC about a year and he had risen up the promotion pole so quickly, 2nd Lieutenant to Lieutenant Colonel, five rungs up the ladder! "Thank you, Sir, for having this faith in me," was his initial response, "I accept the position and hope I can live up to what you expect of me. I am disappointed about the flying aspect, but I understand your motives, and on reflection, I think it is the right decision."

Gordon continued, "You will have five squadrons under your control, and while you will still fly to visit your squadrons in satellite airfields from your HQ, it would be less from now on as you will have a flying leader to lead your wing into battle, and you will have your ground duties to attend as well. But your flying will all be well behind the front lines, safe from enemy action. We expect you not to stray over the front line or got out on patrol either, even on our side of the line, which basically is an order, which I'm sure you will not disobey. When you get there, you will appoint one of the squadron commanders as your flying leader."

While Algernon was sorry to stop combat flying, he made a silent promise to himself, he would try and fly as much as possible, under the terms of his new role, as the Hun hardly ever ventured over British lines, he felt he had now seen the last of them if he stuck to the order he had been given. But what the eye did not see, the heart did not grieve, and as Colonel Gordon would not be out in France, he was determined he would fly on operations over enemy lines if they were short of pilots.

"I'm glad you see our reasoning, and we are sure you are ideally suited for this new role, so don't throw it all away and fly on patrol You will be based in the Ypres area again, so your wing will be known as the *Ypres Wing*." Gordon continued, "Now I understand you were taught to fly at Tommy Sopwith's school at Brooklands, so you must know Tommy and his aircraft."

"Yes, I keep my aircraft at Brooklands, and before I joined up, I often went into see him and was interested in the progress that was being made in aircraft design. We are good friends and we exchange letters on a regular basis, exchanging without giving anything away," he added!

"Well, we want you to go down and see Tommy before you return to France. He has a new aircraft that the RNAS are taking a great interest, and he has asked us if we are interested and could we have one to test. It's an unusual design as it has only one pair of outer mainplane struts and short centre-section struts on each side, so they have called the 1½ Strutter. One aspect that is of great interest to us is it's the first British aircraft to be fitted with a fixed forward gun firing through the propeller arc by means of an interrupter gear. It's a two seater, so whenever you fly around the front, you will have a gunner and observer behind you for your protection! It can do 100mph, so at the moment it's the fastest aircraft we have. We want you to take delivery of this aircraft on behalf of the RFC, and fly out to your new job in it."

"When you have assessed your five squadron commanders," he continued, "we want the one you consider the most competent to test it in action, most properly your flying leader and return it to you afterwards, hoping that it's still in one piece! Does that seem alright with you?" Algernon nodded his agreement. "Finally," Gordon said, "we have selected a very experienced gunner and observer for you who has been flying since the war started, back over here for a short break he well deserved, so he will be going back with you, and you will meet up with him at Brooklands, he's Staff

Sergeant Thorne at the moment, but has been recommended to be promoted to Warrant Office 2 and that could be before you meet him. He will also be your Gunner, Observer Leader for the wing. He will be attached to the squadron which is nearest to your HQ, but will be at your beck and call as you require him."

Algernon was pleased with his new assignment, and readily agreed to fly the aircraft out to his new post after a test flight. It was a better way to cross the channel than in a boat and a rough sea he told Gordon!

On his return home, Keturah was pleased about his new post, as it reduced his chance of being injured or killed. Within the week he got his orders and after a farewell dinner with all the family in Oxfordshire and final goodbyes at Notting Hill, where they were not as worried as they had been the first time, he left and he took a train to Weybridge and taxi to the Sopwith works.

On arrival at Brooklands, he met his other crew member, now Warrant Office 2, and after a quick chat with him, he knew he was the man he wanted behind him. Before he had finished talking to Thorne, Tommy Sopwith came out of the hangar and greeted him as close friends do, then he showed him his new pride and joy, the *1½ Strutter* that was standing out on the apron and invited him to go for a test flight before he left for France. After a thorough briefing, he was impressed to find the aircraft had an endurance of 3¾ hours which meant it could fly over 350 miles without refuelling, which impressed him. A good look round the aircraft carrying out his own inspection as he had learnt at Farnborough, being shown all the controls by one of the mechanics and soon took off on his own for an hour's flying, nothing like the Lloyd Scout that had nearly killed on his first test flight! He didn't take Thorne with him on his first flight; he never liked to fly a two seater aircraft for the first time with a passenger, just in case there were any problems. The WO2 would have plenty of time later flying with him, starting from tomorrow! Before Algernon returned home from the front for good, they both amassed many flying hours together.

On his return from the test flight he expressed his delight with the aircraft and its performance to Tommy, and they agreed he and Thorne would leave first thing next morning. He and his gunner, observer stayed in a local hotel for the night after having dinner with Tommy and his senior staff.

They both departed early the next morning for the 150-mile flight, and with the help of the prevailing westerly wind assisting them, they arrived by mid-morning, all in one hop. The airfield where he landed, was close to the RFC Field HQ where his office was situated, and where one of his squadrons was based, that Thorne would be a member of, while the other four squadrons that came under his command were in easy flying distance away, so keeping in touch was an easy matter by field telephone, but he often flew to visit them regularly, he would never tell them when he was coming, a surprise visit always kept them on their toes.

Once he was settled in to his new post, he was soon off visiting, flying with each squadron in turn to assess their capabilities, and advise on what he wanted done to improve their standards.

Once Algernon had assessed his squadron commanders he passed the *1½ Strutter* to the one he considered most suitable. Within a month, he sent his findings on the aircraft back to Colonel Gordon at the RFC wing of the War Office. The *1½ Strutter* was soon flying in squadrons on the Western Front; Algernon's squadrons were among the squadrons to receive them first.

Once he had decided who was going to be his deputy as Wing Leader, he transferred him from one of the outlying airfield to the one close to RFC HQ; they both used the same Mess and were in daily contact.

***

The first ever raid on England by two German Zeppelins was in East Anglia on 19th of January 1915. Hull was their target, but poor navigation and low cloud, they ended up bombing Great Yarmouth instead, King's Lynn and six other towns in the area also, killing over 20 people and injuring at least 40 others. ■ On the 31st of May, Zeppelins dropped 3000 pounds of bombs on the Capital, killing 7 people and injuring 14 others.

***

The first raid worried Keturah, would they ever venture to London and bomb that? When they did, this was more that Keturah could bear; while she was prepared to stay in London and use her home as her working base for the WEC, she was not prepared to have her children anywhere near the danger and subjected to possible bombing. Very early in June she took them down to her in-laws' home, where they stayed for the duration of the war. The children started their schooling in Reading, Rupert and Benjamin going to Reading Grammar School, while Jane, as soon as she was old enough, and went to Queen Anne's School in Caversham. Keturah wrote to Algernon about all this, he was in total agreement, it was best to take the children out of London and send them to the schools Keturah had proposed, and he considered that boarding school, while it was not what they both originally wanted, was the best solution. They would only be weekly boarders, returning to the Manor at the weekends, being collected and returned by a car arranged by their grandfather. Keturah and Algernon felt being day pupils would not be the best solution, they could see them being spoilt to death by their grandparents, and felt being away from home for five nights a week would do them the world of good.

***

On the 26th April 1915, Lieutenant W B Rhodes-Moorhouse RFC was detailed to bomb the railway junction at Courtrai in Belgium, dropping his bombs at 300 feet; in doing so he was wounded. Instead of landing and giving himself to the enemy, he headed for home at 200 feet and was wounded twice more. He made a successful landing back at base, but died from his wounds the following day. He was awarded the VC posthumously, the first airmen to receive this award. ■ During the Gallipoli Campaign of 1915, the 1/1st Berkshire Yeomanry made an attack on the Turkish lines early on the 21st August, a Trooper, Fredrick Potts of Reading, being among the charge, but he was soon wound in the thigh, the bullet passing through his body. The fighting continued around him where he and a comrade laid nearby, Trooper Arthur Andrew who was more seriously wounded. They had to endure the heat of the day and the cold of the night and Potts decided he could not leave a fellow soldier and dragged him back to British lines, mostly on a trenching shovel, arriving at the trenches of the 6th Royal Iniskilling Fusiliers on the evening of the 23rd 60 hours after the charge. He was awarded the Victoria Cross for his brave unselfish action.

***

On his return from work one evening, the landlady handed Sam a buff envelope with **ON HIS MAJESTIES SERVICE** across the top, the second one he had received in the space of one month. There could not be any more bad news about Bill surely. Upon opening it, it was different from all the other official letters he had so far received. It was a command by King George V to Mr Samuel Bray to attend an investiture ceremony at Buckingham Palace as the Next of Kin of 75281 Sergeant William Perry, DCM & Bar, (Deceased), to be presented with his decoration on 26th August 1915. It advised Sam that he was allowed to bring two guests with him. The letter continued with the date and time, the expected form of dress of both male and female persons and where to present themselves.

The following morning when Sam got to work, he showed the letter first to Alice, then to Bert and Agnes. Bert said he was too busy to go and Agnes said was too scared and did not have the clothes fit to wear to go to Buckingham Palace, so in the end it was only Alice who went with Sam. For the occasion, Sam hired a Morning Suit and Bert gave Alice the money to purchase a new dress with matching shoes, bag and hat. When she was dressed up for the presentation, she said she would feel like a real Lady. Sam did not say anything, but considered she did look like a real Lady all the time; he was growing really fond of her, but could never tell her, well not at the moment, it was another Bill syndrome again!

On the appointed day in August for the presentation, Sam and Alice went there and back by taxi, which Bert insisted he paid for. They got to Buckingham Palace in plenty of time, and Alice was shown to a seat in the presenting room, while Sam was shown into an ante room where all those who were receiving a title or decoration were lined up in order of importance of what was being presented. The ceremony started on time, and it did not seem long before Sam was facing the King, where he bowed to His Majesty. The citation was read out and the King stepped forward and affixed the Distinguished Conduct Medal with Bar, hanging from a mauve, a blue and mauve vertical striped ribbon, onto the right side of Sam's jacket, he spoke a few words and shook his hand. Sam bowed again, took a step back, turned and walked away. All this was watched by Alice with a feeling of pride in all Bill had achieved in his short life. She was still sad at his loss and had tears in her eyes as the King pinned the medal on Sam, but the wounds were now slowly starting to heal.

Before Sam took Alice back home they went to a photographer in Shepherd's Bush and had a photo of Sam in his morning suit, the medal pinned on his jacket, one of Alice seated, holding the medal in its open case, and finally one of them both with Alice again seated holding the medal and Sam standing behind her. On paying the photographer, he advised Sam the photos should be ready in two days' time. When they got back to Frost's, they told Bert and Agnes all that had happened and showed them the medal. Agnes had to wipe away the tear and Bert had a lump in his throat.

When Sam got up to go, Alice went with him to the door, "Thank you for today Sam, and taking me to Buckingham Palace, it was a once in a life time thing for me to do. It was a pity it had to be because of Bill's death that made it all possible."

"If Bill had not been killed Alice," Sam replied, "and he had collected his medal himself, I know he would have taken you."

Sam, knowing that he was going to join up, and might never come back, decided to give Alice Bill's decoration for safe keeping, but he would not tell her this reason. He put his hand in his pocket and withdrew the case containing the medal, "Alice, I haven't got a safe place in my flat to keep Bill's medal, would you keep it safe for me after I have shown it to my landlady, 'cos I know she would like to see it. Any time I want to look at it, I will come and ask, if that's OK with you?"

Alice was thrilled at Sam's request. "Of course, Sam, I would be privileged to look after it for you, I will keep it safe in my bedroom, and you can look at it anytime you want. Thank you so much," and with which she gave him a kiss on his cheek. Alice, when asked by Sam if she would collect the photos they had taken, said she would be only too happy to, prompting Sam to give her the receipt, telling her there would be one copy of them each, plus an extra two copies of them together. When he got back to his lodgings, he showed the medal to the landlady, who's eye started to cry. The following day after Sam had shown everyone in the workshop the medal, he passed it in its box to Alice, who after another long look, kissed it and placed it carefully in her top draw of her chest of draws.

For some time, Alice had seen a lot of the likeness of Bill in Sam, and while she did not let on to anyone, she started to look forward to seeing him most days at work and he helped to fill the gap that Bill's loss had created. When she collected the photos, she purchased a frame for each, giving her parents and Sam one of them both, the one of her to Sam, keeping the third one of Sam for herself which she placed on the table beside her bed where she could see it first thing in the morning and last thing at night. But Sam, like Bill, did not want to get to deeply involved with Alice, as much as he would have liked to, as he was now going to join up, under age or not, and he had found a way, he had to avenge the killing of Bill by the Germans, even if he was putting himself in danger.

***

On 8th June 1915, Flight Sub-Lieutenant Reginald Warneford, RNAS, was the first British pilot to destroy a German Zeppelin as it was preparing to land near Ghent in Belgium. Warneford climbed to 6,000 feet above the airship and dropped six bombs which entered the envelope and exploded, immediately causing a fire to breakout and the airship to crash. He returned safely back to base and was soon awarded the Victoria Cross. On the 19th August, Colonel Hugh Trenchard took over command of the Royal Flying Corps in France and later that year promoted to Brigadier-General.

***

If Sam was going to join up, it would have to be outside London, but not at Aldershot where Bill had enlisted. As the nearest main line station to Shepherd's Bush was Paddington, he started looking for a town that had a regiment and was served by the Great Western Railway. Bristol seemed a good choice, easy to get to and far enough away at about 100 miles. He made inquiries at the Recruiting Office in Shepherd's Bush of various regiments in the West Country and found one titled the West Bristol Fusiliers, based just outside Bristol; ideal, they were on the top of his list!

After work on the first Friday in October he asked Bert if he could have Saturday as a day's holiday, he hadn't taken any days off for some time, and was due for a bit of leave. Bert knew Sam had worked many hours, including overtime, so it was the least he could do for the young lad. Sam decided he would take a train to Bristol the following day and join the Fusiliers there. Before he left work, he made sure his bench was clean and tidy just in case he did not come back. But it would not be Samuel Bray that was joining up, as Samuel Bray was still under age, but as William Perry, because he was of the correct age and Sam still had Bill's Birth Certificate and would claim he was William Perry!

Sam left early and took a fast train to Bristol, getting there mid-morning. On asking directions at the station he was told to take a tram that passed the entrance of the barracks. He had wondered if they would be recruiting on a Saturday, but he had no need to worry. There was no problem, they were recruiting all day Saturday, and West Bristol Fusiliers were desperate for volunteers.

The first officer who interviewed him wondered why at 19½ he had not been called up before. But Sam explained that he had been in a reserved occupation, showing them a copy of the certificate in Bill's name, which satisfied everyone, and told them his firm had now started employing older people so it released him from his job, without any detriment to the firm's war effort. He was accepted on the spot!

He had a medical, like Bill, and "Bill the 2nd" was passed fit and soon swore allegiance to King and Country on the 7th September 1915, signing as:

William Perry

He was given the number:

-	9	3	4	9	4

plus the King's shilling, on the 2nd October 1915. He was in. Next behind him in the queue was a rather scruffy lad, who had just made the legal age for entry, from the Bristol area, Bob Drew by name. He got the next number on from Sam and like Sam he was an orphan too, but, and unlike Sam, he had no friends, not even work mates that he wanted to keep in touch with.

He lived in a village north east of Bristol and was a farm labourer, *'living in'*, considerer a youngster, only being paid a meagre child's wage and the leftovers from the farmers table to eat, so he was only waiting for the day he became of age to join up, he could not get there fast enough, he was very glad to enlist. The pay, the food, and the conditions in the Army were much better than living in a hay loft in a droughty old barn and working from dawn to dusk, seven days a week, for a pittance. All the new recruits were needed immediately, so they were given until the following Tuesday to clear up their affairs and report to the Barracks by no later than 1600 hundred hours. As Bob had left the farm that day for ever, he asked one of the recruiting sergeants if he could stay in the Barracks until Tuesday, explaining he had no where to live. He was soon found accommodation in a transit hut until Tuesday, where they would give him three meals a day, and told to come back when recruiting had finished at 6pm.,

They both left the barracks together early in the afternoon, Sam suggesting, as he was hungry, that they have a bite to eat. Bob was a bit evasive and Sam realised from what Bob had said to him earlier that he did not have any money to spare to buy a meal. Sam said he was getting a good wage and was happy to buy one for him, and if he wanted, he could pay him back when the Army were paying him. They soon found a cheap café to have a meal.

Sam knew his new friend's surname was Drew, but that is all he knew, so he thought he should break the ice. "I'm Bill Perry by the way, I know your name is Drew and you have the next number after me, what can I call you?"

"Me names Robert, but no one calls me that, so call me Bob," was his reply. Bob held out his hand and said, "Let's seal our new friendship with a handshake," which is what they did. They then gave each other a potted history of their past, but Sam's was partly fact and partly fiction!

While he was in the café he asked the waitress if there was any where that did bed and breakfast, as he needed a bed for one night, for next Monday, and was surprised that they offered him a room there and then. When they left the café, they shook hands again and Sam said, "See you in three days time!"

"Great," Bob replied, "Looking forward to it, anything is better than the farm!" On leaving Bob, Sam made his way back to Temple Meads station, and was soon back in the capital.

On Monday he did not go into work, putting what money he had and what Bill had left him into his bank account. He sealed his bank book, Birth Certificate and his Exemption Certificate with his job at Frost's and all his personal documents in an envelope including the photo of Alice that Bill had carried with him. He would only be taking documents relating to Bill Perry with him to Bristol. He would put this envelope in a lockable chest which he had recently purchased. He had sounded out Isaac Eighteen just after he had been to the Palace, that if he was called up, would they be prepared to store a small chest for him. Isaac really agreed, weren't they friends? Sam suggested that when ever he brought it round, the best place for his chest would be under the cutting table, as he knew they stored nothing there, which the Eighteens thought was a good idea. The Eighteens, while they thought Sam looked to young to enlist, never said anything to him about it, it was his business, not theirs!

In three others envelopes were his personal letters, one to Bert and Agnes, another to Alice, all explaining, in a different way to each, what he had done and why, and what to do if he was killed. Finally, was a sealed envelope for Isaac, that he would explain to him that if anything happened to him, he would know as he was his next of kin and he was to open the envelope he would give to him, suggesting he kept it in a small safe that was hidden in Isaac's material storeroom. If Isaac heard nothing from him, they were to remain in the safe and he would collect it when the war was over. He did not tell Isaac that if anything did happen to him, it would not be Samuel Bray who had been killed, but William Perry, which would confuse everyone until they opened the envelope explaining why he had done this. He did not consider what they would do once they knew he was dead, as Bill Perry would have been killed twice and Samuel Bray was officially still alive, according to the paper work. Sam did not consider it was his worry, he had no intentions of dying. The only people he told about his departure were the Eighteens and Sam had made sure that the Eighteens and the Frosts did not know of the existence of the other. The other two envelopes he addressed and stamped which he would take with him and post on the way to the station on Monday morning.

Sam packed up everything he was taking to Bristol in a small kit bag, the remainder he put in the chest with all his clothes and moth balls and his personal possessions, burying them at the bottom under everything else, with a sealed envelope which contained his birth certificate.

He took the chest and envelopes round to Isaac's shop as soon as he knew they were open and said that he had to go away urgently, for at least a month, and was having to give up his flat (that part was true!), explaining that he was not being called up but their main customer, Sopwith Aviation, required him to go down to their works near Southampton as they had lost a lot of staff because of the war. Isaac was a little surprised at this as it seemed to him that this was short notice for Sam, *could they not have told him sooner;* but as Sam explained, there was a war on, things happened fast and one had to do one was told. Isaac was suspicious, but he did not say anything. You were not expected to ask questions when there was a war on, and unfortunately some people were not fond of Jews, so it was best he kept his thoughts to himself

After he had showed Isaac the envelopes he watched Isaac put it in his safe, saying to open it if anything happened to him, like a bombing attack on London or Southampton. They pushed the locked chest under the cutting table. When Isaac was satisfied, Sam gave him one of the keys he had for the chest with a label on it that said **SAM**.

Sam was chatting to Isaac and Joseph just before he left when he accidentally dropped some coins on the floor that rolled under the table, and when he went to retrieve them he hid the second key on hook that was fixed behind one of the legs when the table had been made, impossible to find unless you knew where to look. He had planned this when he had made the table, and the Eighteens had not spotted this when the table was erected.

The evening before he went to his room after work, he told his landlady that he was now old enough to fight for King and Country, he was joining up and would be leaving the following day, but did not mention where he was going, and his landlady was too polite to ask. Bill's room had been let just after he had left, and Sam suggested that she should look for a new tenant for his room as from tomorrow.

He returned to his bedroom and got out Bill's effects that had recently be forwarded to him by the Army in a small parcel that he hadn't had time to open before. There was not much to show, he had already received Bill's photo of Alice form Jack Molineux. He still wondered how Bill had got it, had Alice given it to him, he didn't think he would ever know, perhaps it was best that way.

He opened the small parcel and lay what he had been sent on his bed, there wasn't much there, Bill obviously travelled light! A Boy Scout pocket knife with a thing for taking stones out off horses hooves, a St Christopher badge on a chain which Sam had never seen before, *did he get this good luck talisman before he left England?* There were some English and foreign coins, his cap badge and finally a small brass hinged box, that was the size of a very large tobacco tin, where had this come from? It was a mystery to him, until he remembered that Bill had mentioned it to him briefly in passing in his first letter after Christmas, but with little details. In the centre of the lid was a raised cameo head of a young woman, with an M either side, *who could that be?* At the bottom of the lid was raised writing **CHRISTMAS 1914.** While in each corner and on the other three sides were the places where current conflicts where taking place. He opened the tin and was amazed to find out from whom it had come, Princess Mary, so the M's were for Mary. Inside there was photograph of her and a Christmas card from her also, two packets, each filling half the box, one of cigarettes, the other tobacco, which Bill had not touched, he and Bill never smoked. The only evidence Bill had ever opened the tin was the empty packaging of a bar of chocolate, which Bill must have eaten! The last item in the tin was an indelible pencil, perhaps a gentle reminder to write home!

Sam decided to put the St Christopher badge around his neck; he hoped it would bring better luck than it did to Bill. Everything else he wrapped up in a parcel, tied it up with string and put sealing wax on the knots, and put his name on it, and the Frosts address. He passed this to his landlady, and asked her to post it if she did not hear form him after his month was up in Southampton, which she agreed, and Sam gave her enough money to post the parcel.

The following morning, when he left for Bristol, Sam wore his oldest set of working clothes, and these he would destroy when he was kitted out with his uniform. He took a train to Bristol early Monday morning, and made his way to the café where he was staying the night. After he had left his bag in the bedroom, he explored Bristol and relaxed, as he knew the following day, his feet would hardly touch the ground, well that is what Bill had told him in his first letter to him on joining up!

CHAPTER 8

Another Lamb To The Slaughter?

Bert was concerned that Sam was not at work on Monday morning. He asked around, but no one seemed to know where he was. He eventually went over and looked around his work bench and saw nothing to indicate why Sam had not arrived at work. It was as he normally left it, all tools put away in their appropriate places and all surfaces and floor swept down, as was the norm at the end of a days work. There was no part finished job on the bench, so he must have completed his last task. Where could Sam have gone to worried Bert? He started to have bad feelings to where Sam could be.

When the first post arrived the following day, there were the two letters Sam had posted, Bert recognised his writing. He put Alice's letter in his pocket, he would read his letter first to acquaint himself of the situation, first tell Agnes and then Alice, before passing her letter.

As Bert was opening the envelope, he was 99% sure what the letter inside would contain. As he read the letter, he had to sit down, the shock was so great. All Sam had said was that he was joining up and hoped to see them soon and not to worry. Bert knew he was under age, and wondered how he had hoodwinked the recruiting personnel? He now had to tell Alice and give her his letter to her. He knew there would be more tears again from both mother and daughter, the most from Alice as he knew that Sam had replaced Bill in her affections. Why did Sam have to do this to them, he was too young to go and fight and was in a reserved occupation.

***

Sam had a pleasant time in Bristol after dumping his bag at his digs, going up to Clifton Downs and looking at Brunel's suspension bridge, walking down to the harbour, followed by an evening meal in a fish and chip restaurant on the quayside followed by a couple of pints in a local tavern. He left his digs by 7.30am the following morning and made his way straight to West Bristol Barracks and reported to the Guard Room. He showed them his joining instructions and was directed to one of the many huts, situated on the perimeter of the parade ground. He was met by a corporal who told him he was the first there and he was going to be one of his lads and as there was nothing to do until others arrived he was told to stay with him in the Platoon Hut, and Sam, in answer to the Corporal's question, told him he was 93494 Private Perry W. The corporal had a look at his papers and put them in an empty tray marked 'New Recruits'. "That will be full by the end of the day," the corporal remarked.

"I'm Corporal Cartwright by the way, your half section NCO," and as he spoke a sergeant entered, making Sam stand up to a senior rank, "and this is Sergeant Archer who I report to and is your Full Section SNCO. Now I know the Sergeant wants a cup of char, so do I and I'm sure you do, so make four mugs as the Platoon Commander, our lustrous 2nd Lieutenant Ellis will want one as well. We will be in the office next to the kitchen so when you have made our cuppas, bring ours and yours in here and take the Lieutenant's to his office down the other end of the passage." At this last response, the two NCOs looked at each other and grinned. Sam noticed this and wondered what the interplay was about, he was sure he would soon find out! The Sergeant reminded Sam of the silent film hero Charlie Chaplin, he was thin and wiry with the same type of moustache, and carried his pace stick like a walking cane. The Corporal was a bit like Billy Bunter in shape and manner!

When Sam had made the tea he took three mugs into the Sergeant's office, the forth he took to the Platoon Commander office down at the end of the passage that ran the full length of the hut. Just as he went out, Archer said, "If he doesn't answer after three soft knocks, take it in and put it on his desk, as he is out somewhere and should be back soon." He paused and then added, "Across the passage there is a door opposite the Officer's office, it's our Platoon Store Room, can you check to see if the door is locked, if its not can you go in and see if everything looks tidy, as we have an inspection coming up soon." He heard a quite chuckle from Corporal Cartwright, *what was going on between the two of them.* He was soon to find out!

Sam went down the passage and knocked at the door marked

> **Platoon Commander**
> **2nd Lieutenant Ellis**

once, twice and a third time; no answer, so he walked into an empty office putting the mug of tea on the desk, then left shutting the door quietly behind him on the way out, wondering why there was an officer's hat on the desk and no officer around.

He then saw the door opposite which had a sign attached which stated which he had been asked to check. He thought he heard a noise from inside the room, so opened the door quietly and peered round the door. The room was in semi darkness, as thin material curtains were drawn closed across the single window letting a certain amount of light in. With a quick look round the room it was far from tidy and a set of racks was pushed up against one of the walls. On the floor there was an officer's uniform, with the insignia of a 2nd Lieutenant on the sleeve, a Sam Browne leather belt and shoulder strap, mixed up with a dress and a fashionable ladies hat of the day, assorted underwear from both sexes and lastly two pairs of shoes, brown officer's service issue and ladies dainty trim footwear, all lying about in careless abandonment. The was a noise from across the dimly lit room, he looked up from the pile of clothing and against the wall, under the window he saw a mattress, raising his eye still further he saw on top of the mattress the side of a naked female, lying on her back, his eyes continued to travel up, and on top of the naked female was a naked male lying on his front, face down, both just in the final act of their union.

Sam decided that a hasty retreat was the best solution, but as he went out, his arm knocked a pile of tin plates on an adjacent shelf that went crashing to the floor. Before Sam had made his exit the male person turned to see the retreating Sam, but in the dim light he was not in time to see a face.

Sam now realised why the two NCOs had grinned at each other. He told the Sergeant and Corporal what happened, they thought it was very funny and had a good laugh. They said the girl was Penelope Matchwick, Penny to her friends, and by all accounts she had many! Her father was a Senior Officer, Brigadier General Matchwick and that he far from approved of Sam's platoon Commander and had warned him off on several occasions. Sam said they should have warned him, as he was sure the Officer had seen enough of him to remember a face. The two NCOs said they had the measure of this snotty nosed 2nd Lieutenant who was meant to be their platoon Commander, but was only in name as he was hardly ever there. They assured Sam he would come to no harm while they were there, he did as they told him, or else he would be in trouble, as the said Brigadier General would be informed of what was going on in the store room.

Soon other recruits arrived, including Bob Drew, and they were made up into three squads of 24 men in each, kitted with bedding, their uniforms and mug and irons! After the evening meal they were permitted to use the canteen, but lights out were at 2130 hundred hours, and reveille was at 0630 hundred hours, and woe betide any one who was still in bed one second afterwards!

Later, Ellis saw his two NCOs and asked them who had brought him his mid morning tea, but they both did not know, as there were many solders arriving and they all had been given different fatigues to fill in the time before they were kitted out, and they hadn't kept a list of jobs to soldiers. They would always get the better of this weak and inefficient officer

Sam, like Bill, was a good soldier, and was the top recruit of the entry, but for some reason, this irked Ellis, and the more he saw Sam, the more he had a feeling that he was the soldier who had looked into the storeroom. While Ellis never recognised Sam and could not definitely identify him, he sent for him, and behind closed doors, the officer said if he had ever seen anything by poking his nose into storerooms, he was never to breathe a word about what he saw as his life would not be worth living if he did, and as far as the Officer was concerned, Sam was a marked man.

The Sergeant sent for him as soon as he left the officer and asked Sam what Ellis had wanted him for, and regardless of what Ellis had told him, he told his Sergeant. He told Sam to forget about what Ellis had said; he was a snotty nosed chinless wonder and was not worth bothering about. The officer, they told him, was not a good solider, his parents had purchased him a commission and he was far from suited for Army life. He would skive off, for his own pleasurable pursuits as often as possible and was only seen when he had to put in an appearance. He was in there for the glamour and the uniform. He had persuaded the *'Powers to be'*, through his parents, he would remain in this country for the duration of the war as a Recruit Training Officer at West Bristol Barracks, and never see action on the Western Front. As Sam was to find out in the not too distance future, the *'Powers to be'* had other ideas, to Sam's undoing.

Ellis started to cause trouble, nothing was ever right, the Sergeant and the Corporal were given a lot of stick and Sam started to be picked on. So it was only a matter of time before the word got around of the storeroom activities, not only to the recruits, but to senior NCOs, then Warrant Officers, then Junior Officers, then Senior Officers until it eventually reached the ears of Brigadier General Matchwick, CO of the Brigade. While he though the world of his daughter, he knew she was a bit on the wild side and not a white as the driven snow, but believed she would never consent to anything immoral, and was convinced Ellis must have forced himself on his daughter, most probably plied her with strong drink to get his wicked way with her! When he spoke to his daughter on the subject she lied to protect herself, telling her father she had tried to stop Ellis's advances on her, and was confused after the drink he had given her, but it was to no avail. She had been too muddled to tell him to leave her alone. She had only gone to Ellis office at his invitation on the pretext of him asking to escort her to the next Ladies function in the Officer's Mess. She said he had given her a cup of coffee when she arrived, she thought afterwards that it had a bitter taste and felt he had laced it with something, and she did not remember what happened after that, not sure if he had done anything to her. This her father believed. It was some time after the event he found out that a Private Perry had witnessed this encounter, and the grape vine said Ellis was giving Perry a hard time, why should he do that he asked himself. He did not think it worth interviewing Perry, it would gain nothing, and would probably bring more attention to this sordid affair than he wanted, and could reflect badly on his daughter, but he never forgot the name of Perry, which was a good thing for Sam later on, but he never knew of this. He had no proof to take any official action and it would only be his daughter's word against Ellis's. He would be keeping a close eye on 2nd Lieutenant Ellis from now on, but would not take this matter any further officially, but Ellis was also a marked man from now on!

As soon as word of this got to Brigadier General Matchwick's ears and with his daughter's confession, Ellis was ordered to report to his office immediately, which was 0800 hundred hours the following morning. The Brigadier General decided to let the 2nd Lieutenant sweat it out a bit and stew in his own juice, making him stand for over four hours, and did not get his PA to call him until just before lunch. When Ellis eventually went in he was a bag of nerves, but nothing to the state he was in when he left Matchwick's office half an hour later. He had received a tongue lashing that he would not forget for many a year and had to stand to attention for over half an hour while the Brigadier General told him his fortune with regard to his army career, which did not give him any prospects for any promotion, just as he thought the next rank up was soon to be his. There was other bad news for him; he had lost his soft cushy job at the Bristol Barracks, which he thought his parents had secured for him for the duration of the war, which the Brigadier General had only just found out about. If the Brigadier General had his way, no one should be allowed to buy commissions; he considered a commission had to be earned. He was told not to bother to contact his parents, as he was beyond their help, and by the time they got his letter, if he wrote one, he would be on his way to France. Perhaps his linguistic skills in French would be of use to him? His new position was going to be in the front line, in the trenches, to fight as a Platoon Commander.

If all that was not bad enough, the Brigadier General informed Ellis that he, with a sickly gleam in his eyes, would be leaving for France in the next few days also, where he could keep a close eye on him and he would be away from his daughter and all other decent women.

Ellis was now a much chastened man, but there was evil still much in his heart, he was in a very bad mood. In his opinion it was all Perry's doing, he must have spread the word about his affair with Penny. He knew Perry was due to go to France very soon, so he would try and make sure he was in his platoon when he got there. Perry was now singled out and was top of Ellis's black list, and as far as Ellis was concerned, he would make his life hell, and, if he could, he would get him killed, perhaps a slow death, it would be poetic justice in his book.

On leaving the Brigadier General's office, Ellis was told by his PA to clear his desk immediately and not to contact or speak to any of his Platoon, or ex-Platoon now, reporting back to him within 30 minutes, if not sooner, and providing him with a Captain as escort to see he did not stray. On returning he was told to pack his kit, draw a service revolver, ammunition and holster, pay his Mess Bill, and report back to him in one hour, with his kit. When he returned he was given a travel warrant to Folkestone, and as the PA said to the escort, the Brigadier General did not trust Ellis as far as he could throw him. So the escort was given a return warrant to Bristol and to accompany Ellis to Folkestone. To be on the safe side, the escort took Ellis's revolver from him, to be returned as he walked up the gangplank of the channel ferry, ensuring he got on the boat then wave him goodbye from the quay side as the boat pulled out, to make sure he did not jump overboard! And that is how 2nd Lieutenant left England in less that 12 hours with bitter feeling to wards Brigadier General Matchwick and a certain Private Perry W.

Sergeant Archer and Corporal Cartwright were celebrating, as it was they who had spread the storeroom saga onto the Barrack grape wine which they had achieved after many months of trying. Sam was very much in favour with the two NCOs, but he would soon be leaving them and was in the throes of packing his kit. One thing he was thankful for was that he would not be going over to France for at least another week, and he considered it most unlikely he would ever see Ellis again. Little did he know what the future and Ellis had in store for him.

***

On the 6th January 1916, the House of Commons voted overwhelmingly for the introduction of military conscription by the *Military Services Act* that became law on the 2nd March, stating that all fit male persons between the years of 18 and 41 would be called up unless married, widowed with children or in a reserved occupation. Prince Edward, the Prince of Wales, the son of George V, made his first flight in an aeroplane.

***

It did not take Algernon long to improve the squadrons under his control and they were soon doing sweeps over the enemy territory, shooting down many aircraft with little loss to themselves, the average hit rate for each squadron was increased and they became a force to be reckoned with. They were soon all flying the Sopwith's 1½ Strutters, which they found a great improvement on the Avro 504 that most of them had when Algernon arrived. With the improvement of aircrafts all the time, it was not long that the enemy had better aircrafts than they did, but because of their reputation they were the first to receive the latest aircraft and they were soon equipped in early 1916 with the Bristol Fighter F.2B, known to all as the *Brisfit*, which had a top speed of 125mph, compared with the 100mph of the Sopwith 1½. Things could only get better.

While Algernon's post was mainly flying a desk, he made sure he did as much operational flying over enemy lines as possible and shot down his fair share of the Hun's aircraft. This soon came to the notice of his superiors, and while they agreed with what he was doing, they reminded him he had been ordered not to go on operational flying. They saw his point and felt that the CO of the wing should lead his men, but Algernon was to valuable to go into battle and was told he was to stop operational flying while still in his current post, going no farther that the British front line at the most.

They felt the job of Wing leader should go to a younger man, so a senior Major with a good track record from another wing would be promoted to Lieutenant Colonel as CO of the *Ypres Wing* while Algernon would also be promoted to full Colonel. The first task he was given in his new post was to set up more wings, further afield from Ypres, up and down the rear to the front line which he was to command. He could still fly himself around, providing he did not go anywhere near the front line, or he would be grounded.

While he expressed his sorrow to his superiors, he felt a relief, he had started to feel the strain of leading a wing of up to 60 aircraft and it was best left to a younger man. While he gave up the job with some regrets, he felt he had achieved something in setting up the *Ypres Wing*, which was a first, and had been a success, and reflected well on his abilities. With the success of the *Wing*, he was determined to set up other wings to operate in the area to the same standard as *'His'* wing. He wrote and told Keturah of his promotion, saying he would be doing less flying, which was not quite true, but what flying he would be doing would be well inside the British lines.

Keturah was delighted with the news, and while she was kept busy with her war work, she still worried about her husband, who she loved dearly.

155

With all her work and effort, she was given other tasks to carry out, if you want a job done, find a busy person, which is exactly what they did with Keturah. At least she did not have to worry about their three children anymore, they were safe in the country, either looked after by the two schools during the week, or their grandparents, who spoilt them beyond belief, at the weekends!

***

Sam did not intend to write to anyone while he was at Bristol, he did not want any visitors either. He knew Alice would be tears and pleading for him to return, and Bert would try and pull strings to get him discharged and return to Shepherd's Bush to his reserved occupation. Just before Sam left for the France, he decided to write to Alice explaining why he had done what he had done; it was something he had to do, especially because of the loss of Bill. It was a hard letter to write, saying that what ever happen to him, he would try and return to her when the conflict was all over. He said he would write if it was at all possible, and he intimated that he was very fond of her. The last thing he did when he left the barracks for France was to give the letter to Corporal Cartwright, who had kept a close eye on him during his training, and was only to willing to help the lad who brought Ellis down, and would post the letter for him in a couple of weeks time, so he would be long gone before Alice received it.

After their initial training, Sam, with many others, departed for France, like Bill's train journey to Folkestone, the train had seen better days and the carriages were only one up from cattle trucks. Thankfully there were not many delays, and unlike Bill's departure day, the weather was good and they were not kept waiting on the quay too long either. The crossing was flat and calm and they were soon marched to an awaiting train that took them away from the docks at Calais. Like most troop trains, it was uncomfortable and slow but they got there. They arrived at what was know as the Rest or Holding Area where they would spend a week acclimatising and being instructed on trench warfare and the layout of the Ypres area, as Bill had not too long ago.

***

On the same boat that Sam travelled on, but in senior officer accommodation, was Major General Matchwick, having now been promoted from Brigadier General, to take up his post as a Senior Staff Office at Brigade HQ, also in Ypres. He was a man of action having fought in the Boer War, first as a Major in 1899, when the second Boer war started, and by the time the war had ended in 1902 he had been mentioned in dispatches, awarded the Victoria Cross for bravery on the field of battle and left South Africa as a Lieutenant Colonel. Having attended a Senior Staff Course within a year of his return home, he was promoted to full Colonel. His future, provided he did not make any mistakes, was already mapped out by those at the War Office and he was assured of a position in the top echelon of the army career structure in the years to come.

He had no intention of sitting at a desk all day and would tour the front lines as much as possible. He was far from happy with the conditions the rank and file had to endure in the trenches. The better the troops were looked after, the better the morale would be and you would have a better fighting soldier at the end of the day.

***

Before Sam moved up to the front, he decided to write another letter to Alice, to tell her about his love for her, and from the talk, it would seem that the Germans would soon surrender and they would all be home, but this was white lie, he had heard the stalemate could last for years. He had a problem; he could not give her a name to write back to, so while he was to her Samuel Bray, to the Army he was William Perry, he had to make the excuse that he was moving about a lot, he would keep writing to her, but there was no way at present that he could give her an address to write back. He hoped she would swallow this white lie.

After the acclimatisation period, they were marched down as a platoon to a series of trenches at the front that was going to be their area to defend and attack from as required. They entered the reserve trench, some way behind the front line, making their way down the connecting trenches to the front line trench. When they arrived the platoon was given a 48 hour rest before moving out. Sam's Platoon Commander, Captain Russell, was taking over from the outgoing Platoon Commander who seemed to know everything and was loud mouthed into the bargain. Suddenly Sam's blood froze, he recognised that voice, and it was 2nd Lieutenant Ellis. He looked around for somewhere to conceal himself, but he was too late, Ellis was on his way out and he had to pass Sam to get to the connecting trench. Sam turned away, but it was too late, Ellis spotted him, he stopped and looked at Sam. With a quick look round, Ellis made sure no one was in hearing distance, he shoved his face by Sam's ear and said, "Perry, you are a marked man in my book, I will get you if it's the last thing I do," and on that note left, following his platoon out of the trench complex. Sam was shattered, he knew Ellis was in France but thought the chances were very slim in meeting up, how wrong could one be, it was the last thing he expected. Sam took comfort that he was not in Ellis platoon, and when Ellis and his men returned, they could be in some trench area well away from his current position, there were miles of trenches.

They were told to stand down as they did not expect any action from the Germans and there was no planned push forward from Brigade HQ. Sam looked around him, this was to be his home, on and off for months, if not years, the war seemed to be in stalemate, with all the pushes from both sides, they had not advanced or retreated since the British had taken over the from the French who had dug the series of trenches they were now standing.

He had expected the trenches to be in one straight long line, but no, they zigzagged so one could not see much farther than about 25 yards either direction. There was a good reason for this, if a shell landed and exploded in a trench, if straight, it would cause a blast a long way in each direction, but as it zigzagged, the bends either side of the explosion absorbed most of the shock waves and reduced casualties. There was a dugout on the enemy side of the trenches where the Platoon Commander and his SNCOs billeted. The rank and file lived in the trench, the floor was covered in duckboards so the soldiers did not have to stand in water and or mud and unless it rained so hard it flooded over the boards. Sam thought the sleeping accommodation at Bristol was basic, but they did have beds and palliasse, here they had to get sand bags and form them in some sort of sitting up bed on the enemy side of the trench, between the ladders that leant against the trench wall, ready to climb if they were *Going Over The Top* or sneaking out on a night patrol. They were all on war rations but every so often a rum ration came round, this was good news and bad news, it was good to have some strong drink to warm you up, but the bad news it was usually a prelude of *Going Over The Top*. It was felt. That soldiers who had a few would be more acceptable in climbing up the ladders into enemy fire, giving them Dutch courage, than if you were stone cold sober.

Daily life in the trench was either 10% frantic action, or sitting around doing nothing and being bored out of your mind for 90%, waiting for a brew up or the next meal. Days blurred into days, weeks blurred into weeks, the only break in monotony was either action, which after a time was welcome, or a day or two back at the rest area. They did not have any major action, but Sam was often selected to go out on night patrols into no-mans-land when there was no moon, doing night scouting. As they kept low down and crept everywhere they were seldom detected. If the Germans sent up flares they melted into a shell hole until the flare had gone out and enemy gunfire ceased. In all the time they went out on patrol, they had only one casualty, his best mate from Bristol, Bob Drew. Somehow they got separated in the dark and he was never seen again, it was a mystery. Sam would always remember him, after meeting him when they had joined up, they became good friends and slept in adjacent beds in their billet at Bristol. It was on one of the occasions that there had been no fire, so it had to be assumed he got disorientated and lost in the darkness and wandered into the Germans line and taken prisoner.

About every two weeks, depending on the action, they went on a 24 or 48 hour rest where they could have baths and get all their clothes washed and mended. In the evening there were taverns that they could frequent for what girls there were, but they were not up to much, and there were at least a dozen blokes per girl. Going with girls like that, one never knew what one might catch, some fatal sexual disease if you were not careful. After being in the trenches, going over the top, getting fired at, some did not even care; they may be dead within a few days! There was only one girl for Sam, and that was Alice, he was faithful to her and his affections never wandered. He wondered how she was getting on, and what she thought about not being able to write back to him.

***

A new British invention entered the field of battle on 15th September 1916, under the code name of *Tank*. A tracked fighting vehicle that carried guns and an enclosed cabin for its crews protection, it could bridge trenches as no other vehicle had ever done before, mud and minor pot holes did not hinder its progress, rolling over the German lines at 4mph, crossing over their trenches as if they weren't there, barbed wire did nothing to impede its progress, scattering machine gun crews and crashing through strong points in its wake. Within two hours the British and Canadians had taken over 2,000 prisoners after its first assault.

***

Poor Alice; Bill had left her to join up then got himself killed, now Sam had gone and joined up, she hoped that getting killed was not going to be the same fate for him that Bill had succumbed to. She got a lot of comfort from her mother and Bert and Fred were also sympathetic. She had received a least two letters from the front and she still wondered why she could not write to him. He sounded well and there was little action and he was keeping his head down, which was a comfort, in a way.

The Eighteens were in the same boat as Alice, they were getting the occasional letter from Sam but no address to write to. They knew little about the Army and life on the front line, so they accepted that this was standard Army practice.

***

Algernon was a worried man, he was not short of the latest aircraft but the pilot replacement was bad. He seemed to be losing pilots faster than they could get trained replacements. He kept pestering Brigade HQ but it was to no avail, all the other areas were in the same position, he would have to wait and take his turn as new pilots got their *Wings*. When pilots did come, they had very few flying hours behind them, having only the basic skills of flying, but with no training in combat, that was not enough time as far as Algernon was concerned but he could do nothing about it. He thought this was not the correct way to train pilots, properly trained pilots lasted longer that ones with the minimum training. His losses were in the main from the rookies, not many got to ten sorties, lots did not make the first sortie back, they got called the *twenty-miniters*, as that is how long many lasted in the air on their first mission over enemy territory Many pilots could have been saved by having a parachute. Algernon pestered Brigade HQ time and time again for aircrew to be allowed to wear parachutes, but it was to no avail, those above could not see it his way.

***

Keturah was kept very busy with her work for the WEC during the week, often way into the night while trying to keep her weekends free to go to Grafton to see the children. She was getting very well known in the country with her in-laws friends and within the WEC. She was a fool to herself, the more work that she took on, the more they gave her, but she thrived on hard work, and it took her mind of other things, the dangers that Algernon might be facing daily.

***

Sam had been in the trenches about three months and had been back to the rest area on a number of occasions. There had been no major attacks, but he had been on night patrol a number of times and had their fair share of danger, at least five of his other mates from Bristol had now been killed on these skirmishes. Sam was resting up one morning when the trench area next to him had a change over and to his horror, a familiar voice could be heard shouting out commands, Ellis had arrived back in his area after being allotted to another area since he first encounter him.

Captain Russell was a senior Platoon Commander and was in line for promotion to Major, 2nd Lieutenant Ellis knew this and was soon sucking up to him on two counts, to get those above him to recommend him for better posts or positions and to belittle Sam. Sam thought a lot of Russell, he was kind and courteous to all his troops, he would not get them to do anything he would not do himself and he was always first *Over The Top*. He had been decorated for bravery on two occasions.

As Sam was positioned near the end of his platoon, next to the troops of Ellis's platoon, they got chatting. Sam told him how well liked his Platoon CO was, but what he heard about their Platoon CO, 2nd Lieutenant Ellis, did not surprise him. Whenever they had to go *Over the Top* they told him, Ellis was at the back shouting at the men to get up and get on with it, making threats of courts-martial if they did not get a move on, making sure all the Platoon went over, including the SNCOs, saying, "I'm checking everyone has gone, then I'm right behind you, once you clear the ladders." But they hardly ever saw him in no man's land, bar for poking his head over the trench top. When they got back they found, as he claimed, he was back first, was dirty and dishevelled, looking as if he had rolled in mud, and that is what they were sure he had done at the bottom of the trench while they were gone, but could not prove anything. Even if anyone had reported it, the powers to be would listen to an office first and take his side. He was a waste of time and they would do as little as possible for him, the morale was rock bottom in his Platoon. They were sure it was because of his leadership, or lack of it, that the platoon had so many losses, the highest of all the platoons on the front. From the SNCOs down, no one could stand him, he was a coward. This gave Sam some food for thought; he would certainly keep out of his way as much as possible.

They had just cleared up from breakfast having got their trench ready for another day when Sam was told to report to Captain Russell in his dugout. When he got there he requested permission to enter, as there was only a sack door covering the entrance. Being given permission, he entered and saluted the CO, who was there with both his SNCOs. "Private Perry reporting as ordered, Sir." Russell looked up at him and smiled and told him to sit down.

"Tell me Perry, how do you think you are doing with us?

"Sir, I feel I have done everything asked of me, be it just the normal routine of trench warfare, I don't think I have done anything I should not have, have there been any complaints about me, Sir?" *Had Ellis been telling tales to his CO?*

Again the Captain smiled, "No complaints whatsoever. You have been an excellent soldier, an example to the rest of the Platoon; both my SNCOs have commented on your performance and quite rightly brought it to my notice. But I have also been keeping an eye on you before they mentioned it to me, so all three of us are of the same opinion about you," which was a great relief to Sam.

"But one thing worries me though," the Captain continued, "whenever I get new soldiers I always read through their service history. To tell you the truth, when I saw your report, I was extremely concerned; your Platoon CO at Bristol gave you one of the worst reports that I have ever seen or had to read. I decided you had to be watched closely and I instructed my two SNCOs to keep a close eye on you, as I also did. So you can see why we were watching you. But what we cannot understand is that the report is nothing like how you are because it does not match up with you, as we have seen you. We started to think that the report had been mixed up with another soldier but could find no evidence it was. Have you any comments on what I have said so far Perry?"

Sam knew exactly what had happened, but felt he could not run down another officer in front of his CO. "I prefer not to make any comment, Sir," was his answer.

The CO smiled again at Sam. "I thought you would say that. You do not have to say anything and what I now say to you must go no further, do you understand that Perry?" Sam's answer was brief and to the point, "Yes Sir."

"Perry, I am not going to ask you to comment on what I say, but I have a feeling you must have upset someone at Bristol, and since then that person has been trying to get at you in every way possible. I recently spoke to an officer who gave me the impression that it was something that happened at Bristol. I think I know who the culprit could be from a number of people on the front line, so my SNCOs and I will make sure that this person never gets anywhere near you if we can help it, is that understood?" Sam nodded in agreement.

"Now Perry, you have done so well, and as we have a place for a Lance Corporal, you have immediate promotion, and will be in charge of a half section. My SNCOs will give you a briefing on your duties and the men under you. Good luck in you new post and I will still be keeping an eye on you. One of my SNCOs will give you your chevron and I'm sure you have the means to sow them on. Dismissed."

Sam saluted his CO and left the dugout with the SNCOs stunned, the senior of the two spoke to him, "I know all about what when on at Bristol, you may not know I left a couple of weeks before you, and I knew Sergeant

Archer very well, he told me all, so don't worry, we will make sure a certain officer is kept well away from you, no names, no pack drill!"

As soon as he had sewn his new rank on his arm he was soon briefed and his half section was well away from Ellis's lot. So, early in 1916, Private Perry W (the 2nd) was promoted to Lance Corporal.

Sam read between the lines of what the CO and the NCO had said, he knew Ellis was behind it all. Ellis had passed him earlier that day and went into his CO's dugout. One of the lads on duty near the dugout had done a bit of eaves dropping and told Sam later that Ellis had been warning Russell how bad Perry was, and, if Russell would like to transfer him to his platoon, he would soon sort the slacker out. He had to move away as one of the SNCOs was approaching, so did not hear their CO's reply but later saw him leave with his tail between his legs!

A few days later they saw action, after three days of heavy shelling from the rear to soften up the enemy, they were going *Over the Top*. This was the first time Sam had been involved in any major action and was very nervous, but he felt he must not let this be felt by his half section, he must put on a brave face and show he had no fear. Sam was to lead his half section in the assault, up the ladder adjacent to where Sam had his sleeping sand bags. The evening before, Captain Russell got the platoon together and briefed them on the orders for tomorrow and the object of the mission, to take out the two German machine gun posts opposite their part of the trench and capture the trench they were in if possible. The whistles would blow at 0700 hundred hours for all the platoons to attack. He wished them all good luck and God's speed in their mission and he would be first up the ladder leading the assault. Before the appointed hour, they would all receive a tot of rum.

Sam went round all his men when they had the final brew for the evening, talking to each and every one of them, making sure everything was alright, that they all had cleaned their rifles and got all the kit and ammo that they needed. He then went back to his sandbag bed and settled down to sleep, but sleep did not come, the night was long and dark, and eventually dawn came. Sam went round to make sure everyone was awake and they all had a quick brew, a bit of grub and the tot of rum that sent a warm glow into their bodies. By ten minutes before the off, they were all ready, standing behind Sam who was at the foot of the ladder.

A precisely 0700 hours the officer's whistles sounded all along the trenches, Sam was up and away, running crouched to the ground, zigzagging to stop the enemy getting a good aim and to avoid all the shell holes in the ground. All his platoon were around him, and while he could not stop, he saw soldiers dropping on his left and to right, whether they were just injured or dead, he did not know. He felt a bullet hit his back pack, while it did not do him any damage, the force knocked him over and he lay flat on his back for several minutes. He rolled over onto his front as bullets were still whistling a few inches over his head and found in that short space of time he had been left behind. All around him the ground was littered with bodies, injured, crying out in pain; the dead, or what was left of them, remained dormant.

Sam had only just partially recovered when a shell landed and exploded near to him, the ground being soft, there was no shrapnel, just mud, which covered Sam, blowing him over again, leaving a deep crater beside where he was lying. He eventually got up onto all fours feeling very dazed and shaken, oblivious to the action overhead, luckily, below the firing line of the German bullets buzzing all around him, when another shell a small distance away landed, the force of this explosion blowing him back into the shell hole he was on the edge of again, landing at the bottom, when yet another shell went off on his other side, the concussion of this made him collapse and lose consciousness.

When the whistle went, Captain Russell, further down the trench from Sam's position, was first up the ladder, heading for the German lines, dodging round the shell holes, but he had not got far when he received a bullet in the leg and one in his shoulder. As he fell, he had enough energy to fall down in the nearest hole for protection. He realised that there could be no chance of rescue until dark, so he had to make himself as comfortable as possible for a long wait. He injected himself with morphine and drifted of in a drug induced sleep.

The attack was a disaster; the whole affair was a shambles from start to finish. What was left of Captain Russell's platoon staggered or crawled back to the trenches, including the walking wounded, a defeated band of soldiers as one could imagine. Those who returned could hear the cries of their wounded comrades left in no-mans-land, but nothing could be done about them until darkness fell. By the time the rescue parties went out, they returned first with the injured and as many dead as possible. Captain Russell was soon found and taken to the field hospital and eventually repatriated back to an English Army hospital. As Sam was still unconscious, there were no cries for help from him and he, therefore, was not found, and, if seen, was presumed dead. He lay there all night, through the next day, and as it started to get dark on the second night he began to regain consciousness.

At 0700 hours, Ellis, holding his whistle to his mouth in his left hand and waving his Colt 45 revolver in his right hand, ordered his troops up the ladder with his two SNCOs, saying he would be right behind them, many he would never see again, which did not bother him unduly, he only cared for number one, 2nd Lieutenant Ellis. 2nd Lieutenant Ellis did not get wounded. In fact he did not even make the first foot of no-mans-land, he did not even make the top of the ladder and he did not even climb the ladder, staying firmly in the bottom of the trench, watching his men go over the top, many to their certain death, shouting at them to get a move on so he could follow them up the ladder. He was up to his usual tricks. His platoon did not even get any rum ration, telling his SNCOs there weren't enough bottle for all the troops. Ellis had got their ration and kept all the bottles hidden for himself later.

By evening, a senior officer arrived to take account of the day and to reorganise the depleted platoons. 2nd Lieutenant Ellis saw his big chance to get promotion. He volunteered to take over Captain Russell's platoon and amalgamate them with his. In the urgency of the moment this was granted, little did they know what they had done for those now under him. The senior officer reported back to their HQ, telling his superiors of what the young 2nd Lieutenant Ellis had volunteered for, and praised him for his courage. This information filtered upwards, and got to the ears of the newly promoted Major General Matchwick. He was amazed and horrified, Ellis was the last person in the world who would do anything of this nature and he decided to give Ellis a surprise visit at the earliest opportunity. In the meantime, he would send one of his aides down to check up and report back. He did not think this soldier had changed his spots; he put him down as a coward from the outset. What he found out later proved he was correct.

Back in the trench, much to the dismay of all ranks, Ellis had now taken over, dashing about, shouting stupid orders, which no one took much notice of, and the said 2nd Lieutenant never bothered to check to see if they had been carried out. The morale went down, and the whole platoon started falling apart and was far from a competent fighting unit. There are two parts of an order, the first is the order itself and the second is checking it has been carried out. If the second part is never checked then it's not worth giving the order in the first place. Soldiers in Ellis platoons soon realised this and just ignored orders given by Ellis, knowing they would never be caught out.

When Ellis took over he immediately looked for Sam, but he was not anywhere to be found, believed killed he was told. He was disappointed, not because he may have been killed, but being dead, he could not wreak revenge on him, which is what he had wanted to inflict on him since that fateful day in Bristol when Sam had caught him with *his pants down* in a comprising position with the Major General's daughter!

As darkness came on the second night, Sam started to work out what had happened to him, where he was and what he should do next. He lay there for several hours, waiting for his strength to return and darkness. When they both did he had also got his bearings by this time and crawled up the side of the shell hole and towards the British line. On arrival at the trenches, he found a ladder and half climbed, half fell down the ladder, landing on the duck boards of the trench. He staggered to his sleeping sand bags and collapsed, still concussed.

By morning, Sam was still not with it, found by one of the SNCOs, who immediately realised he was a sick man and made preparations to get him back from the front to a field hospital. Then Ellis arrived, he had got Sam now. He ordered Sam to stay in the trench, even though the SNCO tried to explain that Sam was a sick man. Ellis told the Sergeant to shut up and go away, take all the troops with him and he would sort out Perry's problem. The SNCO could do nothing but to obey the officer's order and departed, making sure all the troops left the area as well. Sam's answer to Ellis's question as to where he had been for nearly two days was that he had been unconscious in a shell hole all the time, which Ellis refused to believe. He now had Sam where he wanted him, he would show no mercy.

"Perry, you are a liar, you are a malingerer, you are a coward, you have been hiding on the front, you have let your comrades fight and die around you. I will report you for this and have you face Court Martial; you will be found guilty and shot at dawn, and it will give me great pleasure to watch you die," was the out burst Sam received from Ellis. Sam in his weak state could take no more and collapsed onto the wet and muddy duckboards, and when he fell he was out of sight and hearing of anyone else. Ellis gave him a good kicking, that gave him great delight and pleasure and made him feel much better.

Ellis had to get enough evidence to convict Sam, as he had not got any at present, and the SNCOs he knew were on Sam's side and would give evidence on his behalf, which did not fit into Ellis's plan. So he would hold placing any charge until he had a watertight case. He had recently seen a *Medical Examining Form* that was used to assess the medical status of a soldier; he had to get one of these to make his plan work. As he had now taken over two platoons, there was an empty officer's dugout at the far end of the trench, which had been Ellis's, but he was now using Captain Russell's dugout that was much better. He dragged Sam to this and took him inside, placed him on a bed in a dark corner, covered him up, and left him on his own. Before he left he wrote out a notice on the card from a box that had contained corn beef:

DANGER
Do Not Enter Dugout
Unsafe
By Order Lieutenant Ellis
Platoon Commander

---

pinning it on the sackcloth door as he left, giving himself promotion which he expected soon to received, but it never happened. He knew there was little chance of Sam being found as the two platoons were short of soldiers and they had giving up using this area until they were back up to full strength.

Sam's luck was running out, everything was going wrong for him. Major General Matchwick's visit to check up on Ellis had to be put on hold, including sending an aide down, as he had been called back to the War Office in London for a high level conference to ascertain what went wrong with the last disastrous attack on German lines. He was away for just over two weeks, time for Ellis to put his master plan into action.

After the last attack, all was quiet on the western front; bar for a low sentry watch, the rest of the men were on stand down. When evening came the day Sam had returned and darkness was setting in, Ellis told his two SNCOs to take over for a few hours as he had been ordered to report to HQ for details of the next action. They thought this a strange thing to happen this late in the day, but did not ask any questions, they knew better. One did ask Ellis about Sam as they had not seen him and Ellis reply was that he had been admitted to the Field Hospital and as it was near the HQ he would go and visit him to see how he was progressing while he was at HQ and let them know on his return. He said he had been told by a senior doctor that Perry's condition was so bad he was expected to be repatriated back home. The two SNCOs were not sure if this was true or not, but what could they do, there was no one else to question and they could not leave the trench area to find out anything for themselves.

Ellis made his way back from the front to the tented field hospital. As he had been there before he knew the tent that was being used as an office where the form he required was kept. Late at night there was no office staff around except the Duty Medical Orderly, a private of the Medical Corps, who was on duty in the Admin Tent.

Ellis, on entering the tent, ordered the DMO to give him a *Medical Examining Form* as he had been asked by a doctor get one for an urgent medical report. The orderly started to object but Ellis said if he did not give him a copy immediately he would be put on a charge for disobeying a direct order. The orderly reluctantly passed over the form asking for the officer's name. Ellis had no intention of giving his own name and while he told the soldier it was none of his business he eventually said it was Captain Russell. He was glad he had had the foresight of putting on a cape to cover his rank.

Afterwards, Ellis made his way to the HQ Officer's mess, which he was allowed to use when on *Rest*. He found a quiet place in the Ante-room where he filled in the Medical Report. He had copies of previous reports on injured soldiers and knew the format and medical jargon used and needed the signature of two medical officers, one who carried out the medical inspection, the other as a witness. What was also useful to him was that he had the signatures of various medical officers from copies of previous medical forms that he had copies of when any of his troops had been injured and hospitalised. He selected two of the medical officers that he had signatures of and he considered would be easy to copy, forging the signatures of a Major Taylor, a senior surgeon who Ellis felt would give more credence to the document, and a Captain Ives, another surgeon, as second medical officer which was required by the *Medical Examining Form* to say Sam was 100% fit for fighting duties and had been faking illness and was not wounded in any way. He had heard that Major Taylor was about to leave for a conference in England, before the CM could be convened, and would not be available to give evidence at the trial if required and felt that they would not bother about Captain Ives. As required by the form, the office bringing the charge had to also sign the form which Ellis duly signed.

What Ellis did not know was the conference dates had been brought forward and Major Taylor had left before the attack had commenced and Captain Ives had been transferred to another hospital, 100 miles away at least a month previous. Ellis completed the form and was pleased with his effort and with the Medical Report, his Statement of Evidence, he would hand this in with his Charge Form, charging 93494, Lance Corporal Perry W. with Desertion on the Field of Battle. As Ellis knew, if found guilty, he would be shot at dawn, just what he had hoped for, the best result he could have wished for.

This type of charge was taken very seriously as there had been a number of deserters, those caught were charged and tried at a Court Martial, if found guilty they were sentenced to death. The result of these Court Martial were often decided before the court sat by the three Presiding Officers taking the charge, they had to make examples of the deserters, to deter others. They usually had a strong prosecuting officer of a senior rank than the defending one; they got the result they wanted in the shortest possible time. The defending officers were given little assistance and evidence, unlike the prosecuting officer, and were often told not question the prosecuting officer's evidence. They would look at the evidence of the defence, and any that could put the prosecuting evidence in doubt, was made inadmissible and had to be withdrawn. The defending officers were left with little or no evidence and defence witnesses, where possible, were deemed inadmissible on some obscure technical reason. The defendant's case was not strong enough to get a Not Guilty verdict very often.

The charge was placed by Ellis to the Provost Marshall's office and Ellis was told to have Perry arrested and taken by army police escort to the town jail where he was to be held until tried. Ellis had not finished yet and said Perry, since his return to the trench from the field of battle, had deserted again and could not be found, but he, Ellis, had an idea where he may be. He was told to take two police corporals and seek Perry out and arrest him.

Ellis returned with the police to the trench, he said he would get to his dugout and start a search that end and directed the two policemen to go to the empty end of the trench. It would look better if someone else found Perry, which after a short space of time they did. Ellis did not go back to his dugout but followed the police at a discreet distance. As soon as they found Perry, who was now only semi conscious, he was dragged to his feet and made to walk. The two policemen thought Sam looked ill, but Ellis said he was just malingering and to drag him away if necessary. Ellis made sure that they took Sam up a connecting trench away from the SNCOs and the rest of the platoon; he did not want anyone else to see what was going on as he had let it be known that Perry was in hospital. He was half dragged, half frog marched to the jail and thrown inside.

Ellis reported to the Provost Marshal, Lieutenant Colonel Harper, who praised him for his good work. Ellis said that Perry was a drug addict and while he was fit, as they would see by the Medical Report he had just obtained from the doctor who had just checked him, he was a bit drowsy from the illegal drugs he had been taking. The Provost Marshal decided this would not make any difference and it was agreed to have the trail in two days time, on the charge as stated on the charge form Ellis had submitted, adding a second case of desertion. There was just time to brief the prosecuting officer, who before joining the Army was a professional lawyer working in Lincoln Inn Fields in London. He hardly ever lost a case.

As Sam lay on the wooden bench that did for a bed, recovering, he looked at the square of sunshine on the wall opposite the window, he realised he would never be free again. He had let Bill down, he had not killed or injured a single German, and he had not avenged Bill's death on the field of battle. Had his life been in vain? Was there no escape from this Hell? What really got him most was that he was innocent, framed by his Platoon Commander in revenge as to what happened in Bristol. He knew before he went into court what the result would be.

CHAPTER 9

On His Own

The Court Martial, held in February 1916, was a complete travesty of justice. The officials of the Court Martial consisted of the President and a Lieutenant Colonel Lucas, supported by two Captains. Lucas was an autocratic disciplinarian who was only to happy shouting orders at his subordinates and seeing them jumping in all directions as they carried out these orders. He had no mercy for anyone who stepped out of line and a CM for a deserter was a situation he relished. His outward appearance was all bravado, a false front, for underneath he was a born coward. He had never been anywhere near any battles including the Boer War in all his 20 years of his army service, wangling positions well behind the action, very similar to a certain 2nd Lieutenant Ellis. He had been the President at a number of CM involving desertion and had found them all guilty and had sentenced all accused to be shot. Behind his back he became know by the rank and file as *Judge Jeffreys of the Army*, a person to be feared. He relished CM and was always badgering the Provost Marshal to appoint him as President of as many CM as possible. Not many officers liked this job, so one volunteer was better than two pressed men, so the PM was only too happy to oblige.

Before the proceedings of the CM opened, Lucas told the two acting Captains, in no uncertain terms, that he was in charge of the Court Martial and they were not to challenge anything he said or did, and they were both to concur with everything that he signed. He told both these two men, who had only just been recently promoted, that if they wished to get further in their career in the Army they had to do as they were told; they were basically there to make up numbers and were to agree with what the President said, they were to be his *"Yes Men"*. Both were too afraid to do anything other than what the he said.

The defending officer had only been commissioned in the army for a few weeks and knew nothing about Court Martial and little of Army Law, he was given a copy Kings Regulations and Army Law, but in the little time before the CM, he had little or no time to read up anything of any relevance to this case. He was told to do the best he could and when he asked if he could have the trial delayed for at least a week so he could get acquainted with the case and the accused it was turned down without any hesitation, and he only granted a couple of minutes to speak to the accused just before the trial began, which Lucas begrudgingly gave permission, but placed restrictions on the visit, on time and not being allowed in the cell with Sam, having to do all the talking through the small cell door window. Sam was still in a partly dazed state, so his Defence Consul gained nothing of the few minutes talking with him.

The Court was assembled, and Sam, while having improved in health for his two days incarcerated in a prison cell, was marched in not wearing his cap, as required of the accused, between two corporals of the military police as escorts. He was not allowed to sit and had to stand by the defending office. The President opened the proceedings by reading out the two charges of Desertion on the Field of Battle and trying to escape after having been detained. He then asked for the Medical Report on the accused. This was given to him by the Prosecuting Officer, he took a cursory look at the form, ascertaining that the accused was fit to stand trial; he never even bothered to look at the signatures of the two medical officers and did not show it to the other two members of board. He then made this as Exhibit No: 1 and recorded it into the proceedings of the CM.

The prosecuting officer outlined the case and then said that the accused was guilty as charged and would soon prove this to the court's satisfaction. The defending officers got up and spoke on behalf of Sam, but it was vague and wishy-washy, it did not impress anyone, especially Sam. The prosecution called 2nd Lieutenant Ellis who repeated what he had given in a written statement, adding a few embellishments that he made up as he went along, saying Perry had struck him when he tried to arrest him and the police had had to restrain him. He said that when he returned to the trench the day after the attack he did not have any of his personal equipment, including his rifle with him, which proved he was trying to desert. This was all accepted by the President and when the Defence tried to repudiate this as it was untrue, it was not even noted in the court records. The two police corporals were called who Ellis had briefed on what they were to say and therefore supported Ellis's evidence. As there was no more prosecuting evidence, the Defence had their chance. He wanted to call Sam first to tell the court his side of the story. The President refused to allow Sam to give evidence, it had been proved by the medical report he was a drug addict and was a known habitual liar, nothing he said could assist him in proving him innocent. As Defence had no more witnesses and had hardly any time to compile a case, he asked for the CM to adjourn the proceeding for a week, so he could gather more evidence from witnesses the accused felt would help him in his defence. This was not granted and the President asked both the prosecuting and defending counsels to give their summing up. The Prosecution took about 15 minutes, while the defence asked as the accused was ill, and had never taken drugs, to consider a Not Guilty verdict. The President, without consultation with his aides, gave his summing up, and said the verdict of the CM was Guilty. The President said the accused had been a disgrace to the Army and the uniform he was wearing. He would be reduced to the rank of Private, telling the Court Orderly to remove the accused stripes immediately. He then pronounced the main sentence that the Accused would be taken from the court to a lawful place of execution and in two days time would be shot dead at dawn by a firing squad, once the sentence had been ratified by the Provost Marshal, which was only a formality. Sam was then marched out and taken to the lawful place of execution.

The President called Ellis forward and praised him on his conduct and placed him in charge of the execution and ensuring the accused was held in custody until the sentence was completed. For Ellis, this was icing on the cake. He departed immediately to ensure everything was carried out as the CM had ordered. Lieutenant Colonel Lucas then closed the CM, got the two other members of the CM Board to counter sign the findings, Lucas being the senior, and anyone his junior, he would let them know it, was he not the President of the CM. He handed the proceeding to the Provost Marshal and told him to sign then so the sentence could be carried out as he had stipulated.

Sam was marched to a remote area about a mile east of the town, beyond all prying eyes, in an enclosed wall garden of an abandoned château near by. When Sam and his platoon had marched from the trenches to the rest area and back, they had passed this walled garden and he had often wondered what was behind these walls, now he was about to find out, *was this where he was going to end his days?* As he was marched into the garden, handcuffed, between two escorting MPs he saw a post standing in the far corner firmly planted in the ground, while at the other end of the garden under a tall overhanging tree was a very large marquee that had been erected, *was this his prison for his final two days on earth.* In the marquee waiting were a number of soldiers who were the firing squad and his guard.

This band of men, who had been chosen for this job as they were all marksman, had never done any fighting, they were privileged and they moved along the front line, executing those sentenced to death by CM. They led a lonely life, no one would talk or drink with them and they were outcasts. They never went to an Army Canteen and only visited taverns to get drink to take back to their billet or to where ever they were for an execution. They never messed with the other soldiers, all their food was delivered. The Sergeant's first task, after the escorts had removed the handcuffs, was to make Sam remove all his cloths, searching for anything that could be used as a weapon or to help him escape, they found nothing, he had already been searched by the military police before he was put in the prison cell and they had found nothing either, including any drugs which Ellis claimed he used. He was then allowed to get dressed.

Once dressed, he was handcuffed by his right wrist, the other cuff was threaded through a ring at the end of a three foot chain, this attached to a stake that had barbs at the lower end to prevent it being pulled out of the ground, where it had been driven firmly down into the earth by at least three to four feet, there was no way anyone could pull it out. If he could, and make a run with it attached, he would never get very far, as the stake weighed about 112 pounds.

Ellis turned up to make himself known to the SNCO in charge of the party and said while he would not be staying, he would return from time to time, checking up to ensure that the condemned man was well guarded and ensure he was given no privileges and only bread and water to eat. Not long after Ellis had arrived a Captain from the Medical Corps turned up to give the prisoner a medical inspection to see if he was fit to be executed. He made Sam strip off to the waist in the cold, but the inspection was brief and the officer soon left. Ellis, with a sickly smile on his face, made Sam stand to attention, removing his identification discs, "You won't want these where you are going, and I will be handing them in to authorities after you have been shot and as you lie dead in your unmarked grave. You are a nothing Perry and have always been a nothing, and, from the day after tomorrow, you will only be a statistic in a ledger," he whispered, leaning close to Sam, so the execution squad could not hear, "Cos I know you are the bastard who shopped me at Bristol and why I got sent here, so I hope your soul rots in Hell."

Ellis's job on the day of execution was first to load all the rifles out of sight of the squad. All the rifles would be loaded with blank cartridges except one which would have a live round. The rifles would be collected by the squad, the men not knowing who had the rifle with the live round in and, in theory, no one of the men would know who had actually killed the accused. In practice the man who fired the live round did, as the kick from a blank cartridge is less than a live round. The squad had a code of practice; the one who fired the live round ever mentioned it to the rest of the squad.

After the briefing Ellis left, only coming back a couple of times on the first day, but seeing there was nothing else he could do, he advised the Sergeant that he would return not until just before dawn the day after tomorrow to carry out his duties as Execution Officer. As the nearest Officers Mess was a long way off, he spent both nights in a tavern, drinking and eventually going to bed with a local wench; his ability to speak French was of great help to him!

The squad's final task before the execution was to dig a grave near to where the post that Sam was to be strapped to for his executed. This took most of the first day, between much drinking. When finished, they retired to the marquee with their shovels, leaving them well away from Sam, and, bar for a sentry, everyone went to sleep. Even the sentry nodded off, Sam noticed.

The Squad had many executions behind them and their method was to place a sentry on the tent door and in pairs take it in turns to get their food rations from the nearest army field kitchen and drink from the local tavern; beer, wine and cognac would keep them going for the evening. While they did this job many times, they had to have a number of drinks before they could carry out the deed of the macabre task. As darkness fell, the drinking was well under way, including the sentry, who had now left the tent entrance and joined the two NCOs' and the rest of his mates for his share of the booze. There was no real need for a sentry if the prisoner was well and truly secured to the stake.

When Sam arrived at the tent he was put into the far corner away from the door. He had two days and two nights before the sentence was carried out. On the ground was a palliasse and couple of blankets for his use adjacent to the metal stake which he had now been attached. Once the SNCO, who was responsible for ensuring Sam was always locked up and keeping the key safe, was satisfied all was well. They left Sam on his own; the rules were that no on would talk to the prisoner unless they had to. Sam was only released when he wanted a call of nature. He had to be unlocked from his stake and then taken outside by two guards to relieve himself into a hole dug into the ground for his use only and watched while he performed, him like a animal, then taken back to be locked to the stake once more. The SNCO delegated this duty to the sentry and one other and the key was left on the ground just out of Sam's reach, where the squad knew where it was but available when the prisoner wanted to go for a walk. The squad relieved themselves at an army toilet near by.

Hot meals were delivered for the troops, to which the accused was entitled but did not get, his ration shared between the squad. Ellis had struck again and had arranged that Sam only got bread and water which was against all regulations as he was entitled to proper food. Ellis was going to get his pound of flesh! The local mess where the food came from, unbeknown to the squad, would slip in a few extras, they felt sorry for the accused; a lump of cheese, a leg of chicken, a cooked sausage, plus anything else they could find that would keep, well wrapped so no smell could be detected. Sam realised on opening the first rations he had extras and ensured they were well

174

concealed from prying eyes when he ate them. Any food left he hid under his palliasse for later as they would take the haversack back to the mess for the next meal. He trusted no one in the squad and they gave him no sympathy! To appease their conscience the Execution Squad considered the prisoner was guilty as charged and shooting was the best punishment for him, so they were doing a service to the Army to purge it of soldiers like Sam.

As Sam had nothing else to do as he lay on his make shift bed, he started to think, how could he escape, he had nothing to lose. He was in the far corner of the tent, well away from the door, with guard's in-between, but well away from him as the marquee was quite large, no way of escape that way. There was a slight gust of wind and the edge of the marquee flapped in the breeze that had not been properly pegged down and he realised that there was enough room to crawl under, but how could he get out of the handcuffs. While he had been checking the flap something dug into his body, on investigation he found it was a long fallen branch from the overhanging tree, dead and devoid of foliage which must have been there some time. On checking the branch, Sam found it was fairly straight with a few and side branches, it gave him an idea. When the marquee was erected he supposed no one had seen it, and if they had, he supposed they would not have taken any notice of it; a small branch was not big enough to defend or attack anyone.

When night came and he had just returned after a call of nature in the garden he was locked up again. After the squad had eaten their evening meal they gave his haversack of fresh water and bread, as they thought, but again, there were extras, a good thing the squad never searched the bag. The firing squad had been drinking most of the day, a good mixture of the local booze which made them in a relaxed and sleepy state. The sentry had taken him for his walk was well away with drink, not even bothering to have another guard with him, things were getting very slipshod. The sentry threw the key to the handcuffs down on the ground, but this time the guard was careless, Sam realised it had been left it near enough for him to reach if he used the branch he found as a hook. Perhaps the tide had turned; luck was now on his side. He bided his time until it was well after midnight and all the execution party were asleep, including the sentry. The sentry was only kept there during the day to impress any visitors, and as there was no visitors at night, including 2nd Lieutenant Ellis, there was no way he was needed at night, the prisoner was well staked out as far as they were concerned and could not possibly escape. The sleeping sentry had left one of two oil lamp burning, one hung just inside the entrance, Sam was in the far dark corner, his movements would, he hoped, be hard to detect.

Sam wondered, if he escaped, where he should go. If he went west, into British held territory, and he was caught, which was very likely, he would be returned and be shot. But he had another idea, at first it seemed a strange idea, but he felt in the end it would be the best opportunity for him if he wanted to stay alive. He may get shot on the way, but it was a chance he had to take. If he stayed here he was definitely going to be shot, if he went west he was sure to be shot, the plan he had was his best bet he considered.

With all the drink inside the squad, they were all deeply asleep by now, snoring away, being little chance they would wake up if he was very quiet, Sam decided it was now or never to make his escape. From the light of the other oil lamp that hung from a roof pole of the marquee that was also kept burning all night he made his move. He slowly rolled over making no noise and with the branch in his hand as his aid he could just stretch out and reach the key ring, He hooked the ring with a side branch off the main stem after the third attempt and slowly, so there was no jangling to wake anyone up, pulled the key and ring towards him. He had got the key! Without making any noise, he inserted the key into the cuff on his wrist and found it fitted easily. Once the key was in the hole he wound it in until the cuff flipped open and he was free. He then relocked the cuff and placed the key far enough away to give the impression it could not have been possible for him to have reached it, that would give the execution squad something to think about! He slid out of his bed, stuffing a blanket under the other blanket, so at first glance it would look as if he was still be under there. He recovered his boots, that he had to remove every night that were put out of his reach and were left beside the keys. He then wriggled under the tent side taking his haversack with him, which contained food and water, and the branch with him, which could give the game away if he left it behind. He quietly walked round the inside edge of the walled garden until he came to the entrance that led into the road outside, looking back at the marquee entrance, the opening flap was closed so no one could see in or out and noises of heavy breathing could be heard from inside, which was a good thing and there was not a soul in sight outside.

He walked along the outside of the wall until it ended then followed it round the corner taking him away from the road, out into the country, tossing the branch away, with a quiet, *"Thank you,"* to it as it landed in the grass as he donned his boots! He had seen a shallow stream that ran adjacent to the road, running from east to west, on their marches into town on the way to the rest area, so he made for this and decided to walk in the water. If they sent in tracker dogs this would lose them and the stream was smooth and cool to walk in. After about what he judged was a mile he left the stream that had now turned south and was now getting to be just a trickle, it had served its purpose as far as he was concerned. He now headed in an eastwardly direction, all a part of his plan, the direction of the front.

Sam always had a good sense of direction and once clear of the stream he started to make his way to the front line, keeping to the fields, but near enough the road for guidance, the same road he had been along many times in both directions, it led to the trenches. He passed a number of cottages where one had washing hanging out on a clothes line, he removed a large white vest with a few holes in it, *this could come in useful later on if he had to surrender.* On his marches from the trenches to the rest area he had noticed a large old barn, by a stream, which was not too far away; he decided that is where he would spend the rest of the following day. Once they found he had escaped, he reckoned they wouldn't think he would have gone west to make his get away, so west would be the direction he hoped the search would be concentrated. He never found out if his theory was correct, but he would have been well pleased if he had seen the hue and cry going in that direction in less than ten hours time, looking for him over the next few days. The search parties never thought of looking for him in the opposite direction, that part of his plan had worked.

***

As there was another day before the execution, there was no hurry for the squad to rise, they would be up early on the following day. They were sure if Ellis did turn up it would be late morning at the earliest. The first of the firing squad to wake up was the Sergeant. He started to wake up his men, all a bit hungover from the heavy drinking far into the night, telling his Corporal to get the prisoner up.

The Corporal looked across to Sam's bed and saw, in the dim light of dawn, what appeared to be the sleeping prisoner completely hidden under the blanket. He went over to give the prisoner a boot in his side to wake up, aiming his kick to sink into him, to what he judged was his stomach, it did not matter if he hurt him, he had no one to complain to, 2nd Lieutenant Ellis would be only too pleased to have him kicked about a bit, and any rate he would be dead in less then 24 hours, so it didn't matter in the least. He swung his leg as hard as he could at the prisoner but as his boot contacted with the blanket, expecting resistance of a solid body, there was none. The corporal lost his balance and fell over and he immediately knew there was something wrong straight away. He scrambled to his feet, bending over he wrenched back the blankets in great haste, only to discover a rolled up blanket underneath. A quick look round the tent confirmed Sam had disappeared. The single handcuff was hanging empty from the ring on the chain attached to the stake.

There was a cry from the JNCO, "The buggers gone, the little sod has legged it, taken his boots and all, escaped. How the hell did he do it? The handcuff is still attached to the stake and both cuffs locked." He looked around and saw the key was at least 10 foot away from the stake, "And the key is too far away for him to have reached it," he continued. The Sergeant was over in a flash, he could see he was in deep trouble if he could not retrieve the situation fast. He woke all the execution squad who were all feeling a bit fragile from their binge the previous night as they had nothing strenuous to do that day bar to keep an eye on the prisoner. The Sergeant asked all the squad if anyone had daft enough to release the prisoner, all denied any such thing.

He sent all the squad out to look for the missing prisoner, both inside and outside the walled garden, but there was not enough light yet to see far, especially as it was going to be a dull overcast day. As none of them could see much they all soon returned empty handed.

The Sergeant and the Corporal got together to work out what they could do to cover their tracks, otherwise they would be deeper in a hole than the grave outside.

"Sarge, I've had an idea," said the corporal. "What if we say when dawn came up and the officer was not here, we shot the sod as was ordered and buried him?"

"No good, that won't do, you have to have an officer present at the execution," was the Sergeant's reply.

"OK Sarge, the officer is AWOL and doesn't want to be found out, so do as I just suggested, but we say he was here, he would not correct us, and he would want to save his own skin. He could sign the document of execution when he comes back later."

"That's no good either Corp, that story wouldn't wash. We don't know it the officer has had an accident or something, or if he is with someone now, that story would not stand up for ten seconds under questioning. Also you have not thought this through properly, if we say we shot and buried him, then some one finds him escaping, we will be in deeper trouble then we are now. No, we have to think again."

The Sergeant did some quick thinking. He got them to dig up the stake, making it look if Sam had worked it loose and taken it with him still attached to his wrist. The Sergeant got them to bury it in the bottom of the grave and cover it over with some top soil, so it could not be seen from above. He then pegged the flapping sides of the tent down securely where Sam had lifted it up by wriggling under and then tore the side of the tent where prisoner had slept, making it look as if he had cut his way out. If he was asked where he got the knife from, it must have had it before he arrived and concealed it well, they could say it was not their duty to search the prisoner, which was untrue as they had searched him when he arrived the day before as a part of their task. They would also say that there had been a sentry on duty at the tent entrance all night, but as the entrance was on the opposite side of the tent to where the prisoner was staked and it was dark in the tent, saying the lamp had blown out with the wind as there was a crack in the glass, the sentries had heard or seen anything.

The Sergeant then sent the Corporal to alert the Military Police, and advise them to instigate a search. Now he had to wait for the officer to arrive, which could be at any time or not at all, he did say he might not return today. If the little bugger was recaptured, which he was sure would happen, he would shoot the little sod him himself if he had half the chance. He knew trouble was on the way for him, he felt his days were numbered if he could not get the prisoner back before too many people got to hear about it. How right he was, and it did not take long to realise the trouble he was in.

About half an hour later the Provost Marshal with a number of Military policemen arrived. The first question they asked was where was 2nd Lieutenant Ellis, as he should not have left the area, as the prisoner was his responsibility. The Sergeant tried to cast as much blame on Ellis as possible, which wasn't hard and said he had left about mid afternoon yesterday and had not been seen since. As Ellis was not there the Sergeant came in for a lot of stick and was put on open arrest until the matter was cleared. The Corporal and the rest of the squad closed ranks and said as little as possible, in any case the Provost Marshal considered the Sergeant had to take the blame in the absence of the officer, the men were there only to do as they were told and could not be blamed for the conduct of their seniors.

The squad was told to stay on site as they expected to capture the condemned man very soon, the execution would most probably be carried out at the earliest opportunity after his recapture. Provost Marshal told the Sergeant that if he saw 2nd Lieutenant Ellis, he was to be told to report to his office at Brigade HQ immediately and, on that note, he left to conduct the search parties, who were now fanning out westwards, which they considered was the only way he would have gone. The Provost Marshal was far from a happy man, he had what he considered more important duties to attend without this distraction of a missing prisoner to contend with and having to now instigate a search.

***

Ellis had a good night with a local prostitute and a lot of local wine to boot. When he woke the girl was gone with her earnings and had not bothered to wake him. Also, his head felt if it did not belong to him and like the execution squad, a bit fragile from their binge from the previous night. The day was well on by now and there was much activity in the street below, locals going about their daily business and a number of military police, which he did not attach much importance to; he then realised that dawn had long gone. He thought he must have a sober evening today as he had to be up early the next morning. He felt he should visit the wall garden sometime during the day after all to see that everything was all right and have the pleasure of having another go at Perry, which would make his day! Another bit of a kicking would give him immense pleasure! He took his time getting dressed and shaved before having breakfast in a local tavern and making his way to the walled garden. As he walked he was curious at the high activity of the Military Police. He eventually stopped and asked a corporal MP why all the action, his reply was short, "Sir, a soldier who was due to be executed tomorrow morning has done a runner and no one knows where he has gone."

It was as if Ellis had been kicked in the stomach, as he had hoped to deliver to Sam, it would have been less painful. He made his way to the walled garden as fast as he could only to find two military policemen, a sergeant and a corporal guarding the entrance, stopping anyone leaving and only admitting those authorised by the PM, Ellis not being one of them. The sergeant asked Ellis for his identity card, he tried to pull rank and say he was an officer and they had no authority, which did not impress the sergeant in any way and he would have arrested Ellis if he refused. Ellis gave in and when the sergeant found who he was, told him he had to report to the Provost Marshal at Brigade HQ immediately and one of his corporals would escort him there as he had been instructed. With his escort, they made their way straight back into town and the corporal handed him over to the PM. His troubles were just about to begin.

***

As the sun set, Sam started to prepare for the next stage of his journey. He had slept well hidden in the hay loft and buried under soft heather smelling hay. It would appear that no one had paid a visit to the barn all day long. He cautiously descended from the loft and looked out of the door, there were soldiers on the road making their way to and from the front, some returning to duty, others starting a short period of rest, he did not expect the road would be empty until well after midnight, he would have to bide his time. He ate the last of the food he had saved and drank the water and was ready to move out when the time came, replacing the bottle in the haversack which he would keep with him.

He left the barn in the dark and the road appeared to be empty. Walking nearer to the road than the previous evening, making his way steadily eastwards, he soon approached the start of the front line area, eventually coming to the reserve trench. Looking around him he saw some cooking pots, one was over the fire and was simmering, ready for early morning tea. If you did not carry anything, you would get challenged, but if you carried anything that looked official, no one stopped you. He picked up the pot, holding the handle with his cap as it was hot; it looked very convincing that way. He went down the trench, along the connecting trench to the front line trench. Everyone was sleeping except one sentry. It was a very quiet night on the Western Front, no action whatsoever. Sam offered the sentry some hot water for a mug of tea, he was very grateful, and Sam stayed and chattered for a few minutes, then excused himself as he had to visit other sentries in the trenches. They bade each other, *'Good Night,'* with thanks from the sentry for the hot water.

He made his way to the area where Ellis had put him before the police had arrested him, which, as there was still a shortage of soldiers since the last attack, was still empty. He dumped the pot and climbed up the first ladder and started to belly crawl, under the barbed wire into no-mans-land and onward to the enemy lines. By keeping flat on the ground he proceeded at a slow but steady crawl, away from his friends and nearer to his enemy. Abandoned equipment was littering the ground everywhere. Sliding into a shell hole he found a full set of British battle webbing, probably discarded from a wounded soldier being taken back to his home trench before hospital. He decided it would look better if he was wearing this, without it they may think he was a deserter. There was also a rifle, which he decided not to take, there was less likelihood of being shot if he was not armed and he was not going to give the Germans a British rifle for free!

When he had kitted himself with the webbing he crawled on, eventually coming to the German wire stretched across the front of their trenches, crawling under as he had done under the British wire. The trench was right in front of him but there was no movement, he was sure there would be Germans below, with a sentry on duty. He decided not to wave the white vest, as he had planned, as they could think he was a spy, so he ditched it in a small hole. When he got to the edge of the trench he half rolled, half slithering down about seven feet, landing on wooden duck boards below, no different than the British trenches. He waited to be challenged, but no one came, this part of the trench was empty, including the officer's dugout which he discovered near by, at bit like where Ellis had hidden him, he decided to investigate further. On lifting the sackcloth that was the door, in the dim light it looked a comfortable place to stay until he was found, which he was sure would not be long, especially as it was getting light. He expected that the Germans would be back at any minute as there did not seem to be any action; they had all probably gone for breakfast before it got fully light. He dropped the door and curled up on one of the bunks and decided to have a nap until found, loosening his webbing, but keeping it on.

He woke up to the noise of movement, daylight was streaming in the dugout as the sackcloth had now been pulled aside, but the light was suddenly blocked out by someone entering. As it was dark in the dugout, a light was shone around until it rested upon him, he was then challenged, but it was all in German and he did not understand anything of the challenge. He threw his hands above his head and shouted, "I surrender, I surrender," which was accepted, he lay on the bunk, not moving. There was a lot of noise, others arrived including an Officer and an SNCO who stood over Sam, both wondering how a British soldier had got into their dugout without being detected. He was dragged to his feet by one the soldier who had found him. He was searched for any weapons or anything that might be useful to them, but they found nothing.

The Officer spoke with a German/American accent, "Vere 'ave you come from?" was his opening remark. Sam tried to explain in works of one syllable that he had got knocked out in *no-mans-land* during the last action and had lost his way and fell into this trench, thinking he had returned to the trench he had left on the last assault, he saw the empty dugout, and an empty bed, climbed in, and fell asleep as he was so tired. He did not know how long he had been unconscious, hours, days, he did not know, must have been some time as he was hungry and rubbed his stomach get the message over.

The Officer accepted his explanation, he felt sorry for Sam, knowing a lot of his men had been captured and were being looked after by the British. He asked Sam when he had last eaten a proper meal and Sam told him truthfully, at least four days ago as far as he could remember. As there was no current action on the front from either side, he ordered two of the soldiers to strip him of his webbing, which he never saw again, and then taken to the mess tent for breakfast while they sorted out where to send their unexpected guest, as he was now a German POW and their responsibility. The officer had to be a bit careful, how could he explain to his superior that a Tommy had got into their trenches without his sentry detecting him. Luck was on his side at last!

***

Lieutenant William "Billy" Leefe Robinson, RFC, was patrolling early on the morning of the 2nd September 1916 over London, sighting one of the 16 Zeppelins carrying out raids over the capital. He had been flying for over two hours and was desperately short of fuel and had little flying time left. Over Finsbury he spotted a Zeppelin making for home after dropping its bombs. He emptied two drums of ammunition into the airship but it did not seem to do any damage. Robinson made one final attack with his last drum of ammo, firing into the airship's twin rudders. As he broke away he saw a reddish glow appear from inside the airship, moments later the whole craft was engulfed in flames and started its final decent to the ground. He was immediately pronounced a hero and awarded the Victoria Cross two days later and promoted to the rank of Captain.

***

Major General Matchwick was having a much needed break from the front and traveling to London for the conference he had been summoned to regarding the last disastrous assault on German lines and the plans for future operations. On the way to England he met a fellow officer on the boat he was traveling, a Major Taylor, who was also going to London, but he for a Medical Conference. They discussed many aspects of the war, in particular the medical implications in warfare, which Matchwick had little knowledge of, and was very interested in what Taylor had to say on the subject. Taylor explained he was a surgeon working only in the field hospital on major wounds. Because of his skills as a surgeon, which was from many years of working at Guys Hospital in London before the war started, he was a valuable asset to the Army. They took the train to London together and found that they were due to return on the same day so arranged to meet up at Charing Cross Station for their return journey a few days later. The conferences were soon over and the two officers met as arranged on the appointed day. The discussions on the return journey varied about army matters to what they both hoped to achieve at the secession of the current conflict, saying their farewells as they left the station in Belgium in separate cars.

As Major General Matchwick approached Brigade HQ at the end of his journey, he was surprised at the large Military Police presence everywhere. On reaching HQ he went to his office calling out to his Aide to join him, the Aide being a Captain by rank, Hopkins by name.

"Hopkins, what the hell is going on outside with MPs everywhere?" he shouted to his Aide who entered the Major General office at the double from a small room that was his office, situated from across the corridor, skidding to a half in front of his superior.

Hopkins saluted smartly and replied, "Sir, it's because a prisoner who was due to be executed has escaped," was his reply.

"It's a hell of a lot of MPs for one prisoner, what's it all about?"

The Aide explained, "While you were in London Sir, a deserter had been caught, a Court Martial was convened and the accused had been found guilty and had been sentenced to be shot at dawn two days later, but the prisoner had since escaped and has eluded all capture at the present. This is why there is a large police present, Sir."

"This has all happened in the few days I have been away? Everything seems to have been done in a terrible hurry," Matchwick told his Aide. After a moments pause he came to a decision. "Get me the Proceedings on the CM right away, I want to know what the hell has been going on since I have been away." A quick exit was made by the Aide to carry out his boss' command.

Major General Matchwick was young for a Major General and not like a lot of the older officers he had to work with. He felt they had not altered their outlook on warfare for 50 years and were very outdated in their ideas of modern combat and field punishment.

He considered a lot of those who had been shot for desertion were far from guilty, but his opinion was a voice in the wilderness. He was sure a lot were suffering from the effects of war with mental health problems and nervous breakdowns, which the old brigade considered was malingering. He had heard that a number of executed soldiers were under age when they to joined up, but that made no difference at their CM, the majority were found guilty, the verdict was execution which was carried out as soon as possible, as a warning to others. He was determined to get to the bottom of this latest episode, it was on his patch. He was not a great supporter of executions either.

The Aide dashed over to the Provost Marshal's office. The Provost Marshal was not there but he was told by a clerk in the Orderly Room that the Marshal was out on the streets conducting an escaped prisoner search, a SNCO was able to pass him the documents. With that, the Aide returned and handed over the proceedings.

Matchwick started to read the report and when he saw 2nd Lieutenant Ellis's name and signature at the foot of the form, as the officer bringing the charges, and a Lance Corporal Perry, the accused, alarm bells started to ring. The first piece of documented evidence was the medical report. When he saw that it had been signed by Major Taylor, who had been with him on the date it was supposed to be signed by him, and a Captain Ives as second Medical Officer, and finally Ellis' signature bringing the charges, Major General Matchwick started to smell a rat. He sent a message to Major Taylor and asked him to come and see him without delay.

When Taylor arrived the Major General showed him the form. "How did you sign this document on the day stated when you were with me, did you misdate it?" he asked bluntly, passing Taylor the medical report to inspect more closely.

Taylor looked stunned. When he had found his voice and gathered his thoughts he replied, "Sir, firstly, this is not my signature, it's a forgery, second, as you know, I was with you on the day it was signed, and third, I am not a Front Line Medical Officer and do not carry out any medical inspections on soldiers who are under sentence of execution. As you know, I'm a surgeon working in hospitals some distance from the front trying to keep as many soldiers alive as possible, not get them killed. Last, but not least, Captain Ives was posted out to a hospital over a 100 miles further down the line at least a month ago, if not more, and has not returned to my knowledge, even for a day, Sir."

"Thank you Major, you have confirmed my suspicions. Will you please write me a report on these events and, if there is a CM, I expect you will be required to give evidence. Thank you, that is all." With that, a much bemused Major Taylor left the Major General's office to write his report.

Matchwick sat in thought, *what should his next move be?* He told the Adie to get him the Provost Marshal without delay. His Aide explained he was not in his office when he got the CM documents as he was leading the search for the escaped prisoner.

Matchwick was beginning to lose patience. "I don't give a toss what he is doing, find that man immediately," he shouted at his Aide. "I want him here before any more damage is done. I don't care what you have to do to get him, but get him here pronto, do you understand?" The Aide understood very well, he knew when his boss said jump, he best jump, and not come down until he said so. He dashed off taking one of the pool motor bikes that were for use of officers at the HQ. After half an hour of searching he was told that the Provost Marshal was about five miles west of the town. The Aide went driving down the road and after some searching found him. He stopped, dismounted the bike, and saluted the PM.

"Sir, Major General Matchwick wants to see you on the double at his office immediately," said the Aide.

"Too busy, I am sure he will understand if I don't come," said Harper, and he turned away to carry on the search.

"Sir, I think that is an unwise decision, I assure you he will not understand, there are problems with the last CM. You must return with me immediately and I will not be responsible for what the Major General will do to you if you do not return with me now."

With ill grace the PM returned and presented himself to the Major General and started to say he felt he should be out looking for the prisoner but was cut short by a glare from his superior before he had started his first sentence.

The Major General then opened up the file on the CM that was in front of him, extracting the medical document and thrust it under the PM's face, and told him it was a forgery and explained why. The PM started to turn pale.

"Tell me Harper, if the accused had been checked and was medically fit, but later the President of the CM would not let him give evidence as he deemed him a drug addict and a habitual liar, he could not have been fit, you can't have it both ways. Also, is this a valid reason for not letting the accused stand up and give evidence?" The PM was now very pale. Before he could answer, more questions were being fired at him. "Also Harper, why were the two SNCOs who reported to Ellis, and knew Perry very well, not present to give any evidence, either for the prosecution or defence?"

The Major General continued in this vain before the PM could utter a word. "Lastly Harper, how was the Defending Office selected, it would appear to me, from reading the evidence and reading between the lines he was a very junior office, who had never defended anyone before, was given no instruction and little time with the accused before the trial. What do you have to say about that Harper?"

Harper had nothing to say, but to accept the words of the Major General. "Right Harper, you will now open a Board of Enquiry into this matter, the whole thing stinks from start to finish, and Ellis is a man I do not trust. Right, now tell me how the prisoner escaped"

When Harper told him, and the part that Ellis played in it all, the Brigadier went spare. "I just told you what I thought of Ellis, this proves it and this is another nail in his coffin. If the prisoner is caught, there is to be no execution until I have reviewed the case, and if there is a charge to be made, a new CM will be convened as I am now overriding the finding of the CM, it is now *null and void.* What you do about the search is up to you, but I suggest it is scaled down, if not called off all together, it's up to you. Regarding Ellis, I want him put under close arrest this instant. And by the by, I don't want Lucas informed about this unless it is really necessary, and that is an order, even if he is a personal friend of yours. When I have enough information from you, I will personally interview him, and if it is as bad as I feel it is, my interview with you will pale into insignificance compared to what I have to say to him. I smell another rat here, a much larger one. Now get on with it and report to my Aide at least twice a day to update him on your progress, and he will advise me as if I should see you. Is that understood?"

Harper understood very well but felt he should try and defend himself. "Sir, I feel I should point out to you that Perry is a deserter and should be apprehended at the earliest opportunity, Sir."

The Major General was starting to see red and his face going the same colour. "I'm not surprised Perry has deserted after having been sentenced to death in an unfair trial," he shouted back at the PM. "He had nothing to lose, if I had been in his shoes, I would have done the same thing. I do not consider him a deserter. Now get out of my office immediately and do something useful with yourself before I have you replaced. I see from your records your present rank is only acting."

Harper left the Major General's office without saying another word, very shaken and realising he was still only a Major, acting Lieutenant Colonel.

***

When Sam had landed in the German trench, there had not been major activity by either side for over a week, so he was their only prisoner. This had an advantage for when Sam was taken back far behind German lines, there was an empty supply lorry returning for another load. It saved his guards and him being marched over ten miles to a large château which seemed to be the German Headquarters building of some sort in the area. On arrival he was taken down to the cellars which they had converted into a make shift prison cell. Wine racks still lined the walls, from floor to ceiling, but alas no wine, the Germans had taken and drunk the lot soon after they took the building over! All he was now left with for company were spiders and other creepy crawlies! There was a bed in one corner and a table and chair. After a little while he was given a meal and drink, so far he could not complain about the way he was being treated.

He expected to be interviewed before he was moved on to a permanent prison camp, but as he was only a private, he did not expect it would last long, as they must have captured many of his rank, who could provide them with little or no valuable information. Firstly they would want to know who he was. He had no form of identity on him, his Pay Book had been taken off him before he left the CM and Ellis had removed his two ID tags. If he told them he was Private Perry, and they informed the British he was their POW, the Army would seek him out after the war had ended. Sam had no doubt we would win and he would probably be shot, so he had to give another name which was plausible. He then remembered his best mate from Bristol, Bob Drew, an orphan, with no family or friends looking for him. He had gone missing soon after they arrived on the front and nothing had been seen or heard of him since, he had been listed *Missing, believed Killed*. Sam remembered Bob's service number as it was the next one on from his so he was all set up. When they were at Bristol for training, they went around together and in their off duty moments, talking about their past lives, Sam got to know a lot about Bob and what he did on the farm, so if he was questioned about where he lived and what he did as Drew the farm labourer, he felt he had enough information not to be rumbled! Sam now had his second alias, unbeknown to him but like his mother; 93495, Private Drew R. He was now ready for any interviews he may have and it was not long in coming.

***

Keturah was concerned about the bombing raids over London, remembering the first raid. Zeppelins were still coming over, and while the RFC and RNAS Home Defence Squadrons were inflicting damage and causing losses on these giant leviathans, London was still being bombed. She felt that their valuables should be packed up and taken to Grafton for safe keeping until the war was over, just like their children.

She would hire a GWR removal container, with packers, that would take all the items of value and other items she felt Algernon would like to be taken to safety, first by horse and cart to Bishops Road Goods Depot, then by train to Reading Good's Sidings and finally by horse and cart to the Manor, as most of the lorries the railway had owned before the outbreak of war had been taken by the army, and what was left was used mainly on war work. There was even a shortage of strong cart horses, the army had taken them and only left them with a skeleton deliver and collection service manned by old men, many ready for retirement, only kept on because of the war. There was a waiting list, things did not get done the next day as it had been before the war started, it was at best the next week, and Keturah was at last given a date. The most valuable items she would wrap herself. She was part way through wrapping up her favourite dinner service that had been a wedding present from a good neighbour close by, and was using old copies of the Shepherd's Bush Chronicle for protection, when an article in one of them caught her eye: The paper was dated Friday, 19th February 1915.

Local Hero Awarded DCM
Sgt Bill Perry
Sergeant William Perry, 4975281, who originally came from Shepherd's Bush, has been awarded the

Distinguished Conduct Medal for bravery in the field. On the 2nd February 1915, at night and while under fire from enemy action, he crawled into no-man-lands, with out any fire arms, to rescue his Commanding Officer who lay badly wounded. With the aid of only a rope he pulled him back to the British front line, without his CO sustaining any further wounds. But for Sergeant Perry's prompt action the Officer would not have survived and would have died from his injuries.

Before joining the army Sergeant Perry worked at Bert Frost & Son, of

Shepherd's Bush as a carpenter. Our reporter went to see Mr Frost and he told us he was an excellent worker, and his job was a reserved occupation, but he insisted on fighting for his King and Country. He also said he was not surprised about Bill's heroic action. He was that type of man, an orphan and had been brought up in the local Dr Barnardo's home before he came to work for me. These are the type of soldiers we must look up to and take their example It is not know when Sergeant Perry will receive his reward. Miss Alice Frost said she hoped he would be allowed home to receive his decoration from the King at Buckingham Palace in the near future.

The Chronicle will keeps its readers updated with the latest information, and hope to interview Sergeant Perry on his safe return home.

Her knees went weak, she had to sit down, she read the article twice more, *was this her first son?* It would not take her long to go down to Shepherd's Bush and speak to Bert Frost, if he was still there. She resisted due to the urgency of packing up all the valuables and sending them off on a booking, if lost it would be about two weeks before there was another slot would become available. With her WEC work it was not possible to seek out Mr Frost that day, but it would as soon as time permitted. She cut out the article and put it into her handbag.

About a week later, in the middle of a sunny afternoon, Keturah took a cab to Shepherd's Bush and on arrival at the Frost's works she went in by a door that was marked **Main Office**, a bell ringing as the door opened to alert that a potential customer had arrived. Inside was a reception area where there were two chairs for customers in front of a short counter which had a clerk's desk and high stool at one end. She was greeted by a smartly dressed young lady behind the counter who welcomed and introduced herself as Miss Frost, daughter of Mr Bert Frost.

"Good afternoon Madam, how can I help you?" she asked.

"Good afternoon. You may think this is an unusual request which has nothing to do with carpentry, but it's about someone who used to work for you. If I may, let me explain it all to you." Keturah paused and Alice nodded in agreement and said, "Yes." She was intrigued.

"I recently saw an article in an old edition of the Shepherd's Bush Chronicle," which Keturah showed her, continuing, "that a Sergeant William Perry, who been awarded the DCM and had worked here before he joined up? I am trying to find him, can you help," she asked the young lady.

Immediately the girl's face crumpled and Keturah realised three things. That Bill must have worked here, the girl must have known him extremely well, and something dreadful must have happened to him.

"I'm sorry, I seem to have caused you great distress. Have I said something I shouldn't, is there anything I can do to help you?" Keturah asked.

The girl spoke through tears, "Yes, Bill did work here, but he was killed three months after being awarded the medal and he got a bar posthumously for bravery in the action that killed him." She paused to regain her composure. "I went to Buckingham Palace to see his next-of-kin being presented with the award and he gave it to me to look after," she blurted out.

Keturah was greatly saddened by this news and felt tears running down her face and collapsed into one of the chairs, feeling very weak, much to the surprise of Alice. She was immediately concerned for this lady, which by her dress and manner she certainly was. "Can I help you in any way Madam?" she said through her tears. "Did you know Bill. I know he was an orphan and he told me he had no family he knew of. Just after he was born he was left on the doorstep of the Shepherd's Bush Barnardo's home, and if I remember correctly he said it was early in 1896."

Keturah felt the girl deserved to be told the truth. "My name is Keturah Cavendish, can we go and talk quietly somewhere?" Alice took her upstairs into their front parlour, the 'best room', kept for the vicar, important visitors, courting couples and Sundays only! She excused herself, but returned immediately with her mother who was looking puzzled. Alice introduced Keturah to her mother and briefly explained everything that Keturah had told her so far. When Alice had finished explaining to her mother, Keturah continued with her story, "It was me who left Bill at Barnardo's, I was a wicked girl in those days and Bill was born out of wedlock and I had to give him away, I could not afford to keep him and I had to continue to earn my living." She did not tell the two women what sort of work she did, but she felt they might have already guessed, telling Alice and her mother the rest of story in the briefest of details.

Keturah paused while they both took all this in, then she asked, "You mentioned that Bill had a next-of-kin, was he an orphan also? Did he also come from Barnardo's before he came to work for you, and is he still here?"

Alice wondered if she should tell this lady any more, but decided she knew a lot, and could see no harm in it. "Yes, he was another lad from Barnardo's, two and a half years younger that Bill, and he did come to work here, but recently left to join up. He use to write to me occasionally from were he was fighting but never gave me his address to answer his letters, unfortunately I haven't received a letter from him for a long time, I am very worried for him, I don't know whether he is dead or alive," and with that she started to weep again, her mother took her in her arms and gave her the comfort that was needed and the tears soon subsided.

While Alice had not mentioned a name to Keturah, Keturah had a good idea who it was. When Alice had regained her composure she asked, "Would his name be Samuel Bray by any chance?"

A look of surprise came to Alice and her mother's face, they were both temporarily lost for words. When Alice had got her breath she asked, "How ever did you know that?"

"Because Bill and Sam are half brothers, I am their mother," Keturah replied. Again in the space of less then a minute, mother and daughter were both speechless. Keturah went on to explain the rest of her story, much to the amazement of Agnes and Alice. While Keturah wasn't proud of her past, it could never be changed, but she was honest enough with herself to accept the facts, what she was then, was what she was. She felt that both the ladies had the right to know the truth, and from what the two women said, the family had been very kind to her two boys and had befriended both of them, for which she would be forever grateful.

But the truth suddenly dawned on Alice,, "Now I understand about Bill and Sam, not only did they look alike, but they had the same temperament and both had the same abilities, and were very close, just like brothers, be it half brothers, which I now know they are. Wait until I tell Dad, I don't think he will be in the least surprised."

As it was now mid-afternoon, Agnes offered Mrs Cavendish a cup of tea which she accepted. While waiting for the tea, Keturah asked Alice after Bill and Sam, she now wanted so find out as much as possible about her two sons past that she had missed and now greatly regretted. Alice showed Keturah the two photos of her on her own and the one with Sam, both showing Bill's medal that was in pride of place, central, in the photos. Keturah saw the name of the photo studio where it had been taken and got Alice to give her the print numbers.

When her mother returned with the tea, Alice dashed to her bedroom and returned with Bill's decoration and the photo of Sam on his own, giving Keturah that photo number also. She then passed the medal presentation box for Keturah to open. She opened the box and removed the medal from its purple silk bed, holding it up, catching the sun light that was streaming in through the window. The medal hung from a ribbon of three vertical stripes, mauve, blue and mauve, surmounted by the two horizontal bars each engraved where the action had taken place. Both the Frost women could see that Keturah was visibly moved at the sight of it and that she had to wipe away a tear or two.

Agnes called Bert up to the kitchen to collect the tea for the staff and asked him to come back after he had taken the tea down. While they were awaiting Bert's return, Agnes felt, after all Keturah had told them about herself, that she should give her a potted history of the Frosts and how they came to employ Bill and Sam in more detail but had not got very far when Bert returned. They quickly explained to him all Keturah had told them.

Agnes and Alice, with the help of her father, explained to Keturah about how the family had met her two sons. "Dad was the handy man for the orphanage and he would take my brother along to help. My brother can't walk very well, so it was a strain for him to go all that way and back, but the orphanage encouraged boys who were interested to help Dad. Dad soon realised that Bill was a natural carpenter and he tagged onto Dad when he went there and soon started to help him, he was very good, Dad saw his potential. After a time my brother stopped going as Bill gave him all the help he needed. But with Bill, you got Sam as well, where ever Bill went, Sam followed, and he turned out to be just as good as Bill. A few months before Bill arrived from the orphanage, just before he was 14, we had to get rid of most of our workers, as there was little work around at the time. We seemed to be only getting small jobs that we could not afford to pay a fully skilled worker for, but an apprentice we could, and as we had two rooms spare off the workshop, we offered Bill a job with full board and lodging free. Sam arrived two and a half years later, he had the other room. When the war started we got a lot of work from Sopwith Aviation and we wanted the rooms back to expand the workshop. Dad found a lady who let rooms not too far away and she took them both in. Dad even paid the rent and Mum still gave them all their meals when they arrived before work started, at lunch and in the evening before they went back to their rooms, it gave them a bit of independence. When the war started their jobs here were a reserved occupation, but they both felt as they were young and fit, they wanted to serve their country. Dad was much upset when they went," she stopped to draw breath, adding that they all felt that Bill and Sam were a part of their family now.

With a lull in the conversation, Bert said he was not surprise that Bill and Sam had some connection as they were so alike in so many ways. He only hoped he could meet Sam again, as he, like Bill, was a part of their family.

Alice continued the conversation with Keturah. "Unlike Bill, who had nominated Sam as his next-of-kin, we don't know what Sam has done. We hope it was my Dad, but we just don't know for sure. We do know he was under age to join up, so he must have lied about this to be accepted. I understand they are so short of troops and if they look the age, they don't ask many questions, if any, they just take them. Now he is old enough to join up without having to lie about his age."

"I suppose you have asked their landlady if she knew where they have gone." Keturah wanted to know.

Alice replied, "That was the first place we started looking, but she knew less that we did. One day Bill was there, the next day gone, he left a note to say he was not coming back and she could re-let his room. It was the same story with Sam. We did think of contacting the War Office, or even the Admiralty, as we did not know which service Sam had joined, he never let on to us what he would join. Asking either of these Ministries to try and find Bill or Sam, we felt was like looking for a needle in a haystack. I expect if we had written, they would say, in so many words, they did not have the time and had much more important things to do, probably they may even say they were not allowed to pass on this information without that persons consent. We did not have anything else to help identify him. So it has all come to a stop, even though we now know from Sam's letters, he joined the army, but not where or what regiment or corps, still not much help!"

Keturah could well understand, and in her position, with Algernon a senior officer, she did not think he could help while he was fighting a war over the Channel. She thanked them for their time, gave them her address and phone number in Notting Hill Gate and asked if they would be so kind to contact her if they heard anything, and, if she was not there, which was often, to leave a message with one of her staff. She would put a few feelers out in her circle of friends but did not expect there would be any positive results but would contact them if there were. On the way home she called at the photo studio and ordered a copy of the three photos which she collected in less then a week and ordered frames for them to stand on her dresser in her bedroom.

When she got home, she decided to write to Algernon, as she had received a letter form him only two days previous, so it was her turn to write.

> *Notting Hill Gate*
> *28 June 1916*
> *My Darling Algernon,*
> *Thank you for your letter, I got two days ago. I did not answer sooner as I was packing all our valuables to send to the Manor, which your father is expecting.*
> *You may recall that when you asked me to marry you, I would not say "YES" until I had told you of my past, and gave you the choice to change your mind, but thankfully you never did. I told you I had two sons, but I never told you their names, and you never asked. They are William Perry and Samuel Bray, and it has been my intention when I had the time to try and trace them, but with all my work with the WEC, that has had to go by the board.*
> *Well, last week, when I was wrapping the crockery in old newspapers, an article in one caught my eye, it said that a Sergeant William Perry had been awarded the DCM. It gave an address where he once worked, Bert Frost of Shepherd's Bush. I will enclose the cutting, but please keep it safe as I would like it back.*
> *I went round to the Frost's today and saw Mr & Mrs Frost and their daughter Alice, who had a crush on Bill. They had some good news, some very sad news and finally some very good news.*
> *William, as you will see, won his medal for bravery, I'm so proud of him. The*
> *sad news, he was killed in action on the 18 May 1915 about three months after winning his medal and got a bar to this decoration in the action which he lost his life.*

Keturah had to stop to wipe tears away from her eyes as she recalled the cold January night she gave Bill away, over 19 years ago, now she would never see him again. She then remembered the time she collapsed and fainted, it was the day Bill had been killed. She also thought of Sam, and hoped the same fate would never happen to him, and hoped eventually they could both be re-united.

> *But the other good thing was they knew of my other son Samuel, who has joined up, under age, he left without telling anyone where he has gone. So I just hope he gets through the war alright, I pray every night and morning that you will get through my darling. I have seen the letter from the War Office to my other son*
> *Samuel telling him of Bill's death, who was his next of kin, and finally the invitation to Samuel to be presented with the medal at Buckingham Palace by King George. Sam went to Buckingham Palace to receive the medal from the King, accompanied by Alice, she showed me the medal, it's lovely. It also had the bar added to the decoration for the action he carried out so bravely fought when was killed. After Sam and Alice returned from The Palace, they had three photos taken, Sam with the medal, Alice with the medal and them both with the medal, I have ordered copies of each and they are now on my dressing table. And I feel it's the first step in finding Sam. At least I know what he looks like now!*

Again she had to stop to wipe more tears away as she remembered holding the medal Bill had won and seeing what Sam looked like for the first time, she felt so proud of them both, serving their country, and this made her soon feel better so she could continue with the more mundane aspects of her letter, the day to day life at home and the WEC.

> *The lorry comes later this week for all the valuables and I will go over to*
> *Brooklands and take our aircraft up, I can see the lorry off and be there when it arrives at your parents. I spoke to your father on the phone, he will never get used to "that thing". He has been so good at finding places to store everything. As soon as the war is over, it will be one*

> *of the first things I will do is to get all our goods and chattels back to London and out of his way!*
>
> *Must go now, I have a WEC meeting, in the kitchen, it's the best place for it.*
>
> *I've given the kitchen staff the night off!*
>
> *All my love Darling, yours for ever*
>
> *Keturah XXX*

***

At the German château, they were not particularly busy as there was little activity on the field of battle and Sam was soon brought up from his cell and put into an interview room and guarded by two armed soldiers. He did not think he was that much of a threat! There was a plain table and two chairs in the room, one on either side of the table, he was told to sit on one, the one that looked the most uncomfortable!

The room was small and looked like it had been a pantry at one time as there were shelves on two walls while opposite the door was a window that looked out on the grounds of the château, which had bars, not put there by the Germans, but by the previous owner to protect their stocks of food, not that it stopped the Boche from helping themselves when they threw the owners out at the beginning of the conflict. Once the château had well tended lawns, now it was filled with army lorries and horse drawn carts, a number of large field guns of various sizes were parked in one area, ready to be sent down to the front when replacements were called for. He wondered where the ammunition was kept, he hoped not to near in case the RFC did any bombing!

After a while an officer entered, Sam stood up, standing to attention, but did not salute as he was without a cap. He had no idea of the rank insignia of the Germany Office Corps, so did not know what he was, but he felt he would be no more that a captain, if that.

The officer sat down but did not introduce himself, but after telling Sam to sit down he just asked questions, speaking good English with an American accent. "Show me your name tags," he ordered Sam. Sam explained that he had laid in *no-mans-land*, it must have been for days and in a semi conscious state and someone must have removed his tags, thinking he was dead. It seemed to satisfy the officer as his next question was, "Number, rank and name?"

"93495, Private Drew, Robert," Sam replied. The officer wrote this down.

"Regiment?" To help with the spelling, Sam was given paper and pencil to write it down.

Then came the questions that Sam was expecting. How long had he been on the front, who was his CO, when was the next attacked planned, and on it when. He gave true answers where it made no difference and pleaded ignorance when either he did not know, or he did not want to give anything away that he felt could help the Germans. The officer had done this type of interview many times before and had got the same results from the lowest of the low, who he knew would be told very little, *cannon fodder* they were, their life expectancy was not very long, some had only been on the front less than a week before they met their maker. To be captured was a safe way out that for a number of soldiers to escape the terror of *going over the top* any more times to certain death; being a POW was a good option, not many tried to escape. They never gave it a thought as to what would happen to them if Germany won the war.

After less than 10 minutes, the officer got up, said nothing to Sam as what was to happen to him, spoke briefly to the guards and left the room. Sam was taken back to the cells. He was there for about a week, taken out each day, under armed escort for exercise in the grounds and given three basic German types of meals a day, a bit better than trench meals in some way and he had to get used to a German diet, especially if he could not escape!

One day he was taken in front of another English speaking German officer and was told he would be moved to a holding camp for POWs tomorrow, from there, when they had enough prisoners, he would be sent to a permanent camp, well away from the front line, where he would be held until Germany won the war, which would be very soon he was told.

As he had been told, the following day he was taken by lorry to the holding camp and when he got there he estimated there were over a hundred British troops, of various regiments, the most senior rank was a corporal, all waiting to be moved to a permanent POW camp. It did not take him long to realise that there was no one there he knew, which he was very thankful for, otherwise his cover could have been blown. All he learnt from one soldier was that there was a change of plan, they would be taken by train to a temporary prison camp that had recently been opened near Brussels before deciding when they would be going to the permanent camp deep in Germany. The journey was not very long in distance but as the railway lines were clogged with supplies for the front, and trains returning to reload, it would probably take days, their train being the lowest priority, even cattle trains where a higher priority than they were, they were food for the soldiers!

Sam remembered his pledge to Bill, he would avenge his death, and being a POW was not the way he could do it, his next plan was to escape and somehow return to England. If the train was going to take many days, and many of it spent in the hours of darkness, stopping a lot of the time, that, he hoped, would be his chance to make his escape. This was all to his advantage.

He started to talk to other soldiers but there seemed there was no one interested in escaping. The majority were happy to waste the rest of the war as a POW, why go back to the front to be killed, they considered themselves to be the lucky ones, they were at least alive, even though it was their duty to try and escape, they were not bothered, the Brits would eventually win the war and their pay would be mounting up for them when they got back to home. While there were no takers of escaping with Sam, some said they would help him if they could, but not if it would cause trouble or any risk for any of them. They stayed in that camp for about a week, the number of soldiers increased every day. Then, early one morning, they were told to parade outside in three ranks. From there they were marched down to the nearest rail head that was about three miles away. In the station sidings there stood a row of very old and battered cattle trucks, but no sign of an engine. They were all put in the trucks, and while they could leave the doors open, any trouble and they would close the doors and lock them in.

During the afternoon, they were allowed out in twos and threes from each truck for calls of nature. When he was behind a pile of metal junk, that was everywhere in the yard, he found a stout metal bar that he slipped down his trouser leg. Sam had a good look at all the trucks on his return and selected the most battered one he could find and took himself back there. As most of the occupants were hanging around the door, Sam had a good look round the truck and discovered that there were a couple of loose planks, and one that was badly rotten in the far corner. It would be no problem to lever up the boards with the metal bar he had hidden, making enough space to slip out, and then one of the soldiers could put the planks back after he had gone, so covering his escape if it was ever noticed, which he doubted. He would have to slip out when it was dark, and when the train was going very slowly or had stopped.

It was not until mid afternoon that they got fed and by evening a very old and decrepit engine arrived that looked if it could hardly pull itself along let alone a train with trucks, steam issuing from various ports which it never had been designed to do when it was new! The guards herded all the prisoners into the trucks, putting up the loading rams that were also the doors and locked them all in. The engine was eventually hooked up to the leading truck and there gathered breath for an hour before finally pulling out of the sidings as it was getting dark. It moved off painfully slowly, being stopped and shunted into sidings to let more important trains pass at regular intervals. There seemed to be many more important trains than their own, taking troops and supplies up to the front and returning empty to collect more supplies and with soldiers on leave, on rest or injured.

Once the train had started, the guards were in two small carriages, one at the front, the other at the rear, none were placed in the cattle trucks with the POWs. While they were traveling, Sam started working at the loose floor boards and it did not take him long to make a hole large enough for him to squeeze through and get out, to be easily replaced when he had gone. The Germans would never discover the hole, as the whole floor looked as if would rot away and collapse at any time. Sam also noticed that while there had been a head count, there had not been a roll call. The count was so casual; it would be possible to fool the Germans Guards by moving in the back of the ranks and one man getting counted twice. It would be days before someone was discovered missing and they would never be sure who it was or where it happened. Guarding a POW train was low on the scale of security and only old retired soldiers, who had been brought back in to relieve the fit soldiers for fighting on the front, were used for this task. They were far from fighting fit, all short sighted and with glasses and to break into a trot caused them to wheeze and groan! To hide their mistake they would probably not say anything and no one would be any the wiser.

Like all cattle trucks, there was an opening all along the upper half of the two sides to let fresh air in for the cattle, but there were bars to stop the cattle escaping and the gaps between the bars were too small for him to squirm through but it gave Sam a good vantage point to look out to see a suitable place to escape.

Just after midnight, as he judged it to be, the train pulled in to a siding, with many tracks and every track filled with trains waiting for engines and available line space to get to the front with supplies or return back to Germany for more materials. Sam saw all this and could see that they were on the outskirts of a large town and considered they may not have much farther to go, so he best make his escape as soon as possible. Once they had stopped, the guards got out of their two carriages and started patrolling both sides of the train in pairs. They did not seem very enthusiastic about the job and were doing more talking than keeping their eyes open, weren't all the trucks locked from the outside, nobody could escape. Sam thought the guards were far from up to do their job properly, not being to see to well in daylight, let alone at night, and he not unreasonably suspected their hearing was not up to much either!

When a pairs of guards passed, Sam lifted the two planks and slipped out through the hole, the planks being immediately replaced behind him by one of the occupants of the van. He lay flat between the tracks and listened for the guards that kept patrolling up and down, so he stayed put. After what Sam judged to be about half an hour there was a blast on the engine's whistle, the guards rushed back to their carriages, climbed aboard just as the train pulled away. Sam stayed flat where he was, the truck passing over his head, clanking and creaking as they went over him. Suddenly the last truck passed and he lay there between the tracks, exposed for all to see. As it was dark, there seemed to be no other guards guarding the depot or the other stationary trains on the six or seven tracks in the yard, he decided it was time to make his move.

***

Sam was never missed when the POW train finally reached its destination. The paperwork listing the prisoners was far from accurate, there were at least ten names that appeared on the list but were not present and just as many who were not listed at all, but were there in body and soul. The receiving POW camp was used to this, it always happened, they considered the old train guards useless, so a head count was taken when they arrived and names taken and the original list was amended to show what soldiers had actually arrived. As far as the Germans were concerned 92495, Private Drew R, with a number of others who were on the list, was not accounted for; they were not there and they were all a nonentity! There was no point in checking up; it would have been a fruitless task.

Sam was now on the run for the second time in less than a month, not wanted or being looked for by the Germans, and it was the same on the British front, while Sam did not know, the search for him, thanks to Major General Matchwick, had now been called off.

CHAPTER 10

One On The Run

Sam raised his head slowly, looking in all directions, there was no one there, not a guard to be seen anywhere. There were a number of trains passing along the main line in both directions from time to time, which gave Sam the direction to go, away from the main line and the noise, which he hoped would be to the boundary of the yard. He could not see very far in either direction for all the goods trains standing there, some with an engine waiting for a clear road, others waiting for an engine. He realised what he had thought was a siding when he arrived, was a major marshalling yard.

Sam started to crawled in the direction he considered would lead to his escape from the yard, as he did from the British trenches into no-mans-land, crawling under two more goods trains, both with trucks of various types, stretching in both directions, disappearing into the darkness. From his hiding place under a long flat wagon that was carrying two large field guns, he looked out realising he was laying on the last siding and from his position saw what looked like a fence, *was this the boundary of the marshalling yard?*

His intention was to make for the boundary fence of the railway yard all along, where he hoped there would be more cover to screen him from any activity that may occur with railway workers attending to trains or any German soldiers that might be patrolling in the vicinity. On seeing the fence, he considered he had made his first goal. Sam thought it was a very quiet night and being so far behind the front line, he wondered if the Germans had standing patrols in the railway yard or in the local town at all.

The Germans did have standing patrols in the yard and throughout the town, by the local defence soldiers. They were old soldiers, too old or unfit to fight on the front line, normally patrolling towns and sensitive areas far behind the front line, similar to those guarding the POW trains. After two years of war, they had got lax and only paid lip service to the guard rosters, and after a cursory patrol two or three times a day, they mainly sat in the town cafés during the day and evening and hiding up in any warm place they could find during the night. They organised a whisper system and as soon as a senior officer in his staff car approached anywhere in the town, word got around and they were out patrolling the streets. The local force must have felt it was safe and a waste of time patrolling the streets and railway yard during the day and especially during night. As far as Sam could see, there weren't any guard patrolling in the yard.

It was night of broken clouds, with a full moon flitting from under the cloud cover every so often to illuminate an overcast night and the stationary trains. Anyone moving could be seen for some distance if the moon was out, so Sam had to be very careful before he moved out into the open just in case there was a patrol about he had not spotted. When the moon came out for a few minutes he could see he had come across the boundary fence which was about six feet high, but over the years a hedge had grown all over it, making it higher and harder to scale. Sam, on looking more closely at this obstacle, considered it would be difficult to climb over and would probably make some sort of noise, safe not to try, just in case there was anyone about he could not yet see. Also he did not know what else there could be on the other side, *look before you leap*, Sam thought!

Before the moon disappeared again, he saw to his right a small brick building. He crawled along under the train until he was opposite the hut. He could now see a door which had a window either side. It would appear from what he could make out that the hut was in darkness. silhouetted against the sky line he saw the hut had a chimney, but he was pleased there did not appear to be any smoke rising from it, two facts to make him think it was empty. He decided it was time to investigate the hut, and, making sure no one was about, he made his way across the few yards to the door. He stopped and listened, heard no noise from within, and tried the door but it was locked. The door looked far too firm to break it down and that would certainly make a lot of noise. Could someone be sleeping in there, if so, there was another reason not to try and break the door down. It would be best if he left the yard as soon as possible and turned to walk away.

As he turned to go, he tripped over something and fell to the ground and on looking round he saw it was a house brick that he had dislodged from a large flagstone. With the moon shining for a moment he could see a key that must have been hidden underneath the brick. So, thought Sam, to save the late shift from handing the key into the Station Master's office, they put it under the brick, for the early shift to open up in the morning. He picked up the key, replacing the brick on the stone as he had found it, and fitted the key into the lock, turning it easily it a full 360 degrees. He then turned the handle and pushed the door open; it swung without a squeak, well oiled with engine oil Sam expected! As he entered the hut, the moon flooded into the room, and as luck would have it, he could see straight away that it was empty. He closed the door behind him, and, just in case anyone came along and wondered why it was unlocked, relocked it from the inside. With the moon being kind to him, it bathed the whole hut with its light. The hut was quite warm inside, he felt the stove that was situated in one corner, it was still fairly warm. He quickly looked round the room. On the far wall were two large maps, one of railway tracks, obviously a plan of the marshalling yard which had at the top a name:

| HALLE |

followed by some foreign words he could not understand. He had no language skills but guessed it could be something like *Marshaling Yard*, so Sam had to presume he was at a place called Halle; all he did know was that he was in occupied Belgium. The second map was of the Belgium railway network, with a red circle drawn round Halle, what a God send that was. He now knew where he was and tracing the main line northwards with his finger, he followed the railway line through Brussels passing Mechelen to Antwerp and ending at the border with Holland. He knew Holland was neutral and was north from Belgium, it would best to make for there. If he ever got to Holland, he would make for a port, there must be one somewhere there; he recalled a place called Rotterdam from his geography lessons at the orphanage. He measured with his finger the distance between Halle and Brussels, the help it against the scale at the bottom of the map, it was between 10 and 12 kilometres.

"What the hell is a kilometre, is it more or less than a mile?" he muttered to himself, he never found out! It didn't really matter. Even if it was over 10 miles, it can't be much more, he should do that in a night, and as there seemed to be no train movement in the yard, he would have to leg it, he had to clear the area, just in case they found he was missing and made a search for him in the yard.

Before leaving the hut he had a good look around, the moon was still on his side, so he could see what he was doing. There was a tap and sink in the corner, and on the floor in a bin was an empty bottle with a cork pushed in it. On opening it, it smelt of wine, he washed the bottle out and filled it with water, had a good drink and refilled it for his journey.

Over in another corner there was an assortment of rail workers tools, on and below a bench, for those who worked on maintaining the railway track, the platelayers. Just as he was about to leave, he discovered behind the door he entered, a number of working clothes hanging from hooks fixed to the top of the door. Most of the garments were dirty overalls, but one hook had a type of donkey jacket and a peaked cloth cap hanging from it, also dirty and well worn. He tried both on, the jacket was not a perfect fit, on the loose side, but passable, while the grubby black cloth peaked cap sat well on his head, not being held up by his ears! This would cover his army tunic with his regimental flashes on. While his trousers were still on show, the army brown was now very dirty and had minor abrasions and snags. He reckoned that if he could find a pair of overalls that fitted, all his army uniform would be hidden, except his boots, and these were looking very scruffy, so no one would look twice at them. He sorted through the overalls, tried on at least three until he had a good fit, and realised it gave him a bit of extra warmth as well and helped to make the donkey jacket a better fit. He felt he now looked the part of a scruffy railway worker. Also, there was old haversack, looking at it, Sam felt it had once belonged to the German army; it had seen better days, but was still serviceable. This he slung over his shoulder and neck, and put in his bottle of water and a part of a stale bread stick he found, he was hungry, so it was better than nothing and would do for later.

To add to this, if he carried one or two tools, he would look even more the part, so crossing over to the bench he picked up a spanner and crowbar, and found an old dirty rag to stuff in his pocket as well, that would help the overall image and they might come in useful at some time. If he carried nothing, he was bound to be stopped and questioned, but carrying tools, you were a worker out on a job, you would usually be left alone and with the haversack slung across his back it all helped. Without a mirror, he could not see what he looked like, but he felt he was not a soldier any more, but a Belgian railway worker. As he had not washed for at least a day, and with all the crawling under trains he had done, he expected his face was a bit grubby, like his hands were!

He felt that he had stayed long enough, and having had a last look at the map, which was far too big to take with him and was well secured to the wall, he committed to memory places going north, deciding that was the best way to go. He unlocked and removed the key from the door with stealth, not wanting to attract attention if anyone was about, then opened it with great care, looking in all directions, ensuring no one was about, before he slipped out of the hut. He relocked the door and replaced the key on the flat stone and the brick on top, then again making sure the coast was still clear all around him before moving out. To his left he saw the yard gates, which were closed. Moving in the shadows as much as possible, he made it to the gate, which was the same height as the fence and was locked with a padlock and chain. On both sides of the gate there were horizontal strengthening bars and this made it easy for him to climb to the top and down the other side, but not before he checked there was no one passing along the road. Another step to freedom.

The gate was set back from the road by a couple of yards, so when he stood he was not exposed to anyone who might be about going along the road unless actually passing the entrance road. He moved slowly forward with caution until he came to a well used dirt track going of in both directions, which the entrance to the yard turned off. He looked up and down the thoroughfare, there was no one about. He realised this was a side road leading probably to other parts of the railway station. As most of the tracks leaving the yard turned left, he made his way in that direction and he had not walked far until he came to a main road, tar macadam. With the moon as his guide, he made what he felt was the general direction of north, looking for any sign for the next town in that direction as he went, which he remembered was Ninove. He was not sure how far he had to go and what did not help was that the scale on the map was in kilometres.

He walked carefully along the road, stopping frequently, making sure he had an escape route if he saw anyone about. He tried to keep as near to the railway line as possible, taking him, he hoped, in a northerly direction, to skirt round the west side of Brussels towards Mechelen, around Antwerp and hopefully across the border. He considered if he kept near the railway, he may find a place where he could hop on board a slow north bound train that would save a lot of walking.

But he had a problem, he had estimated he had left the train just after midnight and it had taken time to crawl to the hut and had stayed in there for a while, time was getting on, soon the sky in the east would start to show the glow of a new day, he had to find somewhere to hide up for the day. He felt barns and abandoned dwelling were a good bet, but he could see none at present. There were plenty of ditches, but he did not fancy one of those, well, only in an emergency. He was now starting to panic, it was now starting to get light, but luck was again with him, he spotted some half collapsed hut in the corner of a field about a quarter of a mile from the road. He made his way there and found while it was in a pretty poor state, there was room for him to crawl in, well hidden, and room to make a nest to sleep in. While he was part covered, he was sure it was not waterproof and hoped it did not rain. With a drink, and a bit to eat from his stale loaf, he was soon asleep.

He slept well into the late afternoon, feeling hungry and ate the remainder of the bread and drank some of his water. As it got dark he moved out, down the field to the road, continuing in a northerly direction. It was not long before he entered a small village.

It was very quiet, he wondered if the Germans had imposed a curfew on the town, but this was soon dispelled when a non-military lorry passed him as he was hiding in the shadows of a deep doorway. After he had been walking for what he considered was about half an hour, about a mile at his pace, he found that there were fewer houses, he was leaving the town behind, and while the road was not a country lane, and more like a minor road, he had not seen any more traffic, bar for the one lorry. He now had a problem, if anything now came along there was little or no shelter to hide in. He kept a very close vigil on anything that might be about.

Suddenly Sam heard screams, a woman's coming from somewhere in front of him. He immediately looked all around him before he increased his pace with caution in the direction of the noise, he did not want to fall into some sort of trap. He had not gone but a few yards when off to his right was a track, down which was an old dilapidated building, once a peasant's cottage perhaps, now with the roof half gone, the frames of the single door and two windows long rotted and fallen out, all flooded in moon light. The screams got louder and appeared to be coming from inside the cottage. As he approached, the screams suddenly started getting weaker and muffled, a man's voice could be heard and to Sam it sounded like German and was raised in anger. Sam approached the building, walking on the grass to deaden and sound of his approach. Looking through the door he saw a German soldier and a young girl in her prime pinned down on the rough cottage floor, the scene lit by the light of a lamp hanging from a beam nearby. The soldier, who had his trousers pulled down, had the girl held down with one hand over her mouth, the other was franticly pulling at her clothes to get to her body.

This was the first chance Sam had to mete out justice hand to hand for what had happened to Bill. Near the door the soldier had discarded his rifle in the frenzy to get to the girl and was oblivious to everything around him. Sam griping the crowbar he was carrying and without any compunction brought the heavy metal rod down on the back of the soldier's head with a sickening thug. The soldier collapsed on the ground falling away from the girl. With a quick look at the body, Sam suspected he was dead, which gave him great satisfaction.

The girl stopped her screaming and looked up at Sam and burst in to tears. Keeping an eye on the German, just in case he was not dead, he went over and comforted the girl as much as possible. After a little while the girl recovered and dressed as much as was possible, pulling her torn clothes over her semi naked body. When she had completed her task as best as she could she started to thank Sam, but not a word could he understand.

"Speak Anglais," was all Sam could thing to say in return and to his surprise the girl replied in fairly good English. The upshot of her story was that she had been returning home and the soldier was walking in the same direction and had offered to escort her there in the dark. When they had got to the cottage, he had dragged her inside and was about to have his wicked way with her until Sam put a stop to his lust and his life.

She told Sam that her parents had been killed in a bombing raid early in the war and she had lived on her own ever since, working in a grocery's shop in the nearby town late into the evening and she was on her way home carrying a lighted lamp to see her way when the moon disappeared behind a cloud, which must have attracted the soldier. She had no relatives she knew and her only friends were her work colleagues; if she ever went missing, no one would know where to look for her, as she had not told anyone at her place of work where she lived, you could not trust anyone these days. She finished by saying she wanted to get home as soon as possible. Sam explained to her he was an escaping English soldier trying to make his way back to England. She asked Sam to walk with her to her cottage for protection, which was about a kilometre further on in the direction Sam was making, which he gladly accepted. But the problem now was what were they to do about the German, he was getting cold and stiff. The girl, being local, knew the area well, and said that there a deep ditch near by that they could dump him in that.

Sam left the girl and went to find the ditch which she had directed him to, it was deep and filled with water. He also noticed some rocks close by. He went back and decided to search the soldier's clothes, but there was nothing that was worth taking, bar for a little local money that he gave to the girl. He had a pistol in a holster around his waist, he thought about taking this for protection, but if caught by the Germans with it he would be in deep trouble, so he left it to be dumped with the body. With her help they dragged the body to the ditch. With an effort, they put the soldier back in his coat and before buttoning it up they put his rifle inside and as many rocks in his pockets as was possible. They then tipped him into a particularly deep waterlogged part of the ditch where he sank from sight. To make sure he stayed down, Sam then threw all the loose rocks they could find around the area down on top of him. He was posted AWOL the next day by his platoon commander, but his body was never found. He was a victim of war!

As soon as they had completed their grisly task, the girl picked up her lamp and they both went back down the track to the main road. Sam told the girl to walk ahead of him and if anyone came he would disappear into a hedge or field, because if they were caught together, she could be shot for helping an escaping British soldier. This was agreed, they made as much haste as possible. The girl had said before they split up there was little or no traffic along the road at this time of night, which was true, nothing passed them in either direction. Sam kept his distance, following the light from the lamp from the other side of the road. The girl said if she saw anything suspicious, she would wave her lamp and it was up to Sam as to what action he should take.

They soon arrived at her cottage, not having seen a soul on their walk, she invited Sam in. He sensed she was still afraid about something. He assured her she was quite safe with him, he had a girlfriend at home in England and would not touch her or do her any harm. He told her he knew that the Germans would doing random checks on houses to make sure the occupants were not harbouring anyone who was an enemy to the Kaiser, so not to compromise her, he would leave her straight away. She thanked him for his good sense and compassion but insisted on giving him a meal before he left. She told Sam she was never without a little food from leftovers from the village shop where she worked that was not sold, which the owner gave her. She considered she could spare some for him, the least she could do for rescuing her from what would have been certain rape and most properly end up being murdered. He knew she was living on her own and her only income was what the shop owner could afford to pay her, so every little helped.

With food enough for at least one day, which she had put into his haversack, he was ready to leave of her, but not before she cooked a hot meal for them both with scraps of pork off-cuts, potatoes and carrots; a stew, the best food he had since the Soldier's Mess at Bristol. Within the hour, he had been fed and was on the road before the first rays of the sun had started to fill the sky in the east. Sam had not walked more than a few miles when he suddenly realised they had not even exchanged names, perhaps that was a good thing

A bit later he passed what looked like a farm house, and about half a mile further on, down a short gated country track too his right, saw what appeared, in the dim light from where he was standing, the third dilapidated building he had seen in so many nights, all was silent this time! He climbed over the gate and made his way up to building that looked like a barn and as he approached it the house looked as disused as the cottage he had found the girl in. The barn had a large open doorway, the doors themselves were long gone, leading into a large passage and then into the centre of the building. He walked into the main part of the barn that extended on both sides to his right and left but straight on was another opening that was a corresponding passage and doorway to the one he had entered, allowing wagons to drive in, unload and drive out the other side, without turning round and sheltered from the elements while in there.

As dawn was approaching, he went into the barn and while there was little or no hay or straw around, he found he could collect enough of what was left for his own purpose, gathering the remains of the leftovers from a harvest of at least two years or more ago. From this he built himself a nest in what he considered the most secluded part of the barn. Before retiring he ate a little of the rations the girl had given him, he couldn't afford to waste any food and washed it down with water from his beer bottle, he would keep the remainder of what the girl had given him for later, it was much more fresh. When finished he crawled into his nest, covering himself with straw and hay, so he could be hidden from prying eyes for the rest of the day, if there were any, which he doubted. The sun was now shining in one of the doorways and the many gaps and holes in the walls. It was now fully light. He settled down for what he considered was a well earned rest and a few hours kip.

Sam was suddenly woken up by the cacophony sound of many aero engines and machine gun fire that he recognised as Lewis guns. He carefully poked his head out of his nest ensuring no one was about. There was not a soul to be seen in any direction, so he went to the front opening looking out with caution; there was no one in sight on the ground or in the air. Going to the rear opening, it was a different matter, no one in sight on the ground but in the air there was British aircraft being attacked by German aircraft, each giving as good as they got as it appeared to Sam. The British were making for home as fast as possible and the mêlée soon disappeared to the west, the sound stopping as suddenly as it had started, all was once quiet again in the sky's above the fields as far as he could see. When it was all over, he checked on the ground just in case the fight had attracted anyone, but there was no one in sight in any direction.

The sun was now high in the sky, he judged it to be mid day, he must have slept for a about five or six hours, he was refreshed, but very hungry, so he feasted on some of the food given to him by the young girl. With his back to the road, looking east across the field, he did not realise how near to the railway line he was. He gathered his water bottle, tools and rag and walked towards the line, keeping very close to a hedge that ran from the barn to the end of the field, which was the boundary of the railway line. The sun was shining in a cloudless day, so Sam kept on the shadow side of the hedge, as it gave him the best concealment that was possible, his dark clothes helping him to blend in to his dull background. With all this extra clothing it kept him warm walking during the night, but he was very hot now, but he could not discard anything, firstly his uniform could be seen, and last he would most certainly need the extra layers at night, especially if he had to sleep rough.

The railway line was on a slight embankment, which he climbed with caution, looking both ways, up and down the track; there was not a soul in sight as far as he could see. He got to the top of the embankment, noting that it was double track, so the line could be fairly busy, and from the position of the sun, it ran approximately from north to south. Taking a last look around, he turned left with his back to the sun, hoping, if his memory served him correctly, towards Brussels; at least it was going northwards, the way he wanted to go. He kept an eye forward and a constant vigil behind him, always keeping on the outside of any bend to see the farthest distance in either direction in case there were any rail workers about. He decided that at the first sign of approach from a train or any indication of a working party on the track, he would make himself scarce on one side of the line or the other, where the best cover lay.

For about a mile everything was OK, but the embankment then ended and the track then entered a cutting. If he went in there, there would be no escape if he met anything, and as the line curved to the right, his forward view was limited. He decided the best plan would be to leave the railway behind and walk on the top edge of cutting edge and come down the other side when the cutting ended. This he did, keeping the track on his right shoulder and it was not long before he realised that the cutting was ending, not as he expected, back down to track level, but at a tunnel entrance. He just hoped the tunnel was not too long and did not curve away sharply to the right or left, as he could easily lose the line altogether, he just hoped he could pick it up at the other end. At least he knew the general direction the line was taking.

The track before it went into the tunnel was on a gentle right hand curve, so he would see what happened and gauging where the sun was he walked through fields, keeping close in, on the shaded side again. He was just half way across the third field, with no sign of the other end of the tunnel, when he heard voices in front of him, on the other side of the hedge in the next field. He fell flat to the ground and tucked himself well into the hedge and froze, waiting for a few minutes, but no one came. The conversation continued, so he hoped no one had seen or heard him. As he could not see them, he reasoned, they could not have seen him either and walking on soft grass he was not making any noise.

When he felt he was safe from detection, he decided to investigate as to what the hedge was concealing from him. Peering through a small gap at the bottom of the hedge, he saw the local farmer and his labourers cutting the corn with big scythes, while the women were gathering up the crop fallen crop, tying them into sheaves and standing them in stooks to dry in the summer sun. The only way he could pass them unseen was to go into the next field, which he was about to do, when he saw that they had brought their food for the day with them. It was piled up in the corner of the field next to him, under the hedge in the shade, some way from the nearest worker.

He felt his need was greater than theirs, share and share alike, so decided how best he could help himself to a little of their sustenance to assist him on his way. He crawled down his side of the hedge until he was adjacent to the corner of the field where all the food and drink were laying, a few feet on the other side of the hedge to where he was. He looked through a break in the hedge, the nearest people were the women, over a hundred yards away, working and chatting away, not looking in his direction. He reached through the gap, grasping the first bundle he could reach and drew it through, with little or no noise at all. A quick look inside the bundle, he found fresh bread and cheese and a bottle of what was probably a local rough red wine, a good size meal for two, husband and wife he thought, and if he was careful, it could last him at least two days. He gathered all this up, looking up to Heaven, whispering a grateful thank you and asking for forgiveness for the sin he had committed, putting all his ill gotten gains in his haversack and made a hasty, but quiet, retreat back to the hedge, then carrying on in the direction he had previously being taking.

He soon made as much distance as possible between him and the farmers and it was not long before he was just over a mile away that he saw a welcoming sight in the distance, a plume of smoke, raising from what seemed like the ground, in steady puffs, a bit to his left. Keeping to the field edges, he made his way in the general direction from where he had seen the smoke that had now drifted away and it was not long before he found the cutting and the mouth of the tunnel down below him to his right, his estimate of the direction of the rail track had not been far out. When he arrived above the track edge the train that had made the smoke was long gone. He continued walking along the top of the cutting as in started to slope down until it was eventually at track level.

When he reached the bottom of the cutting he continued walking northwards along the track and while he was hungry, he felt he must go as far as possible in the daylight and make sure he was safe. The line started to climb round a bend as it passed through a wooded area. He had not gone far round the curve when he saw a platelayers hut on the north bound side of the track and three or four workmen outside; sitting, eating, drinking and talking while they consumed their meal. Sam was in the drainage ditch beside the line before anyone could see him and then crawled into the wooded area, going in until he felt he was well hidden and had good cover but ensuring he had an adequate view of the hut and the men there. He decided this was a good place for a meal, saying a thank you to the farmer and his wife who were probably at this moment wondering where their food had gone!

For the rest of the day Sam either slept or watched the trains going north, all being slowed by the heavy northern rising gradient. The goods trains were the slowest; the heavier they were the slower their speed, some no more than walking pace. To his advantage, he saw that the line curved and he was on the outside of the curve. He reasoned that neither the engine crew nor guard could see the centre part of the train at this point, a good place for him to hop on and hitch a ride. Later in the afternoon, all the workmen got up and stood near the line, not attempting to do any track maintenance, *what was all this about,* thought Sam. The reason soon became apparent; they were getting a ride back to where their base was, Brussels probably, and they were knocking off for the day. It was not long before a passenger train came up the gradient, slowing to a walking pace and as the rear coach approached the platelayers a door was opened by the guard and all the platelayers climbed up the vertical steps in turn to board the train. The guard went to the other side of the train where the driver could see him and gave the all clear to proceed. With a shrill blast on the whistle the engine then started to increase speed amidst clouds of smoke and steam and the slipping of the driving wheels, but as it increased momentum, it was soon lost from sight round he curve and the sound of the engine slowly faded away in the distance. All was silent in the countryside, until the next train passed through.

As the light started to fade Sam decided to make his move. He made his way cautiously to the edge of the wood, all was clear; there was not a soul in sight. He made his way to the hut which was on the outside edge of the curve. While he was waiting for darkness to fall, he felt that the hut could do with a check. The door was not locked; it didn't even have one, just a hook and eye keeping it closed. What was the point, there was no access to the hut except by rail, and bar for rail workers, no one else knew it existed.

Inside there was a bench and a stove, the latter was still alight. There was a kettle and a large can of water, half full and even some fresh coffee grounds in a pot on the only shelf in the hut. He stoked up the fire and the kettle was soon singing away with a bit of extra coal that he found had been deposited outside the hut, probably from a passing engine! He kept a sharp watch up and down the track but everyone had knocked off for the day, the only sign of life was the fairly frequent trains and a certain amount of wild animal life crossing the line in both directions. He made sure there was little or no smoke from the chimney to attract attention to the hut or himself. As soon as he had made his drink, he dampened the fire down. The bad news was the platelayers had left no food but he was grateful for the drink that they had left. He made sure that he left everything as he found it, even refilling the kettle. The only thing that was missing was a small amount of coffee that he was sure none of the platelayers would ever notice that had gone. On leaving the hut he closed the door as he had found it.

As darkness fell the trains were nearly as frequent as they had been during the day, but few passenger trains passed, the majority were goods, the German's needed re-supplying. The passenger trains were far too fast to board in any case, and even if he could get on one, Sam considered it would be far too dangerous as the guard would be patrolling the whole length of the train, and most likely there would also be Germany soldiers in overall charge of the security of the train. Most of the goods trains were not so fast, but still too fast for making it possible for him to board as they passed with any safety. If none slowed down enough for him to board, he would have to start walking again. Sam felt it must be about midnight and he was getting desperate, the trains were less frequent, but hardly any were passenger trains, which was a good sign.

Then he heard the sound he had been waiting to hear, a train was approaching, labouring as it climbed the steep gradient. As it came in sight it was not going much faster than walking pace, now was his chance. As the engine passed, he could see the crew by the glow from the firebox, the driving looking forward up the line, the fireman shovelling coal into a hungry firebox. He made his way out from the side of the hut where he had concealed himself as the engine started to disappear, the rear of the train was not in sight. The wagons were mostly flat beds with loads and there were a few open wagons with he expected a guards van bringing up the rear. He selected a wagon with shallow sides and as it approached he went forward, grabbed a handle and swung himself onto the wagon steps, standing with one foot on the bottom step of a set of three. Getting a firm grip on the handle, he pulled himself to the top edge of the side, heaving himself aboard, to land with a thump on something soft. He had landed on a tarpaulin that was tightly stretch over the whole wagon, acting like a trampoline, breaking his fall.

He wondered why the train was labouring and looking both ways up and down the train and saw what looked like it was carrying heavy damaged guns, he supposed it was going back to a repair depot. As the train continued to labour its way up the incline, he opened up the tarpaulins and crawled under and made a makeshift bed on an unused tarpaulin lying on the floor of the wagon, this shelter would keep out any rain and smoke smuts and also to hide him from anyone looking down from signal boxes or bridges.

At the top of the gradient, the train gathered speed and was rattling along, Sam hoped it was going in the direction he wanted to go. It seemed to Sam that after about two hours, the countryside started to be lost to buildings, and as the train continued, they became more dense, these then gave way to factories and industrial sites, there were more tracks on either side, lines joined them from a number of junctions, while others branched off.

Either side of the main line were marshalling yards, which were dimly lit. As Sam peered over the side of the wagon he could just make out that there had been extensive damage to all the yards he passed, he suspected by British bombing. A number of lines were buckled and bent, craters abound and numbers of damaged trucks could be seen, and at least one engine was lying on its side, looking beyond repair.

Sam expected the train to stop at any time and turn into one of the yards sidings but it passed through and continued out the other side of what he considered must be Brussels main goods train assembly point. It made him wondered why the train had not stopped, *was it's destination not Brussels*, or perhaps, after the bombing damage, there were no free sidings and a possibility of further RFC bombing raids to come?

They were soon back in the country, but they had not travelled far when the train was diverted from the main line into a siding. Sam expected this was to allow a fast train to pass, but no sooner had the train stopped, the engine was uncoupled and left in the siding, crossing over the main track they had been taking to the line going back in a southerly direction. When the engine crew had the all clear, they started to go back the way they had come, picking up the guard on the way. Without a train the engine soon gathered speed and soon disappeared into the darkness of night.

Sam thought about what he should do now. He soon made a decision, once daylight came he could not escape without the chance of being seen and he did not know which way the train would go. There was a high possibility it would go back the way it came to Brussels to reload or be split up and be dispersed in various directions. If he stayed in his truck, he could end up anywhere and be lost! He would have to leave the train for the day, maybe he would return when it got dark, so he climbed out of the wagon, with all his tools and with the remains of the food he had 'borrowed' from the farmers and made his way to the boundary side of the track. There was a low fence that marked the end of railway property and he made his way to this with the railway behind him, climbing over the fence and crossing an arable field, keeping as close to a hedge of just over five feet with his dark clothes he was well hidden.

It was starting to get light, daybreak was on its way, he must hide as soon as possible, even in the field as dawn came up; the chance of being observed became more of a risk, while not in the open, he was not far from it.

As the light increased, he saw that there was someone in the field and in the half light it looked as if it was walking towards him. He ducked into hedge and watched. As it got lighter, the figure now seemed to be standing still, there was something strange about this person, and Sam suddenly realised it was a scarecrow. It made him laugh out loud, it had certainly scared him alright! He gathered his breath before moving on.

It was now near full light on this dull and overcast day, recalling what Matron King had said to him about this type of weather, it was a *'nothing day,'* no sun, no rain, no wind. Looking across to the far side of the field he saw a wood that was bounded by a fence. At great speed he soon reached the fence, which he scaled in one bound and was in the wood. It was not long

214

before he came across a cart track that took him to the far side of what was a small copse. As it got lighter he came to the edge of the copse and saw a fairly large field that was surrounded on all four sides by wood.

He felt that this was a safe place to spend the day. When it got dark, he had to consider his next move. He could return to the railway line and try and hitch another northbound train, but he decided to sleep on that! Sam found himself a nice warm patch to rest up for the day, a few yards from the field surrounded by wood and well hidden. He curled up and was ready for sleep. It was cloudy and warmish, but rain was not threatening. Well he had done well so far, escaped from both the British and the Germans which seemed ironic. As he lay there on this overcast day he remembered something else the Matron had said to him at Barnardo's when things weren't going to well, *'While there may be clouds in the sky, the sun is always shining.'*

Yes, *there may be clouds in my sky,* he thought, *but they were clearing*; things were now going his way, the sun was starting to shine through, on his side this time, and with that thought, he was soon asleep.

***

One of the highlights of Algernon's day was to receive a letter from Keturah. The latest was how everything valuable had been sent to the Cavendish estate in Oxfordshire and all the work she had been doing for the WEC, the letter finished with all the gossip. He could not stay any longer over her letter and afternoon tea, he would read it again when he returned in the evening, he now had work to do.

A few days earlier he had organised a bombing raid on the railway marshalling yards at Brussels, the wing was now going to repeat that raid. From the recent photos, while a lot of damage had been caused, it was not enough, trains were still running, be it at a reduced rate, they had to have another go. The last one had been very early, leaving before dawn; in, out and back before the enemy had known what had hit them, and, which was most gratifying, without any losses but two injured gunners, a proof that they were the early birds who caught the worm! But they had to be more prepared this time, the Boche were not going to get caught with their pants down twice!

He now had to brief his wing leader, Lieutenant-Colonel Andrews, on another raid the following morning to the same location as before, more damage was required, and the yard had to be put completely put out of action. Together they would plan and organise the next show. Earlier in the day, he had instructed his *aide de camp* to contact the five squadron leaders in the wing to report to the Wing Leader's airfield for a working dinner, but not mentioning the reason why, and making sure his gunner Flight Sergeant Thorne was available to fly with him in the afternoon and to insure a camera was fitted. He decided to leave for the airfield after an early lunch.

Taking his staff car, he was driven to his Wing Leader's base and where his personal aircraft was housed and now ready for immediate use. The afternoon and evening was forecast to be clear and he had been told by the weather experts that tomorrow morning would be the same. On his arrival he saw the aircraft was being inspected and the engine being run up with Thorne standing by in his flying kit. Other aircrafts were flying, he presumed on air test, they had no orders to go over and harass the Hun. He found Andrews down in one of the four Bessonean hangars that had been erected on the airfield, chatting to his Captain in charge of aircraft maintenance. Algernon stayed and chatted, interested in all aspects of serviceability, then went back to his car, donning his flying clothes and was ready for a flight.

He took off and circled around until he had reached the aircrafts ceiling, then he made his way over both the front line and to the rail junction they had bombed a few days earlier and was the target for early tomorrow. They were fired on but as they never kept in a straight line, the misses were not even near. Over the target the gun fire was less, they flew in a straight line and took photos and made it for home. The Bosh had been caught by surprise; they were not expecting their enemy at this time of day and were only getting their act together, climbing as fast as they could. As soon as the were getting near, at a much slower speed, the Bristol Fighter was nearly back to their own line, having remained at its maximum ceiling, now Algernon went into a dive for the airfield and left the enemy far behind without firing a shot, their only option was return to their own base without crossing into British territory and anywhere near their adversary.

On return, Algernon had the photos developed before retiring to the Wing Leaders office. They discussed and planned the operation in Andrews's office, comparing the two sets of photos, from after the first raid and the afternoon, seeing what had been cleared up, repaired and under repaired, until the arrival of the four other squadron commanders, each flying in from their own base. When the squadron commanders arrived they all went into a private dining room in the Officer's Mess Tent for dinner where they were briefed by Algernon and Andrews on their next mission. Each squadron had a full complement of the two seater Bristol Fighter, these having a dual role of fighter/photo reconnaissance or bomber, 50% of each type. Some of the fighters would go out on their own to either fight and harry the Hun, the remainder would act as escorts for the slower bombers with their full load of bombs. On return, with no bombs and about 65% fuel left, they could all make a faster get way and hope they all returned unscathed. When dinner was finished, the five Squadron Commanders left to brief their aircrew and ground staff and to prepare for an early start the following day.

Algernon, as he had done before the last Brussels raid, stayed at the permanent mess, a local hotel that the RFC had taken over in a nearby town, overnight, so he could be down at the airfield while it was still dark, to see his crews safely off. He would return to the Mess for a quick breakfast after they had all taken off, returning to the airfield about half an hour before they were due to return, so he could fly out in his own aircraft to meet them, ensuring he did not go anywhere near the front line.

Algernon was one of the first down at the airfield the following morning, just as the ground crew were starting up the aircraft, to ensure everything about all the aircraft was A1 and the engines were warmed to operating temperature. The aircrew soon arrived, getting themselves strapped in and ready for take off.

Five minutes before take off, the runway lights were lit to mark the take off strip; goose necks paraffin lamps with spouts that looked like the bird of the same name that housed the wick. The signal was given and following the CO they took off in turn. The only thing that could be seen as they disappeared into the darkness was the glow from the engines. As soon as the last plane had left, the flare path was extinguished. As soon as they were airborne they would rendezvous at a planned point with the other four squadrons, well inside British lines at the maximum ceiling of the heavy bombers so the Hun would have trouble seeing them until they were over their territory. Every minute they were not seen was an extra minute to their advantage. When Algernon could not hear the sound of engines anymore he went back to the mess for breakfast and as the Wing were expected to be away for about 1½ hours he had an hour to catch up on some paper work.

When the raid was completed, and all bombs dropped, the wing made for home as fast as they could in a shallow dive with the escorts now relieved of the task of escorting the slower bombers. Suddenly they were pounced on by a squadron of German fighters who dove down from above and behind the retreating British planes, firing as they went, passing through both the fighters and bombers, inflicting little damage, they were novices at the game of aerial warfare. The only plane hit was that of Capt Tim Gledhill, the senior Flight Commander of Lieutenant-Colonel Andrews's squadron, causing damage which was not immediately apparent, he was still flying. As the German who had shot him up passed in front of Tim's aircraft, he emptied the remainder of his ammunition from his twin machine guns into the plane and was pleased to see smoke then flames burst out from the engine, the Hun headed earthwards, another kill to add to his total of eight already. But now Tim had his own problem, his engine started to run rough and he was losing height rapidly, luckily no fire at the moment. He had to find somewhere to land without delay or else he would crash and probably be killed. Looking quickly around him he spotted a flat grass field within easy reach, he hoped, which was bounded on all of its four sides by woods. He started to turn towards the field, losing height which he could not afford. He was surprised to see no other aircraft about from either side; he was well and truly on his own. It was touch and go whether he would make the field. As he came in, he just missed the tops of the trees before he made it, crashing to the ground in the middle of the field with a sickening jolt. He remembered no more, he was knocked unconscious by the deceleration of the landing and banging his head on the front edge of the padded cockpit that his safety harness did not prevent.

***

After about an hour, Algernon was back at the airfield having his aircraft started and was soon airborne with Flight Sergeant Thorne behind him, climbing into the rising sun to make the maximum height to meet the returning raiding party. He flew for about 15 minutes from his lofty position and soon spotted the returning aircraft of Andrews's wing. He did a quick head count, there was one missing, he would have to wait until the de-briefing to find out who it was and what had happened, if that was possible. After about 15 minutes, the Wing broke up into their squadrons and return to their own bases. When they approached the Wing Leader's airfield, Algernon kept out of the way letting the squadron land. As soon as they were all down and had taxied to their respective dispersal points, he then landed, keeping well out of the way. Handing over his aircraft to the ground crew, he made his way to the de-briefing hut to find out the success or failure of the operation.

When he entered, the crews were in a buoyant mood. It seemed they had hit the target much better and felt that there were no lines left undamaged, it would be days at least before through trains would be running through the marshalling yard. The two photo reconnaissance aircraft were the last to land and the plates from the on board camera were taken immediately to the mobile processing lab. The prints would be on Algernon's desk by mid morning so he could assess the scale of damage. When he was happy with the results he would select the best photos which would be sent by despatch rider to RFC HQ.

The only down side to the operation was that they had lost their senior flight commander, Captain Tim Gledhill, who had flown without a gunner in the two seater Bristol as the squadron had not received replacements since

218

loosing two injured in the last raid on the rail yards and junction. He had mostly flown single seater reconnaissance and fighter planes since he graduated from the Central Flying School at Upavon so was not unhappy being without a rear gunner behind him and, on the plus side, he needed less fuel without the weight of a gunner, his Lewis gun and all the ammo that went with it. It gave him a little extra speed and more manoeuvrability and was ideal as an escort to the slower bombers. He never had the protection of a rear gunner before, had never been injured and only received a few minor holes in his aircraft where no damage had been inflicted, returning from all patrols to fight another day.

As they were leaving after the raid with little ammo left, having been spent mostly shooting up the marshalling yard, when a squadron of enemy aircraft spotted them and attacked, but it was half hearted affair, it seemed that they were not all that battle wise. There was no point in engaging the enemy as they had nothing to fight back with, so everyone put their noses down and made for home, leaving the Hun far behind. When they all got back together, Gledhill was missing, no one saw him disappear or go down. Algernon contacted the other squadrons, there was no loss in any of them, but they could not help either with any information about the whereabouts of the missing pilot. He was only posted missing, until any other news came in to the contrary.

CHAPTER 11

Two On The Run

Sam had not been asleep very long when he was woken by the sound of aircraft and machine gun fire for the second time in two days. A weak sun was now shining as he ventured out to the edge of the field and he saw a British aircraft being attacked by a German plane not far from where he was hiding. There were also a number of other dog fights going on at some distance away. He saw the German aircraft that had been doing the attacking, turning away from his prey, disappearing behind the far woods, loosing height and trailing smoke; *the prey must have hit back!* The British plane he had seen was now in deep trouble but had disappeared, Sam did not think he had far to go before the plane and Mother Earth met!

From over the top of the tress on the far side of the field from Sam, the British aircraft that was being attacked suddenly appeared, its engine was spluttering, but the aircraft that had appeared to have inflicted his damage was long gone. The aircraft was on its own now and losing height rapidly. As it approached the field, it only just cleared the trees at as it plummeted down towards the ground, it was never going to fly or leave the field again. Sam watched, opened mouthed, from his vantage point. It pancaked in the middle of the field onto the long grass, its propeller stopping dead as it dug in the ground and stalled the engine. The aircraft continued to move forward, bouncing once or twice as it approached a fence some 100 yards from the first line of trees near Sam. It eventually hit the fence that acted like an arrester wire, tearing the undercarriage from the body of the aircraft but the pilot, fuselage and wings continued on their headlong way, their progress little hampered as it reached within yards of the first line of trees, ploughing up the soft ground as it went. Passing between two stout oaks, the plane lost both its wings, and what was left, ended up in a drainage ditch, something like the trenches either side of no-mans-land that Sam had recently left, nose down, tail up! Sudden peace descended over the wood, and thankfully there was no sign of fire. The aircraft was now well hidden in the woods, under other overhanging trees deep in the wood that camouflaged it from the air. It would be hard to spot from the ground, let alone from the air.

Sam could see the pilot slumped over the controls in the cockpit. He dashed over to what remained of the aircraft to find the pilot semi-conscious. As he went to see what he could do to help he found the starboard side of the aircraft had been ripped off by a small tree that had been in the path of the aircraft. This made his task easier for Sam; he undid the pilots harness and pulled him free, dragging him well away from the wreckage, laying him carefully on the ground, he could not be much over 20 years of age. The pilot was starting to come round and looking about. Sam still had water in both his bottles, so dashed back to his den near by and returned with it, pouring some over the pilot and the rest he offered for a drink, which was readily accepted.

The pilot soon started to recover and was now eyeing Sam up and down in a suspicious manner, looking at this scruffy individual with not too clean face and hands. As Sam was still wearing his donkey jacket, peaked cloth cap and working overalls, Tim thought he looked like a local, but which side did he support was the question. By his appearance he was a bit young to be called up, not needing to shave every day but in need of a wash, looking exactly like a manual worker, but he seemed to have nothing to say. Before Tim crashed he knew there was nothing around for miles, only fields and woods, so what was he doing all out here in the wilds, a farm worker perhaps? The pilot felt he should break the silence between them and say something first, if only to give himself up and surrender, he was in no fit state to fight or runaway.

The pilot thought for a moment, what language would he speak, they were in Belgium so there was a good chance he understood French which was a language Tim had first learnt at school, so he would give it a go. What should he say, so he decided to make a neutral statement in French asking him if he understood French. This brought a smile to his saviours face, which he considered an odd reaction. Sam knew as soon as the plane crashed that the aviator was not only British, but from the few pilots he had seen in the flying clothing he wore, it looked like RFC issue, and weren't all pilots officers? Now the officer had broken the silence, Sam felt he should replied, but not wanting to give to much information away. "Sir, I am a British soldier, I was a POW but I escaped and I'm now on the run from the Germans, can I help you?"

The pilot look amazed and relieved, "Thank God for that, I was wondering who the hell you were, I thought you were going to hand me in, you look like a local. Pleased to meet you," and he held out his hand for Sam to shake. "Captain Gledhill of the RFC, so what are you doing in this part of Belgium?"

"On my way to Holland, I hope Sir. I have a hiding place near by, may I suggest we go over there so you can rest a bit, then we can have a talk, best to keep away from your aircraft in case anyone comes to look around," Sam said.

"Good idea, give me a hand as I feel a bit weak at the moment, don't think I've done any permanent damage to myself, but I think I will get over it, even if I may have a number bruises for a few days," was Gledhill's reply.

With that they moved off and were soon at Sam's den, where the pilot laid down and was soon resting on Sam's mattress of grass and leaves. After the pilot had rested awhile and had some food and water, Sam felt he should tell the Captain more about himself, but not as Private Perry but as Private Drew, even if it was going to be a few white lies about who he was, but about how he escaped, some of the truth, a bit of the whole truth and what was left of the truth.

"Sir, I am Private Drew, of the West Bristol Fusiliers. My platoon went over the top recently, I think I must have got concussed by a shell exploding near me when we had nearly reached the German front line, and when I came round I found I was in an enemy trench, the Germans had taken me prisoner. That was what I first remember, how I got there, I will never know, did I crawl in the wrong direction towards their lines or did the Germans come out and pull me in? Who ever they were, they treated me well, and I will say that much for them. I got taken by the Germans to a field hospital for a check up, but they found I was OK. Later they took me to a holding place for interrogation." Here he felt he should tell the officer he had not told the Germans anything that could help them. Sam continued, "After about a week, I, with a lot of others, were taken to the nearest railway yard and loaded into cattle trucks where we were being taken to a prison camp. On the way I escaped from the train, I tried to get others to come with me, but I had no takers; on reflection, I'm glad no one wanted to come with me. They said they would cover up for me, whether they did or not I don't know, but I've seen no high presence of Germans looking for anyone. I've been on the run ever since, at least a week I think, but I have lost all track of time. I haven't had a decent wash or shave for ages which helps with my disguise! I've been making my way north to get to Holland, which I think is not fighting and not on either side, where I hope to find a boat that will get me back to England. I don't know how friendly the Dutch are towards us after the Boer Wars, do you have any ideas Sir?"

The officer paused to gain his thoughts and then commented, "I'm not sure about the Dutch people Drew, at the moment the country remains neutral. If we get there we will have to suck it and see. I suppose you must have some sort of plan as to how you are going make your escape and back to England?"

"As I said Sir, I'm travelling, mostly either walking or hopping on and off trains by night," Sam replied. "To get here I hitched a train ride to some nearby sidings, I would have gone further but the goods train I was on last night was left there and the engine returned from the way we came. I had planned to go back there tonight and hope to pick up another train from there that was going north. The direction I have been going is a lot by guess work as I have no compass. The only problem is I have nearly run out of food. The last lot I had I pinched from some farmers in a field when they weren't looking, including a bottle of red wine, not to my taste, so I ditched it and filled the bottle with water!" He decided not to say anything about the girl and killing the German solider. "So my next problem, or now our problem Sir, is where do we get our next meal?"

"Right Drew, it looks if we are going to spend a lot of time together if we are going to make it back to Blighty, so lets be more friendly, everyone calls me Tim, so while its just the two of us, just call me Tim. If anyone hears your calling me 'Sir', it may make them wonder and cotton on that I might be an officer, which would never do with the enemy all around us, OK." Sam nodded in agreement. "Now what shall I call you?" he finished.

Sam was taken back by what the pilot had said. No officer he knew had ever asked a private to call an officer by his first name, or even call a private by his first name. "I'm Robert, but I'm usually called Bob sir," he finished; he could not yet pluck up courage and call him Tim just yet!

"OK Bob, but please remember I'm Tim, it's much safer for both of us, not sir. Now, first things first. How soon did you see me before I crashed, I ask this because I was wondering if our lads or the Hun know where I crashed?"

"I was only just inside the wood, and as soon as I heard the dog fights, I came out and watched it. I saw a German come down, he must have crashed some way off. Then the dog fight moved away and you suddenly appeared and came down, there was no one else in sight, so I don't think anyone else knows you are here, and as your aircraft ended up in the woods, it can't possibly be seen from the air," he finished.

"Good," said Tim, "the Hun you saw came down, I shot it, but he also got me, the score is a draw. Now as my plane did not catch fire and as it is now well hidden in the wood it cannot be seen from the air as you say, so it won't give away our position, not that we are going to stay here very long. We must see what we can salvage from it, so let's go."

They looked about them before moving off but there was no one in sight from any direction. They soon got to the plane again and Sam saw it was how he had left it when he dragged the pilot out. Tim took a look inside and saw that the instrument panel looked a bit battered and bent but the compass was undamaged but was still well and truly fixed in. "Any idea how we can get the compass out Bob?" he asked.

"I've got a couple of heavy tools I carry to look like a railway worker, could we use these to smash the panel enough to remove the compass?"

"Good thinking Bob, lets have 'em and I will see what I can do."

Sam collected the tools from the den and returned, passing the heavy spanner and crowbar over. It did not take the pilot long to extract the compass that was required to assist them on their journey. "It's a bit bulky, but it will come in very useful. And there are a couple of maps of the general area, but they don't go as far as the Dutch border, which is more the pity, I will just have to trust to my memory as on reflection it could be best if we did not carry RFC maps, if caught it would be our downfall, but I will hang on to them for the moment, but the compass could be a problem if we get accosted, I will try and drop and conceal it before anyone gets near us. Right there is nothing else here for us, and as there is little value for the Hun, its best not to set the aircraft on fire, as it will bring attention to this area and to us if anyone sees fire and smoke. Also it might set the woods on fire that would be the end of us. But just in case someone did see me come down, let's get back to where we have left our things and decide what the best plan of action should be."

Once they got back to Sam's hiding place, Tim got out the maps to pin point where he had ditched. It was not all that easy, as in the dog fight he had lost his whereabouts, and from their position, there were no land marks they could use as reference points.

"Any idea where we are Bob?" Tim asked.

"I know the goods train that got me here Tim, and the siding I got off at is not far over there. We passed through Brussels, but we had not travelled far once we were in open country when we were put into the siding."

They eventually located the sidings where Sam had alighted, which were a little north of Brussels and to the west of the line was the square meadow and woods on all four sides. The line stretched for miles, south to Brussels, north to Antwerp and the Dutch border, their goal. So the siding and woods were the best reference points they had, which was some help and after some considerable time the pilot worked out where he thought the big dog fight was and where he had contretemps with his German adversary.

"We have two problems Bob, while you have disguised yourself well, I'm still in my flying clothing which is easy recognisable and we need to eat, any ideas?"

"I see it this way Tim," Sam was getting used to calling him Tim now, "there is a field I passed nearby, sown with corn with a scarecrow in the middle, which looks as if it has a battered hat and old greatcoat, would that be any good?"

"Just what I need, no one looks twice at a down and out dirty old tramp. When its starts to get dark Bob, I'm going after those. Let's hide up now until then, but we have got to get some grub soon. At least you have your water bottles and I saw a stream nearby where we can refill them." He paused a moment then looked at the map which he had put an **X** to where he was sure they were. He then looked for the nearest village in a northerly direction and worked out a bearing that they should take, the compass would be a God send. One thing the pilot still had with him was a revolver and a torch, which he always carried, especially if he was doing any night flying, the only way to see his instruments if the instrument panel light in the aircraft failed, which had had happened on at least one occasion.

"First I must lose my revolver, never do to get caught with that, a right give away! The other thing I have Bob, is local money, so we may be able to buy some food, if the natives look friendly. Before the war, as luck would have it, I was a teacher at a grammar school in south west London, geography and languages were my main subjects. French was my main language, while German was my second, so this should be a help us."

Tim had been looking at Sam and was starting to wonder about him, he looked a bit young to be eligible to join up, *was he younger than he looked?* "Bob, it doesn't make any difference to our current circumstances, but how old are you, to me you don't look old enough to be in the army."

Sam could see there was no reason to lie; it wouldn't make any difference to the situation. "Yes Tim, you are quite right, I joined up earlier this year, I was only 16, they didn't bother when I told them I was nearly 18." He felt that was enough information, he did not want to say anything about his very close friend Bill being killed and using his birth certificate to allow him to enlist.

Tim thought about this for a moment. "Well, I think you are very brave Bob, and clever to what you have done in escaping. I will make sure we both get back home all in one piece. But you must trust in me to what I think best, as I will trust in you for you help and opinion, OK?" Sam nodded his agreement.

They decided to make as much distance from the aircraft as possible, so picking up all their belongs, they made their way to the other side of the wood, about a mile away, where the field with the scarecrow was, settling down hidden behind a hedge for a sleep until it started to get dark. The could now see the railway line and the siding Sam had alighted at, but there was no sign of the goods train he had stolen a ride from.

***

On Friday, 15th September 1916, a new British secret weapon was first launched on the Western Front at Somme and, with RFC covering support, smashed through the German defences who were powerless to stop them. The code name of this weapon was *'TANK'*, a tracked fighting vehicle that carried guns and an enclosed cabin for its crews protection, traveling at about 4 mph, it could bridge trenches like no other vehicle had ever done before, mud and minor pot holes did not impede its progress, rolling over the German lines, crossing over their trenches as if they weren't there, barbed wire did nothing to hinder its advance, scattering enemy machine gun crews and crashing through strong points leaving them in its wake. Using 32 of these vehicles resulted in the capture of 2,000 prisoners within two hours by British and Canadians troops following behind, gaining seven miles on a 30 mile wide front ■ In another tank incident, this time at Passendale, a number of tanks advanced on the German lines, followed by the Infantry, but a sudden retreat had to be made by tanks and men, but one tank got bogged done in a hollow and could not immediately get itself free. When the coast was clear for the Germans, they attacked the tank, climbing aboard, but to no avail, they could not destroy or break into it or get to its crew. Eventually the tank got started after three days and made its way back to home lines. The tank commander, a bit of a wit, christened the tank *'Fray Bentos'* as it is remembered in history to this day. The eight man crew all received decorations, which has never happen before or since as a single unit. The two officers received the Military Cross, the two SNCOs the Distinguished Service Medal, while the remaining four crew members were awarded the Military Medal.

***

Keturah was bored! When she had joined the WEC in London she was always busy, then she started up the West London Unit of WEC and opened up her own house to help the movement in the west of the Capital. She had started it from scratch on her own and she was initially very busy recruiting ladies to help her. With the various aspects of their work, she had made teams of ladies, each team to look after a particular project. She could not control all this by herself so she appointed a team leader for each one, they became her Lieutenants, answerable only to her. They were all very dedicated in their work and as time progressed they became very efficient in their respective sphere of work. As Keturah was doing a lot more flying for the WEC she was often away so she appointed her second-in-command as her Adjutant to take overall control while she was away. Her Adjutant was very efficient and as time went on, with Keturah being away so often she was less involved, and not as *au fait* with the day to day running and the overall operation of the West London Unit.

So she was bored! Was there anything else that her unit could do? When she went to their central office in London, they could not help either, there were no other major projects that they could give her, all the tasks she had been given were being handled by one of her teams.

As she had time on her hands, she thought she would visit the Frosts again to see if they had received any news. While she spent an hour or more in their company, which she found relaxing, they had no more news at all, Sam had not written for a long time; she returned home, deeply saddened by the lack of any news, *was he still alive?* She hoped so.

Keturah flew to Oxfordshire on one of her regular weekend visits to see her children and in-laws and returned back at Brooklands the following Monday morning. While she was putting the aircraft in the hangar, with the help of some ground crew, she was surprised to see that Tommy Sopwith had arrived, who gave her a helping hand. When all was completed he asked her if she would like to join him in the Brooklands Motor Racing Club House for a morning coffee in the Member's Lounge as he wanted a chat with her. She was intrigued, *what could Tommy want with her?* She only knew Tommy through Algernon and had only spoken to him when with her husband, *so what was all this about,* she wondered. Once they had both settled in comfortable chairs in the lounge and when Tommy had poured coffee from a silver coffee pot into bone china cups with their saucers, they commenced.

"Firstly Keturah, how is Algernon keeping, I hear he is now a full Colonel, he writes to me occasionally."

Keturah was surprised to hear Tommy say this; she had wondered where Tommy got his information from. "Yes, he is pleased with his new post, much more responsibility of course, but no more combat flying, which he misses, and I'm afraid I'm glad and much relieved, but he's still flying around visiting all the squadrons in his wing."

"I am glad to hear that, he is a good pilot, but with all his experience and his age, and no offense intended, he's best keeping out of harms way. Now to get down to business and why I have asked you to have this little chat," and before Keturah had time to speak, Tommy continued. "Now please don't think I have been spying on you Keturah, but I have often seen you flying in and out of here, and, if you don't mind me saying this, and I'm not being patronizing, I think you are one of the best lady pilots I have ever seen, and there are not many men who could better you," he finished.

"Thank you," was her verbal response, the only thing she could think of saying; while her blush was visual, she tried to cover up by looking away. Recovering, she said, "But I am sure you have not got me here just to tell me that Tommy?"

"No Keturah, you are quite right. I have a problem and I think you can help me out. Our aircraft production is increasing all the time, the War Office and Admiralty are flooding us with orders and I'm not complaining. I can keep up with all the orders but my production is such that I have aircraft parked all around the factory and outside, awaiting delivery. I can't get the pilots to deliver them. There is a shortage of pilots on the front, so all the young lads are whisked away to serve for the RFC or RNAS, I am left with male old club pilots, some of them I wouldn't trust with a rubber band driven model airplane."

Keturah laughed but did not answer Tommy, she did not know what to say, but she had an idea what he may ask her next, and she was right.

"Keturah, I know you are doing a lot of useful work at the moment with the WEC as Algernon has told me, but I think I have more useful work for you. If you are prepared to give up this work, would you become a pilot for me and help deliver aircrafts? What do you say Keturah? Will you join my band of Lady Aviators Keturah? Please say yes."

An emphatic **"YES"** was her only possible reply, she would not be bored any more and knew that Algernon would be pleased, as he knew how much she liked flying. It would be a more important part in the war effort to her than the WEC. She added, "The way I have organised all my ladies, I have little work to do and have done myself out of a job! Basically I have become bored and was in the process of looking for some other useful war work to do, so you have found it for me Tommy, thank you," and took his hand in hers and shook it.

"Before I asked you, I wrote to Algernon and he is happy for me to employ you as a ferry pilot, this is what we call our pilots by the way. I know you have three children, this is one concern that worries me, what about them if you are away flying Keturah, on long delivery trips there could be an overnight stay in some God forsaken place."

Keturah was surprised he knew so much about her, working for the WEC and having three children, she wondered what else he knew about her. Algernon and Tommy must have exchange a lot of correspondence

"There is no problem with the children Tommy, they live with my in-laws outside Reading at weekends and are weekly boarders attending schools in Reading during the week, so I usually fly down at the weekends to see them if I have the fuel to spare," she replied, thinking that was something else he now knew about her and Algernon. If she had to miss the occasional weekend in the country with her children, that had to be accepted, she knew they were older enough to understand and there was a war on! It was nothing like the troops had to endure at not having been home for months and years on end. She had no grounds to complain or moan. She was going to do what she liked to do.

"That's OK then. So far I have recruited a number of ladies in the last week or so and I hope to start them delivering aircrafts by the end of this week, or at the latest early next week, I just have to clear this with the War Office and the Admiralty. I don't think they will disagree as they are all screaming out for aircrafts as I have said, they may not like it at first, but they will have to accept it or have shortage of flying machines, as far as I can see, they have no choice. You wait and see, within a month or less there will be a *Sopwith's Delivery Service*, it will be the norm. Now you won't be out of pocket, as we impose delivery charges, so you will get paid by the day while you are out on a delivery, including return the following day if you have stayed over night, plus all expenses that includes lodgings and travel, and if you are not working a daily retainer, how does that sound?"

Keturah was well pleased and thanked Tommy. While she did not need the money, with the generous allowance Algernon gave her, she was not going to refuse; it was the first money she had earned since she had met Algernon when she had retired! This at least she considered was honest money!

Things moved fast as Tommy had predicted, *Sopwith's Delivery Service*, soon to be shortened to SDS, was accepted by the two ministries, and within a week of her meeting with Tommy she became the first of six ladies employed by Tommy to deliver aircraft, soon the numbers increased as the war progressed. Her first task was to deliver a Sopwith Pup to Upavon, the Central Flying School of the RFC, taking her trusted parachute with her which she always had attached too her when flying, returning the same day by train to Paddington.

***

In 1916, Tommy Sopwith designed, tested and offered for approval two different types of aircraft, the Sopwith Pup and the Sopwith Triplane, to the flying arms of both services. It was Keturah that took one of the Triplanes to Farnborough for evaluation. It was rejected by the RFC but approved by the RNAS and entered service with them in early 1917.

***

There were far more planes to deliver than male pilots, so Keturah and all the other lady pilots were in great demand, so much so that she realised she could not do two jobs at once. While she felt her WEC work was important, it was now running with little or no help from her, she had to make a decision which job she should do, *the WEC or flying?* In the end she went to the Central London HQ and explained the situation to the Committee Chair Lady, saying she was happy for the WEC to continue using her home, and when she was not flying, would be there to keep an eye on things, as this was still her London home. She told the Chair Lady that she felt delivering much needed war planes was more important to the running of her branch and that she would appoint one of her Ladies to be in overall charge in her absence, which she had already done, who would run the organisation while she was away flying. The Chair Lady concurred with her decision and Keturah put the new arrangement in place immediately and the lady that had taken over from her would also replace her on the WEC Committee in the London HQ.

***

A week after Sam had escaped, the Sergeant in charge of the execution squad, still using the marquee as their base, wanted to get out of the area as soon as possible, before any trouble started that he and the squad may be involved in. He reported to the Military Police HQ, asking the PM permission to return to their base, about 50 miles away, but was told, under the current circumstances, he was to remain on site where they were all to stay until further notice. He was ordered to leave the marquee up but to remove the execution post and fill in the grave. The latter he was glad to do as the evidence of the stake with the handcuffs on would be lost for ever, he hoped. The execution party started work immediately, first filling in the grave and then removing the post, doing it at double quick time, completing both tasks in under an hour. They then returned the post and other minor items they had drawn from the PM's stores in the truck that they had collected the equipment in the day after the CM. They were held responsible for the loss of the stake and handcuffs, a decision would be taken about how the loss would be written off. While the sergeant was in charge, the corporal had signed for the equipment. When they had all returned to the marquee to await further orders, the Sergeant warned his squad, if anyone of them were asked, the prisoner had escaped handcuffed and attached to the stake. If they said anything else, they would all be in deep trouble. The only one to be questioned about the behaviour of the Execution Squad initially was the

Sergeant. He was far from happy about the situation that was happening around him and felt that the writing was on the wall for him. They were now under close surveillance by the Military Police and there was no more drinking, the Provost Marshall had banned the purchase of any alcohol by any member of the squad, watched over by the MPs guarding the site.

***

Major General Matchwick had now been back from his conference in London just over a week and had had his twice daily updates from Lieutenant Colonel Harper, the Provost Marshall. Progress had been made with regard to 2nd Lieutenant Ellis, who was now under close arrest, while Lieutenant Colonel Lucas was on open arrest. With all the material evidence gathered against both men, without their knowledge, the Major General considered they had enough proof to convict a Court Martial. Ellis would be charged with perjury and dereliction of duty, while Lucas would be charged with failing to conduct a fair trial. As promised, Matchwick had given Lucas good tongue lashing and now he only worn his substantive rank of Major.

Ellis was the first to be charged in front of the Major General. He was advised to find himself a suitable defence counsel. Lucas was the next in, and charged. He was then placed under close arrest and relieved of all his duties and was also told to find himself a person to conduct his defence and not to consort with any other personnel except his council. He had to remain in his room in the Officer's Mess under escort where all his meals would be brought to him and only allowed from his room for a call of nature, under escort, and not permitted to talk to anyone, that meant no tampering with witnesses.

The CM was set for the following week, both on the same day but with a different President and Board of Officers for each. Ellis's case was to be first as his charge was considered the most serious. He had been advised that if found guilty his sentence would be severe and he could be shot.

***

During the Great War the British employed mine warfare. There two major explosions, one in 1916, the other the in 1917. The strategy was to start a tunnel well behind the front line, in some cases over a mile away, dig down to nearly 100 feet, then dig towards the front line, under no-mans-land and behind the German line, in a gentle slope upward, so water would drain away. In Belgium in 1916, six miles south of Ypres, along the Mesen ridge, 17 tunnels were dug; each packed with explosive, culminating in 17

231

explosions, leaving large craters in the ground that changed the landscape forever. ■ A year later in France, in the Somme area, about 10 miles southeast of Verdun there were 19 tunnels dug, resulting in much bigger explosions using 470 tons of explosive, set to go off at 30 seconds intervals at 3am on Thursday, 7th June, the power of which was felt in London.

***

Private Drew and Captain Gledhill woke about an hour before sunset, well refreshed. The pilot's first task was to relieve the scarecrow of his clothes. A quick look round showed that there was no one in sight. "When I go out to get those clothes Bob, you stay here hidden, just in case I get rumbled, so you can be free to continue to Holland. If you do see anyone coming, give a whistle and make yourself scarce, he who runs away, lives to run another day," he misquoted! The pilot gave it a little longer until it was hard to see any distance and cautiously crept out to the centre of the field, about 250 yards away, all in the open. Sam watched him in the gathering gloom, and for anyone else, but he did not expect to see anyone at this late in the evening. Tim soon returned with the holed and battered old knee length heavy overcoat and a beret. He quickly donned his third hand clothes and felt he looked like a typical French peasant. To hide his flying boots, he covered them with his flying suit trousers. He paraded in front of Sam. "I'm set up for the journey now Bob, we look a right old couple! I thought the clothes might smell a bit, but they must have been out in the rain, wind and sun for a long time, and dried, so they have had a bit of a wash! I should be OK. If any Germans stop me, I bet they won't be too keen on questioning me the way I am, which will be all to the good. With the condition of this coat, I look more holy than righteous! The only problem is I've never seen a tramp clean shaven, so like you, I will have to grow a beard, not that I could do anything else about it, we don't carry shaving gear when we fly!" which made them both laugh.

***

After the Germans had captured a downed Sopwith Triplane, Anthony Fokker, a Dutchman, who had left his homeland and set up in a rented hanger in Johannisthal, the centre of German aircraft manufacturing, near Berlin, made a copy of the plane. It did not match up to the Sopwith model that had entered service early in 1917 and remained flying to the end of the war with the RNAS. The Fokker first flew in combat in August 1917 and was retired by the end of that year, except for one aircraft. The German air *"Ace"*

Manfred von Richthofen flew this aircraft with great distinction, Fokker having made a specially modified and strengthened version for him that he flew until he was killed in April 1918. One wonders what the problems were with the standard version that it needed modifications to be safe to fly in combat.

***

When the courts-martial were held, Major General Matchwick decided that he should attend both, an unusual move, but he felt with the problems that had arisen over Lance Corporal Perry's CM, it had to be shown, any rank who broke Army law, especially an officer, was not above the law. The *Magna Carta* came to mind. He also wanted to see Ellis's downfall, he was still very sore over what he had done to his daughter.

Ellis was the first to go on trial. Major Taylor was the opening witness on the stand and was shown the Medical Certificate that Ellis had forged, he stated he had not seen it before and it was not his signature. When he stood down a statement of evidence was presented by the prosecution counsel from Captain Ives, and was read out by him to the court:

STATEMENT OF EVIDENCE
CAPTION R IVES, MEDICAL OFFICER
Dated:- 29 February 1916
I have examined the Medical Examination form, numbered Ypres/235/Feb 16, dated 10 February 1916, relating to 93494, Corporal Perry, William, of the West Bristol Fusiliers. I categorically state that the signature on this form is not mine and I have never witnessed a medical examination supposedly carried out by Major Taylor of the Medical Corps. At the date stated on the form I was at, and still am at, a temporary tented military field hospital set up in the park at Parc Des Buttes Chaumont on the outskirts, on the east side of
Paris, France.
Sir, I remain your
Obedient servant
R Ives

The prosecution counsel handed this to the President of the Court requesting that it was accepted as evidence. The President conferred with the defence counsel and was asked if they would accept Captain Ives's statement to save calling him and delaying the proceedings of the CM, which was accepted by the defence counsel.

The next two witnesses were Lance Corporal Perry's SNCO from the trench. Their evidence was nearly the same as each other. At no time had Perry shown any sign of dereliction of duty or any cowardice or, as JNCO, neglect to his subordinates and as Perry had returned he could not have deserted. They considered, when he returned after about two days lying in a shell hole he was very ill and thought he should be in hospital and were about to take him there when the Platoon Commander 2nd Lieutenant Ellis took him away and told them later he was in hospital and would most probably be evacuated back home, and that was the last they heard of him. When questioned, they both said, that while they had both had gone over the top with the troops, Ellis saying he was right behind them, they had never seen him in the field of battle. When they had returned Ellis had said he had followed them up the ladder, but both SNCOs considered the mud and disarray of his appearance was faked. Nails were starting to be drive in Ellis's coffin.

The next witness was the Provost Marshal, Lieutenant Colonel Harper. Realising the precarious position he was in, he told the court how Ellis had come to him and presented evidence about Perry's behaviour and from this evidence it would appear that Ellis had a case. He admitted that he did not check up on any of the evidence Ellis had presented, was he not an officer? He did not interview the accused and had accepted the Medical Certificate did look genuine. On reflection he felt he should have checked up before agreeing to a CM, but in mitigation said he considered he had had more important tasks to attend at that time than what appeared then as an open and shut case of desertion. The President of the Court told Harper that a CM that could sentence a person to be shot was of paramount importance and he should have looked at all the evidence and double checked it before convening a CM, he was given a formally warning by the court, that was to be enter on his personal documents.

The Sergeant of the firing squad was the last prosecution witness, who gave evidence about Ellis, saying after he had been briefed by Ellis, Ellis had left the site and failed to return again that day to check on the prisoner as was his duty (the Sergeant was trying to get as much of the blame shifted off his shoulders and onto Ellis's), and Ellis turned up next day, late morning on the day before the execution. He was also questioned about the escape of the prisoner, and the President of the Court was not happy about his behaviour and directed that there should be an official Court of Enquiry to investigate the behaviour of the execution squad and the actions of the Sergeant. He ordered the Sergeant to be placed under close arrest.

Lastly, Captain Russell, who had recently been discharged from hospital, was called to give a character reference about Perry, saying what an excellent soldier he was and that he had personally recommended him for promotion to Corporal, and saw his potential and felt he would made a good SNCO, and in time may be considered for a commission. He also gave the court the Character Appraisal of Perry that Ellis had written before he left Bristol, saying it was the complete opposite of the truth and considered that Ellis had a vendetta for some reason with Perry. The Character Appraisal was accepted as evidence by the Court.

The defence had no witnesses and he advised Ellis he would be best served if he did not take to the witness stand. If he did, he would be digging a deeper hole for himself than he was already in! Ellis took his point and kept his mouth shut. This was very out of character for him!

The summing up by both counsels did nothing to take the blame off Ellis. The defence counsel tentatively asked the Court to take into consideration the past record of the accused in the trenches. Major General Matchwick felt like saying if his past record was known, he would be in more trouble than he was already in. The court asked what these were and the reply Ellis's counsel offered did nothing to impress the members of the board. Matchwick smiled to himself, the hole was getting bigger and deeper all the time!

He was found guilty on all charges, his sentence, as the charges were so serious and being an officer, was to be considered by a higher authority. The accused was taken away to be held under close arrest until sentence was passed.

The Court Martial of ex Acting Lieutenant Colonel Lucas, who had now been demoted to his substantive rank of Major and who had conducted the Court Martial that had sentenced Lance Corporal Perry to be shot was only a minor affair compared with the last CM. The CM considered that the trial of Lance Corporal Perry was a travesty of justice and this was not the conduct expected of a President of a CM. He was found guilty of the charge of conducting a CM in an incorrect manner and contrary to Army regulations. The Court ordered that all other CMs conducted by Lucas be reviewed. He was sentenced to be reduced to the rank of Captain and loss of all seniority.

Back in his office, Major General Matchwick considered what should happen to Ellis and Lucas. Captain Russell, Sam's Platoon Commander before Ellis took over because of his injuries, had now recovered from his wounds and was ready to return to the field of battle. Because of what he had achieved he had been promoted to Major and Matchwick ordered that Lucas should now be sent as one of Russell's Platoon Commanders, where he could now fight on the front line, a thing he had never done before. He would soon realise what soldiering was really all about, thought the Major General, and realise the stress everyone was under, and soldiers did suffer damage of the mind.

As for Ellis, he had other plans for him. Sentencing him to imprisonment would not serve the Army well; they were short enough of men as it was. He would be reduced to the rank of Private and he would also fight on the front line. But to be fair to him, he would be sent to another area where he was not known and fight there. He would ensure he was kept updated on how Ellis performed.

Matchwick had now to decide what should happen to Perry, wherever he was. He called the Provost Marshal to his office and on enquiring about the search for him; Harper said he had evaded all efforts made to capture him. They agreed that the CM on Ellis had proved Perry's innocence but a Court of Inquiry was necessary to officially clear his name. In addition he ordered an official pardon would be granted to Perry and his rank of Lance Corporal be re-instated.

The PM said the search had now been called off and the MPs were only keeping a look out for him while going about their normal duties. The Major General said he was to send an open directive to all Military Police posts that Lance Corporal Perry was innocent of all charges and was not to be charged with desertion and call off any local searches that might be ongoing. As Matchwick pointed out, if he had not escaped and had been shot, mud would be sticking all over the place; by escaping he had done them all great favour! Matchwick quietly thought to himself, if Perry had been shot, and all this came out, his career could well be jeopardy. Also, if Perry was found, he was to be returned and he was to see him personally and he would then decide what course of action was to be taken, telling the PM there would definitely be no charges or punishment for escaping, sending him on his way to carry out his instructions. If, as Major Russell considered, he may be sent back to England to take a commission, but that was all in the future, he had to be found first before all this could happen. If Sam knew about all this, he would have been most surprised.

The only other thing that concerned Matchwick was what had actually happened to Perry and how he had escaped. If, as the Sergeant of the execution party had said, Perry was attached by handcuffs to a large metal stake, he would not get very far unless he got it removed, and how could he do that without anyone knowing anything about it. Like everyone else, Major General though Perry would have made his way west and would be passing through the rear of the British line, so how had he escaped with no trace. He felt that the Court of Enquiry that had been set up with regard to the execution squad's actions did not shed light on what really happened, but he was sure that the Sergeant had primed the Corporal and soldiers with a cock and bull story and they would all stick to it. He smelt a third very large rat; he had not joined the army yesterday!

He called for the PM to report to him again and this time Harper came at great speed and without any moans or complaints, he was very worried about his acting rank, *would he ever get it made substantive?*

"Any news of Lance Corporal Perry, Mr Harper?" Matchwick asked. Harper's reply was in the negative. "Mr Harper, there is something very fishy about the actions of the firing squad; I want to get to the bottom of this before the Court of Enquiry is completed. Tell me where did the stake come from, how big was it and what was it approximate weight?"

"Sir, we only keep one at our HQ, with a marquee and a firing post. Our Quartermaster issued them to the Sergeant and was signed for on a loan card. The stake is about 4 foot long, weights about 112 pounds and had barbs on the bottom end like an arrow head to stop it being pulled out of the ground once buried," was Harpers unhappy reply.

"I understand a search was made inside and outside the walled garden by your police and nothing was found?" Matchwick continued. Seeing Harper nod in agreement, there was little anything else he could do! "From the CM the Sergeant stated the stake had been dug out of the ground with a spade. If this is true, why was a spade left near the prisoner which he could have used as a weapon. If we assume that Perry somehow dug the stake out of the ground why did not the sentry on duty stop him and, or, wake the Sergeant of the execution squad. I think all the squad were fast asleep including the sentry. If this was the case and Perry escaped with the stake attached to him, he would have been badly impeded with its weight and size, he would have hardly got very far before being caught, so that story is too tall to swallow, so that theory is out." Matchwick continued to muse over various scenarios while Harper wished the ground would open up beneath him. "Let us consider he escaped but somehow got free of the stake before he left the marquee, it's the only way I feel that he could have got away and disappeared into thin air." He stopped to gather his thoughts.

"The only way that could have happened as I see it was if two things happened. Firstly, I'm sure all the guards were asleep, probably they had been drinking. Was he not properly handcuffed or the handcuff key was left near enough for the prisoner to get his hands on it and set himself free. I don't think the spade was left anywhere near him, but I strongly believe that the key was. The stake must be somewhere on site. I consider the search was not thorough enough, it must be still in or around the garden somewhere. Have you any ideas where it might be Mr Harper?" "No," he replied, with a shake of the head. Harper felt Matchwick had a much quicker mind than he had and was embarrassed by his lack of input.

"My interpretation of the situation is that I believe Perry somehow got the key, it must have been left within easy reach of him. We will never know, and unless we find Perry, the firing squad have closed ranks. I feel he must have removed the cuff from his wrist using the key and made his escape, leaving the stake in the ground, and perhaps I shouldn't say this, but the best of luck to him. Now you say that the stake was designed not to be removed with ease. When the Sergeant discovered Perry was missing, he panicked, dug the stake out of the ground, making it look if it had been pulled out, saying Perry had done it, and hid it, where, if I am correct in my assumption, you have failed to find it." Harper was not a very happy Major, acting Lieutenant Colonel.

"I can only think of one place you have not looked and that is in the filled in grave. Get some trench diggers and take them down there now, not any of the execution squad, making sure you keep them out of the way so they cannot see what you are doing, I suggest they are taken off site somewhere under escort. Then dig out that grave immediately, staying there until they have reached the bottom of it, literally, then report back to me when you have a result, whatever it may be, is that understood Harper?" A reply of, "Yes Sir," was followed by a quick exit by the PM.

Within two hours, Harper returned to the Major General's office a very unhappy man, *why had he not thought of this?* On entering the office he displayed the aforesaid stake with one cuff of the handcuffs attached to a loop at the top of the stake, the other cuff swinging freely and locked. The Major General had the evidence he needed. The Court of Enquiry, when reconvened, did not take long to come to its conclusions and the Sergeant and the Corporal were ordered to be court-martialled for negligence and stating a falsehood. That did not take long either; both were reduced to the ranks and ordered to be sent to the front. Again the Major General did not want to have soldiers locked up doing nothing, they could be more useful fighting, and they may even get themselves shot, poetic justice for all those innocent soldier they had killed. He thought with sadness of all those of our own we had killed who were innocent, who had been medically traumatised, some under age to serve their country. It was a tragedy of the first order. Perhaps the review of all the CMs Lucas would exonerate some of those shot.

But the Major General still wondered where Perry had gone, he could only think he must have slipped through the rear guard, this could have been the only answer, it was not heavily guarded or patrolled. Matchwick never found out the answer to his question. Was he still this side of the channel, or had he somehow may his way back home? Perry had disappeared as far as the Army could establish, for ever. Sam never knew he had been exonerated of all charges and had been re-instated to the rank of Lance Corporal. After escaping Lance Corporal Perry was never found and eventually reported, missing believed killed, without a stain on his character.

***

Before setting off Sam and Tim refreshed themselves with a wash and a drink in the crystal chilled water that flowed in a nearby stream, then replenishing Sam's two bottles for their journey ahead, but both were now feeling very hungry. Before they left the stream Tim threw his revolver into the middle where it was deepest and got some mud and smeared it over his face and hands and on what showed of his boots; no one would expect to see a dirty looking tramp with clean shiny boots! They began with the help of the compass and maps, which Tim had now decided to keep for the time being, both of which he would keep well out of sight, especially if they saw anyone, as they were not sure which side the locals were on. They set out on Sam's next planned stage of his journey back to England, they both hoped.

Their plan was to go in a northerly direction on the main road this time which was not far on the other side of the line, leaving the railway for the time being, there being more chance of obtain food in a built up area than traveling on a goods train. After careful crossing the line, they were soon on the main road, turning north and making for the nearest town of Mechelen, which Tim reckoned was about five miles away. Being late they did not know if any food shops would be open but they would try. From his knowledge of the area, he had a good idea they understood Dutch, being near the border of Holland, it would not be surprising. Tim reckoned if they did not understand his French, there was a good chance they would understand his German, but if they were anti German they could have a problem. As Tim pointed out to Sam, while Holland was neutral, there would be some Dutch who were anti German, while others might be pro German, he could not be sure; they had to be very careful. In the end Tim decided to speak only French, and if they spoke Dutch, his knowledge of German could help him out, time would tell. He would listen but not reply in German, that could be very dangerous especially if they had no sympathy with the Germans.

Tim was also concerned about their appearance; he looked like someone who was down on his luck in his scarecrow clothes while Sam looked like a labourer in work as he was carrying tools. They agreed it would look a bit odd if they were seen walking together, so they decided, as Tim could speak French, for him to go first, while Sam followed up in the rear a good discrete distance apart, on the other side of the road where possible. This had a second advantage, if one was caught the other had a better chance of getting away. Tim would make sure if he turned a corner and there was any likelihood of Sam losing sight of him he would hang around and let Sam pass him before Tim would again take up the lead.

As they arrived in Mechelen it was dark but there were drinking houses open and one or two shops. Sam had dropped back about 100 yards behind the pilot, keeping, as agreed, to the opposite side of the road. Before Tim could take cover a German foot patrol of four foot soldiers came goose marching down the middle of the road towards him in their smart uniforms, their foot steps echoing from the buildings on either side. As soon as he saw the soldiers approaching him he quickly dumped the compass and maps over a convenient low wall he was walking past, which Sam saw before he looked for some where to hide. The patrols were looking out for civilians who looked suspicious and there were not many of those about. Sam had plenty of time to disappear into the shadows of a passage leading down an alley to some old dwellings before the patrol could spot him in the gloom. Tim was not so lucky, he had no time to hide, he could not run away, it would look very suspicious; he would have to bluff it out if he was accosted. When they got to Tim, they looked hard and called him over to them.

By this time Tim was walking with a stoop, looking down at the road and shuffling along. He gave a casual glance at the Germans and walked on, they called him again, no response from Tim. They went over to him and were about to get hold of him when in the light of their torch, they saw what he looked like, a down out and dirty with it! They backed off and spoke again, Tim then replied in rapid French gesturing with his arms, which stopped the Germans in their tracks, they backed off a bit further and told him in German to leave the area and pointed down the road in the direction they wanted him to go, which was the way they wanted to go. Tim shrugged his shoulder, appearing not to understand and shuffled on down the street. This was too much for the German patrol to cope with, it seemed to them that the old tramp could do no harm to anyone and they marched away, leaving him to his own devices!

When Sam saw the patrol march past the end of the passage he was hiding in, he carefully made his way down to the road and cautiously peered up out in both directions, keeping a watch on events. Tim did not dare to return for the compass and maps he had ditched over the low wall, continuing on his way they had planned. Sam crossed the road and followed, picking up the compass and map on the way. By this time Tim had come to a bake house that was in the throws of making the next day's bread. The door was open to the bakery and as he stood there looking in, he saw what looked like the boss.

He asked in French for some old bread, pointing to some loaves, his mouth and rubbing his stomach. The baker took one look at him, he did not want this dirty vagabond hanging around his bakery so the best way to get rid of him was to give him some bread baked early that day, too stale to sell tomorrow and now only fit for chicken or pig feed. The baker picked up two long French sticks from the pile, less for the birds or animals but it would get rid of this dirty dishevelled old tramp, passing them to Tim at arms length and as he did so, gesturing to the door for Tim to remove himself from the premises. Tim took the loaves and the hint, giving the baker many thanks in French and made off down the street.

Sam was back on the other side of the road and had seen what was taking place much to his amusement. As Tim left, carrying on down the road in the general direction of north, there was no one in sight. Tim stopped and beckoned to Sam who caught him up and handed over the maps and compass.

"Thanks Bob, well done, I didn't think you saw me leave them behind that wall. OK, follow me as before. I have heard a train whistle, let's make for railway line and see what is going on there; there must be some sort of traffic going north. The next big town we should make for is Antwerp, we are well on our way to the border. Let's hope our luck stays with us."

Sam continued to follow Tim at a prudent distance listening to the sounds of trains shunting getting nearer. On arrival at the gates of a railway marshalling yard, Tim took a quick look in, but turned away and carried on walking down the road. When he found a quiet spot, he again beckoned for Sam to join him.

"There's too much activity in the yard Bob, while there may be trains going in the right direction, there are too many people there, we would soon get spotted and I don't know what would happen to us if they did. There is little chance of even finding a train going in our direction around here, let alone getting aboard undetected, and I'm sure I saw some soldiers patrolling, what do you reckon we do next?"

"Why don't we walk up the road a bit, keeping close to the line, and when we are out in the country, make for the track and walk along until we come to a steep gradient or some passing loops where we might be able to hop on, that's what I did before and it worked OK."

"Sounds a good idea, can't think of anything better, at least we are still free, if we went into that yard we may soon be behind bars. I will lead the way again, when I give you a signal, join me as I hope to find a way to the line."

Tim ambled off as before with Sam following at a good distance, keeping him in sight. If they came to a bend, Tim slowed down to let Sam catch up so they would not lose each other.

As Tim had a torch, they felt they should have a set of warning codes as they were some distance apart and shouting or using his whistle could attract unwanted attention. Tim devised a code, short flashes on his torch in the general direction of Bob so that he could be located, if he shone his torch all about him, Bob was to hide and observe. If he sent regular short and long flashes alternately, come and join him; long flashes was go back the way we came, Tim would then follow Sam, until they could meet. If Sam could see Tim if he was accosted and there were no signs, Tim was in trouble!

They carried on along the road, keeping a safe distance apart and after about half an hour, at Tim's slow pace, they were leaving the town behind, that's when he received Tim's signal to join him. When he got there, Tim was standing by a lane that looked if it led in the general direction of the railway. A quick look round, as there was no one about, before they set off up it t together. In no time at all they came to the railway, which was on an embankment. They cautiously made their way up the steep side and eventually came the top; no one was in sight, not even a train. Tim checked the compass and made their way northwards and hoped it was the line towards Antwerp.

They had not been going very long when they heard a train coming from the south, by the sound of it, it was not a slow train. They stopped and went back down the embankment a few feet, laying flat looking over the top, and watched. The train was soon on them, belching steam and smoke passed them at great speed, hauling many carriages, no chance of getting on that. Sam explained, he had always kept away from passenger trains, if they were like the British ones, railway guards were up and down the train checking everyone, there would be no place to hide. Plus the fact there may also be German guards on board as well. Tim took his point.

They had done a lot of walking and were now both very hungry so they tucked into a stale French bread stick each and fresh spring water, sitting on the embankment just below the level of the track. When you are hungry anything will do and it didn't taste stale to them! Once they had had their fill, they put the bottles away and the remainder of the bread, ready to continue their journey.

They climbed back up the embankment to the track, all was quiet from the last train and they could hear no further trains approaching. They started walking, keeping an eye open for any trains coming from either direction, but as the line at this point was level even goods trains would be to fast to get aboard, a stiff ascending gradient was what they had to find. They continued on their way and soon entered a cutting. Suddenly they were surrounded and torches were shone in their faces. Tim and Bob froze.

"Bob, very slowly raise your hands above your head," which they both did. They were blinded by the light and could not see who was holding them, but they could not mistake the muzzles of the machine guns pointing out in front of the torches at them. One of the men spoke, Tim thought it was Dutch but was not sure what was being said and whispered out of the side of his mouth, "Dutch." Tim first spoke in French but this did not produce any results. He then tried English, saying, "Englander." He still did not get a reply, but one of their captors called out, as if wanting someone to join them.

While they were waiting for someone to appear, Tim again whispered out of the corner of his mouth to Sam, "Could be the Resistance, I hope." While they were waiting Tim decided to tell the truth, if they had been Germans, their treatment would have been very different. In a short space of time there was movement behind the torches, a tall figure came out past the lights, also carrying a gun, which was pointed at them. In English, with a strong accent, the voice said, "You say you are Englanders?"

Tim replied that they were English, escaped British soldiers trying to get back to England to fight again.

The spokesman laughed, "Neither of you look much like any Englishman I have ever met. If you are you have good disguises, congratulations." He translated this to the rest of the group, and then said, "Prove you are soldiers."

Tim replied, "We are not armed and if you allow us to show you our uniforms under these clothes it will prove who we are. I still have my identification tags around my neck, my companion here had his taken by the Germans before he escaped from them." A few quick words to his colleagues and they were told to remove enough cloths to reveal their uniforms and his tags. This was soon done, their point was proved and there was a relaxation of the tension, the torches facing them were turn downwards or turned off.

"We are the Resistance and we will help you get across the border into Holland. But first we have come here to sabotage the railway line, we are short of men and you have delayed us, so you will help. I am the leader of this group, we never give names so no one can pass information on about us. We do not want to know your names either, for the same reason."

It appeared that the general plan was that for about 200 or 300 hundred yards, they would knock out all the keys from the chair that held the rail in place. When the next train came along, the tracks would open up and the train would be derailed. To further delay repairs to the line and to stop a breakdown train getting down the other line in the front of the derailed train, they would do the same on the other track, starting where they had finished on the other track.

The leader split them into two groups; the first group started on the track where they stood while the other group walked up the line some 300 yards away, both groups then started to knock out the wooden key blocks from the chairs, while lookouts were posted each side of the sabotage. Tim found out they had consulted the time tables before they came and they had less then an hour to complete the task. The resistance would have started sooner, bar for Tim and Sam arriving. As they now had two extra hands, they should get the task completed on time or sooner. Once completed they all walked back along the line to the beginning of the cutting then made their way up the side to where the track had been damaged to look down and to await results.

They did not have to wait long, a fast north bound troop train approached, going at speed round the slight curve as it entered the cutting. The result was as anticipated, the engine suddenly opened up the lines and with the squealing of brakes eventually stopped adjacent to where the other line had been sabotaged, falling across the south bound track, this would cause more mayhem than they had planned, all to the good. The engine crew had been killed outright and the soldiers that were alright or only slightly injured were instructed by the guard and told to make their way on the outside of the track, out of the cutting, all very shaken, only one or two carrying their rifles. The resistance did not have to wait very long as a goods train came the other way, traveling at speed down a slight gradient with a heavy load of large calibre field guns. As like the troop train, the lines opened up, first becoming derailed and then hitting the other engine head on. Both engines were blanked in escaping steam, Tim and Sam wondered how many had been killed. The resistance leader said he hoped many had been killed as they had been told it was a German troop train and the goods were headed to the front, and as far as the two engine crews were concerned, he was not bothered about them either, if they chose to drive for the Germans, they deserved all they got. Then there was a flash and an explosion, red hot coals from one of the engines had ignited escaping gas from one of the carriages lighting system. The cutting was lit up as if it were daylight. The wooden carriages of the passenger train and the trucks of the goods soon caught fire, they would burn for some time. It would be a long time before the authorities got to hear of this and be able to send out rescue crews and cranes.

Both tracks were well and truly blocked; it would be at least two days before even one track was opened. They expected an officer to select a couple of fit soldiers to walk on north and the other south to warn oncoming trains and eventually reach a signal box to close the line and alert rescue squads. The signal boxes either side of the catastrophe would soon wonder why the trains they were expecting had not arrived and would inform other signal box up and down the line and raise the alarm as they could not give the *out of section* to them of their last trains. They knew that sabotage was not uncommon in the area. Meanwhile, all signals were kept at danger.

As soon as the leader was satisfied that they had accomplished what they came for they picked up all there tools and other gear to leave the scene of the incident to make their way down the side of the hill as fast as they could go, just in case anyone from the train who was not injured came looking for them.

One of the resistance gave a last look over the side of the cutting at the two wrecked trains and suddenly gave a shout and spoke rapidly in French. The leader shouted for them all to go as quickly as possible, the group turned and started to run down the hill away from the cutting waving at Sam and Tom to follow. When they had gone some way the leader stopped and told the two escapees that with the whole cutting well lit by the fire, one of his men had recognised the signs on two of the wagons indicating that they were carrying ammunition and were only a few trucks back from the engine, there could be, he hoped, a big explosion any minute, and they were not going to wait to see the results. They eventually came to a rough farm tracks that everyone seemed to know very well. Suddenly there were a number of loud explosions and the sky over the cutting was lit up by a firework display, which caused the resistance to smile, the trucks on the goods train must have caught fire and ignited the explosives, this was a bonus! To Sam it was also a bonus, he had helped to kill many Germans avenging the death of his best friend, Bill.

When they got near a country road they all stopped and one by one each left at intervals, to make their way home, in varying directions and distances. No one had said anything since they had given a cheer when the train blew up, no thanks for a good job well done, when they should next meet, or even a good-bye, all was done in silence, they seemed to work to a much used drill. When all had left, except the leader, he said, "Follow me at a distance, we have just over 5 kilometres to walk on this road, it is very quiet at this time of night, but if you see anything, take cover, there is plenty of it beside the road. I will be taking you to a safe house for the night," pausing to add, "if we get separated and lose each other, you are on you own again."

With that he was off at a good pace which they could both keep up with. As before, Tim went first, with Sam some distance behind. In just under an hour the leader turned off up a cart track and soon they saw the lights in the window of a cottage. He told Tim and Sam to wait there out of sight while he checked to see everything was safe in the safe house. He was gone for less than 5 minutes and was back to take them into the cottage.

Inside it was a simple country cottage, there was a farmer and his wife and a lad of about Sam's age, who they found out later had been on the raid with them.

The leader turned to the two soldiers, "These people will feed you and then you will sleep in the hay loft in the barn, stay there until someone comes to collect you, but you must not more out of the loft until called for, if you do, you may compromise these people who are doing so much for you and risking their lives. How soon will you be collected I don't know, none of my business, in what direction and how far will depend on the circumstances. I do not expect to see you again, but the Resistance will get you into Holland somehow, after that I do not know what happens, it's nothing to do with me, the least I know the safer it is for all concerned. I wish you both a safe journey back to England and thanks for you help this evening," shaking their hands and before Tim and Sam could say their thanks, he was out of the door and gone and melted into the night.

A meal was put on the rough wooden table, a vegetable stew with hunks of fresh bread, and to wash it down, a cheap red wine. They soon ate their fill and with sign language, as the farmer and his family only spoke Dutch, they were told to go to the barn by hand gestures. The son, using a paraffin lamp, led them out of the cottage and across the yard and into one of two barns, the largest of the two, stopping at the foot of the ladder that led up to a hay loft, its floor covering about half of the barns width at the far end. The son gestured for them to go up. There was little light from the lamp below, just enough to make out there was sufficient straw to either make beds and bury themselves if there was a search. When the lad left with the lamp they were in complete darkness. With the aid of Tim's torch they had a quick look round, but Tim soon turned it off to conserve the batteries. They were both soon asleep, helped by the rough red wine and the first good meal they had had for some time; for Sam it was even longer, the last meal of any substance was at the holding camp.

Just as it was starting to get light the following morning the farmer's wife arrived, singing to attract their attention, with bread, local sausages and a pitcher of water leaving them just inside behind the barn door. They did a quick check around before coming down from the loft, collecting the food left for them and returning to their perch. Not knowing how long it would be for their next meal, they ate some and kept the rest for later. They knew they would have to stay in the loft until they were collected, but they could keep a look out through a small ventilation aperture, one of many on each side of the barn, just under the eaves of the roof, over looking the road they had walked down the evening before on one side and the farmer's fields on the other.

They saw the farmer and the lad, they presumed his son, harness up two large shire horses, attaching them to a four wheeled flat cart, then they made their way along a track beside a hedge of one of the fields and disappeared from sight down the other side of a ridge and, like the farmer's wife, they never saw any of them again.

For the two men in the loft it was a long boring day, waiting to be picked up. There was a lot of German activity, they expected it was because of the railway sabotage they had helped to cause. A German lorry arrived about mid morning with an officer and four soldiers. The officer walked straight into the cottage with one of the soldiers without invitation, presumably to search the cottage, which would not take long and soon left, but as neither the woman nor the officer could speak a common language they were no further with their investigation. The soldiers even made a cursory look round farm and in the two barns, one even climbing the ladder, only to poke his head just over the top of the ladder, but did not go any further, it was very casual, they did not find the two Brits well buried under the straw above their heads. When they left, it was quiet for the rest of their time there.

All the two escapees could do was watch over the fields in one direction, where nothing was happening, and the road in the other, where there was a certain amount of traffic, German cars and lorries in the main, but local traffic was sparse, a few dilapidated lorries and a number of horse drawn carts and wagons. After the German visit, the farm wasn't paid any attention by them again, they were far too busy on war work and looking for those who had wrecked two trains, killed many of their own and blocked the railway line for a number of days, they all drove straight past.

Tim got the maps out but they were not much help, all they knew was that they were somewhere between Brussels and Antwerp, whether the road they saw was the main road or a minor road between the two towns he couldn't work out. He told Sam that the maps were of no use to them anymore, they were now off the top of maps, far to north to be any good. He would ditch them as soon as possible or give them to the resistance, with the compass. They were now in the hands of the Resistance from there on.

Just as the sun had reached its zenith, a rundown old lorry, that had seen better days and with solid wheels, chugged down the road to their left, the direction of Antwerp, the way they expected to go. The lorry slowed down and turned up the track to the farm, piled high with straw, roped down to stop it blowing away. It passed the farm cottage and drove up to the barn door, turned around and backed half way inside the building. The farmer's wife was nowhere to be seen, she did not emerge from the cottage to meet the lorry or its driver. The driver, in worn and faded clothes, climbed down from the lorry, leaving the noisy engine running and walked into the barn.

"Englanders, Englanders," he shouted. Tim and Sam looked out cautiously. He called again, "Englanders, Englanders, come out." This time the two young men showed themselves to the driver. When he saw them he beckoned for them to come down. They both realised this was the next stage of their journey back to England, and scrambled down the rickety old ladder from the hay loft with all their meagre possessions. When they got down they found the driver was at the back of the lorry with the tail board down, pointing to the straw and made signs they were to crawl in and under the load, again no word was spoken. As soon as this was accomplished, he covered their entrance, put up the tail board, and was soon off down the track towards the road, where they turned left. Tim checked his compass by the light of his torch; they were going in the direction that would take them to Holland, north.

The ride in the back of the truck was rough, with solid tyres and roads pitted with holes that had not been repaired since the war had started. If the lorry had springs, they did not have much cushioning effect, they were bouncing all over the place and they both hoped they did not have to travel far. Their hopes were soon fulfilled as they could feel they had left the road and were being jolted about again, but very soon they could sense the lorry turning around, stopping, reversing for a short distance and stopping again.

They peeped out from their hiding place and saw they had backed up to a cattle pen. On the far side of the pen was a number of railway trucks, three of which were covered cattle wagons, the doors open, awaiting to receive some form of live stock.

"Come out Englishmen, we are you friends," a quiet soft female voice said, close by. They crawled out from under the straw to be greeted by a pretty young girl in her early twenties, dressed in country garb. She looked them up and down, and laughed. "Not the smart English soldiers I expected." She spoke very good English, with little trace of an accent.

Again there was no introduction, what you did not know, you could not tell! "At present you are in the goods yard at Kontich," the girl continued, "and I will be loading my father's cattle soon to be sent to Roosendaal in Holland, I will accompany the animals there to be sold at the local market by the railway station. The Germans allow us to do this and they inspect each wagon when it gets to the border post between Essen this side of the boarder and Roosendaal the other side. Every week one of the local farmers sends cattle across to Holland and the Germans have become very lax in their inspections. We have to put a false partition at one end of the truck to hide you, there will only have enough room for you both to stand behind and you will be sealed in, it will take a very close inspection to find it. Unfortunately,, it is cramped and with all the cows in the van, it will be smelly and hot, take it or leave it," was her final comment.

The two runaways looked at each other and smiled, they would soon be in Holland. Tim spoke for them both, "We take it, how soon will all this take place?"

"If you look over to the other side of the main road, my father's cows are being driven down from the field next to our farm yard now. The engine with its goods train, which will soon be here to take this train north, started at Amsterdam and will have stopped at one or two goods yards on the way, picking up and dropping off trucks as it went, a slow country pickup goods train, but it won't get held up as even the Germans realise, you can't hold up trains with live stock in, especially as we unfortunately have to give them some of the meal after slaughter, and they want it fresh. Will you now please get into the wagon so we can seal you in."

As they entered the wagon, she called after them, "Some one of the Dutch Resistance will meet the train at Roosendaal to get you out of the wagon, I will nor see you again," was her closing remark.

When they got into the cattle truck they found what looked like two labourers but both must have be members of the Resistance, holding a false partition, waiting for them to arrive so they could fit it across one end of the van once they were in. One of the labourers pointed to the end they wanted them to go, they made their way there, followed by the two men and the false partition. Once settled at the end, the partition was put in place, held in with screws, they were now well and truly sealed in and there was standing room only, just like the Underground! They hoped, like the lorry journey, the trip would not be long. They must have used this trick before; they could not have made such a convincing partition in that short space of time. Sam had noticed, when they had entered the wagon, one side of the partition bore signs of cattle excrement among other marks of hoofs and horns in many places!

Before the cattle arrived the pick up goods passed by on the main line, dropping the guards van, then backed into an adjacent siding with over twenty wagons, leaving three wagons behind. It went forward with the remainder of the train and backed onto the cattle trucks, striking the stationary wagons in a none too gentle manner; if the two passengers had not been wedged in, they would have certainly fallen over. The train was now ready for the next stage of its journey once the cattle had been loaded.

The Old Vicarage

God! I will pack a train, And get me to England once again!
For England's the one land I know, Where men with Splendid Hearts may
go.

Lieutenant Rupert Brooke (1887 ~ 1915)

They could now hear the cattle approaching, and just before they were loaded the girl came in and spoke to them again through the partition, "You will soon be away. We go round Antwerp with out stopping, then there will be four stops before Roosendaal, only three for pickups, Ekeren, Heide and Wildert, and the forth is the border checkpoint, when the train stops there keep very quiet, or sound like a cow," she added cheekily. "The cattle will drown any small noise but talking will travel, no coughing or sneezing either. It is unlikely that the Germans will come in, they just put there head over the half door and try and count the cattle to see we are not smuggling any more that we have applied to send. Good Bye Englanders and good luck," and with that she was gone and the cattle entered, with much noise, pushing and shoving and banging against the partition, much to the concern of those behind.

As soon as the three trucks were filled and the ramps lifted up and put in place, the train pulled out of the siding, backed onto to its guards van and was soon on its way to Ekeren, where it dropped of the guards van on the main line, pulled up to a siding entrance, backed in, collected some more trucks, pulled out, coupling up to its guards van as he had done at all the previous stops and was away to the border. This was repeated at the next two stations, just as the girl had told them.

The border was only a short distance along the line where the train was stopped. A platoon of German soldiers started to check the train. They did this many times a day with both north and south bound trains. They had never found anything; anything that had been hidden was too well concealed for anyone to find unless examined very closely. The Germans were getting bored with their task and the inspection was now very lax and cursory after nearly two years of conflict. Again the guards were the same type that guarded the POW trains and marshalling yards, how many times had they done this before and never found anything hidden. Cattle trucks were dirty and smelly and bottom of their list for checking. They did not wish to get their smart uniforms dirty by going inside, cleaning them came out of their own pocket and wives complained of smelly clothes! Counting the numbers of cattle in the truck was all that they did, from over the top of the half door, like counting POWs; they never bothered if they were one or two out, they never got any of the meat, it was only for the officers! Tim and Sam kept very still and quiet, not even a whisper, the cattle were moving around and making the noises cattle should make, banging against the partition, drowning out other sounds.

They could hear little and the only noise besides the cattle was the slamming of the half door after the Germans had finished their inspection; it had only been a scant inspection. They heard whistles and the train was on its way, soon over the border, arriving at the marshalling yard at Roosendaal. On arrival the train was split up and shunted into various sidings, the three cattle trucks, with others that had been added, were docked at the cattle pens, adjacent to the town cattle market. The engine was uncoupled and driven away to the engine shed to await its next duty.

The cattle were soon unloaded and moved to pens deep in the market complex. All was then silent; both the boys wondered if they had been forgotten, there was no way they could get out on their own. But they need not have worried, within 15 minutes of the trucks being unloaded they heard footsteps enter the truck.

"Englanders, we have come to take you out," whispered a voice and without further ado, screwdrivers were being used to remove the screws holding the partitioning in place and was soon ready to be lifted out. As it was removed they saw three smiling faces of their rescuers but there was no sign of the young lady who had supervised their loading, she had gone off with her father's cattle, taking them to the market pens.

"Hello," said one of the trio, "Welcome to Holland and the last lap of your flight from the Germans. We shall be taking you to Rotterdam and on to a boat for the first stage of you voyage home. There is a small problem but there is no need to worry about it, we think it's all sorted. When the war started, and while we are neutral, the Germans moved in and used our port to bring in their supply ships. You Brits got fed up with this and in 1916 set up a blockade of all our ports to stop the German's receiving their supplies, so little goes in or out now. We will smuggle you aboard a tug that will be allowed out of the harbour to bring a cargo ship in which has been inspected and cleared by your Navy to bring in basic essential food supplies for us. As the tug takes the tow line from the ship, a small boat from one of the naval blockade ships will meet you and you will be ferried to a Navy ship, from then on you will be your Navy hands."

"We have an old cattle lorry waiting for you and we will take you directly to the docks to where the tug is currently at berth. We have to hurry, as she is due to sail on the next high tide in about five hours and we have to take the wall with us, for the next time! This way, please hurry," again no names, the Resistance was a very secretive lot! Sam had still been carrying his 'railway tools' he had 'picked up' in Halle, deciding he did not require them any more and gave them to one of the lads who had removed the partition, he was most grateful, as tools were in short supply and hard to come by because of the war.

The partition was loaded first into the high sided covered lorry, flat on the floor, sacks that had been piled in the front end were put on top, then they were then told to lay on the sacks and then the remainder of them were used to covered the escapees in a small time of cavern, they were now well hidden.

The journey took them through Dordrecht and on into Rotterdam, through the city to the docks beyond, a journey of about 40 miles, taking just under two and a half hours, they were well inside the five hours limit. There was no hesitation when they got there, no stopping at gates to be checked, the driver just waved to the police who let them pass with a wave and cheerful smile in return. They passed along the quay, many ships of all sizes seemed to be berthed there; Sam and Tim never saw any of this under the sacks. They eventually pulled up at the side of a medium sized tug, which seemed to be getting up steam preparing for departure, if evidence of black smoke billowing from the funnel was anything to go by.

The man who had done all the talking removed some of the sacks allowing them to crawl out from their cover and took them on board the tug. He seemed to know his way around as no one challenged him. They were taken below decks and shown into a small crew room, where there were a number of men sitting down, eating a meal.

Tom took out the compass and maps and offered them to their escort, he smiled at them and said they could be useful by someone in the Resistance and would pass them on, he shook their hands, spoke, "Goodbye, have a safe journey home," and Tim and Sam had just enough time to thank him before he disappeared. The Resistance never hung around for very long anywhere! They could see the reason why, less chance of being caught.

One of the sailors who wore a rough serge navy type uniform, and looked more senior that the rest, probably the tugs Mate, spoke to them in broken English, "Ve hear you escaped from Germans, wery goot. Ve vill soon be going to ship soon. Stay here until called," and with that he left with the rest of the crew to take charge of deck operations in leaving port, but it was about an hour before the engines soon started to throb and they were under way.

As soon as the tug had cleared the harbour, they were told to go up on deck which was now in darkness, no deck lights were being used, to prevent their actions being seen by any watchful German spies from their 'secret' harbour lookout posts, the tug only showing its obligatory navigation lights. They approached the cargo ship and a line was soon attached to the tug.

While this was going on, they were ushered to a rope that was hung over the side of the tug, and on looking down they saw the rope disappeared into a void of darkness. The mate gestured for them to slide down, Tim going first, he could see nothing, hoping that there was a boat waiting at the end of the rope. Suddenly, as he was sliding down, hands grabbed him to prevent a hard landing and bar for a whisper in a strong Yorkshire accent telling him to sit where they put him and keep still and quite nothing more was spoken. They left him to catch Sam as he was now on his way down. Once he was seated next to Tim, the coxswain cast off and six hefty sailors pulled on the oars.

Sam and Tim could hardly see anything, but the coxswain must have done, as they were soon along side a large naval ship. The oars were shipped and ropes were attached to stem and stern and in no time at all they were being winched up the side of the vessel to deck level and swung in under one of the ships davits where there was the minimum of deck lighting showing. They were the first to be unloaded and taken to the PO's Mess.

They had not been there very long when a Chief Petty Officer entered. "Welcome aboard HMS Saltash," were his opening words. "We hear you have escaped from the Germans, very well done," and shook them both by the hands. "We have been here nearly a month on blockade duty and expect to be relieved by another of our class so we can return to Blighty shortly, that's why you have come to us. When you have eaten, and we know escaped prisoners must be hungry, the Captain would like to meet you both, but in the mean time, have dinner on us."

Before the meal arrived the CPO had a few questions to ask. "Firstly, can you please give me all relevant service details as it has to be reordered in the ships log," and opening up the book he started with Captain T Gledhill and followed by Private Drew, R. From then on Tim was now 'Sir'.

When they had finished their meal, Tim's first action was to go on deck to ditch his scarecrow clothes over the side of the ship, he still had his full flying clothing on underneath and borrowed some brushes to clean of the Belgium soil from his boots. Sam decided to hang on to his donkey jacket, cap and overalls, he had ideas he would require them later, his uniform being very shabby, having crawled through a muddy and wet *no man's land*, how long ago he could not work out. Also his army jacket still showed the marks on his sleeves where his Lance Corporals strip had been and if anyone in authority saw these, there may be awkward questions to answer, so he ditched that over the side when no one was looking. If asked, he would say his army jacket had been so tatty in escaping that he had discarded it when he found the donkey jacket and he decided to take it on as he considered it better for escaping in and it would not look too good to see a soldier in a tatty army jacket in a very poor state of repair if he had to remove his donkey coat. Hopefully he would not feel the cold to much with the loss of one extra layer of warmth.

Later in the evening the ship's Captain sent for them and quizzed them about their journey, showing much interest in their various adventures. He said he was pleased he could help them in a small way and it would not be long before they were back on English soil. Afterwards, Tim was given a bunk in the Officer's quarter, while Sam was with the ratings, sleeping in a spare hammock that was slung for him!

The CPO said they looked as if they needed sprucing up a bit and lent them shaving tackle, a brush and a comb, and after all this a shower, they both felt like new men!

In less than a week, the change over ship arrived and HMS Saltash pulled up anchor and was on her way to England, making for the home of the Navy. Within two days, after an uneventful voyage down the English Channel, they passed the eastern tip of the Isle Wight on their port side and immediately turning starboard into Portsmouth Harbour where they anchored.

After saying their goodbyes and thanks, they were taken by the same boat in the company of a naval Lieutenant and soon arrived in to the main Naval quay. They were escorted to the Railway Transport Officer's (RTO) office at the Portsmouth Harbour station and handed over to him. They were each taken to separate offices where they were de-briefed about the time they were on the run and any information that was of any use would be passed to the appropriate authorities, this all taking at less than half an hour for Tim, but over an hour for Sam. While the debriefing was easy for Gledhill, Sam had to be very careful, remembering he was still Private Drew and not even Private Perry as he thought he now was, or even Mr Sam Bray as he actually was, too young to enlist! He was asked to show his dog tags to prove who he was but Sam explained that the Germans had removed them when he was captured and never returned them. They were not overly happy with this explanation; it even crossed their mind that he could be a German spy. Sam suggested that Captain Gledhill could vouch for him, which he soon did as much as he could when asked. They had to reluctantly accept Sam was tag less and could be one of them, but a note was added to the de-brief document, unbeknown to Sam, they were not 100% sure he was what he said he was.

Eventually, when it was all over, they were both given suitable clothing to wear for the journey back to their respective bases, Sam being given a naval polo-neck pullover that replaced his 'lost' jacket, but ensuring he kept his cap and donkey jacket. They were also issued with rail warrants to Waterloo and temporary identity certificates, in case they were stopped by Service Police, and told to report to the RTO's office when they arrived at Waterloo station for further instructions. They both caught the same train to Waterloo, but Tim was given a 1st class ticket while Sam had to accept he had to go 3rd class. At least, it was better than all the other railway trucks he had recently been traveling in; it was like 1st class to him!

On arrival at Waterloo late in the evening they went to the RTO's office where they were both interviewed again. When they looked at the sealed documents Tim had given them, Sam was grilled again, they, like the RTO in Portsmouth, had their reservations about Private Drew. Tim was booked into a hotel for the night before going on a weeks leave. While Sam, on the other hand, was ordered to return to his Barracks in Bristol immediately, not even offered leave or a night's accommodation. He was given a travel warrant to take him to Bristol and £1 in coins for incidental expenses, which he signed for and was told would later be deducted from his pay when he got back to his unit, even though he had not been paid for some four weeks, either as Perry or Drew! Little did the authorities know that while they would never get their money back, they would never see who they thought he was, Private Drew either! He was dead, poor chap, somewhere across the channel, a few weeks ago!

Sam was told to report to the RTO at Paddington and again when he got to Bristol on his arrival, they were keeping a close eye on him! The RTO at Paddington, on receiving a call from there counterparts at Waterloo were on the outlook for Drew, but while the message got written up in the log book it some how got lost with the shift change at midnight and it was only when the day shift took over at 8am the next morning did they realise the non-arrival of Drew. Alarm bells started to ring at the three RTO offices. The Military Police were called in and eventually, as part of their routine enquiries, rang the West Bristol Fusiliers at Bristol and were justifiably alarmed when they were told that 93495, Private Drew, Robert, had been killed in action about a month ago, the mud now hit the fan in no uncertain terms! The assumption was that they now had a spy in their midst, but where to start to look, they were lost. The last thing they wanted to do was to inform the press, people would start to panic if they heard there was a German spy roaming the streets of London, a *Jack the Ripper* syndrome. He was still fresh in the memories of many as it had only happened less than 30 years earlier!

Tim had arranged to meet Sam when their train got to London to say good-bye, but they had to wait until they had received their instructions as to where they had to report after leaving the RTO. Once this had been completed they met outside afterwards, for the last time. Tim explained that he had been told after his leave to report to Upavon, which was now one of the main airfields of the RFC on Salisbury Plain. Tim again thanked Bob for everything he had done for him, rescuing him from the plane, which, if he had not, Tim was sure he would have died, and also being a good companion on their journey through enemy country.

Sam, with a grin on his face, took the pilots hand to shake it goodbye and said, "I was happy to have you as a friend, it was a bit lonely on my own, so thanks for everything Tim." Tim smiled at his cheek and with a slap on his shoulder they had a final handshake before taking leave of each other, departing, never to see or hear from each other again!

Before he left he took Sam's details, 93495 Private Drew R, West Bristol Fusiliers, West Bristol Barracks, Bristol, Gloucestershire, so that an official letter of thanks could be sent to him from the RFC to the CO of the Barracks. When he arrived at Upavon he sent his own personal letter to Bob, again thanking him for saving his life and his companionship on their escape together. He added that he considered he was very brave, enlisting for the army under age.

The RTO at Waterloo notified the West Bristol Fusiliers that a soldier named as 93495, Private Drew R, had arrived by boat from Holland and had reported to their unit after escaping from Germany as a POW. The RTO told the WBF that on checking Private Drew found he had no personal service documents with him, claiming that the Germans had confiscated all that he had been carrying, including his ID tags when he was taken prisoner, which was not unusual. That the RTO had issued him with a travel warrant to travel back to his unit at Bristol, and £1 for incidental expenses, and was informed that this had to be deducted from his pay and returned to the RTO funds. They added that Drew had left two days before the letter was dated.

This letter, when received at West Bristol Fusiliers a day or two later, was puzzling in the light of the *Hue & Cry* that had been raised a day earlier, at least to the powers that be it was. They had been informed some time ago that Drew was listed as missing presumed dead Belgium, but if he was still alive and had returned to England, where was he was now, as he had never reported to the WBF, which he should had done according to the letter from the RTO at Waterloo. They could not report him as *Absent Without Leave* as far as they were concerned, he was dead. The RTO was £1 down, the WBF had no intention of paying it back and the £1 was not deducted from the pay that Drew had accumulated from a number of missed Pay Parades. The WBF, claiming he was dead and buried in Belgium, said the Drew who had come back to England must be an impostor, most probably a spy. As the Drew the WBF knew was an orphan, his personal service documents stating *No next of Kin, Orphan,* they were going to look after their own and not give away his accumulated pay to anyone! After a number of years, his pay was never claimed, his pay document was closed and the money returned to the main pay accounts ledger of the WBF. The only strange part of his disappearance, as the Commanding Officer of the Barracks eventually discovered, was Drew was later officially confirmed dead, his ID tags having been recently received and his body buried in a known marked grave in Ypres area, before he had supposedly arrived back in England. The CO of the WBF informed the RTO at Waterloo that they should have been more diligent and handed him to the MP for further investigation, which didn't go down to well with them, but they were not in a position to retaliate.

The private letter from Captain Gledhill to Private Drew R just stayed in the barrack's Postal Room, where the Corporal i/c after a month passed it to his superior officer, who opened it and read its contents. He wrote a covering letter to Captain Gledhill for the CO of the WBF to sign, explain there was a mix up somewhere as Drew had been killed early in 1916, before Captain Gledhill had crashed, and had notification of where he was buried. They treated the official letter from the RFC to the CO of the West Bristol Fusiliers thanking Private Drew R in rescuing Captain T Gledhill RFC in the same manner.

The CO of the West Bristol Fusiliers decided to contact the Military Police and informed them that one of their soldiers, 93495 Private Drew R, had been killed in action in Belgium and they had proof of this, they had his ID tags and knew the location of his grave. It would appear that some one masquerading as 93495 Private Drew R about 3 weeks after the death of the real Drew, claiming to be him and was an escaped British POW, returning to this country via Holland by a naval vessel to Portsmouth, reported to the RTO's office there. He was sent by train to Waterloo and told to report to the RTO there. He was last seen at the RTO's office at Waterloo station where he was given expenses and a train travel warrant to Bristol, being ordered to report to the RTO's office at Paddington when he arrived there. Private Drew had never reported to the RTO at Paddington and the rail warrant was not surrendered at that station for a ticket to Bristol ether. He should now be treated as a spy and apprehended as soon as possible.

The Military Police were looking into the case, but the trail went cold as soon as it had started at Waterloo station as there was no trace of him arriving at Paddington Station. The WBF were contacted, but it was not until the following morning, Saturday, that they were able to obtain details of Private Drew. They eventually traced the farm where Drew had worked before he joined up and later that afternoon MPs from the Bristol area visited the farm and quizzed the owner and when asked he stated that he had never seen Drew after the day he left and had no details of where he went, not knowing he had joined up and, in fact, that he didn't care and wasn't interested and had no feelings of grief when told he had died for King and Country. They reported back to the Military Police in London with their negative finds. When the war was over and it was definitely proved that Drew was killed in action and buried and could not have anything to do with the impostor Drew, who was thought to be a German spy, but never found. They had to conclude that as a spy, he had done no damage to British security as far as they could find. The case was closed as not worth pursuing.

CHAPTER 12

Second Time Around

Sam had plans for his future. He still wanted to get back in the fight and wanted further vengeance for the death of Bill but he had no intention of going back to the trenches and hand to and fighting again. He had his belly full of that and nearly got killed on more that one occasion, both by friends and foes! He may even come up against Ellis again, he had at least twice, and with his luck it could happen a third time, which he considered would be fatal for him, in more ways than one! He had to do something more effective and have more control of what he did, not just be one of thousands of numbered bodies that were moved around a chess board of the battlefields like so many pawns on a chess board that was littered with corpses and shell holes, directed by some nameless chinless wonder of a Staff Officer who had never been out of Britain, let alone anywhere near the front.

While in the trenches he had seen the planes of the Royal Flying Corps flying overhead many times and often dog fights ensued. It was at that time a germ of an idea started, should he volunteer to be transferred to the RFC? He made inquires, which had got to the ears of 2nd Lieutenant Ellis, who told him, in no uncertain terms, there was no chance, he was staying exactly where he was so he could keep a close eye on him! If Ellis was to stay in the trenches, so was Perry! While for the past month he had many ups and downs, he was now free of the infantry, and his past. He was old enough to join up under his own name, so the second William Perry and the second Robert Drew had somehow to disappear if he wanted to continue to fight for his country, but in the air this time. While he was escaping with Tim Gledhill, he had asked him about the RFC, and what he heard, he liked. He had said they were short of pilots, all those who had learnt to fly privately had been called up, so all potential pilots had to be trained by the RFC. Sam had made up his mind, he was free to do as he pleased, so the Royal Flying Corp would soon be hearing from him, he wanted to fly and fight on the front as he had viewed so many dog fights from the ground. Little did he know about the perils and pit falls that were about to assail him until he reached his goal!

As soon as Sam had left Tim Gledhill at Waterloo, he made his way to Shepherd's Bush. It was Friday and he knew of a cheap hotel he could stay for three nights in the area and still have money left over. He started to make his plans for the next few days as he travelled.

He made his way across London, traveling by the Tube, eventually onto the Central London Railway making his way westward. He had already decided not to stay on the train as far as Shepherd's Bush, as he knew too many people there and did not want to meet anyone who might recognise him, so got out at the stop before, Holland Park. On his way he saw on the walls of the underground stations posters that confirmed what he intended to do:

> Join the
> Royal Flying Corps
> Flying or Ground Duties
> Apply at any Recruitment Centre
> or at your nearest
> RFC Station
> Your nearest RFC Station
> to you is
> **Hendon**

On arriving at Holland Park he had just over half a mile walk to the hotel he knew and as he left the station he immediately walked on the south side of the road in the shadows as much as possible, his peaked cap pulled down low over his eyes and the coat collar of his donkey jacket turned up, walking in slouched manner and a shuffling gate, keeping a sharp lookout for anyone he knew, especially as he approached Shepherd's Bush. Having lived and worked in the area all his life there were many people he knew. Satisfied that the coast was clear, he made his way to the hotel he had in mind that he had never frequented, but having often seen when walking round the area with Bill. As far as he could recall it was not used by anyone he knew so there was little chance of being recognised.

When he arrived at the hotel, he booked in as Private R Drew, using that name for the last time. He explained to the attractive middle aged lady receptionist behind the desk, who was part owner of the hotel, that he had been wounded and captured by the Germans and had been a POW before managing to escape and make his way back to England. He was now on a short leave before returning to his unit in England and afterwards to the front.

He explained to her that his uniform had been damaged in his escape and he had acquired what he was wearing while he was escaping and showed her the blue naval sweater as extra proof. He also said that he would be kitted out with a new uniform when he got back to his barracks next week. As he hoped, it went down well with her. He showed her his travel documents and temporary identity card. This satisfied the receptionist on both counts, he was who he said he was. She then asked him how long had he been fighting on the front and how badly he had been wounded. When Sam told her about lying in *no man's land* for two days she was very saddened, but when he explained to her about his wounds that were in places that a lady should not ask, this brought a blush to her cheeks! She felt he was a hero having done all that fighting, he deserved the best she had. She gave Sam her most expensive room that was vacant for the weekend, but only charged him the price of her cheapest one. He certainly had fallen on his feet here; he felt he could not have done better if he tried.

He sat in his room that looked out over the green of Shepherd's Bush, watching the people and traffic go by and thought of the following day, Saturday, the Jewish holy day, and he knew all the Eighteens would be attending the local Synagogue. He also knew what time they left and how long they would be away. In addition he knew where they hid a key to the back door. The Eighteens were looking after all his personal belongings, all placed in his storage chest that was left with them before he joined up and was stored under the cutting table in the shop he had made for them. In the chest was his best suit that the Eighteens had made for him, some other clothes including his better set of working togs, an envelope with his Birth Certificate, the Exemption Certificate stating he had been employed in war work for Bert Frost Carpenters of Shepherd's Bush, personal papers, photos and moth balls!. He would remove the items he would need on the next part of his journey if he was to join the RFC. It was essential that he got them, but he did not want anyone to know he was about, especially the Frosts and the Eighteens. He made his plans for the following day.

What Sam did not know was that the Military Police were looking for Private Drew, they were keeping it a low profile to stop any panic but they had no leads to where he could be, he was safe where he was. The only description of Private Drew the MPs had were taken off his service records, and were nothing like Sam, in height, built and colouring, the MPs were on a hiding to nothing! By Monday he would be safe from then on as Mr Sam Bray, but he never knew his alias was a suspect, wanted as a German Spy!

Spending a night in the hotel that was luxury compared with all the uncomfortable places he had slept in since leaving England. On entering the dining room for breakfast, he found it full of what he assumed were business men, company reps plying their trade in the area, no one he recognised, he was thankful for. After finishing a large breakfast that he felt the landlady had specially provided for him, he made his way to the Eighteen's shop, walking like he had from the station the day before. On arriving there he kept well out of sight in the entrance of a narrow alley nearly opposite the front of their shop. He eventually saw the family leave for the Synagogue from a passage to the side of their building and they would be away for over an hour. As soon as they were out of sight, he crossed the road and made his way down the same side passage, removing the back door key from its hiding place and letting himself into the premises.

He went straight to the shop and pulled out his wooden chest from under the cutting table, removing the key for the chest from the hook behind one of the legs of the table where he had hung it up before leaving to joining the army, which seemed ages ago to him. When unlocked, he removed an old and well used shirt, jacket, trousers and boots that he had used to wear to work and the envelope containing the two certificates he required, Bill's watch and chain and, lastly, the photo of Alice, which he would keep with him from now on. He re-locked the chest, putting it back in the same position under the table as he found it and re-hanging the key on the hook. He went out the way he came, ensuring he left no traces of his visit, depositing the back door key in its hiding place, back the way he found it, all done in less than 15 minutes. As he emerged from the passage, he cautiously looked out to see that the coast was clear, no Eighteens in sight, satisfied everything was how it should be, he then returned to the hotel and his room.

Back in his bedroom he changed into his old working clothes, which he had not worn for over a year. He bundled all of what was left of his army duds together, except the naval pullover he had got at Portsmouth and would dump them in a large bin that he had seen on the way to the Eighteen and was inside a yard, belonging to *The Shepherd's Bush Laundry Service* that was only a few buildings away from the hotel and working full tilt until 5pm on a Saturday. The boundary wall was only about five feet high and he could see old clothes, sheets and other items already dumped there, so he could toss his bundle over, which he would do after the laundry had closed and it was dark, his old clothes would not look out of place with all the other things already dumped in there and he was sure no one would check it. If someone did check and found *William Perry's* service number, it could not be traced back to him. The bin of rubbish clothes would most properly be sold to the local *rag & bone man!* By supper time his uniform was gone, his army career in the West Bristol Fusiliers was now nearly over, and the start of his new career as Sam Bray in the Royal Flying Corps, he hoped, would begin on Monday.

For the rest of his stay at the hotel, except for meals, he stayed in his room. His plan was not to go to the nearest recruiting office, they would place him where it suited the Army or Navy best. If he went to an RFC depot, he reckoned he had a good chance of joining the RFC, one volunteer is better than ten pressed men. He was not sure if he would be accepted as a pilot, but with his skills as a carpenter, making aircraft parts, it would be a good entry point. Once he was in, then he would see what he could do about becoming a pilot, which was his ultimate aim. He had heard of all the flying displays the RFC had done were at the aerodrome at Hendon before the war. Adverts on the Underground he had seen said it was a place the RFC were taking on recruits, so he decided that was the best location for him to go.

Come Monday morning, after an early breakfast, he booked out of the hotel, thanking the lady proprietor for all she had done for him, before leaving behind his last vestiges of the past few weeks of his old late friend Bob Drew, throwing all the documentation he had, all torn up into very small pieces, into various bins he passed and the second Bill Perry had long gone. He was on his way, Sam Bray, wearing his old working clothes, naval pullover and topped by the old donkey jacket and cloth black cap. He made his way back to Holland Park, keeping his head down again, returning in the direction that he had come two days earlier and then making his way on the Hampstead Line to Golders Green, one of their two current northern termini. On arrival there he decided, as he was now running short of funds, he would have to walk the two miles to the aerodrome at Hendon, where he hoped they could advise him how he could join the RFC and not fob him off and tell him to report to a Army or Navy Recruiting Office.

***

Hendon aerodrome was situated about 7 miles north west of Charing Cross, the centre of London, and had opened to flying in 1909. In that year, Everett, Edgecombe Co built an aircraft, and purchased a field at the end of Colindale Avenue in Hendon to fly their aeroplane, which, unfortunately, was not a success. This field soon became an airfield and other organisations were starting to use it, including Louis Blériot who set up a flying school there. ■ What was regarded as the first true flight from Hendon took place in 1910 in response to a prize of £10,000 offered by *The Daily Mail* in 1906 for the first person to fly from London to Manchester in 24 hours. After a number of tries from other aviators, Louis Paulhan, a Frenchman, won the price the same year, taking off from Hendon on 27th April, taking 3 hours and 55 minutes flying time, in two hops over a start to finish period of 12 hours. An early Englishman aviator named Claude Grahame-White also took off on the same day from Hendon, behind Paulhan, and when both had stopped for the night, Grahame-White decided, as he was still behind, to try and catch up, and made the first known night flight, but too no avail, being forced down with engine trouble. Paulham, hearing about White, took off in a storm and won the race.

■ In 1911 Claude Grahame-White purchased the land originally intending it to be the London Aerodrome, serving the capital for all its flying requirements. He set up his own aircraft manufacturing company there on the peripheral of the flying area. He set up a flying school and a number of other aviators also opened flying schools there. Hendon aerodrome had a number of firsts where flying was concerned: An air mail service; the first parachute jump from an aeroplane; night flights; and in 1914 was then the only London airfield and would be a suitable place base for the air defence of London. In 1916, the War Office commandeered all the flying schools for the training of RFC pilots, the start of Hendon becoming a military establishment.

***

As soon as Sam arrived at Golders Green he asked the ticket collector for the directions to the Hendon aerodrome, as he was on his way to join up. Equipped with the information he required, he made his way to the Edgware Road then turned right towards the village of Colindale, away from London. He saw a number of aircraft flying overhead as he made his way there, thinking he must be heading in the right direction. As he was not exactly sure where the aerodrome was, Sam asked someone who looked like a local and was directed down a road a few hundred yards on his right and less than half a mile down this road was the camp, a large white board, painted with black lettering, stating to the world:

> Royal Flying Corps
> Hendon

Behind the notice board, the gates and the perimeter fence laid the aerodrome, hangars, workshops and living accommodation; all seemed a hive of industry.

As he approached the open gates, Sam could see in the distance the four main airfield hangars over on his right, with many aircraft lined up on the apron in front of them ready for take off, some with their engine running, while others were either taxiing for takeoff or having just landed, returning to the apron after a flight.

A sentry who was controlling entry to the RFC complex barred his way with a challenge, *"Halt: Who Goes There,"* blocking his way from further progress onto military property. He was smartly dressed in his best khaki uniform, button to the neck and peaked cap with rifle at the ready, patrolling by the gates that led into the camp proper. To one side of the gate there was a sentry box that would give the sentry little protection if the weather was inclement and blowing toward its front opening.

Sam did as he was told and halted. "I want to join up in the Royal Flying Corps" was Sam's answer to the sentry. "How do I do it, I know I can do it, I saw it in your recruitment posters saying come here, so where do I have to go?" Sam asked him.

"You better come in Mate, go over to that building over there, that's marled Guard Room," he pointed with his free arm, "they will direct you from there, and the best of luck, you can have my job any time you like, and don't volunteer to be a Aircraft Hand if you don't like getting dirty!" was his final remark as Sam passed him making for the direction he had pointed.

On arriving at the Guard Room and he was met by a Corporal MP and explained again that he wanted to join the RFC as he was a professional carpenter who had been making aircraft parts. The Corporal passed him onto the Sergeant in charge of the Guard Room, six foot two in his boots, ram rod straight in his bearing, smartly dressed in his uniform topped by a peaked cap with its red cover. He had been briefed how to handle potential recruits with a list of professions the RFC required, the top two being motor mechanics and carpenters. He asked Sam for any documents he had to prove who he was and on inspection knew Sam's profession was badly needed by the RFC and were in short supply.

He was taken to Station Headquarters by the Sergeant and shown into the Station Adjutant office to Captain Wainwright, a grey haired man with a weather beaten face from years of sailing and a few in open cockpits of aircraft, now in his fifties, having been retained in the Army to allow those younger and fitter men to fly and fight. The Adjutant was the first port of call for anyone wanting to enlist. The Police Sergeant explained that Sam had volunteered to join up as a carpenter and had been in a reserved occupation in that trade, but he, and he looked at Sam, could be better use to the RFC. The Adjutant was also pleased to see him; they were always in need of good carpenters in the Corps. He asked Sam to show him his papers, which he checked. "I'll hang on to these and pass them on to Major Wight, our Technical Officer, who will interview you later." Turning to the policeman, he said, "Sergeant, take Bray back to the Guard Room with you while I arrange an interview, I'm sure you can find the young lad a mug of tea!" with a smile. With that they both returned to the Guard Room, where he got a steaming pint mug of hot, sweet and very strong service tea. His career in the Royal Flying Corps was about to begin.

After a wait of about an hour in the Guardroom, he was escorted back to Station HQ and was shown into a room where a Major was seated.

"Good morning Bray, I'm Major Wight, I'm in charge of all aircraft maintenance, I understand you are a carpenter," said the officer, whose uniform, while not scruffy, had an air of someone who worked with aircraft and engines, there was a certain caster oil smell about him and particles of saw dust adhering to some minor oil satins on his uniform!

"Yes Sir," was Sam's reply.

"Tell me Bray, why are you volunteering to give up a reserved occupation of safety?"

Sam had though of all the questions they may ask as he was lying on his hotel bed and hoped he had satisfactory answers for them all. The first question he had been expecting, "Sir, as you say, I've been in a reserved occupation since the war started and enjoyed my job, but last year I became old enough to join up. In the past year, I've been thinking more and more that I could be more useful serving my country, in a better way than I was working at my last job and allow an older unemployed man with my skills, too old to join up, to take my place, so I'm doing someone and the country a favour as I see it, Sir," Sam answered.

"I see you point of view Bray, a brave decision when you could be sent to an active airfield in France, near the front, where there is every possibility of getting yourself killed. It's very laudable of you Bray, but before I can accept you, I will have to see what your work is like. What work did you do to have a reserved occupation as a carpenter?"

"Sir, I was working for a small carpentry firm in Shepherd's Bush by the name of Bert Frost & Son, we were making aircraft parts for the Sopwith Aviation Company, all manner of items, and I must have made every part of his various aircraft at one time or other since we got contracts from him just when the war started."

This was music to the Majors ears. "Of course I know of Sopwith, and I have heard of Frost, a very good firm I understand, we have a number of spares in stock that have been made by them, even by you if you worked for them, as you say. If I take you on, I expect to see great things from you. OK Bray, I will have you taken down to the carpenters shop and you will be given a drawing of a part of one of our planes, a piece of wood and the tools to make it. Is that OK with you?"

"Yes Sir, but I'll require the jigs if I'm to the job properly," was Sam's reply.

The Major was impressed; the lad knew what he was talking about. He called out and a SNCO came in. "Sergeant Jenkins, take Bray up to the workshop and give him a drawing of a strut, the wood, tools and the jigs to make it, then bring him back with the result," and turning to Sam he said, "How long do you think it will take you to make a strut?"

"Give me a plank of the correct wood Sir, and the correct tools, I will cut the basic shape from that, and in half an hour, or less, you will have your strut to the standard required by Sopwiths."

"If you are back here with in the hour, you will have a place in the RFC, if not the RFC and I don't want you," was his grim reply. Sam knew, with all his experience, he would be back under the half hour.

Sam was greatly relieved that the Major had not asked him when he had left Frosts, he would have had to tell a lie saying it was last Friday, but a check would soon show he hadn't. He was greatly relieved but he had though of that and had an answer ready which he would volunteer at the next interview if was accepted.

Sam was taken to the carpenter's workshop in one of the Bessonean Hangars, allocated to an empty bench, and given a plank of wood and a drawing. Sam smiled to himself, he had seen this drawing many time before and had made many of these struts. He knew he was a bit rusty after about a year away from the bench but he felt he could cope, however, it may take a bit longer than usual. He cut out the shape he wanted on a jig saw and was soon making the spar to the drawing and using templates to ensure the correct thickness and within the tolerances at set position along the spars length. It took him about 20 minutes to complete, he was very pleased with himself and he had not lost his skills. He handed it to Sergeant Jenkins, who checked it against the drawing.

"You've done a good job there son, never seen anything better, you can join my workshop any time you like," and with that he took him back to the Major.

The Major was surprised to see the SNCO and Sam back so soon, but when he was shown the spar and heard the SNCO's high praise, he was well impressed. "OK Bray, you are the type of person we need and we are short of men of your calibre. Now while we recruit here, you have to be sent to one of our Recruits Training Depots, which I expect will be Halton for your initial training for 6 weeks, I will let you know. I will contact them first, explaining the situation and hope they will accept you straight away, and with their co-operation we will get you sworn in and in to RFC uniform as soon as possible. I will tell them you have to be given the trade of rigger and once you have completed you Initial Training I will make sure you come back here as there is no need for you to go on a trade training course. The Police Sergeant will get you a bed for the night and loan you a set of mug and irons. I will contact him as soon as I have any news and he will tell you, so make

267

you way back to the Guard Room and tell the Sergeant what I told you, any questions?"

"Yes Sir," Sam replied, "I did not tell Mr Frost I was going to join up as I knew he would have stopped me, but I know he has a list of some very good carpenters over the age of joining up so he can get replacement at a moments notice, I would be obliged it he was not contacted. I hope what I have just made is a good enough reference of my standard of work."

"I accept what you say Bray and from what you have made, which will be fitted to an aircraft in the not to distance future, it's a good enough reference as you say, so I will not contact Mr Frost, if I do I may lose you!" was Major Wight's reply with a wry smile. "So off you go back to the Guard room and they will get you a bed in the Transit Hut for the night lunch and an evening meal." And with that Sam left.

Later in the day it was confirmed he would leave for Halton the following morrow, after he had had breakfast, first reporting to the Adjutant to collect his rail warrant for Wendover, the nearest station to Halton. He was told he would probably have to walk the mile and a bit from the railway station at Wendover to the camp, where he was to report to the Main Guard Room. As he had already done Initial Training at Bristol, he knew the ropes and what he could expect, but he never let on to any one else.

As well as his rail warrant, he was given ten shillings for bus fares and incidentals on the way, but unlike RTO at Waterloo, it wouldn't be deducted out of his pay once he had *"Signed On"*, the RFC were more generous then the RTO! He was away by nine in the morning, taking a bus to Golders Green and underground trains to Baker Street, where he changed on to the Metropolitan line for a stopping train to Wendover. On arrival at Baker Street he found a number of lads of his own age on the train who were also on their way to join the RFC. At Wendover they were met by a smart looking corporal drill instructor who got them in three columns and marched them the mile or so to the Guard Room at Halton. Sam found he was marching as trained, the rest were all over the place, he thought he better look a bit more like them, otherwise questions could be asked, which could be hard to answer! As he had been told, they were all expected and the corporal left them lined up in front of the Guard Room. A Drill Sergeant was there to meet them, just a smart as the corporal, with a list of names on a clip board and the roll was called, Sam being last as his name had only been entered late the previous day.

Sam was placed in No 3 Squad of 30 men. The first thing was to swear allegiances to the King and given the Sovereign's Shilling, for the second time! Sam was *"In"*. He was now 86877, Private Bray S, of the Royal Flying Corps. He had achieved the first of his two objectives. The squad were kitted out the following day, the uniform was the same as before, but the shoulder flashes were different:

A *Senior Man* was required to be in charge of the squad, to march them around the station from the barracks and between their various aspects of training. And in a few days Sam was appointed to this position as he showed potential and seemed to pick up marching and drilling as if he had done it before! When they had been issued with their uniforms, Sam wore a white lanyard at the top of his right arm to denote his position. One of the perks was that he did not have to do fatigues, just march the squad where they had to go and oversee the fatigue tasks were completed satisfactory.

For the next six weeks it was Bristol all over again, but this time, he knew what was what and what was expected next, and there were no 2nd Lieutenants Ellis's there either to breath over his shoulder give him a hard time! The officers, while strict, were human and treated the recruits fairly. When he had first joined up, like Bill, he wasn't as fit as he though he was, but now, it was all a *piece of cake!*

On completion of his initial training he was posted to Hendon, as he expected per Major Wight's request. He was soon working hard in the workshop, making new parts for aircraft and repairing parts that were broken and required replacing. He soon realised he was much more experienced than all the other men working there and was given all the difficult and plum jobs.

He had been there only a month after completing his initial training when he was called in by the Major. "Bray, Sergeant Jenkins and I have been keeping an eye on you and we felt you should be rewarded for all your hard work and effort. One of our sergeants had been posted away, so a corporal has been promoted to replace him, as a lance corporal to replace him. So we have a need of a Lance Corporal, so from today, you are now one of the JNCOs reporting to Sgt Jenkins. If you do well, which we have little doubt you will, there could be a second stripe on its way, it's up to you."

Sam did well and within a month he was a full Corporal, promotion was often fast in the war. But word had got around of his expertise and the Royal Aircraft Factory at Farnborough was in need of skilled carpenters, ones who could design parts, and a posting soon came through. Sam was on the move again, arriving at Farnborough on a London & South Western train in just over four months of joining up, not bad Sam thought!

In charge of the workshop at Farnborough that Sam had been allocated was Major Kirkpatrick, who had started at the factory as a junior 2nd Lieutenant when they had only balloons. He had worked his way up to his current position and now controlled all new aircraft design and prototype building. Most people regarded him as God of the Royal Aircraft Factory, but while he was in control of over a hundred personnel, he was approachable and would walk the factory floor at least once a day. He knew all his staff by name and would speak to them all on a regular basis. Everyone knew when he was coming as he was over six feet tall and as thin as one of the spars on the aircraft they built and could be seen from one end of the workshop to the other. The workshop was divided into two sections; the bigger part was for the riggers, while the other part was for the engine fitters. In the middle on one side were two big double doors, which led into a hangar, through which all the parts from the workshop would pass to the prototype aircraft assembly area. Sam often worked there, assembling the parts he and others had made in the carpenters workshop. He got to know in detail how aircrafts were constructed which would help him in the future.

When Kirkpatrick first met Sam, he made him welcome and told him that he had come highly recommended by Major Wight. When he had paid one of his many visits to Hendon, Wight had brought Sam to his notice and he had watched him from a distance, not wanting to attract his attention. He was impressed with what he saw and the standard of the parts he had made, he was always on the lookout for expert craftsmen.

Sam then remembered why he looked familiar, he had seen him in the workshop at Hendon, but did not let on to the Major.

On his return to Farnborough, Kirkpatrick decided he needed someone of the skills that Sam possessed. Soon after his visit to Hendon, Sam was head hunted by him, whatever Farnborough wanted, Farnborough got! Sam was soon on his way.

Sam's job was as before, making parts, but Farnborough were designing their own aircraft, so the majority of his work was prototype. After a while, and watching the design team making drawings, he was invited to assist, and started to do drawings of the minor parts, attend evening classes at the factory organised by the Major to improve his skills. He progressed well and was assisting on more important items as time went on. As well as working on

270

the bench making items, he was now working at a drawing board, doing design work. Then came the day when it was suggested that he flew on test flights to see the parts he had designed and made flying, it may be, they told him, that it would give him a better insight and understanding into how an aircraft flew and into the work he did.

The first flight took his breath away and he did not take much notice of the aircraft or how it performed, he kept looking over the side to the small world passing below. He was hooked on flying from that moment on; he decided he had to become a pilot, whatever may happen, *but how* was the question. From Corporal Rigger to a 2nd Lieutenant Pilot was a long way off, but he was determined that he would make it, or at least have a go, come hell or high water! At the moment he did not know how he could achieve this, he would have to make discrete enquires; he didn't want to upset the Major who was doing so much to help him in his current trade. But others in the establishment did, he was being assessed.

After his initial flight he asked to be allowed to make as many test flights as possible as he considered it gave him a better insight to the parts he designed, but in reality he loved to fly. The Chief Test Pilot at Farnborough was a Major Moreton, who took a great interest in the design of any aircraft the factory produced, from the start when new ideas were banded around at a design meeting, the drawing office when the ideas were put onto blueprints, the making of parts, the assembling of them into a flying machine, and finally to his part, when he had to test fly the aircraft. He considered it essential if he was to understand the aircraft he was testing and if any fault developed while carrying out a flight test, he would have a shrewd idea where the problem could lay. Many times he and Kirkpatrick discussed features that Moreton considered a more in depth study was required before manufacture, some remained as designed while others were modified, the two majors worked well together. As such, he spent many hours in the two workshops, watching the aircraft taking shape and seeing the delivery of new engines and watching them benched tested. It was the only way to understand your aircraft thoroughly and Moreton drummed this into Sam, but at present Sam was only interested in the parts he made, the wings and fuselage, engine, at that time, were of no interest to him, they were another world!

Moreton was one of the first pilots in the RFC and had made many ascents in balloons before moving on to the aircraft, but he did not consider the former was flying in the true sense of the word, but he had learnt in those early days. He considered that an aeroplane was the nearest man had become to a bird. After balloons, and before becoming a test pilot, he had been an instructor at Upavon and was a qualified examiner for testing potential pilots wanting to obtain their *Aviator's Certificate*. He was meticulous in everything he did from the very first day he left the ground in a balloon to his job as a test pilot, and being so, he had avoided any bad accidents, and those he had had, he either walked away or bailed out from, a great believer in the parachute. He was the opposite to Kirkpatrick, he was of medium height and built like a rugby player, which he still was, playing for a major London club, and just missing out on getting to play for England in 1912.

Sam had a number of test flights with Moreton and a close rapport between the two men was soon established. Often, while Sam was working, the Major would watch him working, asking questions, sometimes to test Sam, other times to find out information on areas he considered he was lacking. As time progressed he would often give a lending hand in either of the two workshops, he was a hands on pilot and was often seen with overalls on and dirty hands! If the aircraft was a two seater, Sam was nearly always in the second seat once the initial test flights had been under taken.

At this period of the war, pilots were in short supply; they were losing them as nearly as fast as they could be trained, aircrafts were more plentiful. When the war had commenced, all pilots held an *Aviator's Certificate*, it was the only way to be accepted as a pilot into either the Army or the Navy at that time. But times had now changed; pilots were now being recruited either from direct entry or through the ranks. All the pre-war aviators were either building aircrafts for the war effort, as was Tommy Sopwith, or training potential pilots to fly at RFC and RNAS flying school, and lastly, flying into battle on the western front or in the defence of London and the Home Counties, most by now being at least a major in command of a squadron. The main reason for this loss was two fold, current flying training was too short and pilots had little or no experience in combat, lasting only a few sorties, and pilots were not allowed to wear parachutes. Senior officers felt, that if pilots had parachutes, they would, if there was the slightest sign of danger, take the cowards way out and jump, not staying to fight the enemy. As a consequence, if an aircraft was damaged and caught fire, a crash was inevitable, the pilot, if still alive, had three choices, either be to burnt to death in the aircraft, crash with the aircraft, or, lastly you jumped out, either way you usually ended up dead!

To assist in the training of pilots, it was decided by the War Office to have designed, by their Aircraft Factory, a two seat aircraft with dual controls especially for the training of pilots, and when fully tested, set up a production line at one of the many aircraft manufacturers. The task of designing the prototype was allocated to Major Kirkpatrick and his workshop and Sam was pleased that he played his part in all aspects of design and construction and was invite to sit round the table when they had design meetings. It was decided by the top designers that a current two seater did not have enough room in the second cockpit for complete controls as in the pilots cockpit but with a little modification this could be enlarged to the same size to make the rear cockpit identical to the front one. Bar for this change, that included fitting dual controls, a pilot's seat and an extra foot on the length of the fuselage, there was nothing else to be changed as the basic aircraft had been designed for carrying two crew, guns and bombs. Without the last two, there was power to spare. The War office agreed but stipulated that the flying characteristics were to be no different from the two seater, pilot and gunner/observer version.

Once the aircraft type selected for the two seat trainer had been identified, work on these modifications were put in hand, firstly with the drawing, Sam playing his part. As the aircraft selected was in current production at Farnborough, parts required from the production aircraft were set aside while the parts for the two seater trainer version were made. Within a week all parts were made and the aircraft was ready for build. The only noticeable difference to the trained eye between the basic aircraft was that the rear cockpit had to be widened in line with the front one to accept full flying controls and seat and its extra length as the taper after the front cockpit of the reconnaissance aircraft did not now start tell after the rear cockpit, making it the first fully duel controlled aircraft built at Farnborough for training. The workshop was fully employed on the modification, which took just under two weeks. Keeping a close eye on all this was Major Moreton.

The first test flight Moreton would fly solo, but once he was satisfied it was safe and suitable for purpose, he would take passengers. On the day of the initial test flight, the sky was clear blue, not a cloud in the sky with a very gentle breeze coming from the south west. Weights were put in the rear cockpit to simulate a second crew member. Sam, with the rest of the workshop staff, watched the take off; they did not expect any problems as the aircraft was a tried and tested design and they expected little or no extra drag with the enlarged cockpit, but if there was, it was over come by the extra power available without armament. Within an hour the aircraft returned. It was refuelled, weights removed and prepared for the second flight, this with the other Farnborough test pilot, Captain Sunderland, in the seat selected for the pilot, while the trainee would be in the front. The two pilots would take it in turns to fly the aircraft, doing circuits and bumps. On return, both pilots were satisfied with everything except for a couple of minor alterations that would be beneficial when training pilots to fly, one being an improvement to the communication between the two cockpits. The next passenger was Major Kirkpatrick who also found where some minor improvements could be made; these were all made within a few days.

Once the two seater trainer aircraft had been well tested and passed for production to commence, Major Kirkpatrick and his team were not involved any more, they had more important work to do with the design other new reconnaissance aircraft that would be better than the latest the Hun had. It was a see-saw battle, first the Germans had the better aircraft and then the British had a better aircraft than the Germans, this see-saw carried on throughout the length of the war until the Boche had been defeated.

Sam saw a lot of Major Moreton as he was not test flying all the time and everyday. Sam found that he had a good knowledge of tools and woodwork, which was his hobby. Also Sam was now flying regularly getting a good number of flights with him and found that Major Kirkpatrick was quite happy to release him from the bench to let go flying. Little did he know the reason. From his first flight, Sam kept a record of every time he flew in an RFC Log Book that Major Moreton had given him.

Farnborough kept the prototype of the new two seat trainer and it was not long before the test pilot was letting Sam, once they were up and away from the airfield, to fly straight and level in the trainer in the front cockpit, and as soon as Moreton considered he was competent he started Sam doing turns, climbs and dives, and all other manner of manoeuvres. Then came the day he took off and landed the aircraft on his own with the test pilot's hands held above his head unknown to Sam. Moreton considered Sam was born to fly and be a pilot; he had natural co-ordination for the part.

The day after Sam had taken off and landed, Ben Moreton went to see his friend John Kirkpatrick. John's opening words as Ben entered his office were, "Well, how is Bray doing?"

With a smug smile he replied "You of little faith, I told you he was a natural, he could fly out of here unaided if needed. If he is to become a RFC pilot, which I think he should be, he has got to learn about engines, at present he knows nothing and seems little interested, so what are you going to do about it John?"

"OK Ben, as from tomorrow he will be working in the engine shop and you can keep an eye on him as you have done so far. I will get my SNCO in charge to give me progress reports, but if he does not come up to scratch, it all finished as far as I'm concerned."

"I accept and agree what you are saying, but I don't think Bray will let us down."

When Moreton had left Kirkpatrick's office, he called Sam in. "Bray, you have done very well so far but I want to broaden your horizons, as from tomorrow you will be working in the engine shop. Whether you like it or not, I consider its best for you," This was a bullying tactic on Sam's CO's part, to give him a bit of a fright and make him work hard at the new aspect of training. "It's the only way you will get promotion, if you fail me, its back to the chippies shop for the rest of your army career as a corporal, you will see others around you, promoted ahead of you, which I'm sure you don't want?" which was a lie, but he wanted to put the frighteners up Sam to make him do good.

Before Sam could answer Kirkpatrick continued, "Also, I want you to attend evening classes which we hold here on a regular basis for map reading, navigation and basic mechanics, I think this will be of interest to you and you never know when it could help you in the future, so go to it, every night for two weeks, lets see how you do. I know you are a good draughtsman now and as such you will have certain sketching skills. As you have done a lot of flying, you seem not to have suffered from air sickness, which is a good thing, for what we have planned for you."

Sam did not realise he was being tested, if he did it would not have made any difference. But he did wonder what his Boss had in mind by saying, *"what we have planned for you."* After he had left his office he wished he had asked him what he had meant; now it was too late. If he was given an assignment by his CO, he would jolly well carry it out to the best of ability. The SNCO in charge of the workshop had been given instructions by Kirkpatrick to give Sam a crash course on engines, how they worked, and how to recognise faults, especially while in the air, and how to cope and what action to take. The Boss told to his i/c Engines he would look in from time to time and if Bray was not cover in oil and grease there was something wrong with his training.

In the evenings Sam went to classes and enjoyed the subjects he was taught and did well in the exams he had to regularly take.

After about a month Kirkpatrick called Sam into his office and when he entered Moreton was seated in the corner, behind Kirkpatrick's desk. "Bray you have done well, you have not let me or Major Moreton down. Now have you any idea why we wanted you to learn about engines and navigation, while your trade as a carpenter, does not require you to know anything about these subjects?"

"No Sir," was Sam's short reply, but over the past few weeks he had been thinking and had started to put two and two together, and if the answer was what he hoped, he would be pleased.

"After your arrival here, you showed great potential, head and shoulders above the rest of the work force and you took a keen interest in the aircraft and everything about them. From your first flight you have always been keen to take to the air. Major Moreton felt you had something more to offer the service that being a chippy for the rest of your career. That is why I was always letting you off you normal duties to fly as much as possible. The

275

Major has told me some time ago you could fly an aircraft on your own. As you know Major Moreton is an examiner for the *Aviator's Certificate*, as also is our other Test Pilot who I am sure you have you seen but not yet met, Captain Sunderland. Tomorrow you will be given the written exam for the certificate and if you pass that Major Moreton will arrange the flying part of the test with Captain Sunderland in a few days time.

Now if you awarded the certificate and still want to be a pilot you will have to be commissioned, but first you will have to be assessed to see you have the qualities to become an officer in the RFC and the CO will appraise you. If he is convinced you have the potential and with his approval you will be posted to Upavon, attached to the Central Flying School," he paused, then continued, "as an Officer Cadet, we both wish you the best of luck".

While Sam had an idea this was on the cards he did not think it would happen so soon. If he passed he would have achieved the second of his two objectives.

The following day he took his exam which he had no troubling in passing with all the lessons he had been taking. In less than a week the prototype training aircraft stood on the apron ready for the flying test. Sam stood by in full flying kit he had borrowed and did not have to wait long for Captain Sunderland to arrive, like Sam in his flying clothing. Being short in height, his flying suit made him look more rotund than he was, behind his back hew was called *The Michelin Man*! "We haven't met before Bray, but I've see you around with Major Moreton. This is a test for the *Aviator's* Certificate, it's hard, a failure in one area, you fail the whole test. The test will consist of the pre flight, take off, fly it on courses as I instruct, carry out other tasks including a sketch of a landmark I will show you while piloting the aircraft, in a space of no more that a minute (before the enemy get you in their sights!), do acrobatic manoeuvres and recover from a spin and eventually land and do the after flight. I will not tell you until after the flight has been completed if you have passed or failed. If you do fail and you are not safe to fly, I will stop the test immediately. I will tell you why once we have landed, so you will know what you have to do to improve yourself, OK?"

Sam already knew the test already; he had done this at least ten or more time with Major Moreton. "Yes Sir," was his reply. "OK Bray, lets get on with."

Sam gave the aircraft the pre flight check as he had been shown by Moreton and discovered a couple of snags that Sunderland had made earlier and pointed them out to the examiner and corrected them. When Sunderland was satisfied that Sam had done a thorough check they were soon airborne, the first part of the test was various manoeuvres, Sam climbed, dived, banked and turned, stalled, spins and did circuits and bumps. After that he was given a navigation test, navigating in a triangle course from three points as given by the examiner. The test pilot navigated him to a remote Hampshire village and told Sam to make sketches as he circled. After nearly two hours they returned to Farnborough and Sam was instructed to land and taxi over to the apron from where they had started. When they eventually arrived and parked up, Sam cut the engine and they both got out. Sunderland took the sketches from Sam and after studying them was well satisfied, meanwhile Sam carried out an after flight check of the aircraft, reporting to the ground crew any snags he had found on the flight.

Once the aircraft was handed over to the ground crew, Sam went over to Captain Sunderland who had a grin on his face who said, "Well, you will do, can't fault you, Major Moreton did a good job. Congratulations, you have won you *Aviator's Certificate*. Now go over to that single seater 504 over there and make your first solo flight, best of luck, see you back here in about an hour, and when you get back go and see your boss and tell him." As Sam walked to the aircraft he did not see Captain Sunderland give the "thumbs up" sign behind his back to the two Majors who were standing at the window of Kirkpatrick's office, watching. Sam was sure he was still being watched and so did a good pre flight and flew for an hour in the air all on his own, he felt marvellous.

When he entered the office after his flight, both the officers congratulated him. "Alright Bray, you are now qualified as a pilot, but your next hurdle is your interview with the CO to assess you if you have the potential to hold a Kings Commission. I have just been told that you have an appointment with the Station Commander the day after tomorrow. In the mean time, off with your flying clothes and on with your overalls, you are still one of my riggers and there is plenty of work for you to do," and with that Sam was dismissed and continued the job he was part way through, but he did it with a smile on his face and a glow all over.

Sam felt pleased with the interview he had with the CO, he felt he had answered all the questions asked with good answers, some were quite deep; politics, about the war, cause and effect, major aspects in modern history, world geography and current affairs. Most of this he had learn when he was in Dr Barnardo's, which was a great help, and also from when he and Bill were in their 'digs' on any given evening, they would discuss all matter of subjects which covered most topics, all this he felt helped. The CO said he consider Corporal Bray was suitable for a commission and before going for flying training would have to attend a short course at Sandhurst, to prepare him for his new position as a junior officer. Before the war it was an 18 month course, now it was down to six weeks. He would return to Farnborough when he completed the course, remaining as a corporal and on posting to Flying Training his rank would now be Flight Cadet.

When the flying course was completed and he had passed, he would be promoted to 2nd Lieutenant, he was now was equal to Ellis. If he did ever did meet him it would be Officer to Officer. Little did he know, and would never know, that Ellis was now at the bottom of the ladder as a private!

It was about a month later after returning from Sandhurst when he was called into Major Kirkpatrick's office and told that the his posting had come through and was posted out to the Central Flying School at Upavon as a Flight Cadet in a week. He gave Sam a list of things he was to do on the day before he left, one being the removal of his corporal stripes, and being issued the badges and hat of an Flight Cadet. He continued, "Now let Major Moreton tell you what you may expect when you get there."

"I will be notifying CFS that you hold an *Aviator's Certificate* and you will be given an air test to determine what path your flying career should take, that's about all we can tell you really". He did know, but did not want to frighten him, or say too much. "You will miss out the basic training I expect but will train to become a pilot, either flying fighter/reconnaissance or bombers aircraft, who knows. My bet is you will make a good fighter pilot. We both wish you the best of luck. All the raw recruits who gain their wings at Upavon could never gain the *Aviator's Certificate*, they haven't done enough time training bar to get them off the ground, fire their guns and hopefully land in one piece, you are head and shoulders above all of them now, even after they have gained their wings. There is one last thing we have to do," and both the majors got up and shook him by the hand.

Sam declined the 7 days leave he was offered, he wanted get on with the job as soon as possible and was told that within a few days he would be advised when he would be leaving for Upavon and was officially told that on his arrival at CFS, as he knew, his rank would be Flight Cadet. If he passed the course he would be commissioned as a 2nd Lieutenant and be presented with the coveted wings of a fully fledged RFC pilot.

CHAPTER 13

The Last Lap

On the final day at Farnborough, Sam went round the various offices and workshops to say his goodbyes and thank yous. His first port of call was with Major Moreton and Captain Sunderland in the Test Pilots office, he expresses his gratitude for all they had done for him, especially in teaching him to fly and be awarded his *Aviator's Certificate*. The Major had arranged that the certificate would be sent to him, it always took a long time to come through, especially as there was a war on. Once he got it, he would arrange to send it to where ever Sam wanted it. In the meantime, he was given his certificate to take to Upavon to prove his ability.

After spending half an hour, chatting about aircrafts, flying and his future he then left seeking out Major Kirkpatrick, eventually running him to ground in the engine test bay. He and Sam went back to his office and spent at least the same amount of time there that he had spent with the test pilot, thanking him for all that he had done for him and the experience he had been given. Kirkpatrick and Moreton and all his workshop friends all seemed interested in his future and wished him well.

When he eventually left the Chief Engineer's office It was lunch break, so he made his way to the Corporal's & Soldier's Mess where he met up with his pals from the workshop. During the meal, he told all and sundry that he would be in the local they all used when they had the money and time to go out for a drink and that evening when the doors opened, he would welcome any of them there to a farewell drink with him, he offered the first round and suggested they then have a kitty for the rest of the evening.

The following morning, Flight Cadet Bray could be seen in his best uniform, bereft of his badges of rank and dressed as an Flight Cadet with a slightly thick head from the late-night drinking session the evening before, lugging his kit bag over his shoulder, making his way to the nearest railway station. The train he was waiting for soon steamed in, taking him to Reading where he changed trains, stations and railways. He made his way from the SE&C station to the ticket barrier of the GWR and was directed by the ticket collector to one of the three bay platform at the west end of the main platform to take a local stopping train to Pewsey, a small county village in the heart of

Wiltshire. As he had about half an hour to wait, he went into the station restaurant for a cup o' tea and a wad, his head now belonged to him again!

On leaving the restaurant he made his way as directed to the platform for his train. The train had not yet pulled in and waiting on the platform were a number of other cadets, all dressed as like him, who on enquiry found they all hoped to be pilots and would be on the same intake as he was.

When the train eventually arrived, the cadets stood back to allow the arriving passengers to alighted onto the platform, who were either making their way to the exit or changing trains on another platform. Once the crowd had dispersed, Sam and his fellow cadets boarded into a 3rd Class carriage, taking over most of the seats, and they were unlikely to be bothered by any other passengers, as there were not many of them and their compartment was all most full. The engine was uncoupled, ran round the train and was coupled to what was now the front, pulling out nearly on time, and chugged its way through the Berkshire and Wiltshire country side, stopping at all intervening stations on its way except Newbury Racecourse as there was no race that day.

With a crowd of young lads together, the conversation did not stop, the only subject on their lips was the war and combat flying, they all wanted to be fighter pilots. It seemed that the majority had never flown before, those who had, had only been passengers. Sam did not think it right to mention he was a fully qualified pilot with an *Aviator's Certificate*, they would all find out eventually when they were assessed by the CFS. The journey soon passed and they were all on first names terms by the time they alighted from the train.

On arrival at Pewsey station, an hour and a half later, they were thankful to see army transport, in the shape of a very old open back lorry, with solid wheels, waiting to take them the 6 miles to Upavon Airfield; they had been concerned that they may have had to walk all the way! On the country roads the solid wheels were bone shattering but it was better than walking! It reminded Sam of his two journeys in Belgium and Holland when he was escaping, which seemed light years ago. If the weather had been inclement they would have all been in for a bit of a soaking but as the sun was shining, like the mood they were all in, the journey was not too bad, but they were glad to see the station buildings and airfield of Upavon eventually coming into sight.

While the domestic part of the camp was all in the shelter of the valley, the airfield was perched on the top of a hill and open to all the elements. The station opened in 1912 and in August of that year the first flying course started and lasted for four months. The school was commanded by Captain Godfrey Paine RN, whose second in command was a Major Hugh Trenchard.

By the time Sam arrived there the courses were much shorter and the CO had changed and was now commanded by RFC officer.

When Sam and the other cadets arrived they were allocated to their accommodation in the Cadets Wing, which was a collection of eight basic wooden huts, with 20 beds in each hut, 10 either side with a locker each for all their possessions, nothing different from the rest of the barracks he had been in, except as a corporal he had had a small bunk room to himself. The heating was two primitive cylindrical coal burning stove situated in the centre of the room, equal distance apart and they were only to be used between November and March when a meagre amount of coal was issued, but it only took the chill of the hut, and when it had to be put out by ten in the evening, it was cold by reveille, you just slept with all your clothes on to keep warm. In the very cold weather, the condensation from the windows ran down onto the inside window sills and froze! But now it was no problem, the weather was warm. There was one toilet hut for the Wing, situated in the centre, standing isolated with no covered walkway between the huts, a nasty trek in bad weather and all washing was in cold water! Life was tough for a cadet! While they were potential officers, cadets were considered the lowest form of service life; even a Private was above them!

Any Cadet who had held a NCO rank before he came had to remove their stripes, a Cadet was a Cadet, and there was no difference between each other, regardless of what you had been before. They all had white flashes on the front of each side of their collar and on their heads wore a black shiny peaked cap, a white band round the hat denoting what they were *Cadets*. While WOs, SNCOs and JNCOs had to call them all *"Sir"*, the Cadets had to stand to attention to those above them when being addressed or wishing to speak to them. Life as a cadet was not an easy one.

The following day was started with personal interviews to ascertain what, if any, degree of flying skill that any of the cadets may have. Initially, when the war had started, the RFC and RNAS only accepted cadets who had *Aviator's Certificate*. When this source of pilots had dried up and no one had any chance to learn privately as there was no flying schools left open, the two services had to set up their own flying schools taking over the many schools. As such, all flying training was started from scratch at Upavon for the RFC. At this time of the war it was rare to have a cadet with any flying experience so Sam was made very welcome.

As all the cadets on the intake had had a number of interviews, aptitude tests and medicals before they were selected, and if passed all this, it was accepted that they were capable of becoming a pilot after the necessary training. Sam had had a medical when he joined up at Halton and was passed A1; his interview with his CO was good enough for Upavon. The next stage was kitting out with flying clothing, this and the interviews taking most of the day.

As Sam was the only person on the intake with an *Aviator's Certificate*, he was exempt the initial flying training, and after a flying test to ascertain his flying potential, he was given a two week course on combat skills, which was to him was the icing on the cake. On his final flight the senior instructor took him up for one last time and considered he was competent to join a fighter/reconnaissance squadron on the western front. He was assessed as *an above average pilot*, which was considered *the best of the best!*

At the next graduation ceremony Sam, with all the others who had completed and passed the whole six week flying course and therefore had been at Upavon longer than Sam, paraded in their new officer uniforms, all bearing their rank of 2nd Lieutenant, with black hat bands replacing the white and collar flashes removed. They were not *the lowest of the low* anymore and now had to be saluted by all WOs, SNCOs, JNCOs and Privates, who had to call them *"Sir"* and stand to attention when spoke to. How things had changed! Each in turn was called forward and had the coveted pilot's wing brevet pinned on the upper left breast of their tunic. It was a proud moment for Sam, he had now accomplished the second of his two objectives, he could fly, was an officer and a fighter pilot! Before any of the new officers left the station tailor was busy sowing of the flying wings.

The majority of the parade was off across the English Channel to France the following day, joining various squadrons, to fly single engine fighter/reconnaissance aircraft against the Boche, departing from Folkestone by a paddle steamer. As they left the shelter of the harbour, standing on the deck and feeling the swell of the channel waves beneath their feet, they watched the White Cliffs of Dover recede into the background, some never to see them or England ever again. The few who were not selected for fighter/reconnaissance were sent to convert to flying bombers. But Sam was neither of these; he had not been given details as to what his posting or post was, and told to move his kit into the Officer's Mess.

He was called into his Training Squadron Commander's office the day after receiving his wings. "Mr Bray, as one of our more experienced pilot you have been posted to 8 Squadron, which is re-forming at Brooklands airfield before it goes back to Belgium to replace one of the depleted squadrons out there, which will be returning home on rest and re-forming. You will be departing by the end of the week, and reporting to your new Squadron Commander some time on Monday. So as you haven't had any leave for some time, take a few days off now, before you go abroad."

"Now Sam," as a Major would address a fellow junior officer, "Do you know or have ever been to Brooklands," he asked, Sam replied with a shake of the head, "it's south west of London, not too far out, but I expect it will take you most of the day by train as trains helping with the war effort take precedence over everything else. Before you leave, report to the Admin Office and collect your travel documents and joining instructions and they should supply you with a route, if not ask." He paused.

"Your new CO, who I only met when we both junior officers, will be a Major Farquhar, and I am to tell you to report to him where he will be found at the Sopwith Aviation works somewhere, who are preparing a recently new introduced aircraft, the Sopwith Camel, for your squadron. I envy you, I have only just heard about it, but never seen one, let alone fly it; it's the very latest front line fighter. Any rate, best of luck, you have done very well while you have been with us. We all know Major Moreton here, he taught you well, I would expect nothing less of him, I'm sure you will go further in your chosen career." Then he added, "Make sure you look after yourself, watch for the Hun from the sun, keep looking behind and don't fly straight and level for more than three seconds, conserve your ammo, and when it's all gone, head down and make for home," he finished with a smile, they had all been told this many times before! He got up and the two shook hands, Sam saluted and made his way back to the Admin Office to collect all his paper work and directions for Brooklands.

As he did not have to report until Monday, he had the weekend off to stop on the way, but what should he do with this time? He thought about going and seeing Alice, but thought better of it, he had not contacted her for ages and could easily receive a bad reception from her and her parents, best keep out of the way for the moment. He decided to go back to Farnborough and again thank Major's Moreton and Kirkpatrick for all they had done for him and their faith they had in him, knowing what he had achieved, and as a 2nd Lieutenant with pilots wings on his chest, that was their proof and reward.

When he had finished packing his kit he hitched a lift in a lorry that was on its way to at Pewsey station to pick up supplies. He had to wait about an hour for a stopping train and returned in the way he had come just over two weeks previous to Farnborough. He made his way to the camp, booked into the Officer's Mess, and then made his way to the Chief Engineer's office where he found Major Kirkpatrick and was greeted cordially by him, as officer to officer, but Sam still thought of him as the 'Boss'. After a chat he went to seek out Major Moreton, who had just returned from a test flight, and was interested to hear he would be flying a Sopwith Camel, an aircraft he had tested before it was accepted into the service, and he told Sam he thought well of it, but it had its vices for the novice pilot, it had to be treated with both knowledge and respect. In the evening the three of them all dined together in the Mess, very different from his last night at Farnborough.

Sam rose the following morning, with no thick head this time, and spent a leisurely weekend until Monday morning, paying a shopping visit to Aldershot and a lunch in the best hotel, which he could now well afford as an officer.

On Monday morning, he was up early and as he did not know when he would get his next meal ate a hearty breakfast. He left the Mess just after 9am and made his way to the station having found out Brooklands was near Weybridge; the station he required was Byfleet, only three stops up the line in the direction of London Waterloo. The pre-war time table, the last to be printed, could not be relied upon, so one had to wait on the platform until a stopping train arrived, which was nearly an hour, after seeing many troops and goods trains pass through in both directions. It was nearly lunch time when he alighted at Byfleet, and on leaving the station forecourt soon found a small café that served light luncheons, best to eat now as he did not know when he would get his next meal.

While the North West corner of Brooklands racing track was adjacent to the station, the main gates were further away than he realised as he found out from the young girl who took his money for the meal. It was less than a mile away, normally an easy walk, but carrying a fully loaded kitbag with flying clothing, he was puffing and blowing a bit on his arrival, he wasn't as fit as he had been when left Halton!

Sam soon arrived at the complex, approaching down the hill towards the Club House, his first view being the racing circuit with its banked ends and inside this was the airfield while the two aircraft works were situated outside the racing track. Before he had reached the race track, he had spotted aircraft taking off and landing and as he got nearer, the sound of aero engines being run up and tested could be heard. As he entered the flying area, he saw that it was very busy with no shortcut across the airfield to get to the Sopwith factory. From where he stood he could see the company's name blazoned across the front of each of their hangar ends:

SOPWITH

No one could not miss that! The only safe way to get to the factory was walking round the perimeter of the flying area, a mile or so, which took about half an hour, negotiating the various building, garages and aircraft hangars on the way.

When Sam eventually arrived at the premises of *The Sopwith Aviation Company* it was all hustle and bustle; a number of identical aircrafts were lined up in front of the works hangar while he could see others exactly the same inside nearing completion, *these must be the new Sopwith Camel,* Sam thought. A number of RFC pilots were either sitting in or looking around the aircraft, some in flying clothing, other, like him, in their No: 1's. He walked over to them and as he approached a small group of RFC officers, one looked across at him, turned and walked to meet him. He immediately saw he was a Major and felt sure that this was his new CO. He put his kitbag down and gave him a smart salute as he approached, which was returned. "Good afternoon, I'm Major Farquhar, as you are the last one to arrive, you must be Bray, welcome to No 8 Squadron."

"Good afternoon Sir, yes I'm 2nd Lieutenant Bray reporting for duty, sorry if I'm late, Sir," was Sam's reply. As he was speaking another officer approached. "That's OK, I had already been informed you wouldn't be arriving until about this time," and turning to the officer who had just arrived, "Ralph, come and meet the third member of your team, Bray this is Captain Urquhart, your Flight Commander in charge of B Flight. He will show you the ropes and tell you about the Sopwith Camel, a new aircraft which we have the honour to be the first squadron in the RFC to be equipped with. But I will leave you with the Captain who will explain all. We are all billeted in a local hotel in Weybridge where there is a room booked for you. I will see you again when we gather for dinner this evening." And with that he departed into the factory to confer with Tommy Sopwith before Sam could salute him again.

"I believe you name is Sam?" his flight commandeered commented, Sam nodded in agreement. "OK Sam, let me tell you all about the Camel you will be flying. It's a successor to the Sopwith Pup, but it is much better. It's about 10 mph faster and has a better ceiling of 19 thousand feet compared with 17 and a half thousand for the Pup, which is a thousand and a half foot better. The rate of climb is much better also; the Camel is 1,000 ft per minute compared to 650 with the Pup. The only problem is its endurance, only 2½ hours, compared with the 3 hours of the Pup, but for distance travelled at the higher sped it is just about the same. In addition, the Camel is the first British fighter to have two forward firing machine guns, synchronized to fire through the propeller, a great advantage above all other present aircraft, double the fire power. But all in all, we have got the best aircraft in the RFC and better than any aircraft the Hun has at the moment."

"Now the current situation is this," his Flight commander continued, "so far eight planes have been completed, four more are nearing completion and will be flight tested either today or tomorrow, and one of them will be yours," and he looking at a card with a list of aircraft numbers on, adding, "yours is **N715**, so I suggest you go into the factory and have a look at it, see how its progressing and familiarise yourself with all aspects of the plane. So see you later." And with that he gave Sam a pat on the shoulder and a wave and went over to the line of completed aircraft out on the pan to speak with the other two pilots of his flight.

Sam went into the factory and soon found his aircraft, which was just having the engine winched onto its mountings. Once it had been fully installed it would be taken outside, ground tested and when past fit to fly, all the covers would be fitted and the flight test would be carried by the Sopwith test pilot, and once it had been passed fit for purpose, it would be handed over to the RFC, when the CO would sign the *Acceptance Certificate*. He stayed watching the final assembly and when possible asking questions about the aircraft and looking it over. When all had been completed, it was too late for any tests and they let Sam get into the cockpit and *get a feel* of the layout, get to know where all the *taps* were. It did not take him long to memorise the position of all the controls and, closing his eye, he went around saying a control and reaching out to find it, he soon got the hang of things. He remembered that Tim Gledhill had always carried a torch with him for pre dawn takeoffs or night landings, he never trusted the cockpit lights and he said they always seemed to fail when you most needed them! He would have a look round Weybridge when they got back to the hotel to see if he could buy a small one that could fit somewhere in the cockpit or a pocket of his flying suit.

The CO had arranged transport to the hotel, and on arrival there, Sam went out into town and soon found a shop open that sold torches and lanterns. He purchased one with a bull's eye lens which was housed in a wooden square shaped case, first produced in 1914 for war use by the police and service personnel being manufactured by *British Ever-Ready Company.* The torch had a handle at the top which Sam attached a strap which he could fit to a ring he saw when familiarizing himself with the layout in the cockpit, adjacent to his seat.

The squadron gathered in the hotel dining room later that evening for dinner, where all the pilots were staying over the last few days as they arrived in dribs and drabs. The CO and his three flight commanders were all very experienced fighter plots, each having many hours on the Western Front, while the rest of the junior pilots had few or no combat flying hours behind them, Sam being in the latter bracket, a novice, but he knew he was rated as above average pilot and he hoped it placed him in good stead and could prove his worth.

When they all met up in the hotel in the evening, Sam as a newcomer, was made welcome as the latest member of the squadron, everyone mixing well. Sam soon made friends with Lieutenant Peter Holland, Pete to his friends, who was already been blooded in battle.

He had been a pilot with the squadron they were due to replace but he had been sent home early to join up with 8 Squadron. He had joined the battered, beleaguered and depleted squadron in Belgium at short notice, to fill a place of a *twenty minuter*, being thrown into the fray with little help or encouragement of the few remaining pilots left who were fit enough and still able to fly. He was told not long after he had arrived, they would soon to be withdrawn and swapped with a fresh squadron from Blighty. As he was not as battle weary as the rest of the returning squadron were he was told he posted to No: 8 and was very pleased to do so. He had limited battle experience, but experience nonetheless, and while he had not shot anyone down, he had not been shot down himself. The squadron was so depleted and when they were withdrawn from active service, Pete was sent home in one of the few aircrafts fit to fly to Bircham Newton in Norfolk where the returning squadron was posted, but the aircraft did make a few alarming noises on the journey and Pete was glad to see firm land beneath him after crossing the Channel and Bircham Newton come into sight.

When the CO allocated pilots to flights, the flight commander had one combat pilot and two novices, so this made a good balance, working out as one experienced pilot to look after one novice. He was glad that Pete Holland was in his flight and he was told he would be Pete's wingman while the other novice pilot in the flight would be Captain Urquhart's wingman, who was 2nd Lieutenant Alan Dawlish.

The following morning Sam saw his aircraft going through its ground test and when completed to the satisfaction of Harry Hawker, Sopwith's chief test pilots, he was taken up for an air test. Within the hour the aircraft was back and Hawker signed the *Acceptance Certificate* for **N715** and the CO duly counter signed it, the aircraft was now on the RFC inventory. Sam then was required to sign the factory Acceptance Register stating he had taken personal delivery of **N715** and, putting *RESTRICTED* in the place of destination, first as he was told to do so, and secondly he did not know where he was destined. Once this had been signed, he was given the aircraft log book and all other documentation to be handed over to the Engineering Office on arrival at their new base, somewhere in Belgium he understood

That evening as they gathered for dinner, Major Farquhar took them into a private room where he divulged the arrangements for the next two days. Tomorrow all pilots were to test fly their own aircraft for at least an hour, doing all the movements they had been taught, any problems to be sorted out on their return, especially if it was to do with the aircraft. He reminded them that they had to cross the channel in one hop the following day!

They would all be leaving the day after tomorrow after an early breakfast; transport would collect them no later than 08.00 hours. Once all the *'before flights'* had been completed, they would be taking off in flights, no later than 10.00 hours, at intervals of 2 to 3 minutes, he would lead the way with A Flight, followed by B flight and C flight bringing up in the rear, each flight keeping each other in sight. So far no one knew where their destination was on the other side, but they were not kept in the dark any longer, they would be one of five squadrons that were part of the *Ypres Wing*, which they were told was currently commanded by Lieutenant-Colonel Cavendish. Only the CO had met him when on a brief trip to the front to reconnoitre the area when he had been of advised of his posting to 8 Squadron. The CO understood he was an experienced combat pilot, so you wouldn't be able to pull the wool over his eyes! Their airfield would initially be near Poperinge, a few miles west of Ypres. The CO reminded everyone that this was secret information and they were not to divulge this to anyone and that included Tommy Sopwith and any of his staff.

The rest of the evening was spent in the hotel bar drinking English beer, only two more evening they would spend in England, they did not know how long they would be away for, some would have *'Return Tickets'* for others it would only be a *'Single'*, never to return home across the British Channel. The CO made sure that the drinks were limited and they all were sent for an early night. Sam was quite happy with this, he was tired, and it had been a long day. He did not want to wake up with a hangover as he had following the farewell evening drinks at Farnborough!

They were all bussed down to Brooklands and set about testing their aircraft. As soon as N715 was ready, Sam did a pre-flight and was soon off. He decided he would first fly over Hendon, followed by Shepherd's Bush, to see the orphanage, the Frosts and the Eighteens, then fly west to Upavon, and finally Farnborough before he returned to base, taking about just under 2 hours, an enjoyable morning flight, one he would not get once they had arrived at Ypres.

The following morning they all gathered on the pan where all 12 aircraft were now lined up, fuelled and ready for takeoff, all guns fully loaded, just in case! They were all dressed in their flying clothing and their personal kit now stored safely in their own aircraft as with the aircraft log book. It was a clear morning, ideal conditions to cross the channel. Sam felt he was now on his way and hoped to avenge those who had killed his best friend Bill.

While they were awaiting the CO's command to depart, Sam saw half a dozen other single seater aircraft of various types, in RFC markings, parked up on an adjacent pan to where their aircraft were, all appearing ready for takeoff as well. Just then he a saw movement of two cars coming round the peri-track towards the Sopwith Factory, the cars pulled up outside the Despatch Office and three pretty young ladies alighted from each car and walked into the hangar where 8 Squadron had all recently signed for their aircrafts, all wearing flying clothing which did nothing to enhance the female figure!

Sam peered over the tail of his aircraft that he was leaning on, *what could these ladies be doing down here.* "Pete," he asked his new found friend, "what's all that lot doing, is someone taking them up for a jolly?" was his question.

Pete looked at Sam with surprised amazement. "Don't you know, they are so short of blokes to ferry aircrafts to the squadrons from here they have had to recruit the fair sex to do the job for us, and very good they are too, Tommy Sopwith calls them the *Sopwith Delivery Service,* or *SDS* for short. I went out with one once, she was a darling, but it didn't come to anything, our paths never crossed again, more or less ended before it had begun, more's the pity!"

The CO and A Flight Commander, with the other three pilots of the flight climbed into their respective aircrafts, started up and were soon away in a **V** formation, with the CO out front. They was no time to try and chat up these girls, as much as they would have liked to as Captain Urquhart called them to get started up. It was not long before Brooklands was receding into the background as they headed for the channel. As they crossed that stretch of water, which had only been flown for the first time eight years earlier in 1909 by the French aviator Louis Blériot, Sam thought of the two previous times he had crossed this stretch of water, but then it was by boat. First going out as Private Perry, preparing to fight in the trenches, returning as Private Drew as an escaped soldier. Now it was his third crossing, this time as a 2nd Lieutenant Bray, a pilot in the RFC, using his own name. He knew which he liked best, and hoped he could do what he had set out to do in the first place, to avenge the death of Bill. He looked down and could see a number of boats plying the waves in both directions; he did not envy any of them!

***

The six pretty young ladies that Sam and Pete had seen, that included a Mrs K Cavendish, entered the despatch office of Sopwith's factory to sign the Acceptance Register for the aircraft they had been allocated to deliver, which they had done many times before. Keturah was the first to sign for a Sopwith Pup, an aircraft that had entered RFC service late 1916 and had just been superseded by the Camel but was one of the last ones in production. She was to take it to the RFC station at Narborough in Norfolk and having completed her entry, she was just about too picked up her aircraft documents

289

from the foreman when an entry from the previous day, two names above hers caught her eye:

Date	Aircraft	Number	Pilot	Purchaser	Destination
17 Jul 17	Camel	N699	Major G Farquhar, RFC	RFC	Restricted
17 July 1917	Camel	N689	Captain R Urquhart, RFC	RFC	Restricted
17-7-1917	Camel	N721	Lieutenant P Holland, RFC	RFC	Restricted
17 July17	Camel	N715	2nd Lieutenant S Bray, RFC	RFC	Restricted
17 Jul 1917	Camel	N711	2nd-Lieutenant A Dawlish, RFC	RFC	Restricted
18/7/17	Pup	M579	Mrs K Cavendish, SDS	RFC	Narborough

Keturah dropped her goggles, gloves and documents and leant on the table for support but soon recovered before anyone noticed. Was this the son she had given away? She asked the foreman if he could remember who 2nd Lieutenant S. Bray was, but with so many pilots collecting aircrafts, it was not possible, especially when in full flying clothing. Further enquires to him were only very vague while the foreman was never told, he reckoned they were off to France. Keturah would write to Algernon as soon as she got home, which would be tomorrow as she was doing a delivery that would entail an overnight stop and ask him if he could find out anything about a 2nd Lieutenant S Bray, was he going to the front in her husbands area? From the Acceptance Register, all she knew was his name, no squadron or destination, not much to go on!

When she got home the following evening, she found a letter waiting for her from Algernon; he was posted home to work in the RFC section of the War Office in London, promoted to a Brigadier General. He was told he was to head up a certain new project, but they would not tell him until he was home and in post. He was handing over to a newly promoted Colonel, Colonel Andrews, and part of the handing over was taking him round to each of the five squadrons in the *Ypres Wing*. This would take about a week and he would be home within two weeks he thought. With a weeks leave, he would be in post in less than a month. He finished by saying this would be his last letter to her and it was not worth while in replying as it probably would not reach him before he was on his way home.

To Keturah this was excellent news, he would be out of danger, he would be home and they would be together every night unless she had a long delivery to make. She hoped his new job would not take him away from home overnight, she wanted to look after him and to give him all the loving tender care he deserved for all he had done for her and his country and sleep together again after what seemed a long time. The only down side, he would not be able to look for 2nd Lieutenant S Bray for her; it was a small price to pay. Perhaps Algernon could contact his successor when he had settled in at some time, if the war would allow it.

***

On arrival at Poperinge, the squadron taxied in and were parked adjacent to the three khaki canvassed covered Bessoneau hangars, their sides and roof flapping in the light afternoon breeze along side the remains of departing squadron. Once 8 Squadron had officially taken over, the departing squadron started up and were all soon on their way back to Bircham Newton for rest, new aircrafts and pilots before returning to the front again.

They all soon settled into their new surroundings, the departing squadron having left their ground crew and all facilities and servicing tools, including the specialist tools for the Camel that had been sent ahead and had arrived a few days previously.

After an initial two days of settling in, flying around to familiarise themselves with the area and over flying the other four airfields where the other squadrons of the wing were based, they were considered fit to take part in action over enemy lines as a wing, putting up on average 50 aircrafts plus between them.

Sam had looked down on Ypres a number of times from his aircraft and once driven into the town passing the wall garden he thought he was going to ends his days, things had not improved since he was last there, in fact they were much worse, not only for the few remaining civilians, but the fighting troops on the ground.

Sam and all the pilots were each given a printed sheet of paper, written by a Colonel Cavendish, the outgoing Wing Leader of the *Ypres Wing*. This he had written from advice that had been given to him by *old hands* and personal experience:

The Fighter Pilot's 10 Commandments

(1) Beware of the Hun in the Sun.
(2) Never fly straight and level for more than 3 seconds.
(3) Shoot as close as possible, in short bursts to conserve ammo.
(4) Keep watching your tail.
(5) A good wingman protects his master.
(6) Fight in pairs, one attacks while the other protects.
(7) If after the first shot, be ready to break away.
(8) If damaged, heads down, make for home, don't stay and fight, lives to fight another day.
(9) He who flies straight & level won't live to fight another day.
(10) Never do victory rolls, your aircraft could be damaged and Weakened, that could be your last manoeuvre.
A. D I Cavendish
A. D I Cavendish
Colonel, RFC
Ypres Wing Leader

The first patrol over enemy lines soon drew up the Boche but the enemy were out numbered and departed before the wing could attack. The following day was different and they were matched one to one, the ensuing dog fight only lasted a short time but to Sam seemed like hours, both sides losing aircraft and pilots. Sam kept close to Pete and watched him shoot down one aircraft while he defended Pete's tail, keeping at least one Hun aircraft away. On return they had lost one novice pilot in C Flight. After his first combat action he felt knackered but he knew he had to forget about this and get on with the job he had been trained for and was there to carry it out. If you fall off the horse, get straight back on the saddle!

During the first week, the out going Wing Leader, now Brigadier General Cavendish, accompanied by his replacement Colonel Andrews, on recent promotion from Lieutenant-Colonel to command the Ypres Wing, visited each of the five squadron under his command in turn before the Hand Over. They had to attend a Dining in Night at each one. The evening at 8 Squadron proved a good break for the aircrew and the two guests mixed well with the assembled officers, speaking to everyone there. Sam, in turn, spoke to both the guests, but he had more rapport with Brigadier General Cavendish than Colonel Andrews. Little did he know that the retiring Lieutenant-Colonel was his mother's husband, his stepfather!

Soon after the visit Sam was promoted to full Lieutenant and decided it was time he should write to Alice.

My Dearest Alice

Please forgive me for what I have done to you, you do not know how upset I was at the loss of Bill,

I just had to do some thing to avenge his death, I could not let the Germans get away with this.

Initially, I have been in an army unit, don't ask where, but I was doing little to get at the Hun, but for everyone of their ground troops we killed, they seemed to kill one of us, it was fruitless, and we had been in the same trench line since the war began in '14, it was stalemate. I started as a Private, and could see no way forward, no promotion,

so I decided to make a change

A white liar about promotion, but it was best that way.

I am now a pilot in the Royal Flying Corps, commissioned, and have recently been promoted to full

Lieutenant. I feel I am doing something useful now, I haven't shot down any German aircraft so far, and we are over enemy lines everyday bombing, doing reconnaissance and photographing and anything that our HQ wants us to do, so I hope it won't be long before I do.

The Officer's Mess is about 3 miles from the airfield in an old French château, a real home from home.

We sleep in beds and have proper cooked food, it couldn't be better; compared to what we got in the trenches, its bliss!

> Our squadron is one of 5 which is made up into a wing, instead of 12 aircrafts going to chase the enemy, and with these numbers, they usually chased us off, we now go out at least 50 aircrafts, and this frightens the Hun off, and we get a better chance of shooting them down. I am in No 8 Squadron, in C Flight of the Ypres Wing.
>
> Captain Urquhart is my Flight Commander and Major Farquharie the Squadron Commander. In charge of the wing is Colonel Andrews and right at the top is Brigadier Tucker at RFC Brigade HQ. Colonel
>
> Andrews has served very well so far, but hardly ever flies operationally, he takes us on training exercises, when we are not chasing the Hun. All the officers are a good bunch, and in the evenings, we have some good parties in the Mess and I have partnered up with Pete Holland, a pilot more experienced that me and I am his wingman.

He read what he had just written, perhaps he should not have told Alice all this but he was sure the Germans knew all this anyway and he felt that the end of the war was in sight and victory was on its way.

> If you feel after reading all this, that you can't forgive me, I will understand, and I cannot blame you.
> So
> please don't read the last paragraph.
> Again, I do hope you will forgive me. When I was given Bill effects, there was a photo of you that I have kept with me all the time. I love you so much, and when this terrible war is over and done, and hoping for a brighter future
> when this happens, and if you will consent, I would like to marry you.
> Sent with my love   Sam

***

Keturah was overjoyed, Algernon was working in the Ministry in London and home every night, be it often rather late, but that did not matter, he was home and safe, and later, they were in bed together, in a lovely big four poster! She still had her onward quest to find her second son Sam but Algernon was far too busy to find anything out, and as he pointed out, all his work was concentrated on the war effort, finding her son did not come into this category. She was a bit miffed with Algernon on this point but she quickly realised he was right, much to her own annoyance!

On the 4th June 1917, King George V created another award, for people who had served their country well, the Order of the British Empire. In the New Years Honours List of 1918, one of the recipients was a Mrs Keturah Sophia Cavendish, for her services to the Women's Emergency Corps and delivery of much need aircrafts to the armed services, much to the delight of Algernon and their children.

***

Alice was sorting through the days mail one Saturday morning, about a week after Sam had posted his letter to her, when she came across an envelope only used by service personal writing home in a hand she recognised. A thrill passed through her body as she slipped the letter in her dress pocket and continued sorting out the rest of the official Frost mail, taking the appropriate action where necessary. When there was a lull in her work and she was on her own, she opened the letter and saw that it was from Sam. When she read his letter her feelings were mixed. She realised when he had first joined up he must have been under age; *was he being brave, revengeful to make up for the loss of his best friend, or just down right stupid.* Sam didn't yet know that Keturah was his mother and he and Bill were half brothers; and Bill would never know.

Initially her first reaction on reading the letter was anger; *why had he done this to her? Why had he not told her? Could she ever forgive him?* She nearly screwed up the letter and threw it in the bin but stopped herself in time. She realised deep down she loved him. *What was she to do?* Through out the day she mulled it over in her mind. While she had no intention of showing the letter to her parents, she would give them the main gist of its contents after dinner later that day, finally saying that Sam had proposed to her.

After the factory had closed down for the day, the four of them sat down for the evening meal. Bert and Agnes had been married long enough to know that their daughter was excited about something by her demeanour; she ate quickly in small mouthfuls, as if she wanted the meal over and done with as soon as possible. They said nothing to each other, just passing knowing glances across the table. When the meal was finished and cleared away, Bert

295

winked at Agnes, then looked at his daughter and said, "Well, what's on you mind young Alice, you've been like a cat on hot bricks ever since we knocked off work!"

She gave a quick nod. "Mum, Dad, Fred, I've had a letter from Sam," she blurted out. "Is that all?" Bert teased. Agnes gave Bert a swift kick under the table for his troubles and told him to leave the girl alone and let her speak. Alice then told them most of what Sam had said in his letter that she had taken out of the pocket of her smock, but kept it in is envelope, not saying anything about his proposal.

There was much discussion, as the pros and the cons of the situation were thrashed out. As Bert summed it up, "I see his point Gal, and I also understand how you feel, but put yourself in his shoes, what would you have done?"

Alice realised her Dad had a good point, a very strong point in fact. She had the Suffragette spirit in her. "I know where you are coming from Dad and I suspect, in the same position, I would have made the same choice. Thanks for all you help, I will write back tonight telling him I forgive him, and, if you both agreed..." She paused and held her breath for a few seconds and then blurted out, "Sam has asked me if I will marry him, and if you both agree I will accept his proposal, and tell him I want to marry him the day he comes home," finishing in a rush with a blush on her cheeks and a sparkle of tears of joy in her eyes.

Her parents and brother were all overjoyed, they all thought a lot of Sam. Many months ago, Agnes and Bert had thought there was something between Bill and her, but that was not to be. "This calls for a celebration drink," was her Dad's response, and with that Bert poured four glasses of port, calling the toast to Sam coming home safely and a happy marriage between Alice and Sam in the near future.

They agreed that Katurah should be told as soon as possible and Alice should go round and see them, but phone them first, which she did straight away. She spoke to Keturah who said she would be welcome to come any time as they would love to see her as they were staying in London this weekend, she suggested she came the next day after church. Keturah could tell by the excitement in Alice's voice that something good had happened, but as much as Keturah tried, she could get nothing more from Alice, she would say no more.

Later that evening Alice wrote back to Sam, saying she forgave him and giving him a minor scolding for not telling her sooner. The next problem she had was what to tell him about his mother. In the end she said nothing and would hope to make the introduction face to face when he next came home.

***

As they were both working long hours, Algernon at the War Office and Keturah delivering aircrafts for Tommy Sopwith, mostly six days a week, they did not get down to the country as often as they would like to see their children or Algernon's parents either, their war work kept them based in London. Keturah could not relax after returning from church while waiting for Alice to arrive, but Algernon took it in his stride, and both breathed a sigh of relief for different reasons when there was a knock on the front door that one of their maids went to answer.

Leaving Alice in the hall the maid entered the dayroom and announced that a Miss Frost had called as arranged. Keturah was on her feet before the maid entered, feeling excitement and anticipation, Algernon smiled behind her back and sat back waiting for their guest to arrive.

Alice had never come here before, and because of pressure of work, it had been ages since Keturah had last visited Alice at her home. Alice was still in her Sunday best after attending church with her parents when she arrived and was overawed by her surroundings. *If this was the hall, what was the rest of the house like?*

Keturah felt if Alice was coming to see her then it must be good new and excitedly told the maid to invite Alice in. Algernon rose as Alice came in, she was all smiles, convincing Keturah that it must mean it was good news. The first thing Keturah did was to give Alice a hug and a kiss then introduce her to Algernon, as they had never met before, he just gave her a restful shake of the hand. She soon felt less intimidated by her surroundings. With the preliminaries over they all sat down and Alice launched into her good news.

"Yesterday, out of the blue, I got a letter from Sam," she said all flustered, her words falling out of her mouth, this bringing tears to Keturah's eyes. "Where do I begin? He is in the Royal Flying Corps, now Lieutenant Sam Bray with 8 Squadron in the *Ypres Wing*."

"My God, that was one of my squadrons in the wing until I left a few months ago," Algernon interrupted, "I dined with his squadron and I remember having a chat with a young chap called Bray after the meal. He was new out there on his first tour, hadn't done many sorties, but his Flight Commander told me later he was an above average pilot and had great potential. He was unusual amongst all the new young pilots that we were currently getting, he held an *Aviator's Certificate*. I never found out how he got it, as far as I know there were no private flying schools still open after the war had started. When I meet him I must ask him."

"Algernon, do be quiet and let Alice get on with her story, you can have you say later, I want to hear all about Sam," she scowled at her husband, and turned to her visitor with a smile on her face, "do go on Alice." Algernon knew he best hold his tongue for the sake of peace!

Alice continued, "He does not know when he will come home next, he cannot be spared because of the shortage of pilots, but when he does," she stopped, held her breath for a few seconds and blurted out, blushing as she had done the previous evening "and he has asked me to marry him and I have written to him accepting his proposal".

Keturah was over the moon with the news, tears streaming down her cheeks now. "Alice my darling, I'm so pleased for you both, and I'm thrilled to bits, you will soon be a part of our family," and gave her a big hug and a kiss, followed by Algernon who felt he was entitled to kiss her know. When they were seated again, two things suddenly occurred to Keturah.

"Alice, my love, there are two things I want to say, the first is what should we do about telling Sam who I am? At first I thought I would like to write and tell him, but he does not even know me, and I think that is a bit unfair, so I think its best if we hold our first meeting with you to introduce us when he returns home next," which Algernon and Alice agreed. She did not say to them that she had already decided this before writing her letter to Sam. "The other thing is, would you like us to hold the reception here?"

There had not been much discussion in the Frost household about the marriage arrangements the day the letter arrived, except it was decided the wedding would be at St Stephen and St Thomas, the Frost's church, but what about the reception, in the church hall, perhaps. While she was happy with the arrangements that Keturah had proposed, Alice said she did not want to agree to anything without first consulting her parents and getting their approval, as it was the bride's father's responsibility to make all the arrangements. This they agreed was the correct course of action.

"Would you like to come home with me and discuss it with my parents?" Alice asked them both.

The both agreed and Alice was soon on the phoned to her parents and told them the news and asked if she could bring Keturah and Algernon back home straight away. They said give them half an hour, which meant they would have a quick tidy up, check that the parlour was spick and span and still being in their *"Sunday Best"* having attended church, they did not have to change. In just over half an hour Algernon was driving them to the Frost's home which was about 20 minutes away by car.

Before they left, Algernon phoned his parents with the good news, telling them all about Sam and explaining everything. His parents and their children, who could meet their half brother for the first time, would all come down to London for the wedding, which would be on Sam's next leave home, whenever that may be as the war dictated.

Unbeknown to Keturah and Alice, Algernon had picked up a couple of bottles of champagne and glasses before putting them in a wicker basket, which he smuggled out when he went to start up the car. Algernon left in the knowledge they could all drink a toast to the forthcoming marriage of Alice and Sam in the correct manner when they got there.

***

In September 1917 the Royal Flying Corp set up a special flying school to teach aerial combat, the first *"Top Gun"* conceived. ■ In October a secret report was presented to the British War Cabinet recommending that an autonomous air force should be created, separate from both the Royal Navy and Army.

***

Over the weeks that followed the pattern was the same, they went out to draw up the enemy to fight; they also escorted reconnaissance scouts who were taking photos of the trenches, battery positions, railway installations and anything else that caught the eye of the trained flight observers.

They suffered many losses, mainly from the newcomers. The replacements that they received were very green. To get more pilots to the front as quickly as possible flying training hours were cut back at the training school to what the pilots at the front considered was a dangerously low level. They were proved right, the new comers did not last long, Not many made 5 sorties, if that; a number did not return from their first flight, but now they were flying in big wings they had a better chance as was starting to show, they could protect the sprogs to some extent.

Sam soon got the hang of things, and in the first month he had bagged two of the enemy, with only a few bullet holes in his wing and tail, none of which stopped him flying, but he made a dash for home as advised. He lived to fight another day. He always kept in mind what Colonel Cavendish had written *'The Fighter Pilot's 10 Commandments'*. His tally of German aircraft shot down rose steadily.

They had been there about six weeks when they lost A Flight Commander. Promotion was rapid on the front; places had to be filled immediately. Pete was promoted to Captain and became A Flight Commander while Sam was now the senior pilot of the flight after Captain Urquhart. Not long afterwards, Major Farquhar was injured while in a dog fight, he managed to get back to base and was taken by a horse ambulance, all that was available, to hospital. He survived his injuries but never returned to flying duties. Promotion was rapid again, Captain Urquhart took over as CO of the squadron, becoming a Major, and Sam was raised to the rank of Captain, moving across to B Flight as its Commander and received news that he had been awarded his first decoration for bravery, the Distinguished Service Order, a cross that hung from a purple ribbon, with two narrow vertical blue strips on either side. When and by whom it would be presented no one said, or perhaps no one knew.

Sam, now in command of his own flight progressed rapidly; he thrived on authority and leadership. These qualities were soon recognised by Major Urquhart and were passed on to Lieutenant-Colonel Andrews. Andrews noted him down to be a potential Squadron Commander when a vacancy occurred in any of the front line squadrons. This never seemed to be a very long way away with all the aerial combat that they had to undertake.

But Sam had other things on his mind, besides running his flight and flying, he had received a letter from Alice, and joy of joys, she had agreed to marry him, and as he had a photo of her, could she have one of him. An answer was soon winging its way back to her, with a photo of him sitting in the cockpit of his aircraft, saying he could not return home soon enough, unfortunately he had no idea when that would happen. But the day after he had sent his reply to Alice things changed.

Sam returned home sooner than he thought. One day on patrol over enemy lines in early 1918, when there was little or no opposition from the Hun that day, the squadron headed back to base and while flying over the British trenches someone opened fire, thinking they were German aircraft. A number of bullets hit Sam's aircraft, one passing through his thigh, but luckily not hitting any bones. In considerable pain he signalled to his wingman he was hit and was to take over as leader and escort him back to base, which was less that ten minutes flying time away, but to Sam it seemed like ten hours. He landed safely, be it with a few extra bounces, stopping where the landing finished and cutting his engine. This wingman had sent up a red flare to indicate there was a problem and an ambulance was beside Sam's aircraft by the time the propeller had stopped turning.

He was gently taken out of the cockpit, put into the ambulance, and before moving off he was given an injection of morphine and shell dressings were applied to both sides of his leg. He was then taken to a field hospital about 5 miles from the airfield and after a brief look by the doctors there, he was sent further back behind the front line to a major hospital safe away from any action.

He was X-Rayed to confirm that there were no bullet fragments in his leg and the leg was stitched up both sides and clean bandages applied. By the following morning, he was back in the land of the living and on morphine pain killers. When the surgeon saw Sam on his morning rounds the following day, he was told that he would be on the next ambulance train and ferry back to Blighty for convalesce. When he was medically fit it would be up to the *Powers To Be* in the RFC as to what he was fit to do next, but he was expect he would be back to the fray as soon as possible, pilots were urgently needed.

To Sam this was bad news and good news. The bad news was that while he had shot down a number of German aircraft and strafed many ground targets, and therefore must have killed and injured many Germans, he still felt he had not avenged Bill's death to his satisfaction. The good news was he and Alice could get married sooner than he had hoped. When Alice had consented, he did not think they would get married until the war was over. He got pen and paper and wrote a short letter to Alice telling her of the situation and asked her to start looking to get the banns called in her local church.

***

Alice received Sam letter before he had left the hospital and was very upset to hear that he had been wounded but understood it was not life threatening, he would have a limp and walk with a stick for a while.

No sooner had she read Sam's letter, she was on the phone to Keturah reading out what Sam had written. "He got shot in the leg by friendly fire, it was only a flesh wound, but they are sending him home to convalesce and he wants us to are get married as soon as he gets back and I will start to arrange the wedding at the our church today," she finished. Keturah, like Alice, was upset Sam had been injured, but pleased it was only minor wound and he would be home soon to recuperate and to get married.

Alice went down to see the vicar of St Stephen and St Thomas church and between them they worked out a plan of action. No dates could be set until Sam had returned and had been discharged from the hospital, he would only then be sent on convalesce leave, she hoped it would not be too far away. Another phone call to Keturah, keeping her in the picture. Keturah felt that there could be no better wife for him, she was very found of this young girl. Like her parents, the Frost's were working class; she had nothing against that, the salt of the earth. Wasn't she from a working class family, she would never forget her roots, and looking back on it, she was proud of her upbringing, even though she had been a troublesome child to her parents.

CHAPTER 14

The Final Hurdle

The War Office sent a message to the RFC Brigade HQ in the Ypres area calling for them to recommend an above average pilot of Flight Commander Status and inline to be a Squadron Commander. They stipulated that the person nominated will be required for special duties in a new sphere of flying, returning to England for conversion to a new type of aircraft. On receipt of this message, the Brigade recommended a Captain S Bray, DSO, of 8 Squadron, who had recently been slightly wounded in the leg, and was soon to be repatriated from hospital in the local area and will soon be on his way back to England for recovery in a home hospital followed by a short spell of convalesce leave, and would probably be fit to fly, according to the medics, within the month. As he was due to return to his squadron on completion of his leave, please advise if he has been selected for these special duties. In reply they confirmed they would be interviewing the said Captain S Bray and that they would duly inform them of their decision in due course.

***

As soon as they considered Sam fit to travel his return was swift. He was told he would be going to a military hospital just outside London. An ambulance train took him to the channel port of Calais, a naval hospital ship across the channel to Folkestone, and finally another ambulance train across the Home Counties to Reading. The ambulance train was warm and comfortable, as was the boat on the channel crossing, the best the three journeys he had by boat, and the final stage by train was just as comfortable. It was not that long ago he recalled he had travelled 3rd class after his escape from being a POW. All in all, this journey was much more comfortable, with doctors and pretty nurses to give him loving tender care all the way!

On arrival at Reading, he was taken by ambulance to a hospital west of the town off the Oxford Road to keep him fairly close to London and the RFC Headquarters. This building he went to was completed and opened in 1867 as the Reading Union Workhouse and after passing through a few minor changes over the years, which included adding an infirmary in 1889, became the second hospital in Reading, the oldest being the Royal Berkshire Hospital, south of the town, that had opened in 1839. Within a year of the war starting, there was a desperate shortage of beds for the wounded returning home from across the Channel and the buildings within the site off Oxford Road were taken over by the military that became know for the duration of the war and afterwards as the Reading War Hospital, where Sam found himself ensconced at the end of his long journey. The Royal Berks also took in a number of military patients but still catered for the local population.

On his arrival he was put in a side ward on his own and he immediately asked the Ward Sister if he could phone his next of kin, briefly explaining the situation. They considered this a priority as it would help the patient's health if he had no worries. He was now on the mend and off all painkillers.

***

From the outbreak of war and its duration, it was difficult, if not possible, to get a telephone installed unless it was a priority case. After Bert had been accepted by Sopwith, he was getting a lot of orders and had to give daily updates on progress of work to them, it was an essential tool, letters were too slow, taking a day at least to reach there destination. He applied to the local telephone exchange, his application was turned down by the phone company, until he got the backing of Sopwith and the RFC section of the War Office and he was soon connected as a 'war priority'.

It was mid afternoon when the call came through from Reading but Alice was out at the local post office with all the days outgoing mail, Bert having taken her place keeping up with the paper work and listening for the phone. When the phone did ring, expecting it to be Sopwith about some work or problem, he was surprised to hear Sam's voice who told him where he was and gave him the hospital phone number where they could reach him. He also told him he would be released soon and asked, once he had found somewhere to stay, if he could see them all while on his convalescent leave before he had to return to Belgium. Bert was overjoyed to hear from Sam and nothing would make him and the family happier to have Sam come round visit. When Alice returned home she was very annoyed at have missed talking to Sam and had to be satisfied with the news that he would be coming to see them. She had a quick chat with her mother about accommodation but with the loss of the boy's rooms being converted to workshops when Bert had expanded just before the war started and their house now only had three bedrooms, the two that Alice and Fred used, and these were only small singles, they would have to look elsewhere for Sam to stay.

Alice phoned Keturah as soon as she had had her chat with her mother to tell her the news and she would let her know when visiting hours were so they could make arrangements for them to visit him and Keturah and Sam could have their first meeting, after nearly 20 years. She told them that they were going to look for somewhere for Sam to stay when he was released from hospital. Keturah had other ideas, but she did not say anything she would discuss her ideas with Algernon when he returned from work.

After Keturah had told Algernon about Sam being back and in a Hospital on Reading, he had other ideas that she got very excited about and could not get to the phone quick enough to tell Alice of Algernon's idea. Algernon had phoned the hospital and got the times of visiting, pulled a bit of rank and got permission for three of them to visit, not the regulation of two visitors at a time. It was Thursday, he would take Saturday off and they would all drive to Reading in his London car and give Sam a pleasant surprise.

On Saturday, Keturah and Algernon, in uniform, left just after eleven, only stopping to pick up Alice on the way, who had been told by Agnes that she and Bert sent their love. The nearly 40 mile journey took just over the hour, arriving at Reading for lunch at the Great Western Hotel in station square across from the station. The hotel had opened four years after the GWR reached Reading in 1840, one of the earliest railway hotels in the country, and reputedly I K Brunel had a large input into its design.

By 2 o'clock they presented themselves to Sam's Ward Sister. Sam had not been told of the visit, they wanted it to be double surprise, which it was. When they arrived at the ward they decided that Alice should go in first and have a little time alone with Sam, she deserved it. The sister took Alice to the side ward that Sam was in, opening the door telling him he had three visitors, on which Alice entered, and the sister went out closing the door behind her, she knew when she was not wanted!

Sam was surprised and was lost for words when he saw Alice. After a long hug and many kisses, Sam then found his voice, "When did you leave home, it's a longish journey by train, and the sister said I was expecting three visitors, have your Mum & Dad come as well?"

Alice had a secret smile on her face. "No," she replied, "I came by a car, with a very smart chauffeur in uniform, driven all the way, door to door, what you think of that Sam my darling?" This was a white lie, but not far from the truth!

Sam did not know what to think of that and did not know her well enough to know when she was telling white lies so he decided to have another kiss and cuddle. After a few minutes, when Alice eventually got out of Sam's clutches she said, "I have a surprise for you Sam," and she went to the door and opened it to let Algernon, without his cap on, and Keturah, the latter who had been hopping up and down, waiting for Alice's call. "Sam," she said in a very emotional voice, "this is Brigadier General, the Honourable Algernon Cavendish, my chauffeur," turning to Algernon with a big grin and cheeky smile, "of the Royal Flying Corps and his wife, Mrs Keturah Cavendish."

Sam looked bewildered at Alice and at the couple who had just walked in. He noticed that the lady, while not crying, had tears in her eyes and a smile on her face, *what could this be all about?* And the gentlemen looked vaguely familiar; he had seen him before somewhere, *but where?* As no one spoke, Sam felt he should say something and then he remembered where he had seen the man standing at the end of his bed. "Sir, were you not the outgoing Colonel of the *Ypres Wing* just after I arrived on the Western Front?" to which Algernon agreed with a nod and a grin, but still no one spoke.

Sam was getting frustrated with silence and asked, "Will someone please tell me what's going on, why are you both here? What's all the secrecy? I did not know you were friends of Alice, Sir, and who is Mrs Cavendish, Alice?"

"Of course you may," said Alice with a happy smile, her eyes shining with tears, taking Keturah by the hand, leading her over to Sam's bedside and placing Keturah's hand in Sam's, said, "because Sam, this lady as I said is Keturah, and before she married Algernon she was Keturah Bray, she is your mother."

Sam was struck dumb, but not so Keturah, "Sam, Sam, my darling Sam," she cried and bent over and took him in her arms, tears running down her face as she hugged him like there was no tomorrow, she was then struck dumb with emotion, tears were now running down all faces, there was not a dry eye anywhere. When they had all gathered themselves, they all sat down around Sam's bed, Alice holding one hand while Keturah was holding the other and Algernon looking on with a smile on his face. "It seems if I have gained a stepson today," he remarked with a smile, "and what I hear a very brave one too. I hear you were recently awarded the DSO; I'm very proud of you and I welcome you into our family. As soon as you are well enough, you must meet my parents; spend your convalescent leave with them." More tears and hugs all round.

After about an hour all had been explained, Keturah gave her son an honest account of her life, not omitting out the early days, she felt he was entitled to know this part of her life. She also told Sam she was Bill's mother as well, and therefore Bill was his half brother and knew all the sad news about him, which in a way made Bill's loss even worse, a few more tears were shed. Sam then realised why he and Bill always got on so well and were so alike in looks, temperament and ability, it explained everything after all these years.

In return, Sam told them about Bill and their time at the orphanage before the Frosts came into the picture. Alice had already told them about the time they worked for her Dad and Sam gave a very brief resume of his army career as well, not mentioning how he enlisted using Bill's birth certificate, the time he was arrested, the Court Martial and finally his escape back to England. All he said of this episode was he had applied to re-muster to the RFC, was accepted as a rigger and after training become a pilot. His three visitors never asked any questions and accepted his story, not asking for anymore details, they could not see any reason why they should, which Sam was glad, the more he told white lies, the more chance of a slip up. This was his secret he would keep as long as he lived, but perhaps he would confide with Alice at a later date, but for the time being, it was best left under the blanket! He knew he could never hide anything from Alice, especially after they were married!

"Sam," said Algernon, "you can't keep calling me *"Sir"* for the rest of you life, I would like you to call me Algernon if that is alright with you?" Before he could reply Keturah chipped in, "Sam, I think you are too old to start calling me Mother now, I think Keturah would be better, and that goes for Alice as well, we would both like you to use our Christian names from now on, I hope that's all right with you both."

Sam looked at Alice, she was smiling, and they both looked at Keturah and Algernon and nodded their agreement, their eyes shining with tears.

When they left, after over two hours, well past the end of visiting time, Brigadier Generals get dispensation, all the wedding arrangements had been made and the banns would be called for the first time tomorrow and Sam and Alice would be married in three weeks time. Sam had been told he would be walking within seven days, but with the assistance of sticks at first.

They had discussed the wedding, presents, reception and guests, Algernon's family on his side and Alice's on hers. Sam wanted some personal friends, a number of RFC officers he had become acquainted with, they would form a Guard of Honour after the wedding, which did not surprise any of them. What did surprise them was when he mentioned the Eighteens, who his visitors had never heard of. Sam explained how he had met them, telling them who they were and how they had come into his life and how very good they were to him before he joined up. Because he would not be able to get to see them until he was discharged, he asked Alice to go round to see them and explain everything to them and also and invite them to the wedding.

In the general conversation, Alice had told Sam that her Dad had now had their own transport, which was obtained with the aid of Sopwith and the War Office, a solid four wheeled lorry for making deliveries, and as a driver an ex-army soldier who had been discharged on medical grounds, but fit enough to drive. Sam thought it would be a good chance to pick up his chest and suggested to Alice to approach her father to see if he would help.

As she wanted to see the Eighteens, she asked her Dad when she got home if she could, when the lorry was passing in that direction, go with them to collect Sam's chest from there. He was happy to do this small service for Sam and the next time the lorry was out she went with it, knowing the chest was under the cutting table, where, if she looked hard enough, she would also find the key! It was not long before Sam's chest was in Alice's bedroom, ready for Sam to have a look. This was the only place they could be alone together, her parents had complete trust in them both.

Alice's first call on Sunday, before going to the morning church service at St Stephen and St Thomas, was to arrange with the vicar for the banns to be called that day. On the way back from church she went round to see the Eighteens, introduced herself and explained the good news to them that she and Sam were getting married, telling them about the wedding and telling them they would be special guests. They were all thrilled and would be only to happy to attend. Then the question of wedding presents came up, but Alice said she had not given much thought to this question and would let them know it good time. While they all had been chatting, Marie was getting an idea. Before she had married Isaac she had trained to be a dressmaker and still kept up her skills for herself and friends, it was a bit of extra money. "Alice," she said, "would you like me to make your wedding dress as our wedding present to you?"

For a moment Alice was speechless. She got up and hugged Marie with tears in her eyes. "Thank You, Thank You, Thank You," was the only reply she could think off. Marie was so pleased, while she had made a few wedding dresses in the past, she had not made one for many years, and was thrilled with the opportunity to do so again. Marie and Alice took their chairs and went into a huddle in the corner, away from the men, and made the plans and arrangements for getting the dress made, looking at current wedding dress designs in trade magazines. Maria would design the dress herself with Alice's input.

Sam recovered well and was discharged from hospital within the week. Algernon again drove to Reading with Keturah and Alice, collected Sam from the hospital and were soon at Grafton for lunch. The first of many visits to the Manor Alice made.

Algernon had rung his parents asking them if Sam could spend his convalescent leave recuperating there for a week and they were only too willing, when the grandchildren were away at school during the week they had little company and welcomed some one to fill in the time from Monday to Friday. Algernon had told his parents about Bill and Sam some time ago and they accepted the situation, as their son had. No sooner had he arrived, Sam was chatting to the Earl and Countess like he had chatted with his mother and Algernon. Sam had been asked to call them Jonathan and Isabel, they felt adults should be on the same level, a modern way of thinking, not by the current thinking of separation by generations. They asked him a lot of questions about warfare on the front and were both proud to have him as a member of their family, which they now considered he was, but were horrified when he told them about the atrocities and conditions some of the troops had to endure.

***

Early in the day of 28 March 1918, the German Chief of Staff, General Erich von Ludendorf, deployed troops which carried out a successful onslaught on Vimy Ridge. Three days later, with re-enforcements from the Eastern Front, his troops shattered the British lines in France in the Arras area hoping to reach the English Channel. Instead of a massive infantry charge new tactics were employed; short bombardment of high explosives, smoke shells and gas, followed by shock troops to probe weak spots to be exploited by infantry combat teams, the forerunner of the German *Blitzkrieg*... ■ The Government in 1916, headed by Prime Minister Lloyd George, were unhappy about the two separate flying forces, the Royal Flying Corp and the Royal Naval Air Service. Each was desperately after aircraft and engines, in detriment to the other, which did not help the war effort. The current thinking was for an independent air force. A committee was set up by the PM, General Jan Christiaan Smuts and General Sir David Henderson, and during the summer of 1917 two meetings took place which finally recommended that an independent air force be set up, partly in response to the public outcry for retaliation for German bombing raids on British cities, especially London. It was planned that on the 1st April 1918, the Royal Air Force would be formed out of the two air services, RFC and RNAS. ■ Also a new service was formed for women, the Women's Royal Air Force, Sylvia Hodkinson being their first recruit.

***

Sam had not been long at Grafton when he had a visit by a RFC Colonel from the War Office, who arrived in an official staff car. He soon got down to business, he had no time to waste he told Sam. "Bray, I have been interviewing pilots and gunners for special duties in London, but as you are convalescing I have had to make a special visit to see you, it gets me out of

308

the office for a day, which I'm glad of. You have been selected for these special duties because we consider you are an above average pilot". Sam could feel his ears burning. "The Germans have bombed us and our Government and the civilians of this country want retribution. We will be creating a new squadron, a bomber squadron here, more highly trained than previous squadrons, concentrating on navigation, bomb aiming, night formation and flying at high or low level, with the latest bomber we have, much superior to the current bomber. When trained you will be based initially in France, within striking distance of suitable targets in Germany, and carry out bombing raids in an attempt to destroy as many selected targets as we possibly can. Your main targets will be their supply routes, mainly marshalling yards and railway junctions, to stop supplies getting through and empty trains returning for more and secondly industrial targets such as factories and storage areas in the main.

"Now, this is where you come in. When you have finished your leave you will report to CFS at Upavon, which I see from your records you have been there before. When you get there you will meet up with other pilots who are also training to fly our new bomber, the Handley Page HP O/400, which has a crew of three, made up of a pilots and two gunners, you will get more details about the aircraft when you get there. We are over subscribed, intentionally, so we end up with the cream of the cream. There will be six potential flight commander pilots and 12 potential junior pilots and 30 well seasoned gunners on the course. The numbers will be whittled away until we end up with the number we require, in your case four flight commanders, eight junior pilots and 24 gunners, the remaining pilots and gunners will be helping as replacements, which we hope will not be needed. If you complete the course and pass, you will then be a fully fledged captain of a HP 0/400 bomber and you will be one of the four flight commanders," were his closing remarks.

With a twinkle in his eye he continued, "I understand from your step father, who I know very well, you are getting married soon. He works in an office a few doors from mine, we have no secrets in that department, family wise that is! Congratulations."

Sam stammered out his thanks but the Colonel had the last word, "You will have to fit in you wedding around your service commitments, there is just enough time to get married and have a short honeymoon before your course starts. When you have completed the course, you will go to the Handley Page factory at Cricklewood, in North West London, with the other pilots who have passed the course and there you will then test fly your allotted aircraft. When all is ready you will fly out as a squadron to a staging post in France. All the aircrafts will be ready by the time your course had been completed, which we hope will not be more than a month, less if possible. Lastly, your Squadron Commander, Major Anthony Norton, has already converted and you will meet him at CFS where he will be keeping a close eye on you all and making his selection, anyone who does not come up to mustard won't be on the short list, so watch yourself. If you want to be a part of this new unit, pioneers, make sure you do well! I'm off to see the other five potential Flight Commanders. Any questions Bray?"

"Sir, if I don't pass the course, what will happen to me then?" Sam asked.

"You will be back on the front flying fighters again, but if we lose a pilot, we may call on you as a replacement. If that's what you would prefer, tell me now and I will cross you off my list?" was his reply.

"No Sir, I like the idea of a new challenge, I have every intention of being one of your new bomber flight commanders," Sam answered.

"Glad to hear that, it was the answer I was looking for," and with that he took his leave in the car that had been waiting for him, making his way back to his office in the War Ministry in London.

***

At the end of the week, Algernon arrived at the Manor by car to take his parents, children and Sam back to their house in Notting Hill Gate in preparation for the wedding. When they arrived back there Keturah was there to greet them all at the door. In the evening she had arranged a special dinner and had invited the Frosts and the Eighteens. It was an evening enjoyed by all, everyone getting to know each other, which saved a lot of ice breaking on the wedding day.

After the meal was over they all retired to the lounge for coffee, talking about the war and war related tales and when there was a lull in the conversation Algernon remembered a story he had recently heard. "I've heard a strange tale the other day," he said, "true, but strange, as told to me by one of my ex-Flight Commanders, now a major, who was my *Ypres Wing* when I was there and I recently met him again when I was on a visit to the Central Flying School at Upavon where he is now a flying instructor."

"I was sitting in the mess after lunch when he walked in. I was very surprised to see him, you could have knocked me down with a feather, as the last I knew of him was that he was lost in action, missing believed killed. I hadn't heard anything of him since, dead or alive. It was while I was in command of the *Wing* that I first met him and it was towards the end of my tour there I planned a major bombing raid on a railway junction with all five squadrons. The first raid did not do all the damage I had hoped for, so I sent them in for a second go, which was very successful, put the junction out of

310

action completely for nearly a week, and before it was partly repaired, I heard when I got back that we kept having another go at it from time to time. Now back to the story. Unfortunately this chap I met was the only one who didn't return from my second raid. We never heard what happened to him, no one saw him go down, had he been killed or captured and taken prisoner? We didn't get anything from the Germans via the Red Cross. So that was the situation when I left Ypres and came home. His CO sent his next of kin a letter saying he was posted as missing and would let them know as soon as they had anything more definite," pausing for breath.

"Alg, what's the name of this pilot? Don't keep it a secret, do I know him?" Keturah asked her husband.

Algernon laughed, "Sorry, got carried away, no you don't know him Ket, he was Captain Tim Gledhill then and was a senior Flight Commander in one of my squadrons, in line for promotion I understand, when he was lost doing escort duties to the slower bombers," he told them.

It was lucky for Sam they were all looking at Algernon, if they had looked at him they would have seen his face was drained of colour, how would his stepfather finish this tale? He hoped nothing was given away or connected with him in this part of the story.

"To continue," he said, while Sam looked on trying to hide the worried look on his face, "when I was rudely interrupted," and immediately got a rebuke from his mother and wife, to his amusement! "This is what Tim told me. His aircraft was badly damaged on their return to base, his engine was shot up, but he did manage to shoot his opponent down with the last of his ammo but he soon lost him from sight going down in smoke in the opposite direction. But Tim had his own problems to worry about to care what had happened to the Bosh, there were no British aircraft in the vicinity to help or report his crash, but his main objective was to get down in one piece and stay alive, he had to find a suitable place to land. Just to his right was a small field surrounded by woods and he was able to crash landed in this with little or no room to spare, ending up in the woods at the far end, hidden from above, which was lucky for him as he was in enemy country, also, luckily, there was no fire, but he was knocked unconscious so did not realise this until after he had been rescued. When he came round, he found he had been dragged from his wrecked aircraft and taken a safe distance away by a scruffy young lad, who Tim said looked very shifty and was standing over him in a peaked cap, donkey jacket and overalls. To cut a long story short, this lad was English and a POW on the run trying to make his way back home, called Drew of the West Bristol Fusiliers, and Tim found out later that he had joined up under age. They both made it to Holland and somehow got a RN boat back to Blighty. Drew had been on the run for about a week before Tim met him, he had been captured by the Germans when he had fallen into a Hun trench after a charge on enemy line, he must have become temporary disorientated by shell shock and went the wrong way as so often happened. He became a POW then escaped from a train taking him and another couple of hundred POWs to permanent camp well behind the German front lines. Tim was very impressed by what he had done, he considered him very brave for someone his age as no one else on the train wanted to go with him. When they got back to England they went their separate ways, Tim taking his details so he could write to his CO to praise him and say an official 'Thank You' and to say he felt he deserve some sort of decoration for what he had done, but he did point out he was under age."

"Now here comes the strange part. He got a letter back from the CO saying that the soldier who Tim wrote about, a Private Robert Drew, giving his service number, had been killed in action about a month previous to when Tim had been shot down and his body had been recovered from no-mans-land and buried with military honours and they had recently received his ID tags to prove this. Also they had proof from his joining up papers that he was over 18 years of age when he joined up many months previous. That was all they could tell him and felt that Tim had somehow got the wrong soldier. There was nothing more Tim could do."

Algernon looked around his silent and intrigued audience. "So," he said, "how can a dead man be a POW on the run at the same time as being dead. Tim could not say enough in his favour and thought he had potential for promotion. The only thing that could be proved was that the real Drew was over 18 and dead, while the Drew Tim knew admitted to him he was under age when he joined up, so who was the second Drew, and where is he now and why had he disappeared? He must have been masquerading as Drew, but why? So who was he? Has anyone have ideas?" They all discussed the whys and the wherefores, but no one could provide a solution that ticked all the boxes. No one noticed that Sam kept a very low profile on the whole affair, the only one who could tick all the boxes!

***

A few days later, when they had not been back long in London, Sam asked Algernon if he could borrow his car and visit the Frosts and the Eighteens on their own ground. He first went to the Eighteens and on entering the shop was given a warm greeting by father and son, which was the norm for them. They invited him upstairs, Sam giving the cutting table a shake as he passed, it did not move, solid as a rock. As he arrived at the top of the stairs, Marie was there to welcome him and he was soon in her embrace. But she barred his way into the room pushing him pack with her hand on his chest. "Sam, you can't come in, I am making Alice's wedding dress in there, and you are not to see it, this is as far as you go!" she said with a smile on her face and a chuckle in her throat. Sam knew when he was beaten, so he, Isaac and Joseph all retired down stairs to the shop for a chat. Isaac felt they all deserved a drink and while pouring a sherry asked Sam what he would be wearing to the wedding and did he require a suit? Sam said No and Yes. He only had one suit that they had made over three years ago and felt he would like a new one, but at the wedding he would be in his best RFC uniform, the RAF had not yet got around to issuing their uniforms, well not to the lower officer ranks!

After about half an hour he left for the Frosts home. On entering the workshop there was a big cheer by all the staff who knew him, including Bert and Fred. Alice came out of the office to see what all the noise was about and soon found out, which caused her to turn back into the office to hide her blushes! He shook hands with them all before going up stairs with Bert and Alice to see Agnes. The living room was up to neck in preparations for the wedding; everywhere he went it was the same! Even at Notting Hill he was only allowed in certain rooms. What was the world coming to, surely weddings were not all like this, but he kept his thoughts to himself. After giving Agnes a hug, he embraced Alice and kissed her, to her embarrassment in front of all her family, her face changing to a delicate shade of pink, and when she could get out of his grips, pushed him away with a playful slap on his arm!

***

The wedding of Alice and Sam took place on the afternoon of Saturday, the 6th day of April, a bright blustery day for the month; March had gone out like a lion! The ceremony was conducted at the Frost's church, St Stephen and St Thomas, near Shepherd's Bush and was full with the families and close friends of Cavendish from the Reading area and the Frosts from around Shepherd's Bush. Also invited were Mr Newbury and Miss King, who had been the Governor and Senior Matron at the Bernard's Home, when Bill and Sam had been there, now both retired. They both knew about Bill's death, having seen the same article that Keturah had, and were both saddened by the loss, like many other lads from the home who had lost their lives, but were compensated by seeing Sam, alive and well, and a hero to boot. Also invited were a number of officers, Majors Kirkpatrick and Moreton from Farnborough and his friends he worked with there, other RAF officers home on leave or reoccupation after being wounded, and anyone else who had helped Sam to get to the position he now enjoyed.

On the day of the wedding, the bride, escorted up the aisle by her father, looked splendent in her shimmering white floor length wedding dress with a train all which had been designed and lovingly created by Maria, which everyone thought they had not seen such a pretty gown before. The train was held by Keturah and Algernon's daughter Jane Ellen, followed by Benjamin as a pageboy. As Alice approached the alter she saw Rupert, Sam's Best Man, and Sam in his best uniform. The groom, now in the RAF since last Monday, but still wearing his RFC khaki uniform, rank and insignia of a Captain, with medals hanging from his left chest.

On leaving the church as man and wife, the bell rung a greeting that could be heard over a mile away. The RAF officers formed a *Guard of Honour* with swords unsheathed, forming an arch for the *Happy Couple* to walk under, being showered with confetti as they made their way through. A photographer had been hired by Algernon to record the occasion, with his large plate camera and hood. The now Captain and Mrs Bray were taken by open carriage, pulled by two horses, to the Cavendish residence in Notting Hill Gate where a lavish wedding dinner took place. After the dinner concluded the guests retired to the lounge for drinks and socialising while the bride and groom went up stairs to change for their honeymoon.

When they descended the stairs all were gathered in the hall to wish them *bon voyage*. A taxi was waiting for them and with a second shower of confetti they left for their honeymoon destination of Brighton, making their way to one of the London rail terminal servicing the south coast, Waterloo.

Their honeymooned at the Grand Hotel overlooked both piers, Palace and West and the sea, it was a period of bliss as they could get better acquainted and to know each other more intimately as husband and wife. Neither of them had been to Brighton before, going out each day exploring different parts of the town, they practically liked the *Lanes*, fascinated by all the small shop and the range of goods one could buy there. After much deliberation they purchased a small round mahogany coffee table, not to large to carry home, but it being their first item they had bought together and a starter for when they set up home as soon as the war was over, but that horizon could not yet be seen. The week soon sped by and on the following Saturday they returned to Notting Hill.

In the evening of their return, Alice and Sam went to see her parents, for Sam to say goodbye, as he was leaving the following day for Upavon, and returning to Notting Hill to spent the night together.

The following morning Algernon drove Sam, with all his kit, to Paddington, accompanied by Alice and Keturah. As the train left, with everyone waving goodbye, there were tears in both girls' eyes. Afterward Algernon drove Alice back to her parents home where she would stay, continuing to help as the firms secretary at the factory, until Sam returned home permanently, to set up a home together, hopefully still in the RAF as it was now, to wherever he may ever be posted, with their newly acquired coffee table!

***

The war was not going the way the Government or the service Chiefs had wanted or planned. By about mid April von Ludendorf struck again, he broadened his offensive in another area, breaking through at Ypres and further north. Was this man turning the tides of war in favour of the Kaiser and the German fighting forces?

***

On arrival at Upavon, in the early afternoon, Sam was billeted in the Officer's Mess, much better accommodation than the Cadets Mess he had stayed in on his previous training course there. Before dinner, with the five other potential Captains on the course, they strolled up to the airfield to get their first view of the Handley Page 0/400, a twin engine tractor biplane. None of them had flown anything as big as this before, only a single engine, one or two seater aircraft, and as one of the pilots remarked, "With two engines you must have a better chance of getting back home if one packs up," which they all agreed was true.

The following morning all the pilots on the course were assembled in the main lecture hall. The course Commandant welcomed them to Upavon and the HP 0/400 Conversation Course. "Gentlemen," the Commandant addressed the assembled pilots and gunners. "First I would like to introduce you to Major Anthony Norton, who will be your Squadron Commander to those who complete and pass the course. As well as the instructors here, Major Norton will also be assessing you for suitability."

He paused and looked around the 36 trainees. "You are attending the third of a number of courses we are holding over the next few months for conversion to the HP 0/400. The HP 0/400, which is an improvement over the HP 0/100, and has more powerful engines, faster speed and a larger bomb load. It has one pilot position, the duration of the flight can be anything up to eight hours. Armament, the aircraft can carry up to about 1 ton of bombs, 20 x 112 pounds or 8 x 250 pounds internally, not hung from your wings causing drag, and you will use the Mk 1a Drift bomb sight that the front

315

gunner will operate, and you the pilot will release the bombs. There are two gunners, all with Lewis guns, one in the nose, one behind the pilot's cockpit, and lastly one gun firing down through a trap door in the fuselage, to catch anyone coming from behind and below, all firing .303 ammo, the rear gunner has to decide which guns to use, upwards or downwards. The aircraft is powered by two Rolls-Royce Eagle VIII engines of 360HP, it will fly on one if you have trouble, best ditch all bombs and if you feel safe, guns and ammo. Max speed is 97.5mph, ceiling 8500ft and it will take you 23 minutes to reach 5000ft. Because of this, all airfields where the bomber will be based, are some distance behind the front lines to allow you to get as high as possible before crossing over to the other side. More details of there aircraft you will get from your pilot's notes with which you will be issued as you leave the hall. Finally, this aircraft is better that what the Germans currently have, the Gotha. Any questions?" Dead silence. "OK, if there are no questions get your flying kit on and let's start the training."

The two weeks soon went, the first week was taken up flying over Salisbury plain in daylight with two different ex-fighter gunners firing at targets towed behind the aircraft and dropped bombs on dummy building, results ranging from average to very good, and soon the poor performing gunners were identified. The second week was devoted to night flying, Sam's experience was very limited in the fighter aircraft, mainly either on a pre-dawn take off or being delayed after an evening patrol when darkness had fallen, he had never carried out any all night patrols. An airstrip was laid out with *goose neck* flares facing into the prevailing wind. The takeoff gave him little or no problem but navigating in the dark required all the skills he had learnt at Farnborough and now this was in the dark, thank goodness there was a good downward facing light in the cockpit, essential in the work they would be doing! They were given triangular courses to follow, different each night. The last problem was landing,as the flares only gave enough light for the pilot to home in and line up on the landing strip, judging the height and landing on the first pair of flares caused most difficulty. Before they took off, they were told in no uncertain terms, if in doubt, abort and go round again, it was not a mark against them, it was more the opposite. Sam, like all the others there, had a few aborted attempts but no crash landings. By the end of the week he was quite confident, and on the final night he came straight in and landed, much to his satisfaction. Sam was very comfortable with flying this aircraft, it was slower and heavier than the nimble fighters he had flown but this was a different challenge.

The course soon came to a conclusion. On the final day they were all tested in both daylight and night time flying to whittle the number down to what was required, Sam was the top pilot on the course and with two other pilots received an above average rating. While they were on the course their new Squadron Commander had been keeping a close eye on the potential pilots and with input from him and the flying instructors, soon whittled away at the potential pilots and crew and had selected the personnel they required, those who had not 'made it' were put on the reserve list.

After the farewell dinner Major Norton took Sam to one side. "Sam, I am very impressed with your performance and as such you are appointed as senior pilot after me, and if anything happens while we are airborne you take over. Once we have done a few raids, I will let you lead while I take you place to let you get experience, how does that sound?"

"That's OK by me Sir," was Sam's reply. "I am very pleased in this change of flying, but as they say, the proof of the pudding is in the eating!"

Those graduating from the course went *en bloc* by trains to Cricklewood, arriving late afternoon and booking into a hotel where they were shown to their rooms that had being booked for them for as long as was required, probably three or four nights. In the evening they all met in the bar where the CO only allowed one round of drinks! The following morning, early, transport was waiting to take them to Cricklewood where the Handley Page had their factory and airfield. As they alighted from the vehicles outside the workshop hangars they were greeted with all 12 of the HP 0/400 aircraft lined up on the apron. In the Aircraft Reception Office they were told all the aircraft had been tested, any snags were rectified and they were ready to handover to the RAF. They were given their log books of their aircraft and told to report to the ground crew who would show them round and prepare the aircraft for their test flight. By mid morning they were ready to take to the air in their allotted aircraft, just like Brooklands when he collected his Sopwith Camel, but this was on a bigger scale! They took off in turn, first the CO, followed by Sam as senior Flight Commander. The plan was, once they were all airborne, to fly in pre-planned formation for about an hour then break up and have an hour on their own, each having been given an area to themselves to fly in, before returning to base for a late lunch. The rest of the afternoon was spent checking the aircraft over and sorting out any snags that had arisen from their flight. The next day was reserved for any more flight test arising from any snags found on the previous day, once these had all been cleared up they were stood down.

The Squadron Commander, knowing tomorrow was the last chance any of them would be able to see their loved ones and friends again for God knows when, maybe for the very last time; they were all released from duty until early the day after tomorrow. By mid afternoon all was completed at the Handley Page works and everyone, including the Boss, all went their various ways.

317

Sam made his way as fast as he could to Notting Hill, where he was not expected, but nonetheless given a warm welcome. Keturah's children and Algernon's parents had returned to the country seat, the children then having to go back to school, so there were only the three of them there. Sam took the car to the Frosts to collect Alice and say his goodbyes to her parents. On the way back he called in to see the Eighteens to say goodbye to them also.

Sam had to be back at Cricklewood late the following day so Algernon took them all to the Savoy for a final dinner that evening. Before they went Algernon asked Alice if her parents would like to accompany them, but Alice knew it would be a waste of time, they did not have the correct clothes to wear and they would feel uncomfortable, the Savoy was not for them!

When Alice and Sam were together, they now always stayed at Notting Hill; Alice's room back in Shepherd's Bush was far too small for both of them and the walls were thin! When they eventually went to bed, alone in their bedroom, before they undressed, Alice took both Sam's hands in hers and looked into his eyes, "Sam, my darling, I hope I have some good news for you. I went to see the doctor this week because I was starting to be sick in the mornings, I thought there was something wrong with me at first," Sam was now looking very worried. Alice saw his concern, "No Sam, there is nothing wrong with me except I'm expecting our baby, are you happy?" Sam was overjoyed with the good news and told her so. "No one else knows Sam, except you and the doctor, he said I'm doing fine and the baby is due in late December, early January, well that's the best he could tell me. I've heard that the majority of babies are later than the forecast!"

"Alice, we must celebrate this now as I will be away tomorrow evening," and knowing that Keturah and Algernon were still up, he dashed down stairs, two at a time, followed by Alice at a more sensible and sedate pace. Without ceremony he flung open the lounge door making his mother and step father both jump, disturbing their quiet night cap.

"Keturah, Algernon, wonderful news, Alice has just told me she is expecting a baby sometime around the New Year," to which Keturah let out a scream of delight, got up from where she was sitting and hugged Sam as hard as she could and giving a good motherly kiss, and as Alice entered the door she also got a hug and kiss from Keturah. Algernon gave his stepson a hug and firm hand shake and for his step daughter-in-law a kiss and hug also. "This calls for a bottle of Champagne to celebrate. Alice, if your parents don't yet know, would you like to phone them up now?"

Alice laughed, "You don't know my Mum and Dad, they are early birds, they will have gone to bed long ago, I'll tell them in the morning, we will try and catch them and Fred at breakfast, that should make for a noisy meal!"

The following morning Alice and Sam went down to see her parents, not in time for breakfast because of Alice's sickness, but in time for the mid morning break, giving them the good news; they again celebrated with a drink, a glass of port each! They returned back to Notting Hill for the rest of the day and Sam and Alice were left on their own, which for Alice was not too soon, not knowing when and if she would ever see her husband ever again, what price war!

That evening Algernon drove Sam over to Cricklewood with Alice and Keturah. Algernon was able to book two double for Keturah and himself while Alice slept in Sam's room, only a single bed, but that was all they needed! An early call was booked for breakfast to make sure they got Sam ready with the rest of the squadron. All the crews were up early, as was Alice, Keturah and Algernon, to say their goodbyes. The crews left in a bus while a black car followed behind. Algernon was well known in flying circles and they were allowed into the complex and watched from a hut adjacent to the airfield but could only see Sam from a distance. The last they saw of him was a wave as he climbed up into the open cockpit, where only his head, in goggles and flying helmet, was now visible.

They took off as the CO had planned. They knew which aircraft Sam was in, watching it start up, taxi round and line up on the grass runway to await the green light. When it came, Sam opened up the two engines; there was a roar and flames issued from the stub exhausts, followed by much exhaust smoke as the aircraft started to roll. As it gathered speed, the aircraft rotated running on its main wheel until it left the ground, crossing the boundary fence, climbing away and was soon lost from sight to those left behind.

The squadron flew directly to their base at Ligescourt in France, a long way from enemy lines and very safe from raids and shell fire. Every bombing raid would start and end well in friendly territory so they could reach their maximum ceiling before venturing over enemy territory. The camp was a more permanent structure compared to a fighter/reconnaissance units Sam was use to, all the personnel were billeted in requisitioned houses and as usual the Officer's Mess was a Château about two miles away.

In less than a week they were off to fly over Germany, linking up with other bomber squadrons, so that they had between 40 and 50 aircraft in all, depending on serviceability, to bomb what was considered major targets which would help to win the war. These targets that the Staff Officers included on their list of required hits were chemical factories first, where it was known poison gas was being produced, aircraft factories and blast furnaces, which were easy targets as they showed up even in daylight, and finally railway junctions. The main towns that were on the end of this onslaught were Frankfurt, Düsseldorf, Cologne and Mannheim.

319

The first raid they went on was an aircraft factory near Düsseldorf with two other bomber squadrons' station in the near vicinity. As they approached the enemy front they picked up an escort of over 50 Sopwith Camels who gave them escort to and from the target. The raid went well but they were harassed by enemy fighters, losses on both sides including two bombers, but none of Sam's squadron.

***

On the 3rd June 1918, a new medal was created, the Distinguished Flying Cross ■ Late in June, Paris was shelled by the German long range guns, the 'Big Bertha' from about 65 miles away. By the end of July von Ludendorf eventually drove across the Marne for 4 miles, but three days later the Allies counter attack, the Germans being driven back and their advances since March had soon all been eroded. The tide was now turning in the favour of the British forces ■ At the beginning of August, British, Americans, Canadian, Australian and French troops attacked at Amiens while 400 tanks spearheaded the initial advance ■ Fighter aircrafts of the RAF were undertaking daily low level machine gun strikes at German infantry columns ■ The enemy were now back to the position they were when they first attacked in late March.

***

Sam's squadron was seeing action most every night using the *goose neck* runway. While some of the other bomber squadrons, the less experienced in night flying were carrying out daylight raids, Major Norton's squadron was detailed, with other squadrons, to carry out night raids. The bombing of the enemy was relentless, day and night, there was no let up and they pounded the enemy in its heartland. In one day, the day raiders dropped 26 tons of bombs while the night raiders, who were nearly double in numbers, dropped 43 tons.

This continued throughout the summer, some raids they suffered no losses to the squadron, on others, they lost aircraft. It was in late August on a raid to Frankfurt that they encountered heavy opposition and to hinder the raid the weather suddenly turned bad as they approached the target. The target was lost in low cloud and Sam dropped his bombs by guess work, he did not think he was anywhere near the target, like the rest of the squadron, he had no intention of taking his heavy load of bombs back home. It was not safe to take bombs home and try and land with them on board, especially at night so they jettisoned their loads as near to the target as they thought was possible. But with the harassment they were getting he wanted to return back to base as soon as possible. Everyone had scattered over the target and Sam found he was on his own, no escort, but thankfully no Huns.

When he got back over British territory and into France the weather cleared enough to see his way home visually and a number of his squadron were to be seen flying around him and they all joined up for the long journey back over enemy territory to the save haven of France and their base. They were the first to land and once they had taxied to the pans and handed over to the ground crew Sam, as senior member of the squadron until the CO arrived, did a head count on who had so far returned. The CO had yet not arrived but more aircrafts were in sight, some damaged but landing safely, some carrying injured crew members. Sam stayed at the airfield until the last aircraft had returned and no one else was expected, as they would be out of fuel by this time. They had three aircrafts unaccounted for; he hoped that those who had not returned had either landed at another airfield or crash landed safely on this of the front.

Sam reported the loss to the RFC Brigade HQ later that morning. There were no raids planned for the next few days, allowing the ground crews time to repair aircraft and get replacements flown in and crews to fill the gaps the losses had created.

The following morning he was told that two of the three missing aircraft were now located, one, while damaged, had landed safely at another airfield, the other had crash landed, minor casualties, but no fatalities, the aircraft a right-off. The third there was no news. He was given no information of which crews were in which aircraft. Later in the morning he was told to report the HQ immediately.

On arrival there he was taken to the office of the Brigadier in charge of all the bomber squadrons. He was a rotund gruff man with short dark hair with streaks of grey already showing, below which were dark bushy eyebrows above a neat military moustache. On his uniform he wore a set of pilot's wings and three rows of campaign ribbons below, some from the second Boar War where he had been in the infantry and in the current war acting as a pilot; obviously he had seen a lot of action, had done very well and had been suitable rewarded for all his efforts. Sam also noticed a walking stick hooked over the back of his chair which made Sam think that after his last sortie he had probably been badly injured and was now flying a desk. Sam entered with a smart salute to the Brigadier, he said nothing to Sam but a wave of his hand, indicating he was to sit in the only other chair, opposite him on the other side of his desk, in the small cold office, the open window contributing to the low temperature. The colonel still liked the cold air he had experienced when flying. When the Brigadier did speak, he spoke in mini sentences that came out from his mouth like bullets from the machine guns he use to fire in his fighter plane, in short rapid bursts, he had never wasted bullets and did not intend to waste words or breath either!

"Bray - - - Bad news - - - sorry to tell you - - - - your CO - - - - - reported missing last night - - - - - been doing checks - - - - - found his aircraft early today - - - - - crashed - - - - - on our side of the lines - - - - - all killed - - - - - aircraft a right-off." He paused to reload for more breath. *"You are senior Flight Commander - - - - - as from today - - - - - promoted to Major - - - - - CO of Squadron - - - - - see my PA, he will give you all the info you require - - - - - best of luck - - - - - carry on".*

The Brigadier did not rise but extended his had to shake Sam's hand but said no more, then waved the same hand at the door indicating the interview was over. And that was how Sam became a major, just short of his twentieth birthday. He reported to the Brigadier's PA and after giving him the 'info' he required, he was then told to see the officer in charge of personnel who told him to select his best Lieutenant for promotion to Captain to take over his flight, and he would send three replacement aircraft and crews to fill the gap created by their last raid, which would be by tomorrow.

Before returning back to the squadron Sam wanted to have his new rank sewn onto his uniform. There was a soldier in HQ who was a high class tailor before he was conscripted and had been installed in a small room in the basement where he had a sewing machine and all the paraphernalia of his calling, a bit like the Eighteens! The Staff Officers in HQ found it highly desirable to have a service tailor on the premises, not only to look after their uniforms but to make civilian clothes for them, the soldier getting the odd back hander for his work. Most HQ officers returned home with a sizable and adequate wardrobe of mufti. Local clothes shops that had been deserted by their owners were a good supply of free material which the tailor made good use of.

While he was waiting for the changes to be made to his uniform he got on the field telephone to his Adjutant telling him he was now a Major and CO of the Squadron. On his return he told the Adjutant he would first meet him in his new office as CO and named the Captain who was to be second in command and the senior Lieutenant to fill the Captain vacancy, both to be there also. Afterwards, to have all the squadron officers to assemble in the Mess ante-room, as he wanted to address them on his return, which should be in about an hour's time.

On his return, after meeting the new senior Captain and the Lieutenant in the CO's office and briefing them of their duties he told the new captain to get his new rank sown on his uniform immediately He then spoke to all his officers in the Mess, followed by all NCO and privates, aircrew and ground crew in one of the hangars, telling them both there would be no initial changes but once he had settled in, he would then appraise the situation; he would not make changes for changes sake. Any changes would only be made to make improvements to the Squadron and he would welcome any ideas anyone may have. He was that type of person. He was easily accepted as CO as he had on many occasions been acting CO and the whole squadron assumed if anything happen to Major Norton, Sam would take over.

As there was total blackout over enemy territory, night bombing raids had to be carried out with a certain amount of moon light, which restricted operations. It had a plus and a minus, the plus they could navigate with a reasonable amount of accuracy and find the target, but the minus was that they could easily be spotted by the enemy. To overcome this they flew as low as possible. So none of the big guns had much time to take aim and fire with any accuracy, they had come and gone before the Hun knew what happened, but rifle fire was their main problem. Had not Sam been wounded by rifle fire from the ground? German fighters were of little problem in this stage of the war with all the bombing they were in short supply, as were German pilots who could fly safely at night. The Boche Air Force reserved their flying for day light use in the main where they obtained their best results, as the RAF fighters and bombers knew.

The first raid that Major Samuel Bray led his squadron was to Mannheim, with four other squadrons, the leading squadron led by a Lieutenant Colonel and a fighter escort. The moon was full and they arrived at about 500 feet above the target after a zigzagging course to confuse the enemy as to where they were heading. The target was spotted and marked by the leader, the rest of the squadron dropping bombs on or about the markers, lighting up the night sky as they hit the ground and exploded. Sam's squadron was third in and what he saw of the results, he felt that they all should have done better; to him it looked as if they were way off the target. The leading squadron should have marked the target more accurately, it was their job to pin point where they wanted the bombs to land for those following in their wake. It was the same on the next two raids, the targets were not being marked with any degree of accuracy, thus the results were poor, nothing was hit fair and square. A waste of crew, aircrafts, bombs, fuel and time, and some times lives and planes into the bargain.

RFC HQ was far from happy with the poor results the Lieutenant Colonel had achieved either and he was replaced by one of the squadrons CO's. On the next four raids each squadron commander took it in turns to lead, with Sam's turn at leading getting the best results. He was told by HQ to lead the next two raids and he obtained good results each time, had he not been the top pilot at the CFS conversion course?

Promotion was swift, Sam, for all his efforts and achievements, was promoted as Wing Leader of the night bomber group with the rank of Lieutenant Colonel. It was a visit to the tailor again! The first raid as leader was just as successful as all the following raids he led.

It was not long after taking over as Wing Leader that Sam was awarded the Distinguished Flying Cross, one of the first recipients of this new decoration, which hung from a ribbon with narrow blue and white diagonal strips.

***

By the end of September the Germans were in full retreat with a crushing defeat in Flanders and pulling back out of Belgium, things were not going to improve on the German side, all their allies were now starting to desert them, they were now virtually on their own.

***

As day light raids were more effective than night ones the latter were discontinued. Sam still continued as Wing Leader of his squadrons, taking it in turns with the day bomber groups. The bombing raids continued, the opposition by enemy fighters was little or nothing and was easily crushed with the superior number of the latest fighters defending the bombers. These raids were therefore on a much larger scale, deeper into the enemy's territory, targets were seldom missed by any bomber and their only problem was the guns on the grounds that were still very active. A number of aircrew suffered wounds, some even dying of their injuries, and aircrafts seemed to always suffer some damage while they still lost the occasional aircraft, but the German war machine was slowly grinding to a halt.

***

By the end of October things had become so bad that the once hailed German hero back in March, General Erich von Ludendorf, was now in disgrace being replaced by General Groener. All the German allies had now quit the field. Groener was put in far too late, with little or no resources, he could achieve nothing. Everyone now realised the writing was on the wall for Germany, it would not be long before hostilities were over.

***

In 1918, in the 11th month, on the 11th day, at the 11th hour, the war to end all wars came to an end, the Armistice being signed in a railway carriage in the forest of Compiègne. The troops started to come home to a country that was not fit for heroes as the Government had promised it would be. The losses to both sides were terrible. The British forces were led by Generals who should have been pensioned off at the turn of the century, basing their tactics on warfare from an earlier age with horses as in the two Boer wars. They ruthlessly sent troops in waves from trenches to be shot down, pilots to fly, being refused the safety of a parachute.

***

Lions led by Donkeys!
Max Hoffman *(1869 ~ 1927)*
***

Good morning, good morning, the general said,
When we met him last week on our way to the line,
Now the soldiers he smiled at are most of them dead
And we're cursing his staff for incompetent swine.
But he did for them both by his plan of attack
Siegfried Sassoon *(1886 ~ 1967)*
***

One realises how lucky we were to have won, many times, it could have gone the other way, and the Gods must have been looking on us more kindly than the Kaiser and his defeated German empire.
***

When you go home, tell them of us and say,
'For your tomorrow these gave their today
John Maxwell Edmonds *(1878 ~ 1958)*
***

CHAPTER 15

After The War Was Over

The day before the Armistice was signed Kaiser Wilhelm II, who had started the conflict, had fled by train to Holland, never to return to his native Germany, and would have only done so if the restoration of the monarchy was respected, it never was. He never set foot again in Britain or ever saw either of his cousins again, King George V and The Tsar in Russia. On 28th of November 1918, he signed a document of abdication. For what he had done by starting the Great War, there were various consideration what should happen to him; left alone, brought to trial, imprisoned for life or executed. Queen Wilhelmina of the Netherlands refused extradition so that is where he stayed to end his days. He first settled in Amerongen and in 1920 moved to the municipality of Doom as Wilhelm Hohenzollern, a private citizen, where he stayed and spent the rest of his life there at his house *Huis Doom*. When he died Hitler wanted to bring his body back to Berlin for a state funeral as he considered Wilhelm was a symbol of Germany and Germans during the Great War. This never happened and his body was interned in a mausoleum in the grounds of his house, his coffin being draped in the Nazi flag (for which he did not want) after a minor state funeral.

***

And the Imperial German Flying Corps was condemned to the scrap heap, as was a much disillusioned Bavarian army corporal by the name of Adolf Hitler. Was the price of war really worth it?

***

O Death, where is thy sting-a-ling-a-ling?
O grave, thy victory?
The bells of Hell go ting-a-ling-a-ling
For you but not for me.
The Holy Bible, 1 Corinthians; Chap 15; Verse 55
S Louis Giraud ~ {Songs That Won the War ~ 1930}
***

What had happened in Hartingford after Sarah had left in disgrace? Her family were shocked and the scandal she brought on them swept throughout the village, but it was only a nine day wonder. It wasn't as if she had had a baby out of wedlock as happened on a number of occasions in the village, she had only gone off with a married man and was his mistress, but this was a sin, especially to their Baptist upbringing and the Baptist Minister's. Other things happened in the village and it was soon forgotten in the community, but never by the Smiths. With the second Boer War in South Africa still raging over the turn of the century and soon to be followed by a world war, Sarah's scandal which had brought shame on the Smith family was soon lost in the mists of time. There were others families in the village, before and after her, who's daughter's brought shame on their families, with a many a hasty wedding. Sarah had only left home under a cloud, no one ever found out what had happened to her after she gone. The Smiths defiantly did not want to know, they were a respectable family.

In 1899 Sarah's father Thomas died and his eldest son Mathew took over the running of the Smithy, ably helped by Mark, and their youngest brother Luke who had started working there a year previous. All three brothers and their mother continued to live at the Smithy, and when in 1900 Mathew was married, his wife came to live with them. A year after Mark was married; he took the plunge and moved into a rented cottage in the village that had been vacated on the death of an old widow. While they wanted children, none ever came. In 1903 their mother, Eliza, died, and Mathew and his wife took over the whole house, with their four children who were born over a period of five year from 1901.

When they entered the 20th century the motor car was becoming more prevalent. Also farm tractors were on the horizon, the days of the horse as a means of motive power was on the decline. This meant the village Smithy started to see his work decline and the youngest brother Luke had been laid off, as available work for a village blacksmith was declining.

Luke had secured a job as an under groom at the local manor and was living in a room for the outside estate workers above the stables, he was paid a small wage and earning extra for shoeing the few horses they now had. He started courting one of the under maids and was married in 1906 and given a tied cottage within the Manor grounds. Like his brothers over the years he had four children but two died within the first year of life.

By the time the war started in 1914 work had reduced by such an extent that the jobs could be undertaken by one person. Mark, the second son, on the outbreak of war, decided to volunteer for the Army. At the age of 38 he was considered too old for fighting, they had more young men below 25 than they could initially cope with but they had a vast number of horses and farriers were essential in keeping them in good working order and shod. It was not long before he was across the English Channel plying his trade starting as a Private in the Veterinary Corps and finishing as Warrant Officer, operating well behind the front line. He came home at the end of the war, having never seen action, had no wounds or injuries, but was considered a hero by all the villagers of Hartingford, with ribbons on his chest to prove it. Within weeks of peace being declared he was discharged from the Army, his services were now no longer required as the army was demobilising thousands of fit and able men and with it went the horses; motor transport was taking over. He was meant to be returning to a *Land Fit For Heroes,* as the Government in power was proudly pushing for millions, but for Mark and millions of others it was not there, and in addition, his wife, fed up with being on her own, had found a younger man and left the area with him, never to be seen or heard of again. To find work he had to go far field and went to live and work around Bedford never to return to the village of his birth except on business. In Bedford he found a war widow ten years his junior and they set up together, to the outside world they were man and wife. To get employment he decided the up and coming thing was to drive. He did so and with his discharge pension purchased one of the many army buses being sold off. He soon started to operate a service between Northampton and Bedford. Within years he had a fleet of modern buses and coaches and was doing nicely, he had a large modern bus depot on the outskirts of Bedford, where he and his 'wife' lived with their son above the *'shop'*. When he was about to retire, the second Great War started, his services were much needed by the arm and air force. He made his son the chairman of the company, a reserved occupation, and he was there to assist until he retired when the war ended.

For Luke it was different matter. He was only 30 when the war started, he did not get into uniform until late 1915, being trained to fight in the trenches. On *going over the top* on his first assault he was killed within a few yards of the trench he had just left. His name was later engraved on the Hartingford War Memorial that was erected early in the twenties at the top of the village green, opposite St Mary's Church. His widow continued to work at the Manor so kept her cottage. As so many of the staff had children and had also lost their husbands in the war the Lord of the Manor and his wife had a crèche made in the basement of the building manned by a permanent Nanny so the widows could keep their jobs and earn much needed money. He had a good and faithful staff and this was the best way to retain their services. He was a forward thinking man and he and his family were much loved by the village folk for what they did and had done for them.

The two Smith daughters went into service at the manor also and were soon married, one to a stable lad and the other to a junior butler. Like their parents, they produced a number of children between them. The Smith family continues to live on in Hartingford.

**

With the entry of the new century it heralded the exit of the stage coach, to be taken over by the omnibus, people movers, plying their way between Bedford and Luton and beyond and later by charabancs for sightseeing and trips to the coast. When the stages ran there were 10 to 15 minutes stops out side the Black Horse for change of horses, but buses only required two or three minutes at the most to unload and load their passengers. The stage coach trade for Doughy collapsed and Sarah's small two wheeled covered pushcart laid abandoned and rotting behind the bakery. He purchased himself two army surplus lorries, thousands having been sold off at a knock down price when the war had finally ended. He used these to take his produce to all the local towns and village markets in the area, his output had changed to suit his new clientele and he found this was for the better.

Early in 1919 he purchased land behind his premises and expanded the bakery, his production increased 10 fold in less then 12 months, but he had an outlet for his extra produce, two large shops that the owners had vacated as they had gone our of business because they loss their war work, one in Bedford, the other in Luton, both now run as bakers shops managed by his two sons, one in each. They still lived in Hartingford, and early each morning, they would load up their lorries with the fresh produce for sale that day, returning with flour from the local mills to save cost on delivery and a good profit of cash. Doughy and his two sons where making a good living. Doughy had now increased his staff, firstly as he felt making bread was to much of an effort for him as he got older, now delegating the hard work to his new staff, and second looking for some one to manage the bakery in preparation for when he retired He was popular in the village as he now employed only villagers, taking them as they left school, the girls either in the shop or light work in the bakery, cakes and all sorts of buns, while the boys supplied the muscles for the mixing of dough for all the bakeries needs, a heavy task, the early shift starting at midnight, the second shift taking over a 6am. At the turn of the century changes were on the horizon for the bakery trades, electric dough mixers and large steam ovens to name a few new innervations in the trade. Also gas was soon to arrive in Hartingford, soon to be followed by electricity. Doughy and his two sons were looking to the future, machinery to mechanise dough mixing, bigger and better ovens to increase their capacity for baking were on the menu, this would help them two fold, increased production and a reduction in staff by about 50% through the baking industry. With cheaper sugar, there were taste changes sweeping the country also, bread production dropped and sweet products were now on the up; tarts, pastries, buns, doughnuts and lardy cakes to name but a few. The middle and upper class now held afternoon teas and sandwiches were now very much in demand.

***

Like Doughy, the butcher did the same and got himself a lorry and did his weekly journey to Luton and Bedford markets with home made products such as sausages, pork pies and faggots to name a few; bringing back carcases of beef, pig and sheep for his next weeks work. But never expanded as did the bakery, he did not have the foresight or inclination and only had a market stall; there was no one in his family to hand the business down to. In the fullness of time he sold the shop as a going concern to Doughy and his two sons. With their contacts, they soon found a butcher in Bedford who was very able but was held back by his employer; they soon took him on and found another vacated shop in Bedford for him to manage and it was not long before they opened a shop in Luton. They were on the up and up and would expand as they had done with the bakery. The two businesses now employed many staff, having eventually to seek workers from outside the village. Theses worker in time married locals and lived in close proximity to their work, the village was increasing in population, bringing more money and trade into the village shop, and the *Black Horse*. The two churches had bigger congregations, the school more pupils.

The trade for the carpenter remained small but steady, mainly from the Manor, but Mathew could see the writing on the wall for the local blacksmith. He was approached soon after the war had ended by one of the local lads recently out of work. He told Mathew he was a trained motor mechanic in Army Service Corps, he could see the trade was going down for blacksmith and suggested he joined forces and set up a garage for the repair of cars and other motor vehicles. Like the bakery, the venture flourished and they were in turn employing a number of skilled mechanics.

***

With the railways spreading across the land like spiders webs the usurp caused the downfall of canals traffic, similar to the stage coach network being displaced by both the railways and later motor transport. The first casualty in Hartingford that the villagers felt was the demise of *The London Flyer*, but this was not a problem for the village people as not many made the

330

trip to London when it was running, but as the century moved on more and more inhabitants of Hartingford were making the trip, but by train, at much less cost than by the coach and in less that an eight of the time. The villagers at first had to put up with the walk to the local station, but soon the railways laid on a regular bus service to the local station, to board the comfort and speed of the train as opposed to the stage coach. There were three classes, luxury closed in carriages with windows and padded seats, at one end of the scale, open truck, initial with no seats at the other end of the other end, but things soon improved for the 3rd class.

***

The sergeant and the corporal of the execution squad, both born cowards, who together had volunteered for the macabre task of killing their fellow men, considered they had a safe job from all the fighting for the duration of the war, were sentenced by the Courts Martial to be demoted to privates. Their punishment was to be sent to the front and fight alongside soldiers all braver than they ever would be. Later both were killed, in separate incidents on *"going-over-the-top"*, a part of the 888,246 killed in the *Great War*, perhaps for them this was poetic justice. The rest of the squad were disbanded and sent to the trenches to fight, some were killed, others were maimed or injured, and what was left returned home, broken men, never to answer the question from their children *"Daddy, what did you do in the war?"* □ They never gave a true or full answer to that question to any of their family, especially their children!
    □ *'Daughter to Father'* in a Great War recruiting poster.

***

Major General Adrian Matchwick returned to England, a year after *'The War to End All Wars'* had ended, completing his days in the Army at the War Office in London, finally obtaining the rank of Field Marshal and a Knighthood, retiring at the end of his career to his county of birth, Kent. In his absence, his daughter Penny played the field while her father was safely out of the way in France, her mother too busy with war work to notice what her daughter was up to! By the time he had returned she had found herself a man, a son of an Admiral, himself a career Naval officer, and destined, like both fathers, to rise rapidly to a very senior rank in the Navy. Both families were very happy with the union. On his retirement, he wrote his memoirs, and one subject was one he could not answer to his satisfaction, what had happened to Lance Corporal W Perry. He considered the only way he could have gone when he escaped was West, but why had no one caught him? He realised Perry would have thought if caught he would be shot, so he had to make his escape through the various army camps and installations behind the front line. He must have been successful as there had never been any report of his capture, which had been promulgated to all units to detain him, but not as a prisoner. He felt he must have somehow got back to England, but was never discovered. The Military Police made discrete enquires in the Shepherd's Bush area and discovered a Sergeant William Perry, deceased. He made enquires to his regiment, the West Bristol Fusiliers, but there was nothing that they could do to help. The only interesting thing was that a certain Major T Gledhill of the RAF had also been making the same enquiries. Adrian contacted the Major, but neither got any further, their joint investigations both came to a dead end.

***

Lieutenant Colonel Harper, the Provost Marshal, stayed in the Army after the cessation of hostilities, returning to the home of the Army in Aldershot to end his service life there, but his career in France put an end of reaching great heights and he only rose to the rank of Colonel He felt he had been passed over and deserved better, leaving the Army at retiring age in the early 1930s, a rather bitter ex-soldier. He never married and was without any family, his only friend was a Lieutenant Colonel and they retired within a year of each other. They got together and emigrated to South Africa and both ended their days there working in the Colonial service, Harper holding a rank equivalent to his Army position.

***

Lieutenant Colonel Lucas, the President of Sam's Court Martial, demoted to Captain by the sentence handed down at his Court Martial, was sent to fight in the trenches. On one of the many *"going-over-the-top"* incidents, he was badly wounded and sent home with one leg less than he left England with! He was discharged from the Army with a disability pension and with the help of SAAFA was found employment as a clerk in the Post Office, eventually rising to only lower management status. He, like the Provost Marshal, felt embittered at the way he had been treated, especially over the last CM he officiated at, feeling the accused was guilty as sin, but heard later that the accused was acquitted and promoted back to Lance Corporal, that was really rubbing salt into the wound, while he was demoted and sent to fight on the front line, injured and left a cripple for the rest of his

332

life, it was all the Army's fault. There was no justice, not like the justice he had been trying to hand out!

***

2nd Lieutenant Ellis, on being demoted to the rank of private, was also sent to the trenches to fight. Realising the dangers his body may suffer, he deserted as soon as it got dark on the first night he arrived there, he did not want anyone seeing him making his exit. He was immediately listed as deserted the following morning after his SNCO found his field equipment, and most importantly, his rifle, abandoned in the mud of the trench, but he was never found. Ellis made sure of that, making his way back to Ypres where all his troubles started, but he had contacts, he knew a few locals and prostitute there and he hoped one of them would help him.

As he entered the metropolis he found an old man who had collapsed, the worse for wear for drink and lying in the shadows by the side of the road. Ellis searched the man and relieved him of a small amount of money that would come in useful and decided this was an easy way to make a living. Arming himself with a makeshift club he soon found himself another victim who happened to be about the same size as Ellis. He was soon despatched and taking his outer clothes he made his getaway before his victim returned to the land of the living! At a safe distance, Ellis stopped, removing his last connection with the army, dumping his uniform in a ditch and donning his new possessions, cloth cap, jacket and trousers, so he could now blend in like a local and get lost in the crowd! On searching the garments pockets he found a considerable amount of money and a fully loaded 45 service revolver with a small amount of spare ammunition. He did wonder who the bloke could be, but not for long, now he was well prepared.

Now officially a deserter, if caught and convicted he would be sentenced to death by a firing squid, how the tables had turned! With his skills in speaking the French language he decided to stay in France until the conflict was over, whichever side won. He felt he was best off to bide his time until the fighting had finished, then he could stay with the victors, which ever side that my be. With his ability to learn languages he reckoned he could soon learn German if necessary. He never stayed in one place for long, he did not want to get tied down, especially if he got one of the many girls that he had slept with pregnant, which unbeknown to him, there were a number of young Ellis' strewn in his wake!

Now clothed, flush with money and armed he was ready for anyone. He made his way to a brothel and asked for a 'lady' he had had many times and spent the night with her. They both woke early and on looking out of the

333

window he saw the British military service police doing a house to house search, Ellis knew they were looking for him but he was cunning and knew the town well, including its back alleys. Once the police had searched a particular area and were getting nearer to the brothel which would soon be searched, he slipped out the back and made for a partly ruined house that he saw that the MPs had already investigated, staying there in the cellar until the coast was clear, only venturing out to a near by café for a meal, returning to hiding place until it got dark. By the following morning Ellis had put many mile between him and Ypres, making his way west to France.

To earn a living he did odd jobs where he could find them to pay for food, drink and women, but was quite happy to steal any food, drink and money that came his way and take the virginity of any young pretty girl that crossed his path without any compunction, either with cunning or force. When the war had ended he paid to get himself smuggled out of France by a fishing boat to England, eventually returning home, expecting his parents, his father a recently retired Major General, to welcome him with open arms, how wrong he was. Ellis was descended from a long line of Generals and Admirals on both sides of the family and his parents disowned him on the spot in no uncertain terms. They had heard about his misconduct and when they were told he had been court-martialled, reduced to the rank of Private, then had gone deserted, they did not want to know him ever again. He was a disgrace to the family. His three brothers had all done well in the army, survived the war and all held senior ranks and were an asset to the family, boys to be proud of, he was the proverbial *'black sheep'!* He was not made welcome at the family home when he returned and was immediately ejected by two young strong lads who worked in the garden and, by the orders of his father, was roughed up enough to make sure he got the message never to return home again, relieving him of the contents of his pockets, very little as it happened, some loose change and a revolver. One of the lads broke the weapon open and found two live rounds and four spent in the chamber. He smelt the gun, it had been fire recently, they both wondered who had been on the receiving end, they never asked or found out. While he was still their son his parents did not have the courage to turn him in to the military authorities; it could raise problems for them if this got out with their relations and friends if they heard of their son's dishonest behaviour. He was last seen as a down and out, wandering the back streets of London, then disappeared. Later, word got back to the family that he somehow got himself back to Paris, where he had *'friends'*, and ended his days with the arty set. With wine, drugs, prostitutes and sexually transmitted diseases, he was dead by his mid 20's, buried like so many of the soldiers he had sent *'over the top'* to their death, in an unmarked, unknown and uncared grave.

***

Once Keturah had been re-united with Sam, but still mourning the loss of Bill, she started to have guilty thoughts about their upbringing in Dr Barnardo, each of her sons had been there for 14 years, she had given the home nothing in return. She discussed this with Algernon, and they felt they should do something. For the rest of her life Keturah contributed anonymously to the home of a monthly donation of the sum equivalent to the cost of the upkeep of two boys for the same period. Sam only found out after his mother had died and he was clearing up her estate as chief executor.

***

At the earliest opportunity Algernon applied for his discharge, his father was now feeling his age and wanted to hand over the running of the Grafton Magna Manor estate to his son as soon as possible. Algernon's discharge was granted early in 1919 and after that he and Keturah moved out of their Notting Hill home to reside in the Manor, which became their permanent home while the London house was only used when either of them or Algernon's parents had to return there on business or for pleasure. As the children got older, and eventually married, they also used it as a London base. After over four years of war, the house at Notting Hill had taken its toll with the *WEC*, later becoming the *Women's Volunteer Reserve* using it as their base. Algernon had the house refurbished and redecorated throughout, electricity, central heating and all other *mod cons* installed.

***

At the end of hostilities the *WVR* was disbanded and all their temporary war time offices were closed down and handed back to their original owners, except the central HQ which reverted back to the Suffragettes. As soon as the war was over the Suffragettes started their protests again. *Votes for Women* won a partial victory for their cause, getting the right to vote for all women over the age of 30 as against 21 for men, this age limit restriction was partly to avoid an excess of women in the electorate because of the death of so many men in the war. Women first voted in the General Election of December 1918, won by David Lloyd George's Liberals party in coalition with the Conservatives. They were still not satisfied and carried on their campaign until women got parity with men in 1928, when both sexes over the age of 21 years being allowed the vote. In 1919, Lady Astor became the first women to sit in Parliament.

***

In late November 1918, Sam was ordered to fly home with his squadron to their new base at RAF Narborough in Norfolk. As the squadron was now not part of a wing, the CO's position reverted back to a Major and Sam handed over the Squadron to the new incumbent. He was offered a permanent commission in the peace time Air Force and would retain his current rank of Lieutenant Colonel, later to the new Royal Air Force equivalent rank of Wing Commander, Sam and Alice were both delighted with this offer. To their delight, in early January 1919, Alice gave birth to a girl, Abigail Camille, and nearly three years later they had a son, William Albert. Both children, when old enough, learnt to fly and when the war started in 1939, Abigail joined the Air Transport Auxiliaries Woman's Auxiliary delivering aircraft from factories to airfields, as her grandmother had in the Great War, in the British Isles and later over the channel to France. William joined the RAF as a coastal command pilot, flying patrols over the Atlantic in Sunderland flying boats, protecting the supply convoys and looking out for and attacking any 'U' boats they discovered, sinking a number, and like his father and grandparents, received a number of decorations.

Sam looked through his Flying Log Book soon after he had returned home, seeing all the combat missions he had undertaken, and between flying fighters and bombers, he had carried out over 100 sorties, 30 was considered a good average, and amassed over 1,000 flying hours, on at least 10 different aircraft. While Sam had been awarded the DFC and DSO, he had never been presented with the crosses. Early in March 1919, Sam was summoned to attend an investor by King George V at Buckingham Palace which he, with Alice, Keturah and Algernon, attended. Alice considered the chance to go once to Buckingham Palace once wonderful, but twice was out of this world!

Sam's first peace time appointment was to 10 Group HQ at RAF Calshot, the main RAF station for all types of float planes and their repair and maintenance. He went there he went on a Test Pilots course at RAF Upavon as his appointment at Calshot was to test fly all types of float planes, after major servicing and new ones that were offered to the RAF for evaluation, a similar job his step father had carried out at Farnborough. At the culmination of his 2½ year tour of duty there he was awarded the Air Force Cross in recognitions of his duties in that post. Sam still held a civilian pilots licence that was to become useful when he left the Air Force; on leave he often flew Algernon's latest aircraft from the Manor airfield.

Alice had never asked Sam about his *'missing years'* in the army when he had just disappeared from her fathers workshop and suddenly turning up out of the blue, over a year later, having joined the Royal Flying Corp. One day, while they were away on holiday and on their own, without the children, he quietly and slowly told her his story. She was much moved by his tale and of the harrowing experiences, the Court Martial, his escape and eventual return to England. From the start of the tale her eyes were soon moist, by the end the story her eyes were filled with tears. When Sam had finished, she hugged Sam like there was no tomorrow, clinging to him while she cried her heart out telling him how brave he was. They both never told anyone about his army days, taking their shared secret to their graves. They both knew there was no possible way to trace Group Captain Samuel Bray, as he now was, as being either Private Robert Drew of the West Bristol Fusiliers, Lance Corporal William Perry of the same regiment, or even Sergeant William Perry of the Berks and Hants Light Infantry. It was then that Sam showed Alice the letter that Lieutenant Molineux had sent him after Bill had been killed, more tears flowed, and they both consoled each other.

***

On trying to trace Private Drew after the war had ended, Captain Timothy Gledhill, now Lieutenant Colonel, could never understand why that Bob Drew, who had saved his life, then helped in his escape from capture and return to England with him, had been killed, a month before he crashed his aircraft. An official letter from Drew's Commanding Officer at West Bristol Barracks stated that:

Private Drew was reported missing, believed killed and eventually his body was found some time afterward. He had been shot and wounded, falling into a water filled shell hole, where he had later drowned in, May 1916. This has had been confirmed by the Commonwealth War Graves Commission and he was later buried in one of the British Cemeteries in the Ypres area in about June 1916, before you claim to have met this soldier. Currently a wooden cross marks his grave, but eventually a grave stone will be erected. On application to the War Graves
Commission, they will be able to tell you the cemetery he is buried in and the plot number. I feel that you must be looking for the wrong Private Drew of a different regiment.

Gledhill knew Drew's service number and could not understand how there could be a mistake. West Bristol Barracks could offer no more help, even after a second letter from him. This threw up more questions than answers for him! He never got to the bottom of this mystery. A year later he visited Private Drew's grave, now with a proper headstone, bearing the number he had been given by his fellow escapee. Many years later, after he had retired from the Air Force as Group Captain Gledhill, he was made an Honorary Member in the Officers Mess at the station at which he had retired as Station Commander. It was on one of his weekly visits to the Mess when leafing through an internal RAF magazine in the ante' room when he saw a photograph of a Group Captain Samuel Bray. While looking a few years older, he was the spitting image of Private Drew, but this must be just a coincidence, everyone is said to have a double somewhere! It was not worth pursuing the matter any further. It was all in the past, there was nothing to be gained by further investigation.

***

Sam was looking through the London Gazette and saw promulgated that Wing Commander T Gledhill had been promoted to Group Captain to take commander of an RAF station in East Anglia. He made a mental note not to visit that station. Just over two years later he saw that Tim had retired and wondered where he had retired to and did he ever marry. While they were together, many years previous, he never mention a lady friend. Sam never saw or heard about him again. He did wonder if Tim had seen his many photos in 'Air Clues' as he rose through the ranks, but he would never know.

***

After the war had ended, early in 1919, the War Office set up a sub section in the Personnel Department in Whitehall to list all Army personnel who had been killed in *The Great War*, regardless of what regiment that they may have belonged, stating their rank at the time of their death. The department was small and under manned for the project in hand, which the powers that be had hoped would have been completed before the end of the year, but was not. It was done alphabetically and after 18 months they were only up to the **P**'s. A junior clerk of the section had got to the Perry's, which there many, and Perry W's were nearly at the end of that particular surname. There were at least 25 Perry, William, but something caught the eye of this young clerk. There was: Barnardo Shepherd's Bush

Name	Number	Rank	Service	Demise	Birth Details
Perry, William	75281	Sergeant	Army/B&HLF	Ypres/19 April 1915	Barnardo's, Shepherd's Bush, London. 18/1/96. No: 586.
Perry, William	93494	L/Corporal	Army/WBF	Ypres/ca May 1916	Barnardo's, Shepherd's Bush, London. 18/1/96. No: 586.

He showed this to his superior, a very harassed Civil Servant coming up to his retirement and being pressured by his superiors to get this task completed. He had been a *job's worth* all his life and worried about his pension. When the junior clerk showed his supervisor what he considered were anomalies between the two Perrys he was not in the least interested and made little of it, they were only there to make a list of the dead, not to ask questions. They were both dead and it was not their job to hold a *Court of Inquiry* on who they were or how they died or where. The junior clerk was told in no uncertain terms to get on with the job and not to pursue this line of enquiry any further. He had his retirement to look forward to, he did not want to blot his copybook at this time of his career, he was due a retirement present which he was not going to jeopardise!

The junior clerk returned to his desk and carried on with the list as he was told and soon finished the rest of the Perry's. But he could never understand why these two particular William Perry's had the same name, the same Birth Certificate number, were both born on the same day and both came from Shepherd's Bush in London! It was not worth pursuing the matter any further if he wanted to retain his job.

When the War Memorial was erected in Shepherd's Bush, it carried the names of two William Perry's, but they both had different numbers and belonged to a different units. Alice and Sam went down to the memorial; they were the only ones who knew about the two Perry's.

***

In 1919, Prince Albert (later King George VI) transferred from the Army and joined the Royal Air Force and became a pilot.

***

It wasn't long after hostilities had ended, that all the wounded had been repatriated from the front. As the patients were repaired, put back together as far as possible and discharged, the beds started to become vacant in military hospitals that had taken in the wounded. The Reading War Hospital was now able to have room to start treatment for the local civilian population again. In 1920, in memory of what the hospital had done for the wounded of the Great War, the hospital was renamed the Battle Infirmary.

***

Rupert, Keturah & Algernon's eldest son, showed great interest in the estate and when he left school he became Algernon's assistant, to be groomed to succeed his father in due course. Rupert's grandfather, Jonathan, was now feeling his age and once Algernon had returned he was glad to hand over the running of the estate. The war years had taken a toll on his health; he was 71 when the war had started. Over the next few years or so he grew weaker and weaker and died in 1921. Algernon succeeded to the title of the 7th Earl of Caversham and Keturah became Countess of Caversham and their son, the Honourable Rupert Cavendish, the new heir to the Earldom. Isabel, Jonathan's wife, now the Dowager Countess of Caversham, died about 10 years later, continuing to live at the manor for the rest of her life.

***

Algernon found the estate, with the very competent staff who worked for him, did not require him full time, and having an excellent young estate manager, who had recently replace the retiring manager, he was able to take on other projects. Because the estate was well run the profits were very good. Algernon decided to increase his holdings and over the years he purchased a number of run down estates, turning them into profitable ventures run by tenant farmers. They were scattered about the country, some many miles away, and to help visit them, he set up a landing strip at each, allowing him to fly to any of them with the least possible trouble.

Algernon continued flying and extended the landing field and replaced the small hangar with a larger one in the Manor grounds to take larger aircrafts. He purchased a succession of aircrafts over the years, each carrying a larger passenger load, eventually ending up with an 8 seater De Havilland Dragon Rapide in the mid 30's so that he could take his family and staff by air between their two homes, saving them time and the train journey, and away on holidays, at home and on the continent. For his personal use he purchased a DH Tiger Moth, a two seater that was an excellent run around, having short take off and landings, and as he and Keturah had enough of force fed fresh air they had a canopy fitted and used the heat from the engine to heat the cabin. So the could be easily recognised they had their initials painted on the tail and painted bright yellow!

In the late 1930's, Algernon's failed a pilot's eye test and had his flying licence withdrawn. Keturah took over all the flying from then on with the help of Sam when he came home. By the time WWII had ended the Rapide was getting old, tired and slow compared with the newer aircraft that had been developed during and since the war so Algernon decided to change it for another De Havilland plane, so in the late 1940's he acquired a DH Dove, a 10 seater aircraft. This he felt would be a better aircraft for Keturah to fly, be more comfortable for them both and their family and staff, no draughts, it also had heating and a retractable undercarriage. Algernon often flew this in the co-pilots seat with either Keturah or Sam in the pilot's seat beside him!

***

When it was announced that Alice was expecting a baby late 1918, early 1919, she told her father she would like to retire when summer came, all the steps she climbed between the office and their home above the workshop everyday were steep and she was afraid of falling down as the baby grew. Both he and Agnes agreed as they were also concerned about the steps and the welfare of their daughter and felt that the offer by Keturah that she should now live with them a good idea. She could visit them by being driven there by Algernon's chauffeur, or they visit her in turn, a short ride by bus.

Bert soon started looking around for a replacement for his daughter while Alice still worked there so she could train the new incumbent, which they all felt would be best filled by a young lady. After a number of interviews Bert employed a girl between Fred's and Alice's age, who had been doing essential war work in Acton a few miles away, replacing a man when he was called up, but he had now returned and she was out of a job. Her name was Anne Caroline Davidson and Fred soon took a fancy to her and they were *walking out* within the month of her arrival. In less than a year they were married and in the same space of time they had twins, a boy and a girl, Peter and Pamela. Bert's business, unlike others, grew; planes were still being

341

made, but mainly for peaceful purposes, and the firms profits grew after every succeeding year. He was very busy; output had increased, but had changed from military to commercial and pleasure aircrafts, not only for Sopwith but now other aircraft manufactures. A factory next to Bert's premises closed as all its war work had ceased and the owner was not forward looking like Bert and had not made any continuance plans for peace time operation. Bert was in need of more space and took over the site and it was soon filled with new machinery and new carpenters, the Frost's were on the up and up. As soon as the war had been won, the Government started on a new houses building scheme, a building programme was formulated. The Frosts were at the forefront of this making essential parts and delivering them to site, making sure they had more than one iron in the fire. When Bert retired Fred took over and his son was in the pipe line to eventually carry on the family business from him.

***

As Isaac had now employed more staff, there wasn't room for Alice to help in the shop any more as she had in the past, so she now had time on her hands. She could not just sit around, she was too much of an energetic woman to do that, but an idea was forming in her head, its seed was the making of the wedding dress for Alice. After discussion with her husband and son, it was agreed that she should go back to the profession she had been trained for, dressmaking, but there was a problem, there was not enough room in their current shop for both tailoring and dressmaking full time. Recently the shop next door had became vacant as the owners had retired, and would have retired sooner if it had not been for the war work they did, making webbing parts for the army. There was no one to hand the business on to, his single source of work, army webbing, had now been terminated by the Army, they had more surplus webbing than they could handle. His staff, all women, had had to be made redundant to return to look after the home and their returning husbands. He offered Isaac the opportunity to buy the premises as he knew Isaac was expanding his business and Isaac and Marie immediately took up his offer, both parties were happy.

It was just what Marie required and the Eighteens took it over as a dress shop for the upper class clientele, catering for the same class of people as in Isaac's tailor shop and it became:

Marie Eighteen ~ Ladies Dressmaker

The two shops complemented each other; trade increased for Isaac and Marie and the only solution, with all the extra work that they were attracting, was to employ two young dressmakers and an apprentice tailor. Not long after taking on the extra staff their son Joseph had started courting one of the young dressmakers, Ruth Cohan, and they were soon married and were living over the dress shop which was vacant as the Eighteens had no use for it. With the increased income, Isaac and Marie purchased a cottage not to far away in Ealing where they moved, making it easy to travel by train to get to work each day or return to see their friends in Shepherd's Bush, whatever the case may be. When they retired it became their retirement home.

When Isaac and Marie eventually retired, Joseph and his wife took over the running of the two shops, by this time they were employing three dressmakers and two tailors. Because of the increased workload, work space was becoming a problem, they did not have enough room, they could not meet customers' delivery dates and they were starting to lose trade. They had to move to larger premises and it was not long before Joseph and Ruth found a suitable property in Notting Hill, a much better area to be based, a more purposeful clientele and much more room for both parts of the firm, and a much larger living quarters over the *'shop!'*. After the move, trade soon returned, and increased, as did the staff. Sam's table, still with a hidden hook under it, went with them; they could not bear to part with that. Unlike the old premises, Sam's table was now not big enough for all the work but Bert Frost obliged and made them another table from Sam's old drawings. Sam and Alice kept up their friendship with the Eighteens and remained loyal customers. The two tables out lived Joseph and Ruth and his son, who took over the business from his Dad, and their daughter when Ruth retired, and there were grandchildren coming along to take over from them!

***

Benjamin Charles, Algernon and Keturah's second son, on leaving school went up to Oxford and after graduating joined the Colonial Service, and before departing for India, married a distant cousin. Joanne Ellen, their daughter, did the debutante circuit, was presented to the King, found a suitable young man with a title and service background living in a large manor house in easy reach of Grafton Magna Manor.

***

When the war had ended, the Cavendish, Frosts and the Eighteens were very busy during 1919, both adjusting to their new world. Algernon was now running the estate full time and Bert his factory and Isaac and Marie the two shops. All were very busy in their own fields of work. As Christmas approached, at the instigation of Algernon, his family and the Frosts gathered at the Cavendish home. Algernon had an idea he wished to discuss with them all. The outcome was that in about mid April the following year, they would all visit Bill's grave, the fifth anniversary of his death on the 19th of April.

In April, Sam and Alice, Keturah and Algernon, and their three children, Agnes, Bert and their son Fred, made their way to Dover staying over night in a hotel. They crossed the Channel the next day by an early morning ferry to Dunkerque and travelled the 35 miles to Ypres by road, in two hire cars that Algernon had had the foresight to book earlier.

On arrival at the cemetery where Bill was buried, armed with the plot number that they had been given, they soon found the grave they were looking for, now with a proper headstone, surmounted by the Infantry crest with the following inscription carved below:

☐
75281 Sergeant
W Perry
DCM & Bar
The Berks & Hants Light Infantry
19 April 1915

They all knelt down and said their final prayers to him with tears running down their cheeks, laid their final tributes of flowers, one from each of them, including the children. On a small purple velvet cushion that Alice had brought with her, she placed it in the centre of the flowers on which she then laid all Bill's war decorations, the Distinguished Conduct Medal, now with the Bar he had received in the battle that he had been killed, taking pride of place. Photos were taken of the grave that both families kept in remembrance of a brave hero. The flowers were left but Bill's decorations returned home, to be kept by Alice and Sam, being passed down to the eldest child of each generations.

The Soldier

If I should die, think this only of me;
That there's some corner of a foreign field
That is for ever England. There shall be
In that rich earth a richer dust concealed:
A dust whom England bore, shaped, made aware,
Gave, once, her flowers to love, her ways to roam,
A body of England's, breathing English air,
Washed by the rivers, blest by suns of home
And think, this heart, all evil shed away,
A pulse in the eternal mind, no less
Gives somewhere back the thoughts by England given;
Her sights and sounds; dreams happy as her day;
And laughter, learnt of friends; and gentleness,
In hearts at peace, under an English heaven.

Lieutenant Rupert Brooke (1887 ~ 1915)

For The Fallen

They shall grow not old, as we that are left grow old.
Age shall not weary them, nor the years condemn,
At the going down of the sun and in the morning
We shall remember them.

Laurence Binyon (1869 ~ 1943)

CHAPTER 16

The Years Roll By

Peace in our time came and went, where in 1939 had all the peace gone. Sam rose steadily through the ranks, the 1939/45 war helping him along.

Sam and Alice had not been long at Calshot when they decided to try their hand at sailing and both joined the RAF Calshot Sailing Club and were soon competent sailors, deciding that they should own their own craft; they purchased a small sailing boat and were sailing up and down Southampton Water, along The Solent and over to the Isle of Wight. By the time they had completed their tour there they had a 30 foot sailing yacht and had sailed over to France on a number of occasions.

On the death of Algernon Cavendish, the 7th Earl of Caversham at 82 in 1956, Rupert became the 8th Earl of Caversham, his wife the new Countess. Keturah became the Dowager Countess of Caversham. Sam retired from the Air Force in that year, having risen to a senior position with an air rank and a Knighthood.

Because of Algernon's death, Keturah decided at 78 it would be best if she gave up flying, she had hardly done any flying for some time. Sam still held a civilian pilots licence and the new Earl asked him if he would take over as the estates pilot as there was much flying to be done as they had invested well and purchased a number of farms across the country that made a good return from tenant farmers that had to be visited on a regular bases, flying was the only way, in their trusty Tiger Moth Algernon had bought many years ago, being kept warm and draft free now with a heater and cockpit canopy. The farms ranged from the north of England, the West Country and East Anglia. Not only would this give Sam something to do but he was getting paid for it as well. For the last few years in the RAF he had continued to fly to ensure he kept his flying qualifications and was also glad on leaving the service not to have the pressure of work required by his rank and as a civilian he only had to fly and navigate a plane.

The next item they had to think about was where to live; their children Abigail and William were both married, having left home long ago and living in the Reading area and were often bringing their children to the Manor for a day out or to stay on holiday, helping out on the farm! Rupert had offered

346

Alice and Sam the empty wing in the Manor to live, free as he was employed by the estate, but they declined his offer as they wanted be to on their own in a self contained home. It was not long before they found a house a few miles away, near Caversham, and a short drive either to the Manor or into Reading. The grounds of their house fronted the north bank of the River Thames way out on The Warren, up stream from the third Caversham Bridge. In memory of their first home at RAF Calshot in an officer's quarter at Eagle Camp, the domestic site that overlooking Southampton Water and the flying boat base on Calshot Spit, with Calshot Castle a prominent landmark for pilots to home onto on their return, they named their new home Calshot.

On arrival at their new home they soon purchased a four berth sea faring launch that they could pursue their love of *'messing about on the water'*, which had started 36 years ago at Calshot, going up stream as far as Lechlade and down to the mouth of the river Thames at Southend and across the channel to France and beyond.

***

On 19th February 1919, Captain John Alcock, piloting a modified Vickers Wimy bomber, navigated by Lieutenant Arthur Whitten Brown, completed the first Trans Atlantic non-stop crossing from Newfoundland to land in an Irish bog. They were both knighted for their achievement.

***

Treaty of Versailles was signed in June 1919 by the Germans who eventually accepted the terms after two months of haggling and failed negotiations with a threat of military occupation if they did not sign. It was a peace treaty to stop any further wars after the Great War, which cost over 10 million lives on both sides. The document was 200 pages long, contained 75,000 words and 440 clauses. The *Victors* won, the *Vanquish loss*, from this the seeds of the second Great War were sown, cultivated by an unknown Bavarian ex-army corporal from the Great War by the name of Adolf Hitler

***

London's first airport, as against airfield, was opened in 1919 on Hounslow Heath, west of the capital, but in less than one year services transferred from there to London's new airport at Croydon and officially opened at the end of March 1921. The distance from Croydon to Paris was shorter than from Heather row. The Control Tower was the only modern building, standing tall on stilts, all the other buildings were of the army barrack type huts, but plans were afoot to make the whole site of modern buildings to suit the art-deco period in the style of the De La Warr pavilion at Bexhill-on-Sea.

***

The Schneider Trophy competition for 1927 took place in Venice in September, the Royal Air Force team winning with a Supermarine S.5, designed by R J Mitchell at an average speed of 281.65mph. The pilots were Flt Lt's Webster and Worsley. Having won the competition in 1927, the next venue for the race in 1929 was on home waters, at the Solent, between the Isle of Wight and Southampton Water. Again the RAF team, based at RAF Calshot, won the trophy, flying a Supermarine S.6, piloted by Fg Off Waghorn and set up a new world speed recorded of 328.629mph and lapped the course at 331mph. As the winners in 1929, the competition was again held at the same venue along the Solent in 1931, but the British Government pulled out and would not provide financial backing of £100,000 to support the British entry. This upset many people, especially Lady Lucy Houston, who provided the money required for the provision of a new and improved version of the previous Schneider aircraft, the Supermarine S.6B. The pilot was Flt Lt Boothman, winning the competition at an average speed of 340.08mph, with a world speed record of 379.05mph on one of his runs. Having won three consecutive races, the RAF retained the trophy for prosperity and in four years they had raised the air speed by 50mph

***

In November 1923, the small but extreme Nationalist and virulently anti-Semitic party stormed Munich's biggest beer hall, *Burgerbraukekker,* where Gustav von Kahr was just starting to present a lecture. The storm party was led by a certain Herr Adolf Hitler, jumping on a chair, firing a shot into the ceiling and shouting, *"The National Revolution has begun."* The seeds of the 2nd Great War had now started to germinate.

***

The future fighter aircraft, monoplanes, built to take us into the next war were to the Air Ministry specification published in 1936 open to all aircraft manufactures, this being F.36/34, requiring 4 machine guns mounted in each wing. The Hawker Aircraft Company produced the Hurricane designed by

Sydney Camm (later Knighted) and was first flown in 1935 and entered RAF service in December 1938 at RAF Northolt with 111 Squadron. The Supermarine Company's contribution was the Spitfire, first flown in 1936, to the same specification. It was a development of the three Supermarine Schneider Trophy aircraft, both designed by Reginald J Mitchell, who died in 1937, never knowing the contribution he made to the war to come and entered service August 1938 at RAF Duxford with 19 Squadron. Both aircraft carried the same engine, the Rolls Royce Merlin. The Hurricane was cheaper to build, requiring 10,300 man hours, while the Spitfire totalled 15,200 man hours, but in the end the Spitfire became the better aircraft.

The Avro Lancaster bomber, the most famous of all WWII bombers, made its maiden flight in January 1941 and was operational by March 1942; like the fighters, it had Rolls Royce Merlin engines.

***

Tommy Sopwith, aviator and aircraft designer, born on 18th January 1889, later knighted, died on 27th January 1989, just surpassing the age of 100 years.

***

CHAPTER 17

Epitaph

In 1966, Samuel, Rupert, Benjamin, Jane and the late William, lost their mother, aged 88 years:

Sarah Smith
1878 ~ 1895

Jane Perry
1895 ~ 1896

Keturah Bray
1896 ~ 1901

Keturah Sophia Cavendish
1901 ~ 1921

7th Countess of Caversham
1921 ~ 1956

Dowager Countess of Caversham
1956 ~ 1966

The End

APPENDIX 1

Who's Who

Name Status/Title Life Details

Andrews, Lieutenant-Colonel Wing Leader, Ypres Wing
Archer, Sergeant Bristol Barracks, Section SNCO
Ashworth, Abraham Hartingford's village baker, known as Doughy
Barnardo, Thomas John, Dr [b] Founder of Dr Barnardo Homes 1845 > 1905
Bray, Abigail Camille Sam & Alice's daughter 1918 > 2005
Bray, Keturah Sophia [a] Mother of Samuel Bray 1878 > 1966
Bray, Samuel (Sam) {93494} {586877} Keturah Bray's son 1898 > 1977
Bray, William Albert Sam & Alice's son 1921 > 2003
Bray, Abigail Camille Sam & Alice's Daughter 1919 > 2005
Bayliss, Private Algernon's batman
Brown, James, Major OC 5 Squadron, Ypres
Butler, Sergeant Section NCO, Ypres
Cartwright, Corporal Bristol Barracks, ½ Section JNCO
Cavendish, Algernon Daniel Ian Keturah's husband, 7th Earl of Caversham 1874 > 1956
Cavendish, Benjamin Charles K & A's 2nd child 1905 > 1987
Cavendish, Joanne Ellen K & A's 3rd child 1908 > 1992
Cavendish, Keturah Sophia [a] Mother of Rupert, Benjamin & Joanne 1878 > 1961
Cavendish, Rupert John K & A's 1st child, 8th Earl of Caversham 1903 > 1982
Cavendish, 5th Earl of Caversham Algernon's grandfather 1825 > 1899
Cavendish, 6th Earl of Caversham, Jonathan, Algernon's father 1850 > 1921
Cavendish, 6th Countesses, Isabel Wife of Jonathan Cavendish 1855 > 1931
Cavendish, 7th Countesses ,Keturah [a] Wife of 7th Earl of Caversham 1878 > 1961
Cohan, Ruth Joseph Eighteens wife 1893 > 1971
Davis, Corporal Victoria Barracks, Aldershot
Davidson, Anne Caroline Fredrick Frost's wife 1895 > 1970
Dawlish, Alan, Sub Lieutenant Pilot, 8 Squadron, Ypres

Drew, Robert (Bob) {93495} Private Sam's mate from Bristol 1898 > 1916

Eighteen, Isaac Tailor, Shepherd's Bush 1860 > 1937

Eighteen, Joseph Tailor, Isaac's son 1886 > 1962

Eighteen, Marie Isaac's wife 1859 > 1939

Ellis, 2nd Lieutenant Bristol Barracks, Platoon CO 1896 > 1921

Eveleigh, Company Sergeant Major Victoria Barracks, Aldershot

Farquhar, George Major CO, 8 Squadron, Ypres

Frost, Agnes Bert Frost's wife 1863 > 1935

Frost, Alice Frost's daughter 1898 > 1978

Frost, Bert Founder of Frost Carpenters 1851 > 1921

Frost, Fredrick Frost's son 1882 > 1947

Frost, Pamela   Fredrick Frost's daughter

Frost, Peter Fredrick Frost's son

Gledhill, Timothy, Captain Flight Commander in Squadron of Ypres Wing

Gordon, Colonial Staff Office, War Office, London

Harper, Lieutenant Colonel Provost Marshal, Ypres

Hawker, Harry [b] Sopwith's chief test pilots

Henderson, Lieutenant General Sir David [b] CO of RFC in France until August 1915

Holland, Peter, Lieutenant (Pete) Pilot, 8 Squadron, Ypres

Hopkins, Captain Aide to Major General Matchwick, Ypres

Hughes, 2nd Lieutenant Bill's Platoon Commander, Ypres

Ives, Captain, Robin {25941} Medical Officer, Field Hospital, Ypres

James, J M War Office, London

Jenkins, Sergeant Workshop SNCO, RFC Hendon

King, Senior Matron Dr Barnardo Home Shepherd's Bush

Kirkpatrick, John, Major OC Workshop, Farnborough

Long, Beth Girl friend of Jane [a], Marylebone

Lucas, Lieutenant Colonel President of the Court Marshal, Ypres

Matchwick, Adrian, Major General Bristol Barracks

Matchwick, Penelope (Penny) Daughter of Major General Matchwick

McGhee, Corporal Bristol Barracks, ½ Section JNCO

Molineux, Jack, Sergeant Bill's Section NCO, later Lieutenant, Ypres

Moreton, Benjamin, Major Teat Pilot, Farnborough

Newbury, Governor Dr Barnardo Home, Shepherd's Bush

Norton, Anthony, Major CO 207 Squadron, Ligescourt

Oliver, James, Sub Lieutenant Pilot, 5 Squadron

Parsons, Joseph Jane Perry's friend; Merchant Venture, London

Perry, Jane [a] Mother of Bill Perry 1878 > 1966

Perry, William (Bill) {75281} Jane Perry's son 1896 > 1915

Richardson, Lance-Corporal JNCO i/c Section 5: D Squad, Aldershot

Roberts, 2nd Lieutenant Bristol Barracks, Platoon CO
Russell, Captain Platoon Commander
Rolls, Charles [b] Co Founder of RR cars 1877 > 1910
Royce, Henry [b] Co Founder of RR cars 1863 > 1933
Short, Eustace [b] Aircraft manufactures 1875 > 1932
Short, Horace [b] Aircraft manufactures 1872 > 1917
Short, Oswald [b] Aircraft manufactures 1883 > 1969
Smith, Eliza Sarah Smith's Mother 1846 > 1903
Smith, Luke 6th child of the Smiths 1884 > 1915
Smith, Mark 2nd child of the Smiths 1875 > 1935
Smith, Mary child of the Smiths 1880 > 1942
Smith, Mathew 1st child of the Smiths 1874 > 1931
Smith, Maud 5th child of the Smiths 1881 > 1950
Smith, Sarah [a] 3rd child of the Smiths 1878 > 1966
Smith, Thomas Sarah Smith's father 1841 > 1899
Sopwith, T O M (Tommy) [b] Aircraft manufacture 1888 > 1989
Sunderland, Captain Teat Pilot, Farnborough
Taylor, Major   Medical Officer, Field Hospital, Ypres
Thorne, Sergeant Algernon's Observer, Ypres
Trenchard, Hugh, Brigadier-General [b] CO of RFC in France from August 1915 1873 > 1921
Tucker, Colonial RFC Brigade HQ, Ypres
Urquhart, Captain, Ralph Flight Commander, 8 Squadron, Ypres
Wainwright, Captain Station Adjutant, Hendon
Wight, Major   Maintenance Officer, Hendon

Key

[a] Sarah Smith; Jane Perry; Keturah Bray; Keturah Cavendish:
[b] Actual persons that features in the main story.

APPENDIX 2

Holders of the Victoria Cross

Awarded during the Great War to RFC, RNAS, and RAF aircrew.

Surname, Forename, Rank, Service, VC, Life.

Ball +2, Albert, Capt. RFC 1917. 1896~1917 †
Barker +1, William, Major (C) RFC/RAF 1918. 1894~1930
Beauchamp-Proctor, Andrew W Capt. (S) RFC/RAF 1918. 1894~1921
Bishop, W A, Lieut. (C) RFC/RAF, 1918. 1894~1956
Hawker, Lanoe G Major. RFC 1915. 1890~1916
Insall, Gilbert S M, Lieut. RFC/RAF 1915. 1894~1972
Jerrard, Alan, Lieut. RFC/RAF 1918. 1887~1968
Leefe-Robinson, William, Lieut. RFC/RAF 1916 1899~1918
Liddell, John Aidan, Capt. RFC 1915. 1888~1915 †
Mannock+1,+2 Edward M, Major. RFC 1917. 1887~1917 †
McCudden +1, James B, Major. RFC/RAF 1918. 1895~1918 †
McLeod +1, Alan, Lieut. RFC/RAF 1918. 1899~1918 †
McNamara, Frank H, Capt (A) AFC/RAAF 1917. 1894~1961
Mottershead, Thomas, Sgt. RFC 1917. 1892~1917 †
Rees, L W B, Major. RFC 1915. 1884~1955
Rhodes-Moorhouse, William B, Lieut. RFC 1915. 1887~1915 †
Warneford, Reginald A, Flt Sub. Lieut. RNAS 1915. 1891~1915 †
West, Ferdinand, M. Capt RAF/RAF 1918. 1896~1988

† - Posthumous award of the decoration.

Other Awards

Distinguished Flying Cross
Only NCO to win the VC
Military Cross
Distinguished Service Order
Distinguished Conduct Medal
Air Force Cross
Order of the British Empire
Croix de Guerre ~ French
Legion d'honneur ~ French
Order of St George ~ Russian

Country of Origin

(A) Australian
(C) Canadian
(S) South African

Apologies

The author wishes to apologise to any holders of the Victoria Cross in any of the British flying services that I have omitted,   and of any other awards that they have received that I have not given credit.

APPENDIX 3

Map of the Great War Battle Areas

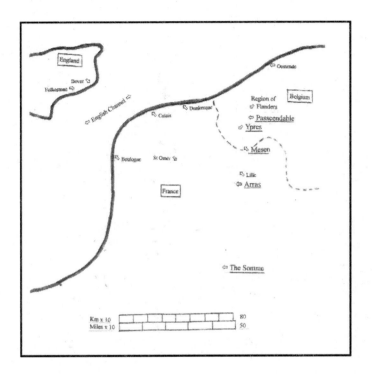

England

Dover

Folkestone

English Channel

Oostende

Belgium

Region of
Flanders

Passchendaele

Ypres

Calais

Duinkerque

Mesen

Boulogne

St Omer

Lille

Arras

France

The Somme

Km x 10   80
Miles x 10   50